SASKIA SARGINSON

♦

THE BENCH

Complete and Unabridged

CHARNWOOD
Leicester

First published in Great Britain in 2020 by
Piatkus
an imprint of Little, Brown Book Group
London

First Charnwood Edition
published 2020
by arrangement with
Little, Brown Book Group
London

The moral right of the author has been asserted

Copyright © 2020 by Saskia Sarginson
All rights reserved

Lyrics from 'Leaving on a Jet Plane' on p. 108 by
John Denver. Lyrics copyright © BMG Rights Management, Reservoir Media Management

All characters and events in this publication, other
than those clearly in the public domain, are fictitious
and any resemblance to real persons, living or dead,
is purely coincidental.

A catalogue record for this book is available
from the British Library.

ISBN 978–1–4448–4642–3

Published by
Ulverscroft Limited
Anstey, Leicestershire

Set by Words & Graphics Ltd.
Anstey, Leicestershire
Printed and bound in Great Britain by
TJ Books Limited, Padstow, Cornwall

This book is printed on acid-free paper

SPECIAL MESSAGE TO READERS

THE ULVERSCROFT FOUNDATION
(registered UK charity number 264873)
was established in 1972 to provide funds for research, diagnosis and treatment of eye diseases. Examples of major projects funded by the Ulverscroft Foundation are:-

- The Children's Eye Unit at Moorfields Eye Hospital, London
- The Ulverscroft Children's Eye Unit at Great Ormond Street Hospital for Sick Children
- Funding research into eye diseases and treatment at the Department of Ophthalmology, University of Leicester
- The Ulverscroft Vision Research Group, Institute of Child Health
- Twin operating theatres at the Western Ophthalmic Hospital, London
- The Chair of Ophthalmology at the Royal Australian College of Ophthalmologists

You can help further the work of the Foundation by making a donation or leaving a legacy. Every contribution is gratefully received. If you would like to help support the Foundation or require further information, please contact:

THE ULVERSCROFT FOUNDATION
The Green, Bradgate Road, Anstey
Leicester LE7 7FU, England
Tel: (0116) 236 4325

website: www.ulverscroft-foundation.org.uk

SPECIAL MESSAGE TO READERS

THE ULVERSCROFT FOUNDATION
(registered UK charity number 264873)
was established in 1972 to provide funds for
research, diagnosis and treatment of eye diseases.
Examples of major projects funded by
the Ulverscroft Foundation are:—

* The Children's Eye Unit at Moorfields Eye
  Hospital, London
* The Ulverscroft Children's Eye Unit at Great
  Ormond Street Hospital for Sick Children
* Funding research into eye diseases and
  treatment at the Department of Ophthalmology,
  University of Leicester
* The Ulverscroft Vision Research Group,
  Institute of Child Health
* Twin operating theatres at the Western
  Ophthalmic Hospital, London
* The Chair of Ophthalmology at the Royal
  Australian College of Ophthalmologists

You can help further the work of the Foundation
by making a donation or leaving a legacy.
Every contribution is gratefully received. If you
would like to help support the Foundation or
require further information, please contact:

THE ULVERSCROFT FOUNDATION
The Green, Bradgate Road, Anstey,
Leicester LE7 7FU, England
Tel: (0116) 236 4325

website: www.ulverscroft-foundation.org.uk

THE BENCH

It begins at the end.

It begins on a bench, on a heath, where a woman waits for a man.

Ten years ago, they made a pact: On this bench, on this day, they will end a love affair that's spanned three decades, or start again.

They should never have met. They should never have fallen in love.

But they did, until a lie separated them for a lifetime.

Can they fix the mistake, forgive the lie, erase the years in-between? Can what was lost ever truly be found?

ON THIS BENCH, LIFE SLOWED, LOVE
BLOSSOMED, AND MEMORIES WERE MADE.

Prologue

Hampstead Heath, 2004

Panting a little from the climb, she reaches the bench and drops onto the wooden slats. She sits with her knees together, back straight, hands linked in her lap. Only her thumbs, moving restlessly across each other, betray her nerves. She closes her eyes, shutting out the view of scrub-covered hills, woods of ancient oaks, ponds filled with the dark waters of the Fleet.

Is he here already? Walking one of the paths, passing joggers and dog-walkers, mothers pushing prams. If she had super-powers, could she discern the scrape of his feet against the gritty surface, dislodging tiny stones? A football match is in mid flow on one of the pitches at the foot of Parliament Hill, and she hears their shouting, and the yell of distant sirens.

She opens her eyes, scared that she might somehow miss him, and runs her hands along the engraved letters on the back of the seat. A long time ago, Cat read the inscription aloud to him, and then each of them made up their own versions, like spells, making the other laugh. But the last time they met on the bench was the last time they saw each other, and by then words had become powerless. Instead, they squeezed as close as they could, his fingers holding her face, silently wiping away tears, salty thumbs grazing her cheeks. Ten years ago.

She places her hand on the wood, almost as if she expects the warmth of his body to have lingered in the grain. Countless people will have found refuge here, eating a sandwich perhaps, reading a newspaper, pleased with themselves to have found such a good spot, alone or in company, holding a child on their lap or stroking a dog at their knee, looking down into the valley.

Will he come? Fear tightens her throat. Maybe he's forgotten. Maybe he's found someone else. She spots a man making his way towards her. He's doll-sized at the moment; as he approaches, she strains to make out details. Even from this distance and angle, she's sure he's the right height and build. Wait. No. This man's hair is grey. But he's nearly fifty, she reminds herself. He's coming closer across the meadow. Is it him? She frowns and uses her palm to shield her gaze. Then she sees the child traipsing behind, sees him running to catch the man's hand. They have a kite, a red triangle of plastic with a fluttering tail. They are laughing, this stranger and his grandson. Disappointment stings her eyes.

She tries to steady herself, thinking of the diary, how it was all written down; the story of them, from the very beginning.

The first time Cat and Sam sat on this bench, they couldn't stop talking, there was so much to tell each other. The second time she was angry with him. Very angry. The third time they met here, life was a muddle, but not impossible, and the sheer joy of being together eclipsed the rest.

'A hundred years ago,' he told her, 'there would have been cattle grazing here, locals coming to dig up sand, collect wood for their fires. Just think, we could have been a couple with a smoky cottage to go back to, standing out here, feeling the sun on our faces, the scent of the new ponds in the air. Me reaching for your hand, kissing you, your hair, your mouth, and not caring who saw.'

She stayed quiet, imagining them in rustic clothes, living a simple life, no lies or deceit or thoughts of betrayal, just the pure comfort of each other, cows grazing around them, swaying slow and sure. Cat loved the poetry in Sam, how it came out in the lyrics he wrote, the sentences he spoke. How everything became a story, a song. With gleaming eyes, he explained that Guy Fawkes and his gang had planned to watch Parliament blow up from this vantage point; that there was a myth that Boudicca was buried here.

'Boudicca! Are you making this up?'

He showed her a battered book in his coat pocket. *Hampstead Heath: The Walker's Guide.*

'Very sex, drugs and rock 'n' roll,' she teased.

He made a lunge then, and Cat slipped out of his grasp to run down the hill, stumbling over tussocks, feet slurping in and out of mud pools, arms flailing for balance, longing for him to catch her, anticipating the first thud of his body against hers, the judder of rib bone against spine, one heart behind the other.

⋆　⋆　⋆

It is his shadow that touches her first, lassoing her inside its darkness, making her look up. He's breathing heavily. He must have taken the steep slope at a run, sprinted up it like a young man to find her.

His hair is not grey. It's thick and black, with paler streaks at his temples. He runs a trembling hand through its damp strands, pushing it back. They stare without speaking. She has so much to tell him, but the words have caught in her throat.

He does not look away or even blink. His stare holds her at its centre. Feelings flash across his features, one after the other, like a pack of cards falling from an opened hand. And despite everything, the last one that settles on his long mouth and around the creases on his forehead and inside his black eyes is hope.

Part One

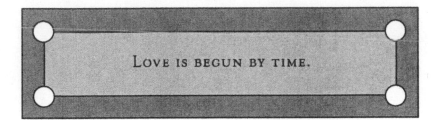

LOVE IS BEGUN BY TIME.

1

Cat, March 1983

To Mom's eternal disappointment, all the men I meet are dead. But that's what happens when you work in a funeral home. Even the guys I spot on my days off strolling the boardwalk in their flared pants and open-necked shirts, smirking at girls and eating handfuls of salt-water taffy, look hardly alive. Of course, to be fair, they're tourists, here for the gambling and the fun of the arcade. They're in Atlantic City to escape reality.

There are never any tourists around when I get up and head for the beach. It's not just the early hour, the sky pink with dawn light, it's because our neighbourhood's considered out of bounds. Don't go more than one block from the beach, is the general recommendation. 'Heavens to Betsy,' the old ladies in their plaid pants tell each other, 'be sure not to stray too far.'

But once I've crossed the wide strip of Atlantic Avenue, the clapboard houses and vacant lots fall away, and I'm in the area people think of as Atlantic City: big casinos and towering hotels, doormen in uniforms yawning on their patch of red carpet. By now I can smell the briny tang of the ocean, and soon I'm on the long line of the boardwalk itself, the sea murmuring beside me. The weak spring sunshine doesn't take the chill out of the air, so no one else is fool enough to

7

think of swimming. As I pass shops with *Closed* signs on the doors, chained-up surfboards rattling in the breeze, it's just me and the night cleaners, and a few stray cats.

Green wooden benches are positioned all along the front, facing the ocean. Every morning, I stop beside the exact same one, resting my hand on its curved back, touching its little bronze plaque. And down by the shoreline, the sea waits: the comforting *hush, hush* of the waves, the never-ending stretch of blue on blue. I hold my breath, because I'm hoping for a sight of fins, and I gasp as I spot them: three dolphins ducking in and out of the waves. I know I won't be able to get close, but the joy of seeing them propels me down the steps and onto the sand. At the surf's edge, I strip down to the swimsuit I'm wearing underneath my jeans and sweatshirt, and before I can gauge the exact level of biting cold, I plunge straight in.

Nothing else exists except green-blue water and mind-numbing cold. I swim fast, my arms carving a path through the low waves, keeping the shore in sight, counting the empty lifeguard stations in order to know when to turn and swim back. By the time I'm out and towel-dried, clothes pulled on over skin tacky with salt, the early crowds are gathering. I hear the familiar chink and clatter of the arcades opening for business, awnings being winched over shop-fronts, racks of postcards and novelty souvenirs wheeled onto the wooden boards.

As I head for home, the scent of coffee wafts from the Beach Shack, reminding me that I'm hungry. In front of me, a tall guy rests his guitar case and a huge rucksack on the ground, then rolls his shoulders and gets a map out of his jeans pocket. He looks to be in his mid twenties, and I like his face. He has a long mouth that seems made for smiling. He bends his head to examine the map, floppy dark hair falling into his eyes. I slow my steps, thinking I could offer him directions, but a couple have already stopped. They hold a camera out to him, gesturing. As I pass, I hear his voice replying politely. He's English. His voice sounds as I imagine those old-fashioned heroes in my favourite novels might.

Immediately, I have this scene in my head — a kind of mash-up of *Pride and Prejudice* and *Rebecca*, Mr Darcy crossed with Mr de Winter: a man with beautiful manners and a stately home. A man with a wide mouth and an easy smile. In my head, I watch him striding off into the distant green of an English countryside to right an injustice, to win the heart of the woman he loves.

I wonder what the tall guy with the guitar would say if he knew that hearing a snatch of his British accent triggered a fantasy in the space of five seconds. But that's what's so great about an imagination, the freedom to roam inside your own head. Without it, I'd probably be certified by now.

★ ★ ★

Dad's slumped on his chair on the porch, and it's clear he hasn't been to bed. He's been

9

playing blackjack or poker at one of the casinos. Red-eyed and dishevelled, he gives me a weary glance.

I take his hand. 'Come on, Dad. You need to eat something. You can't be late for work again.'

'I was on a roll, Kit-Cat,' he says in a hoarse voice. 'It was my lucky night . . .'

'. . . and then it wasn't,' I finish.

'Yeah.' He pushes a hand through his thinning hair, then fishes a crumpled packet of cigarettes from his pocket and attempts to light one with shaking fingers, the flame stuttering out. I crouch beside him and hold his lighter steady. He smells of stale sweat and nicotine. He takes a deep drag.

There's a small birthmark on my forehead shaped like a star, or it is if you squint and use your imagination. 'My lucky star,' Dad likes to say. I don't ask him how much he lost. He wouldn't admit the truth anyway. No need to panic, I tell myself, my wages will cover the rent. Just as well, because there's nothing of value left in our house to sell or pawn. Mom's piano went months ago. She says it's easier now, better without the worry of losing it. But sometimes I catch her running her fingers over the kitchen table, sounding notes in her head.

* * *

After a quick shower, I'm dressed for work in my uniform of black shirt and trousers. In the kitchen, Mom's bustling about, a white apron over her sprigged cotton dress, a blue ribbon in her hair like a young girl. She's cooking grits and eggs for my father. Coffee boils in a pot on the stove. I pour myself a cup.

She gives my steel-capped boots a sorrowful glance. I've given up telling her that I wear them for protection. It's mandatory. She longs to see me in elegant pointed slippers with delicate heels.

I take a sip of scalding liquid. 'It's got worse, hasn't it?' I lift my eyes to the ceiling. Above our heads, Dad's heavy footfall creaks across the boards.

She turns, hisses, 'You think I don't know?'

'But Mom — '

'There's no point, Catrin. No point talking about it. We manage, don't we?' Her words trickle into silence. Neither of us speaks for a moment. 'He found it hard after little Frank died.' She flutters her fingers. 'Then you were so ill . . . at death's door. It took a toll. And there were the medical bills. It's been a struggle ever since. I think that's it. I think that's why he does it.'

'I know he doesn't want to hurt us . . . '

Mom grimaces. 'I have one of my sick heads.' She touches her temples with the tips of her fingers, rubs in tiny circles. 'Just do one thing for me,' she says.

'Mom?'

She comes close, and I think she's going to ask me to massage her feet or fetch a damp cloth to cool her brow. 'Don't be hasty when it comes to finding a husband,' she says. 'Not like me.' She grips my wrist and squeezes hard. I didn't realise

11

she had the strength. 'Make the right choice. Use your head, not your heart. I want you to have a good life. I want you to be secure.' She lets go of me. 'Safe.'

'Safe?' I repeat. 'Mom, I'm not going to rely on a man for that.' I frown, rubbing my wrist. 'Do you . . . regret marrying Daddy?'

She looks at me with something like pity. 'Regret is pointless, Catrin. Best just to make decisions that will save you from the sorrow of it.'

'But . . . you did love him, before?'

'Love?' She clicks her tongue impatiently. 'Love's not real, Catrin. Not romantic love.' She turns from me, busying herself with putting crockery away.

★ ★ ★

I spent so long wishing Baby Frank hadn't died, imagining how he'd have turned out, that the wanting has made him real, real enough that I can conjure him at will: a lanky big brother giving me bear hugs, dishing out advice along with plenty of teasing. He sounds deep and slow, with a hint of the South; not country, but that lovely, lazy stretch to his vowels like Mom's.

Mom's fallen out of love with Dad, I tell him. *Do you suppose Dad knows?*

I imagine Frank wrinkling his eyes in irritation. *What's to love about a man who lies? Dad hasn't got a clue. Haven't you been watching?* He whispers into my ear. *Listen, you can't fix Mom and Dad. You need to fix yourself, Cat. You need to start living.*

12

I suspect Frank disapproves of my job. Which is ironic, when you think about it. Like Mom, he probably worries that there's not much of a social life attached; I'm the first to admit that most people I meet aren't exactly raconteurs. Corpses tend to be on the quiet side.

I get to Greenacres on time, clumping up the steps to the front entrance, past the sign saying: *Funeral Home. Est. 1927.* Pushing open the door, I'm in the hushed, respectful silence of the foyer, lilies upright in a pale vase.

At the end of every working day, there's a silky dust on my skin, a grey tinge of something that looks like soot. Human ash gets everywhere, flying free just as soon as the door of the retort is opened, riding on a wave of heat.

'Oh Catrin,' Mom said when I first told her about the job. 'How are you going to find yourself a husband working in that place?' She shuddered. 'Never tell a soul you work there.'

'Isn't it a sin to tell an untruth?' I teased her.

'Well, this is different.' She gave me a sad, damp look. 'A gentleman would think it odd.' She sucked in her cheeks. '*Anyone* would think it odd.'

She can disapprove of my job as much as she likes; truth is, it's the best-paid option for someone like me, with only a high school education and no qualifications. Don't get me wrong, I wanted to go to college to study English and American literature. 'Plenty of books in the library,' was Dad's helpful take on it.

Mom's right, of course. I never will meet a man at a funeral parlour. But her Southern upbringing has made her believe a woman isn't complete, or even capable, without a man at her elbow, protecting her virtue, paying her bills. Only I wasn't brought up in the Deep South. I was brought up on the road, fending for myself at new school after new school, never settling in one place long enough to make real friends or finish my studies. More than acquiring a man, I'd like to acquire a talent.

At Greenacres, I'm often the last in this world to touch a person, and it's as if their spirit haunts my fingers. I have to find a way to release them through writing. After work, I go home and scribble out ideas for stories, writing those lost souls back into existence as brand-new characters. Maybe that's it — maybe that's my talent. I want to believe it.

14

2

Sam, March 1983

A sea breeze salts the morning air, tugging at his hair. Sam wishes it would blow away the clatter and beep of slot machines. There's a smell of coffee coming from somewhere, making him realise he hasn't eaten since lunch yesterday. People around him all seem to be chewing bagels, or munching salt-water taffy out of paper bags. His mouth waters. He puts his guitar down carefully, unhitches the rucksack from his shoulders, letting it drop onto the boardwalk with a grunt. The weight has got lighter with each week he's been travelling, but it's still vertebra-crushingly heavy. According to his guidebook, there's a hostel not far away. He takes the map from his pocket and presses it flat with his palm; the place is within walking distance.

He's calculating just how much he has left to spend on food when a couple stop to ask if he'll take a snap of them; they pose beside a neon casino advert shaped like a huge dollar sign. He aims the camera at their shiny smiles, directing them to stand closer.

After they've gone, he hoists his rucksack up, adjusting the angle of his body to balance out the familiar weight.

★ ★ ★

15

He's lucky, one bed left. A bottom bunk. He asks the woman at the front desk of the hostel what the local attractions are, and where he should go to get a flavour of the city. His stomach rumbles as he says the word 'flavour'. She admires her painted fingernails. 'Just stick to the boardwalk,' she says in a bored voice. 'Don't go past Atlantic Avenue. Not if you wanna keep your watch and your billfold.'

The dormitory is empty apart from a young man in Y-fronts doing press-ups in the middle of the room. Sam puts his guitar case on his bed. Sleeping in communal rooms is a bit like going back to his boarding school days, long over. Waking to find himself in a tiny bunk with someone else snoring close by came as a shock after the privacy of his airy flat in Barnsbury, the comfort of his and Lucinda's double bed with its Egyptian cotton sheets. But he's got used to travelling on a tight budget; he's even come to like it, because it means he appreciates luxury all the more on the odd occasions he has it, and because having limited means forces him to use his imagination.

The young man doing press-ups gets to his feet with a grunt. He glances at Sam. 'One hundred, every day.' He smiles a little self-consciously, inclining his head in greeting, 'Levi Hansma.'

'Sam,' Sam says, craning his neck to look up. 'Sam Sage.'

'Sam Sage,' Levi repeats, exaggerating the hissing sounds. 'Nice name, buddy.'

'Your English is good. You're German?'

16

'Dutch. Are you here for the gambling?'

'No. Just passing through,' Sam says. 'Leaving tomorrow. Planning on visiting Miami, then New Orleans.'

Levi pulls on a pair of jeans, shrugging his head through a checked shirt without undoing the buttons. 'We're here for the casinos. There's three of us. You want to join us tonight?'

Sam is tempted. He likes Levi's big, open face, his straightforward friendliness. He imagines Levi's companions will be similar amiable blonde giants. He's missed male camaraderie, his friend Ben and his constant banter, taking the mickey out of everything. But he shakes his head. 'I've got no money left. Nearly at the end of my visa. Just three weeks left.' He sits on his bunk. 'I've been in the wilderness. Haven't slept in a bed for a while.'

'You're a musician?' Levi nods at the guitar.

Sam pauses. 'Yeah,' he says. He sits up straighter. 'I am.' He opens the case and puts his hand on his acoustic instrument, pats it affectionately.

'Cool. We were in a bar last night. The music was good,' Levi says. 'It was on Pacific Avenue.' He frowns. 'What was the name . . . ' He holds up a finger. 'Ally's. That was it. Not far from here. It was like, um, rock music? Live. It was good.'

'If it's free entry, I might give it a try,' Sam says. Then he sniffs his underarms and rolls his eyes. 'Think I'd better take a shower before I eat something. I've gone feral the last few weeks.'

'Feral?' Levi raises his eyebrows. 'I don't know this word.'

17

Sam grins. 'Wild.'

Levi opens his mouth in an 'ah' of understanding. 'Communal showers down the corridor. Hot-dog stand on the corner of the street.' He gives Sam a thumbs-up. 'See you later.'

The shower room is deserted. There's a public swimming pool smell of feet and disinfectant, and the drip of a leaky shower head. Sam steps out of his well-worn jeans, dropping his black sweatshirt onto the tiled floor, kicking off his trainers. He stands under the stream of water, letting it hit his scalp, his sore shoulders, the base of his neck.

He looks down at the scum of water running down his skin, his gaze falling on his new tattoo. He grimaces. Lucinda will hate it. The thought gives him a familiar twist of guilt; he needs to find a phone booth. He promised he'd be in touch every week. He knows each time he rings that she's hoping he's ready to return to their life together. Ever since they started to date in their last year at Oxford, Lucinda always had grand plans — for going to London and applying for their first jobs, for moving in together, for decorating their new flat, and now for him to rise to partner in the law firm he works for. He's tried to explain that he doesn't want that. But she won't listen. He dreads their stilted conversation, pauses magnified through the crackle of the long-distance wire.

3

Cat, March 1983

I'm still a rookie at the funeral business. The young ones are especially hard. 'No sense in taking on their grief, isn't room enough in your heart for it all,' Ray tells me. But unlike him, I haven't spent forty years adjusting to the matter-of-factness of death.

After work, I take the jitney to Maryland Avenue, heading for my favourite bench on the boardwalk. I like to spend a few minutes sitting there, looking out at the ocean. It makes me feel better.

Get out in the evenings, Frank keeps telling me. *You got to live a little*. I want to do exactly that: find a drink in a bar, loud music, the rowdy press of other living humans at my elbows. I long for the casual touch of someone's hand on my shoulder, to share a joke or two. The only people I know here are Ray and my boss, Eunice. Neither of them is going to be my drinking companion. And much as I know Frank would love to oblige, circumstances mean he can't.

I walk down the steps onto the beach. At the edge of the surf, I slip off my shoes and sit on the cold sand, wiggling my toes so that my feet are half submerged.

'Wanna get a drink with me?' I ask a nearby seagull, and he fixes me with a sceptical eye, flaps his great wings and takes off over the blue. 'Well, I was only asking,' I murmur, wrapping my arms around my knees.

Behind me, people scream on the big dipper, the arcade machines ring and the crowd on the boardwalk chatter and whoop. The wind has got up, blowing gusts of grit into my eyes, scraps of rubbish from the boardwalk. As I head for home, a piece of paper slaps against my ankle, sticking there. I bend down to peel it off. It's a flyer for a club: Ally's on Pacific Avenue. Free entry. A live band. I go to screw it up to throw in the trash. Then blink at the words again.

Go on, urges Frank's voice. *This is a sign, right? Take a little risk. Who cares if you go to a bar alone? This is the eighties, kid. You might meet someone, make a friend.*

I crumple the paper.

I dare you, his voice insists.

I don't remember when I first invented my brother's voice; I must have been pretty small, I guess. Now he's a character all of his own. He's been with me for years, giving me strength each time I crouched in some dark place, listening to Mom sobbing in another room, with Dad promising her he was gonna stop, that this was absolutely the very last time, hand on heart, that he was gonna see the inside of any goddam casino. Dad's lies taught me not to trust, but Frank has never let me down. He was with me on every midnight flit we made from rental places, whispering comforting words as I struggled to keep up with Mom and Dad, hurrying through the night, Dad loaded down

20

with cases. I worked out early that I couldn't hang on to anything precious; even my old plushie, a torn dog with one ear called Titch, got left behind in one of those houses we abandoned, in a city we never revisited. Anything of financial value could disappear into Dad's pockets, and anything I loved could be lost at any moment. Nothing was safe. But Frank couldn't disappear, because his voice was inside my head.

I look down at the crumpled paper in my hands. Frank knows I'm not going to wimp out of a dare. All right, I tell him. You win. You're a goddam bully. But I'll go to this club.

4

Sam, March 1983

The hostel bed proves too tempting to resist. After his shower, and a hot dog eaten too fast, he rolls into the bunk and closes his eyes. Just a couple of hours, he thinks.

When he wakes, bleary-eyed, with a taste of onions in his mouth, mustard dried to a crust on his cheek, it's early evening. He fumbles for his trainers and finds a piece of paper tucked into one of them: *See you at Ally's tonight! Levi.*

He calculates that he's got a little time to explore, find somewhere to eat, see what this place has to offer before he meets Levi and his friends. He puts his guidebook in his pocket.

He walks the boardwalk for a while, checking out the arcades, craning his neck to stare up at towering casinos, and then, with a jolt of something that feels like electricity, he sees her. She stands up from a bench. She's hard to miss: tall and slim, dressed entirely in black, and with such a sad expression he wonders if she's just been to a funeral. His fingers fall still and his shoulders straighten as she walks by, so close that he catches the slant of her cheek in profile, the shine of bare skin. Sunlight picks out golden glints in her light brown hair, pulled off her forehead, tied at the nape of her long neck. Nobody else appears to notice her. It's as if she's a ghost, he thinks. He watches as she goes down the steps onto the beach, big workman boots clumping un-ghost-like against the wood, and his gaze follows her across the sand towards the ocean. He feels an urgent need to go after her, and his body flickers into involuntary movement, but she looks as though she needs to be alone. He turns away.

It's getting chilly, the last dregs of sunlight seeping away. He settles himself at a corner table of a café called the Beach Shack, where he buys a plate of chips and ekes out a flat white, watching the deserted sand. He's hoping to see the girl again. He imagines that he'll spot her easily in her black clothes. But she doesn't make another appearance. Disappointed, he reads through his guidebook again. He loves facts and stories about the places he's visiting. He orders another coffee and reads about the Mob shooting each other on the streets of Atlantic City in the twenties.

After the waitress has asked for the fourth time if he wants anything else, he closes the book with a snap and stands up, stretching stiff muscles. When he finds Ally's on Pacific Avenue, he asks the bouncer what the band is. The roar of chatter from inside is already deafening. The hulking man in black pea coat and dark glasses frowns, cupping his hand to his ear.

'Who's playing tonight?' Sam shouts again.

'The Magic Men,' the bouncer says. 'Cover act.'

'Cover act?' Sam's heart plummets. He hesitates. Maybe there's another band, something authentic and interesting, playing somewhere nearby? On the other hand, it's cold, and entry is free. He dithers, trying to make up his mind.

'Sam! Sam Sage!'

Levi looms over the shoulder of the bouncer. He steps forward, flanked by two ruddy-faced young men, his companions so exactly as Sam imagined, it makes him laugh.

'Hey, buddy.' Levi gives him a playful punch on the shoulder. 'You came. You won't regret it. It's a cool place.'

And Sam is corralled into the club by three blonde giants, all of them clapping him on the back, offering to buy the lagers.

5

Cat, March 1983

The security guy waves me through; no cover charge. Inside, it's small and loud.

I am bumped and jostled by shoulders and elbows as I make my way towards the bar, where I buy a Miller Lite. The crowd are clapping and whooping. I turn towards the stage and see four guys arranging themselves at drum kit and keyboard, grinning over their guitars. One of them grabs the microphone and shouts, 'Atlantic City! We're the Magic Men. And we're here with all your favourite songs tonight.'

They begin to play a version of Aerosmith's 'Walk This Way', and the room goes wild. I take a gulp of my beer. At first, I'd thought the slurring lead vocals was down to faulty equipment, but when the singer stumbles over his guitar flex, I realise he's drunk. There's laughter and catcalls as he gives the audience a thumbs-up before launching into another song. Halfway through, he staggers forward, appears to attempt an Elvis-like hip gyration, catches his foot on a speaker cable and, with a surprised squawk, pitches head first over the side of the stage. The music screeches to a halt, a guitar twanging tunelessly, a last clash of the hi-hat, as the rest of the band members peer over the edge at their fallen singer.

Burly security men move purposefully forward. There is an eerie silence, and then the buzz and mutter of conversations starts up.

'Shit,' someone is saying. 'Maybe he's unconscious.'

'Nah, the dude's wasted,' another voice says. 'Won't have felt a thing.'

There is laughter and booing as the singer is half dragged, half carried between the flanking shoulders of the stony-faced bouncers. A man in a suit climbs onto the stage and waves his arms for silence. 'Management,' someone says. But the noisy crowd refuses to shut up. The band members are conferring in a huddle, worried faces in the strobe lights. Another man has appeared on the stage, and I'm guessing he's a roadie, as he's wearing a black T-shirt and jeans. He says something to the nervous man in a suit, who scratches his head. Now the new guy is talking earnestly to the band. They discuss, gesticulate. The new guy comes to the front and picks up the microphone.

'Hi,' he says. 'It seems that your singer tonight is . . . a little indisposed.' Hoots. Whistles. He waits for them to die down. 'My name is Sam Sage. If you'll have me, I'm happy to front a couple of covers for you tonight.'

'I'll have you!' a woman calls. There's more laughter.

Sam Sage smiles. He has a long mouth and a crooked smile. And it adds up fast in my head: that mouth, his accent. He's the same guy I saw on the boardwalk this morning. I remember the guitar by his feet. He pushes a hand through untidy black hair, and closes his eyes for a moment. Then he nods his head, and clicks his fingers. One. Two. Three. The room falls silent. The band look at each other and shrug, and the keyboard begins, a gentle swell of notes. Sam opens his mouth and launches into a Patti Smith song, 'Because the Night'. One of my favourites. By the time the drums kick in and his voice blasts into the chorus, the room is singing along with him, and I want them all to shut up, because he's good. Really good.

★ ★ ★

Sam Sage sings more covers. When the band stops, there's a frenzy of relieved high-fives between them. The audience clap and cheer. Sam springs off the stage into the crowd, and I see hands reaching to pat his shoulders, a tall blonde man thrusting a beer towards him.

'Must be nice being the hero,' the man next to me says.

'He was amazing,' I say.

'He's too cocky,' says a guy to my left. 'I could have got on that stage and done the same.'

'But you didn't,' I say.

The restroom is full of girls jostling for space at the mirror. As I sit in the stall, disembodied voices float over the door. 'Cute,' one of them says.

'I'm a sucker for the accent,' sighs another.

'I'm gonna get his number.'

Out of the cubicle, I wash my hands, bending towards the faucet to take mouthfuls of lukewarm liquid. I straighten up, wiping my lips and chin with the back of my hand. The girl next to me is tilting close to the glass, batting blackened lashes. She straightens up and winks at me, 'That English dude has started a riot. But I wouldn't say no.'

I go back into the club, but the band have packed up. I don't want to stand in this crush, drinking by myself. I catch sight of Sam Sage in the crowd, people grabbing his hand to shake, patting him on the back. He deserves it, I think. He saved the night.

I did it, I tell Frank. Spent an evening in a bar on my own. But now there's disco music playing and everyone's hammered. I'm going home to check on Mom.

Way to go! Frank sounds a little surprised. *Step in the right direction, sis. Hell, I'm proud of you.*

★ ★ ★

Outside, the lights from the boardwalk trail glitter across the dark sea. The beach between me and the water is a shadowy swathe of empty space. I know that junkies loiter under the pier at night, kids with flick knifes in their back pockets, but I go down onto the sand anyway, slipping off my shoes and socks. I want to walk by the sea and think about Sam Sage, the way he sounded up there on the stage, the way he smiled into the audience, and how, just for a moment, it felt as if he was smiling right at me.

6

Sam, March 1983

As soon as the lead singer had fallen into the audience, Levi was poking him in the chest. 'Get on the stage!' he insisted. 'They need you up there, buddy. You can sing, yes?'

He resisted. But as soon as Levi had communicated the fact that Sam was a singer, the three of them lifted him and set him down gently behind the speakers. He blinked in the lights, stunned by the new perspective. Then instinct took over. It felt good to be in front of an audience. There was only a brief moment of dry-mouthed horror before the words came rushing through him. The band, apart from their idiot lead singer, were professionals. Afterwards, the manager stuffed a wad of dollar bills into his palm, asked if he'd sing for the rest of the week, or until the band got themselves sorted.

As the blonde giants batter his shoulders with congratulatory punches, he squints towards the exit at a familiar figure. His heart skips. It's her. The tall girl from the beach. He catches a glimpse of her face as she stares into the crowd, and remembers her expression from before: her terrible sadness, her stillness. He needs to talk to her. She's leaving. Panic stirs in his gut.

He makes his way as quickly as he can towards the door, but people are keen to be his best buddy. He pushes on, away from expectant strangers and clutching fingers, words crowding him, questions spilling before him like obstacles.

★　★　★

Dammit, he thinks, breathing hard outside the club. He's lost her. The avenue is frantic: a crowd of holidaymakers pushes past, features distorted by the electric pulse of casino lights. There's a stink of fried grease and alcohol. He sniffs, hungry despite himself, and smells something else. The Atlantic Ocean. He follows the scent, his steps merging with the flow of the crowd, and finds himself back on the boardwalk. He dodges drunks, following the smell of brine towards the dark spill of sand and sea and night sky. He leans on the rail of the boardwalk, clutching it like a raft in a storm. Out there is the blackest navy, a glimmer of starlight. Movement catches his attention and he looks down. A figure is moving away, along the beach.

★　★　★

'Hey!' He's blundering after her.

She whips around with shoulders squared, fists clenched, and he realises she's terrified. 'Sorry.' He stops, holding his hands up. 'I'm not going to hurt you. I just . . .'

She's staring at him. Her fear has turned to caution, a flicker of curiosity making her frown. 'You're the guy from the club.' She tilts her head to one side, hair sliding across her cheek. 'Sam

30

Sage.' She says his name as if to prove that she can remember it.

He feels a tug of shame in his throat.

'It was cool,' she says, 'what you did back there. Took some nerve.'

'Actually, I didn't have much choice . . . but thanks.' He shrugs. 'Funny, but I saw you this afternoon.'

'*You saw me?* This afternoon?' Her eyebrows shoot up.

He's not sure why she's so surprised. 'Yeah. You were sitting on a bench a bit further along the boardwalk from here.' He gestures vaguely in the direction. 'You went down onto the beach.'

She takes a step backwards, folds her arms. 'You were watching me?'

'I noticed you,' he says quickly. 'You stood out a bit, you know. I mean, everyone else was all excited and laughing, and there you were in black from head to foot, walking like you were on a mission. And you looked . . .'

'What?'

'Sad,' he says.

'Oh.' It sounds as though all the air has left her with that one sound.

'Had something . . . bad happened?' he asks.

But she says at the same time, 'That was my bench — '

Their words cross, and it makes her laugh. Him too. Nerves zing in the air between them. She has a nice laugh, he thinks. It's big and honest and she doesn't put her hand in front of her mouth as so many people do.

'Your bench?'

'Not mine personally, no. But I've gotten fond of it. It has a great view. And there's the inscription . . . '

'Inscription?' He takes a couple of steps closer. She has a gap between her front teeth, and he finds it incredibly endearing.

'Yeah, you know. The plaque on the back. I love reading them. Each one is like a little story. Love and loss. I always wonder about the people they're for — make up stories about them in my head.'

'Yes,' he says, startled. 'I know what you mean. It's funny. I do the same thing.'

'You do?' She widens her eyes. 'I thought I was the only one.'

He notices that a few strands of her hair are caught in her earring, creating a delicate loop that he wants to touch, to unravel. Her hair is halfway between blonde and brown. What name do people give to that colour? Honey? he guesses. Amber?

'What does the inscription say?' he asks. 'On your bench.'

'"For Frank, who loved the view from this bench. I know you are still sitting beside me."'

His pulse jumps with recognition. 'It says that?' Then he registers the first bit of the inscription. 'But did you know this guy . . . Frank?'

'No. Just, he's got the same name as someone . . . someone important to me.'

'A boyfriend?'

She shakes her head. 'Nothing like that.' She rubs her nose. 'You're English?'

Relieved, he nods again. 'From London.'

'On vacation?'

'Kind of. I've been travelling. Nearly at the end of my visa.' Is that disappointment he can see in her eyes? Maybe it's just his wishful thinking. But he makes a decision in that second. 'I'm staying here for the rest of my trip,' he tells her. 'Got a job at Ally's until they find a permanent replacement. I've never been in Atlantic City before. Fancy showing me around?'

'Fancy?' She turns the word over, smiling to herself. Then she gives him a long, penetrating look. 'Why me?'

Sam's heart has started to hammer at his ribs. 'I don't know anyone else.'

'You don't know me.'

'No, but I . . . well, I hoped that you might be kind enough . . . '

'I'm not a groupie. Just so we're clear.'

'No.' Sam widens his eyes. 'God, no. I didn't think . . . '

She shrugs. 'Not much to see. Tourists stick to the boardwalk and the casinos.'

'Well,' he says slowly, doing a good impression of casual, 'maybe you could show me the real city, then?'

'You wouldn't like it much.'

He looks at his trainers, kicks them into the sand. Is this her way of saying no? He glances up. She's bending down, and he realises that she's pushing her feet into her shoes. Not the clumpy men's boots from before, but red pumps. She's not in black any more; she's wearing glittery ankle socks and a red and yellow dress. She

33

straightens up, brushing her hands against her dress. 'After work,' she says. 'I can meet you after work tomorrow.'

'Great.' He tries to stop himself grinning too hard. 'Can I walk you home?'

Her head jerks and she angles her body away. 'No need.'

'It's just . . . well, isn't it dangerous on the beach at night?'

'I can look after myself.' She gives him another penetrating glance. 'And we've only just met, so I'm not sure if I should trust you to get me home safe.'

'Of course. Sorry. I didn't mean . . .'

She softens. 'I live here. I can handle myself.'

'Yeah.' He puts his hands in his pockets.

'Goodnight then.' She begins to walk away.

'Wait!' His hands are out of his pockets, his voice rising to a squeak, all pretence of cool gone. 'Where do you work?' He clears his throat. 'So I can meet you?'

She frowns as if it's a difficult question. 'Just find me on the beach,' she says after a pause. 'Where you first saw me. Around five thirty.'

'Great,' he repeats. He can compose rhymes on the spot, but this girl has reduced him to monosyllables. Before she can turn away, he says quickly, 'You never told me your name.'

She looks wary, as if it's another trick question, and then nods. 'Catrin Goforth.' She pushes her hair behind her ear. 'Some people call me Cat.'

★ ★ ★

He waits, watching her disappear into the shadows. Above him, the screams and clatter of the boardwalk are like noises from a nightmare; flashing lights illuminate slices of sand and then cast them into blackness. He doesn't like the idea of her walking alone under the pier. But she must know what she's doing, he reassures himself. She's nearly as tall as him, and moves with long, firm strides. Remembering her words, the way she faced him with her chin up, ready for confrontation, even though she was scared, implied she was confident. It was just something in her face that made him think she was vulnerable — a bit wary; as if she was hiding a hurt.

Catrin Goforth. Like the name of a heroine in a play, something historical and witty. An Oscar Wilde, maybe. Some people call me Cat, she said. People. It strikes him as odd now that she didn't say *friends*, or *family*. There's nothing feline about her. She doesn't have a button nose or slanting eyes. She has strong, straight features, a wide mouth with white American teeth, just the gap between the front two lending a little necessary imperfection, and that steady blue-yellow gaze, unnerving in its openness.

As he turns back to the boardwalk, the simple joy of getting her to agree to meet him is dissipating. He shouldn't have pursued her. He's not in a position to begin any kind of relationship — not when he's got a girlfriend at home. He can't cancel; he doesn't have her telephone number. He'll have to meet her on the beach. A vague arrangement, it occurs to him now; perhaps she won't turn up. If she does, they can have a coffee and go their separate ways, no big deal.

Except the thing is, it feels like a big deal. Over the last months, despite his intention to avoid meeting anyone, out of necessity he's come across a lot of strangers on the road, good people who gave him advice or directions, people who shared their life stories, who gave him lifts, even donated their lunches; but he hasn't met one person that made him feel like this. He tries to work out what 'this' is, and decides that the nearest he can describe is an unexplained familiarity and at the same time an exhilarating sense of standing at the top of a mountain looking down into a spinning abyss.

He thinks of her response when he offered to walk her home, as if he'd insulted her; perhaps he came across as controlling, too macho. Whereas of course he was just trying to do the right thing. Walking a girl home safely to her front door is one of many rules instilled in him by his upbringing. But the world that taught him those rules lies in ruins. He hears his father's voice in his head urging him to be a man, to do the right thing, to behave with honour. 'Fuck off, Dad,' he hisses under his breath.

★ ★ ★

Sometimes a whiff of scent will send him back, quickly and unexpectedly, as if he's fallen down Alice's rabbit hole. Even all these years later. *Whoosh*. Straight to hell. There are several

36

components to that particular perfume. Chalk. Silver polish. The stink of hormones leaking from armpits, skin raging with acne, sweating palms. Fear. He'd never realised before that fear had a smell, but his first day at boarding school, he understood.

It had been his father's school before him. His father had been head boy. His name was inscribed on the honours board. Holder of the Fairly Cup. Captain of the cricket and rugby first teams. His record for the 400 metres never beaten. A couple of the masters were old enough to have taught them both, and when they realised the connection, they looked down their noses through smeary glasses and said, 'So, you're his son? Well, well.' And he felt that he'd missed the mark. A disappointment, as he was at home.

He was a late developer, small for his age. It was a huge disadvantage when most of his peers seemed to grow inches overnight, were busy sprouting hair, calves and forearms thickening with new muscle. He was dropped from even the third teams, his gym shoes flung into the topmost branches of a tree.

The beatings happened almost daily. Fag Master Salt with a belt in his hands. Seven of the best. The reasons were many: daydreaming, smiling, burning toast, not properly polishing Salt's CCF buttons. And then again, for resisting when a hand slipped into his trousers, for flinching at the groping and rubbing. So he ran away. It took him six hours, terrifying hours of walking through the dark and the rain, falling to his knees in ditches, hitching lifts on a blustery motorway. When he reached home, wet and exhausted, and explained why he'd done it, his father beat him for being a dirty little sneak. And then he was returned, like a parcel. Shame consumed him, shame for his weakness, for the fact that he could never be like his father.

★　★　★

Back at the hostel, Sam crawls into his bunk and pulls the covers over his head. The Dutch posse are still out. He hears the rustle of a body moving on the mattress above, and a muffled snore. He won't think about his father. Outside, there is a roar of traffic. The hostel is near the freeway. He wishes he could hear the low moan of the sea, but all outside sounds are funnelled into the hiss of rubber on asphalt and engine roar. The city is an unexplored mystery to him. Somewhere in one of the unknown streets will be the girl. Cat. Hopefully safely arrived at her destination. She must be in her own bed by now, in her own room, dreaming perhaps. The thought of her is oddly comforting. He wishes he'd touched that untidy loop of hair, felt the texture of it between his fingers.

7

Cat, March 1983

I couldn't sleep when I got home. Meeting that guy on the beach — it was almost as if he'd been looking for me, as if I'd been the only reason he was there in the dark and cold. But that can't be true — can it? Meeting him has put me in a state of shock. It feels as though I've been hit with a pancake block. I'm scrabbling around for a way to get back into play. Sure, I want to see him again. But I'm disbelieving. Who wouldn't be? I was relying on Frank's voice popping into my ear to tell me that yes, this is really happening, and dammit, Cat, you deserve it. Only he's remaining stubbornly quiet.

Girls fall over themselves to sleep with men like Sam Sage — I heard those comments in the john. I should forget I ever met him. Walk away before it's too late. He'll be arrogant, superficial; he's bound to be, looking like that, sounding like that. I don't need a man in my life. I'm not like Mom.

★ ★ ★

Ray sucks air through his teeth and shakes his head in disapproval when I bring the wrong body out of the reefer for the second time. 'What's up with you today, girl?' He sends me off to do a makeover on a middle-aged woman whose relatives are insisting on saying goodbye to her face-to-face. She's been dead three days, and without the help of embalming, she's not looking her best. Lime-green fungus blooms across her cheeks. She's on the cuddly side, and I've found that larger ladies decompose quicker.

I settle myself at her side and snap open the large make-up bag. It's full of the tricks of the trade: mouth formers, needle injectors, and eye caps with tiny spikes to keep eyelids closed. Plus an array of commercial cosmetics: bottles of foundation, tubes of lipstick, even mascara. It's going to take a lot of work to disguise the decay. Her name was Cindy, I see from her toe tag. 'Okay, then. Let's do this, Cindy.' I lean closer. 'I don't have a magic wand,' I tell her, 'but I've got a few tricks up my sleeve. I'm gonna send you to the ball looking your best.' And I begin the task of closing her mouth, setting her lips into a winsome half-smile.

As I work, I'm imagining a story where she's alive and centre stage, the main character in a plot where she gets her heart's desire, like a modern Cinderella.

* * *

I get off the jitney with the holidaymakers in their brightly coloured leisure pants, shiny windbreakers and mirrored sunglasses, and pause by my bench looking down onto the beach. There he is, gazing out at the rolling breakers of the Atlantic. I recognise the back of

40

his head immediately, the same untidy dark hair, now blowing about in the sea breeze.

Frank whispers, *This could be the one.*

Fairy tales aren't real, I remind him, as I go down the steps onto the beach, my heart smashing into my ribcage. And it's common knowledge that any Prince Charming comes with a massive ego. My reinforced shoes crunch over the sand. As I get closer, I'm trying to think of something clever to say, something witty.

Sam Sage turns before I reach him. 'Hello,' he says in his English accent, all the sounds standing upright. 'You came.'

'Yeah,' I manage to croak. 'I did.'

'So . . . ' He gestures towards the city. 'Where are you going to take me?'

Take him? I haven't given it a thought. Not allowing myself to get further than this moment. 'Um. Let's sit on my bench awhile,' I say quickly. 'Then . . . I can tell you what's worth visiting. The best attractions and stuff. And . . . you can choose.'

'Passing the buck,' he says with half-closed eyes.

When I take him to the bench, he pauses a moment to read the inscription to himself. Sitting together, with the sound of the ocean breathing and seagulls shrieking overhead, my nerves retreat. He seems pretty relaxed. I guess this kind of thing is all in a day's work for a guy like him. His sleeves are rolled to the elbow, and I notice a tattoo of musical notes curving across his forearm.

'If someone played them, would they make a

tune?' I ask, wanting to run my fingers over the quavers and crotchets on his skin.

'That would have been a good idea, wouldn't it?' he laughs. 'But no. I didn't really think it through that well. Considering it's going to be with me for ever.'

'Have you had it long?'

'About a month.' He rubs his thumb over the tattoo. 'You can probably guess by now — it was a spontaneous decision. Although, in my defence, I wasn't drunk.'

'But was there a reason for it? Does it . . . you know, represent something important?'

'It's supposed to mark a turning point,' he says slowly, his voice becoming suddenly serious. 'I want to stop doing what everyone expects me to do, and do what I want instead.'

'Music?'

'Yup. So the design isn't exactly original, but . . .'

'To the point.'

He laughs again. 'You know, it's odd,' he says slowly, 'I meant to say before, but the inscription on this bench reminds me of one on Hampstead Heath.'

I startle. 'This inscription?'

'Yeah, it's got the same bit in it, about the person still sitting beside you. I like that idea. Someone who's gone, their spirit just sitting there, the memories of them keeping you company.'

'That place you said? Hampstead Heath?'

'It's in London. North London. It's this big open space with hills and trees and woods.

42

Ancient land.' He pauses and looks at me, smiling. 'I think you'd like it. It has lots of benches. Lots of inscriptions.'

'Maybe I'll get to go there one day. I've always wanted to go to London. I've read all of Dickens. And one of my favourite novels is *84, Charing Cross Road*.'

'About the old guy in the bookshop and the woman, writing letters?' He looks at me. 'I liked that too. So how come you've read so many English novels?'

'I've always had a thing for them. Especially the classics. Way back, Dad's side of the family were from England,' I tell him. 'According to him, we're descended from Normans. Dad likes to boast they settled in Buckinghamshire, became landed earls and lords.'

There's blue blood in our veins, Kit-Cat.

I gesture towards the boardwalk. 'How about I tell you what there is to see?'

He shakes his head. 'How about we just wander?'

He stands up, putting out his hand. I take it, and his fingers close around mine, warm and certain. As I stand, we lock eyes. My stomach lurches, and we both glance away.

He nods towards the expanse of camel-coloured sand and spiky grasses. 'Must have been beautiful before it got built up,' he says. And then his voice softens. 'Hello, kitty.'

For a second I think he's getting inventive with my name, but an actual cat is slinking from the gap beneath the boards. I squat and hold out my fingers towards her. She sniffs regally and turns her head away. 'There are dozens of them living wild under here,' I tell him. 'They're a kind of fixture. There's a programme to catch them and spay them, but there are always kittens.' On cue, a tiny creature totters out of the shadows, meowing. The mother gives its rear end an efficient licking before picking it up by the scruff of its neck and removing it from sight.

'I swear she just rolled her eyes,' Sam laughs.

God. He likes animals, too. Could he get any more perfect?

Shut up, I tell Frank. Not now.

We walk on, the bustle of the boardwalk fading away. It feels like we're the only people here: his arm brushing mine, our steps keeping time.

'So what do you do?' he asks. 'I mean, for work.' He puts his head on one side. 'I'm guessing it entails wearing black?'

I swallow. Here it is: the million-dollar question. I remember Mom's warning. I hesitate. 'I work in cosmetics,' I tell him.

'Selling them? Or . . . making them?'

'Um. Neither . . . I just use them to make people look their best — even if they're . . . ' I cough, 'kinda off-colour.'

'A make-up artist?'

I make a non-committal noise, clearing my throat. 'It's not that interesting,' I say quickly. 'Not like being a singer.'

'Actually,' he frowns, 'I'm not. I'm really a lawyer. Only . . . I've begun to think I made a mistake, you know, going down the safe route. Pleasing my parents, when I always had this dream of being a singer-songwriter.' He stops

44

and rolls his eyes. 'Sounds clichéd, I suppose.'

I don't know if this is the famous British self-deprecation or genuine humility. He must know how great he is. 'You *should* be singing,' I tell him. 'It's not just my opinion. The club went wild for you. All the girls, anyway,' I can't help adding.

He rubs his nose, looking bashful. Then he pushes a hand through his hair. 'Hey — do you want to come to another of the shows? I could get you a backstage pass.'

I take a deep breath. 'Sure.' There has to be a catch. And then I remember: he's leaving soon.

'Where are you from in England?' I ask, thinking wouldn't it be funny if he was from Buckinghamshire too.

He looks down. 'We lived in the countryside, but I was away from home a lot when I was a kid.'

'Oh . . . why?'

'Boarding school.'

'Holy shit! You went to boarding school? I wanted to go when I was a kid,' I tell him, unable to contain my enthusiasm. 'I found some Angela Brazil novels in the library. They made it sound so cool, you know . . . midnight feasts and playing pranks. The characters all said 'golly gosh' and 'jolly good show'. I began talking like that for a while. People actually thought I was some weird kid from England.'

He laughs.

I fiddle with a strand of my hair. I used to think that going to a school like the ones in the books would solve my problems, that I'd get to

45

sleep in the same bed every night, have real friends.

I don't want to ruin the atmosphere, so I don't say any of that. I smile instead, and notice where we are — right outside Ripley's Believe It or Not! 'This is where all good tourists go,' I tell him. 'But I've never been.'

'Tourist heaven? First time for both of us then.'

As we look at a wax model of the world's tallest man, I ask, 'So now you're aiming to be a musician, not a lawyer?'

He nods. 'Not an obvious career move, but . . . ' He shrugs.

'It's who you really are,' I say quietly.

'Yes.' He rubs his chin. 'That's it. Whether I'm successful or not, it's only when I'm singing my own stuff that I know I'm *me*.'

'You will be successful. I have a good feeling about it. Hey — maybe you'll even be famous.'

'I don't know about being famous,' he says slowly. 'But the stakes seem higher because I'm older. I'm not a kid any more. But of course,' he opens his arms, and his mouth splits into that wide, crooked smile of his, 'I want as many people as possible to hear my music.' He nods at me. 'What about you? Any ambitions for worldwide fame and domination?'

I shake my head, laughing. 'I'm not good at anything. There's nothing I could be famous for, even if I wanted to be. Which I don't.'

'I'm sure there's something you're good at . . . You're just being humble. Unlike me.'

I can operate a retort, make a corpse look

46

respectable for the relatives. Not exactly talents to shout about from the rooftop. I'm not going to mention my scribbled stories — that would be embarrassing. Sam has a real gift.

'What do your parents think of your new career path?' I ask.

'My parents?' He stares at me. 'They're . . . they're dead.'

'Oh my God!' My hands fly to my cheeks. 'I'm sorry.'

'It's all right,' he's saying. 'But if you don't mind, I . . . I can't talk about it . . . '

'No,' I say, flustered. 'Of course.' My gaze flails about for a distraction. I notice two wizened brown balls behind glass. Black hair sticks out at jaunty angles. 'Look,' I say brightly. 'It says here that they're ancient shrunken heads from an Amazon tribe.' One sports a substantial moustache, and is wearing a kind of funky patterned headband around his mop of hair. 'John McEnroe style,' I say.

'Whaaaat? You cannot be serious!' Sam shouts, doing a good impression.

We're both laughing, and everything is all right again. As we leave the museum of curiosities, happiness opens inside me like blossom, sweet and natural and wondrous.

He stops on the boardwalk, and he's not laughing any more. 'I've just realised something,' he says.

'Yes?' Our faces are close, and my heart thickens and slows so that I can hardly breathe.

He gestures with his fingers, counting. 'Not one, but two decapitated heads on a first date.'

He grins. 'Must be some kind of record. And I've discovered something about you. You're not at all squeamish.' He smiles. 'Both my sisters would have found it creepy.'

The lack of the expected kiss makes me feel unbalanced. Then I remember that he called this a date.

'Well . . . maybe it was a bit creepy,' I concede, trying to sound like I mean it, trying not to think about Cindy's sad face with her rouged cheeks and stiff expression. At least I got her skin tone to look more pink than green. I shut the image out of my mind. Right now, all I want is to concentrate on this moment, on this man walking beside me.

8

Sam, March 1983

The club is jammed. Sweat trickles down the side of Sam's face. He wipes his sleeve across his forehead. The crowd are clapping and whooping. He can't see anything out front except a riot of silhouettes. Cat is standing just behind the strip of curtain that serves as backstage space. She grins when he turns to look at her, and he's jolted all over again by that sudden wide, gap-toothed smile. She looks amazing: long legs in bleached jeans, honey hair falling across her shoulders. He hardly knows her, but there's nobody else in the world he wants here with him, sharing this.

He grasps the mic, brings it close and says, 'This one's for Cat. Bad Company's 'Feel Like Makin' Love'.' There's an expectant din from below, and he glances at Len the drummer, who taps the beat with his stick. Then all thought is gone, because he has a bellyful of words; he tilts his head back, eyes closed, and opens his mouth. But the image of Cat remains, blowtorched onto his mind.

★ ★ ★

He escapes straight after the set, turning down the offer to hang out with the rest of the band.

49

He makes his way through the crowd as she waits by the bar. He's enjoying glimpsing her in snatches, over the shoulders of others, in the sudden flash of strobe, knowing that he'll be with her any minute, the whole of her revealed. When he reaches her, he whispers in her ear, 'Let's get out of here.'

The air outside is cool, sounds muted after the clamour of the club. Cat zips up her jacket and shivers. 'Let's walk,' she says. 'Warm up.'

'Or we could go inside?' he suggests. 'Find another bar?' He wonders if she'll invite him back to her place. He doesn't even know if she lives with someone else — or multiple someones.

'Can we look at the ocean first?'

They make their way onto the sand, grey and gleaming in the moonlight. He can't see another person. In the distance, the Ferris wheel is still working. She's right. It's good to be next to the ocean. The rush of waves soothes his pounding ears. They walk beside each other, hips and shoulders nearly level. 'We'd smash any three-legged race,' he says.

'What?'

'English tradition. You run a race with another person with your inside ankles tied together. Do you have that in America?'

'Oh, yeah,' she laughs. 'We have that here too. It's kinda funny to watch. I've never run in one, though.' She's pulling off her scarf. 'Hey, let's test out your theory.' She's kneeling at their feet, wrapping the scarf around her right ankle and his left. He feels the knot tighten. She stands up. 'Now what?'

'Well . . . I need to put my arm around your waist. And you do the same.' He pauses for a second before he slips his hand around her ribs. Her breath rising and falling under the fabric of her top makes his senses reel. He forces himself to concentrate.

She places her hand lightly on his waist, then turns her head to look at him expectantly. 'And now?'

He wants to lean in and kiss her, but instead he shouts, 'Ready, steady, go!'

There's a moment of complete disconnect. They wobble and nearly fall. Then he grabs her tighter, and they find a rhythm. His teeth jolt as they gallop with three legs over the sand through the dark, and it feels as though his heart is going to burst.

At the shoreline, they stagger to a stop; a big wave swills over their feet, freezing water soaking Sam's trainers and the bottoms of his jeans.

'Shit!' he yelps.

Cat is laughing. She crouches down and unties the scarf, takes off her shoes, kicking them away from her. Her eyes are bright as she rolls up her jeans.

'What are you doing?' he asks.

'Getting wetter,' she says, as she wades into the black water. 'Jeez, it's cold,' she exclaims. 'But it feels kinda amazing. Come in!'

'Is there something you need to tell me — this weird compulsion to take your shoes off all the time, does it have a name, or a cure?' He stands at the edge. She's only a few feet away, but he feels the sorrow of a separation. Waves splash against her legs, sending spray up her thighs. She shrieks and laughs again. Silver light catches in her hair.

'Sharks can get you in the shallows, you know,' he calls out.

'God, that film has a lot to answer for.'

'But there are Great Whites off this coast,' he perseveres. 'Aren't there?'

'I guess. But more sharks get killed by fishermen than the other way around. I've seen dolphins, though. Early morning's best.' She splashes out of the water. 'I swim before breakfast most days.'

She's shivering, teeth chattering like maracas on speed, and it's a great excuse to wrap his arms around her and pull her close. Honey hair tickles his mouth and he takes a deep breath, inhaling the seaweed saltiness of the ocean. Like holding a mermaid, he thinks. His hands are inside her jacket, around the softness of her waist. Desire kindles in his groin. She breaks away, bending to put on her shoes. 'Let's find a bar that's open,' she says.

Holding hands, they walk briskly up the beach towards a flight of wooden steps and the lights of the boardwalk. He's wondering if she felt the same careening into lust, or if it was just him. How can he feel this familiarity, and at the same time such hopeless ignorance?

As they pass the dark overhang of a pier, movement jags at his peripheral vision. Two shapes unfurl from the shadows. He grips Cat's hand tighter. 'Don't look round. Keep walking.'

'Hey!' A shout. Rough, urgent, slurred. 'Got a smoke?'

52

'No. Sorry, mate,' he calls over his shoulder, without pausing.

The men are walking with shambling but fast strides towards the steps. They're parallel and gaining, and there's an intention there; he can feel the arrowed certainty of it and he knows they're planning on cutting them off. Adrenalin screams through him, instinct telling him the situation could escalate quickly. There are two of them. They might have knives. They're probably high on something. He can't take a risk, not with Cat here. 'Run!'

Without a word, she leaps forward, sprinting beside him. He's grateful for her lack of confusion, and her speed. They race for the steps, hand-in-hand. The shadowy figures are running too, a cackle of laughter from one of them. Sam's chest is tight, Cat's breath comes fast. He can hear the men behind, thinks they've fallen further back. But it's not safe to stop. Not yet.

Panting, they take the wooden steps two at a time, staggering onto the boardwalk, hands on their knees, catching some air. 'Shit.' He glances around. It's deserted. 'Where are the bloody tourists when you need them?'

'Follow me,' she's saying. She heads down a narrow alley between two buildings. It's pitch black, but her hand steadies him. On the other side, they're next to a wide street. Cat slips in between two parked cars and crouches down, pulling him after her.

They press together, trying to control the sound of their breathing. Her jeans are wet. All

53

his senses are on high alert, his heart banging in his ears. Everything is clearer, louder: the purr of passing vehicles, the rasp of tyres, distant voices, distant sirens. 'We lost them,' she says, and begins to laugh. Relief crashes through him, and he is laughing too. His belly aches with it.

Their laughter fades to hiccups. Her face is right next to his, and all he can see are her eyes, dark pupils pulling him in. He leans towards that twin darkness, and their mouths meet. They are kissing, and he's falling through the kiss into her body, her soul, their tongues and lips saying everything he's been feeling since they met.

They pull away, staring at each other. 'Wow,' he whispers.

'I need to tell you something.' She drops her gaze. 'I lied,' she says.

'What?'

'I'm not a make-up artist.'

His brain can't seem to catch up. The kiss has disabled the connections somehow, made him feel drunk. 'What?'

'I work in a funeral parlour.'

He still can't react. The words clatter in his mind, not making sense.

'I'm sorry.' She's shaking her head. 'I knew you'd be put off. You're creeped out, right? It's not exactly . . . I don't know . . . sexy.'

'I don't understand what it means,' he says slowly. 'I don't understand what working in a funeral parlour means.'

'It means I spend a lot of time with dead people,' she says. 'Corpses. I collect them from their homes or hospital. I cremate them. I scrape the ashes out of the retort. I fix them up to look better for their relatives after the rot sets in. I get them ready for burials.'

'Okay.' He takes a deep breath. 'That's . . . wow . . . that's . . . '

'Sick?' she suggests. 'Weird? Disgusting?'

'No.' He grabs her wrist. 'It's necessary, isn't it? And it's . . . well . . . it's brave. I don't know if I could do it.'

She swallows. Closes her eyes. 'Kiss me again,' she says.

★ ★ ★

They spend a lot of time kissing after that, leaning up against parked cars, sitting in doorways. She's a good listener, and he hasn't spoken to anyone in a long time, so in between the kissing he finds himself telling her how he wrote song lyrics when other boys were playing rugby, how he played the guitar alone in his bedroom, teaching himself riffs.

'But why didn't you do music after college then, if it was what you'd always wanted?'

'My father made me feel like I'd be letting everyone down if I didn't follow him into the law. Generations of our family have been lawyers. Barristers. Magistrates. It's tradition.'

'But just because something's a tradition doesn't make it right,' she says. 'There are lots of traditions that are just plain wrong.'

'I don't know.' He rubs his forehead hard. 'Is it really that simple? I'll be letting people down . . . my family . . . the law firm I work for . . . '

'Sorry to be blunt, but . . . ' her voice softens, 'your parents are dead.' She shrugs. 'And a law firm will find another lawyer to replace you. If you want it, you should go for it.'

He smiles, pulls her in to kiss her hair. 'What makes you so wise?'

She shakes her head. 'I'm not wise. But I know what it's like to be held back. I'm stuck at home with my parents because my wages pay the rent.' She looks down, twisting her hands. 'I wanted to go to college, to study English and American literature, but I couldn't.'

'There isn't an age limit on going to college,' he says, trying to give her the same encouragement she's given him. 'Maybe you don't need to go to college anyway. Sometimes I wonder what good it did me.'

She sighs. 'I guess. So . . . are you going to play me some of your own material some time?'

'I will,' he says. 'Promise.'

They're walking the long, straight line of Atlantic Avenue, arms entwined, stumbling against each other. He's exhausted, but at the same time buzzing as if he's taken drugs.

'Can we go back to your place?' He's too tired to think of a more subtle way to put it.

'No way.' She sounds appalled. She shakes her head. 'My parents. Remember?'

'Damn.' He bites the inside of his lip. 'We can't go to the hostel.'

Cat is silent. They walk on slowly. They pass a deserted bus shelter, a yellow fire hydrant, Popeye's Louisiana Kitchen, with a homeless man sitting on the step. Looking up, Sam reads

56

the names of hotels and casinos emblazoned at the tops of the buildings, blinking in neon, endlessly beckoning. They stop outside a convenience store, and kiss again. 'I have an idea,' Cat says when they break off. 'I have keys for work. We could go there. Tomorrow night.'

'Work? You mean . . .'

'The funeral parlour. At least we can be alone. Safe.'

'Won't you get in trouble?'

'Only if we're caught.' She squeezes his arm. 'Don't worry. The dead are all safely locked away. You won't see anything gruesome.'

He starts to laugh.

'What?'

'I just remembered yesterday — worrying you'd be squeamish about those shrunken heads.'

She smiles. 'I've never fainted at the sight of blood. But it is upsetting to see bodies when they've died young or violently.' She glances away. 'Being around death makes me hungry to make life count. Only,' she shrugs and looks at him, 'my days are . . . I don't know . . . slipping through my fingers.'

'Because you have to look after your parents? Are they ill?'

'My dad . . . well, he's kind of sick, I guess. He's a gambler.' She says it in a matter-of-fact voice, but he sees the pain in her eyes.

'I'm sorry. That . . . that must be really rough.'

'It's not that he doesn't love us,' she says quickly. 'He tells me and Mom all the time. He's the generous type, you know, full of grand gestures and bear hugs. He likes to ruffle my hair and call me pet names. Once, when I was little, he made me a go-cart out of wood and an old tyre. But gambling comes first. And he lets me and Mom down every time.' She looks at her hands as she continues. 'Talk is cheap, right? Saying you love someone and showing you love them are two different things.' She shrugs. 'We move a lot. We don't always have money to eat. Then suddenly he wins big-time and buys us extravagant gifts.' She looks at Sam. 'Then we're broke again. Mom's stuck in the past. She's never earned a cent in her life. So it's down to me.'

Her words have come out in such a rush, he can hardly understand what she's telling him. He can't imagine how she lives with such uncertainty. Although to be betrayed by the person who's supposed to protect you — he has some understanding of that one. But in the face of what she's just told him, he feels inadequate. He frowns. 'I wish there was something I could do to help.'

'You are helping,' she whispers. 'Just talking to you helps.' She blinks at him. 'I've never told anyone before.'

'I'm glad you did.'

'Not too much information?' She sounds hesitant.

He shakes his head. 'Nothing I can't handle.' He wishes he could find something better to say, something that would explain how honoured he is that she's chosen to confide in him. This is why writing songs is so much easier, he thinks.

The melody is a way of sounding out the unspoken, the part of the story lyrics can't reach.

The street lights flicker off.

'I didn't realise it had gotten so late.' She rubs her eyes. 'I need to get home, take a shower.' She twists her hair into a long tail and pushes it over her shoulder. 'I have to go to work.'

'I'll walk you back.'

'It's nearly daylight. Quicker if I go by myself.'

'I want to make sure you get home safely.' He raises his eyebrows at her. 'Think you can trust me now?'

She lets her hands rise and fall, and yawns.

'Can't you call in sick or something?'

She shakes her head. 'It wouldn't feel right.'

He feels a sudden stab of something that feels like home-sickness. 'Cat?'

She twists around, her face expectant.

'I'm . . . I'm glad I met you.'

She gives her gap-toothed smile, ducks her chin and walks on, hands in her pockets.

As they head away from the coast, each new street is more down-at-heel than the last. Shabby houses, bins on their sides with rubbish spread over the pavement. Empty lots fenced off with wire. A heavy dog with a blunt head barks at them from the end of a chain. Graffiti sprawls across walls.

'It seems worse than it is,' she says. 'But be careful on your way back.' She grins. 'Luckily, you don't look like a tourist. You forgot your velour tracksuit.'

She stops outside a small clapboard house. Bright geraniums spill from pots lining the steps.

He doesn't want her to go. He pushes a strand of honey hair back from her face. 'You're beautiful,' he says.

She blushes, glances away.

A screen door opens and a pale, frowning woman stands in the doorway in a long lacy dressing gown. She wraps it closer as she peers at them suspiciously.

'Damn,' Cat hisses under her breath. 'My mom.'

Sam smiles at the woman and puts up his hand in greeting. 'Good morning,' he calls.

'Hey, Mom.' Cat leaves him, climbing the steps towards her mother. 'Sorry if you were worried. My friend just walked me home.' She pauses, as if considering whether to introduce him. 'This is Sam,' she says quickly. 'He's from England.'

'Young man.' The pale woman stares at him. 'No gentleman brings a lady home at this hour.'

'Mom,' Cat hisses.

He opens his mouth to explain, apologise, but Cat gives him a warning look, mouthing *See you later*, as she hurries her mother into the house. The door swings shut behind them. Sam stands for a moment, feeling the small shock of her mother's words, the sudden loss of Cat. He stands taller. He's confident that he can overcome her mother's prejudice. He's always been good with mothers.

He's whistling 'Morning Has Broken' as he retraces his steps, longing to collapse into his bunk, to close his eyes and go over the details of the evening, remembering every moment, recalling every curve and plane of her face, every nuance of her expression. Waiting at a stop light, the whistle falters on his lips. He rubs his eyes with the heels of his hands. Why on earth did he lie about his parents? It was a sudden impulse, the words out of his mouth before he could stop them. And she needs to know about Lucinda. But it's okay, he reasons; it's not too late to put it right.

9

Cat, March 1983

Mom's hair falls around her shoulders. Her gown gapes, showing bird-thin collarbones. She blocks my way to the stairs like a gatekeeper to the underworld. I knew that if she saw Sam, she'd add up his tattoo and earring and scruffy clothes and come up with the wrong answer.

'Can we not do this now?' I ask wearily, knowing she's going to insist that we do. 'I have to get ready for work.'

She doesn't move. 'Who is he?' Her face is tense. 'What are you doing with a man like that?' She peers at me. 'Have you been with him all night?'

'We were just walking and talking. I lost track of time. He's a singer from England.' I rub my knuckles over my brow. 'He hasn't done anything wrong. And the way he looks . . . it's just . . . fashionable.'

'Fashionable?' She spits the word out. 'Looked like he'd crawled out of a dumpster. A man like that — he'll be on drugs.' Her mouth twists. 'Catrin, I know that sort . . . he'll drag you down.'

'You don't know anything about him. He's going back to England soon. I'll probably never see him again. But right now, he's the first good thing to happen to me.' I pause. 'Anywhere.'

'Well, my goodness, if he's just passing through . . . ' Her voice has softened. 'What's the point in seeing him again?'

I am so tired my eyeballs feel as if they've been rolled in salt. Nausea thickens my throat. 'Mom, please don't try and persuade me out of this. I'm going to meet him again. You can't stop me. I'm not a child.'

She lets out a sound halfway between a sob and a gasp. Her hand presses against her heart. 'I have a pain — right here.'

Gently, I take her hand from her chest and rub it between my own. 'We've been to the doctor. He said your heart was as strong as a twenty-year-old's. You're just tired. I promise, there's nothing to worry about. Go back to bed.' I brush past, catching a mouthful of her sour breath as I climb the stairs.

'I didn't figure you for a fool,' she shouts after me.

I don't have the strength to pronounce words any more. 'Mom,' I whisper. 'Please. It's my life.'

'Just remember, I warned you.' Mom jabs at her loose hair with twiggy fingers, sniffs, and gathers the trailing hem of her gown to mount the stairs after me. 'Don't come crying to me when he lets you down.'

'Sam isn't Dad.'

Shock darkens her eyes. She flinches as if I've struck her.

Dad comes barrelling out of their bedroom. 'Jesus Christ! Can't a man sleep in his own home?'

Defeat lurks in the lines on his forehead, in his

thinning rumpled hair and bloodshot eyes. He's spent all night losing at whatever game he thought he'd get lucky playing.

'Catrin's been out with a man,' Mom says. 'I know white trash when I see it. Tell her to be sensible, Arthur, tell her — '

'Goddammit.' My father scowls. 'Kit-Cat's old enough to know her own mind.'

I tiptoe away. Behind the closed door of my room, I want nothing but the luxury of thinking about Sam. *You're beautiful.* I want to hold the memories close, write them in my diary, find the exact words to describe everything that's happened. I open my diary and turn to a clean page, pick up my pen.

I got him so wrong. It's shocked me to my core that he's not what I thought: full of himself, a womaniser. There's something inside him that makes him doubt himself. He's funny and kind. And it's weird how at home I feel with him — this English guy who's lived a completely different life from me.

Exhaustion overwhelms me and I slump onto my bed, sprawled sideways over rumpled covers. I'll just close my eyes for a minute, I think, as the diary slips from my fingers.

* * *

I slept, of course, waking hours later, still in my clothes from the night before, drool slick on one cheek. I grab the clock and stare at it as if I could will the hands to spin backwards. No time for a shower. But the dead don't care how bad you smell. I pull on my work clothes, grab a handful of crackers and sprint out of the door.

* ★ ★

Ray shakes his head sorrowfully. 'What's up with you, girl? You been acting weird for a couple of days now.'

I would like to take his hand in mine, turn it over and stare into the leathery palm, and explain about Sam. But I can't give Ray any reason to be suspicious. He rules this place like a castle. Knows it like his own skin. If I disturb the dust in a corner, he'll guess it was me, and he'll wonder why I was sneaking around here after hours.

★ ★ ★

We don't have the luxury of time, the privilege of counting out days and nights, ticking them off until he's allowed to get to first base like we're in high school, waiting the correct amount of time before we have sex. We only have three weeks. I don't want to waste a second agonising about whether I'm doing the right thing, or what anyone else will think, or whether he'll respect me in the morning. I am going to have sex with Sam. Period. I just don't want it to be a disaster because of my lack of experience. Since coming to Atlantic City, I've only had one boyfriend. When we finally got around to it, we were both so nervous we drank a bottle of tequila between us, and the squishy fumbling that followed didn't seem to add up to anything in particular.

I'm pretty sure I've never had good sex. It didn't start off well, daring myself to lose my virginity to a football jock at high school. Mission accomplished at a party on a bed lumpy with other people's coats. He couldn't remember my name afterwards. Then there was that guy in Reno I liked. He made me laugh. But he drank too much, and that scared me, because his lack of control reminded me of Dad. Sam's different. I want to be as close to him as it's physically possible to get. The whole point of sex (apart from procreation) has become clear as a lit-up bulb.

* * *

The day passes slowly and then quickly, like a ride on a crazy house at a funfair, the floor lifting and falling beneath me. At the end of the afternoon, Ray tells me, 'You did good, Catrin. You're learning how to handle death with dignity. I'm proud of you.'

Guilt sweeps through me, guilt at what I'm about to do. The sacrilege of it. Frank comes to my rescue. *Lighten up, kid. You're not doing anyone any harm. The stiffs won't mind. And you need somewhere to be with this guy. He's one of the good ones.*

On the way home, I hold those funeral parlour keys in my hand like a talisman, clutching them as if they're the holy grail itself.

* * *

I meet Sam at the club. After the set, he pushes his way through the crowd to get to me, looking sweaty and happy and pleased with himself. As soon as he reaches me, he folds me into such a passionate embrace, he rocks me off my feet, which makes me laugh and clutch his shoulders. I catch other women giving me dirty looks. I'm spinning away into an alternative universe. I want to enjoy every single moment, so I can relive them when he's gone.

'So,' he says, outside the club. 'Are we really going to the funeral parlour?'

I take his hand and squeeze. 'You bet.' I hope he doesn't feel the tremor in my fingers.

★ ★ ★

When we get to Greenacres, I see with relief that the windows are dark. The tree on the corner bends a little in the breeze, a silent sentry. I take the keys out of my bag.

'Wait,' Sam says. 'This is it?'

I nod.

He gazes up at the gables. 'I was expecting something different.'

'There's outbuildings at the back built for purpose,' I say. 'But this is what the public see. I was surprised too, when I first saw the veranda and shutters. Just seems like a regular home, doesn't it, not gloomy at all.'

We go up the steps and I slip the key into the lock, repeating the code for the alarm in my head, punching in the numbers. Nerves tingling, I'm suddenly hyper-aware of him right behind me. The ticklish weight of my hair on the back of my neck makes me breathless to feel his touch there.

Sam steps ahead of me as I deal with the alarm. He's walking through the lobby, past the heavy desk with its vase of white lilies and helpful leaflets. 'I had no idea there were so many choices,' he says in a subdued voice.

I remember what he said about his parents. I wonder what kind of funeral they had and if they died together in an accident.

'Are you close to your sisters?'

'Eleanor lives in Australia, so I don't see much of her. Mattie's in London and married with a kid. We're pretty close. Why?'

'Just wondering . . . with your parents being dead and all . . .'

The atmosphere has changed. There's an awkwardness again, a sense that he's retreating from me. I look at the ground.

But then he's in front of me. He takes my chin and tilts it upwards, looks into my eyes. 'Cat, are you okay?' His voice is gentle. 'We don't have to do this, you know. Only if you want to.'

My arms go around his neck, and we're kissing. The yeasty taste of lager on his tongue. He pulls me in so we're rib to rib. I break off just enough to say, 'I do. I want to.'

His fingers are fumbling for the zipper on my corset dress, getting tangled in my long necklaces. 'Jesus,' he gasps. 'What are you wearing? Is this a chastity belt?'

I'm tugging at his sweatshirt, finding the taut skin of his stomach underneath, how warm it is, how smooth, the trail of hair leading from his belly button downwards. Then we're naked on dark blue carpet tiles, under shelves carrying examples of cremation urns.

'I've got a rubber in my pocket,' he pants. 'Do you want to put it on?'

My mind is blank. 'On . . . me?'

He bursts out laughing, 'Don't worry. I'll do it.'

And immediately I understand my stupid mistake, but it doesn't matter. I laugh too, we're both laughing, and he's rolling the damn thing on, and telling me to stop, because he has to concentrate.

We're kissing as we embrace, tipping one way and another.

The other occasions were nothing like this. I rise to the joy of his fingers and tongue inside me, the slide of his legs and arms against mine, setting my skin alight. It's impossible to stay quiet. I can't stop myself crying out.

We lie panting and slick with sweat, limbs spread-eagled as if we've been dropped like puppets from space. The tiles are itchy beneath my bare buttocks. I shift onto my hip. I want to tell him that I love him, love him, love him. Instead, I bury my mouth in the hollow of his collarbone, lick the salt from his skin. 'Think I have carpet burns,' I murmur.

'Me too.' He reaches around and fumbles with our clothes, dragging his sweatshirt and my jacket over us, tucking them around our chests. His fingers brush my stomach, pausing over my scar. 'What's this?'

'I had a ruptured appendix when I was eight,' I tell him.

'A ruptured appendix? But . . . you could have died, couldn't you?' He moves his head downwards, and I hold my breath while he kisses the jagged line across my belly.

When we're settled in each other's arms, I say, 'I nearly did. It was touch-and-go. Must have been hard on my parents. They'd already lost their baby son. I don't remember much.'

He lets out a long sigh. 'I'm very thankful to the person who saved your life.' Then he waves his arm above his head, calling loudly, 'Whoever you are, wherever you are — THANK YOU!'

I shush him, laughing, my hand over his mouth. 'Crazy. You'll wake the dead!'

'Wish I could be a surgeon. Save lives. That's something, isn't it?'

'Music saves lives too,' I tell him. 'The right song at the right time. It could make all the difference to someone.'

He squeezes me closer. 'You never told me who Frank is.' His voice rumbles through his chest, vibrating in my ear. 'The name in the inscription?'

'He was my brother,' I say quietly. 'The son my parents lost. I never met him. He died before I was born. But,' I swallow, 'he's in my head all the time. I hear his voice talking to me.'

'Like . . . an imaginary friend?'

I nod. 'I must have invented his voice at some point, ages ago, and then it kind of took on a life of its own. He feels very real to me. Sometimes I wish he'd shut up.' I peer up at his

70

face. 'Do you think I'm mad?'

'No.' He smiles. 'You needed him. And you found a way to answer that need.' He sweeps a strand of hair from my forehead. 'I think it's great that you still have Frank with you.'

I put my head back on his chest.

'Has he . . . said anything about me?' Sam asks in a voice laced with slight anxiety.

I smile. 'That would be telling.' I poke him between his ribs.

'I see what you're doing here,' he says, tickling me. 'Two against one. That's not fair.'

I'm laughing, but tears prick my eyes, and I feel them spill silently onto my cheeks, running along the side of my nose. I don't know why I'm crying. He's leaving soon, but it's not just that. We've only had two days together, I tell myself. You can't love him. But I think I always knew that I did, from the moment I saw him standing on the boardwalk being polite to a couple of tourists.

10

Sam, April 1983

The summer holidays let him escape the misery of school for six long weeks. Days opened their wings like butterflies, everything a dazzle of colour and light: spending afternoons with Ben, his friend from the village, poking about in the woods with sticks, building dens and coming home for tea, Mattie and Elle grinning at him from the other side of the table. His father worked up in town during the week, so it was just his mother and sisters at home, the Great Danes slobbering and farting.

Sundays, they had a family pew right at the front of St Mary the Virgin church. He sat with his sisters on a hard bench, his collar rubbing his neck and his shoes laced tight. While the priest droned on from the pulpit, Sam pinched his wrist in an effort not to daydream. Being at boarding school had taught him about power, about the body language of those who had it, and those who didn't. When their family climbed into the Daimler to go home, the priest raised his hand in a special blessing, and the people in the churchyard dipped their heads as the long black car passed by; all except Ben, who stuck out his tongue.

During lunch, slices of roast beef eaten at a white tablecloth, his father tested him on the contents of the sermon. If Sam got an answer wrong, his father rapped his knuckles with a knife. 'I'm not spending a fortune on your education for you to be a slacker and a fool,' he said. 'An Englishman is a leader.' The dogs, waiting hopefully on the floor, whimpered. Dropping slivers of bloody gristle into their jaws, his father kept on with his own sermon: 'A decent man leads a life to be proud of.'

★ ★ ★

That child — the one in Sam's memories — is growing fainter, disappearing like a figure seen in brilliant sunshine, edges blurring until he's swallowed by the light. But his father's voice will not shut up. Sam can't waste any more time thinking about him. He only wants to fill his mind with her — Cat — with what they did last night, with the weighted substance of her bones, the flawed beauty of her golden skin, the mole on her right buttock, the crease above her lip when she smiled her gap-toothed smile. He hasn't felt that connected to another human being since . . . He runs through the relationships he's had, and realises that he's never felt it, not with anyone else. Not even with Lucinda, not even at the beginning, in Oxford.

They were in the same production of *Romeo and Juliet* at university. He was playing Mercutio; she was producing the show. She was frighteningly efficient even then, all five foot nothing of her. Everyone was in awe. He was flattered at first, when she showed interest in him. Once they started going out, he recognised how her need for perfection hid her fear of not being taken seriously. But when she let her guard down, she could be funny and sweet. He liked being the only one who knew the real Lucinda. Nobody else got close; she was too good at keeping her guard up.

Her face floats before him now, looking at him; her mouth, bright in her trademark Chanel scarlet, turns down, disappointed again. It's an expression he's come to know well. When did they become different people? And why didn't they understand before? It's been obvious for ages that they'd be better off apart. He feels bad about her, about the timing of things, but he can't regret meeting Cat. He still hasn't plucked up the courage to explain about Lucinda, and the longer he leaves it, the more impossible it feels. He's afraid of ruining the time they have left together.

He counts the days on his fingers, and knows there are not enough.

★ ★ ★

Levi and the Dutch giants leave for home, poorer for their nights at the casino, but implacably cheerful. Levi clasps Sam's hand. 'So, you never got to New Orleans, buddy?' he says. 'I heard you singing the other afternoon. That was your own song, right?' He gives Sam a keen look. 'I think you've fallen for someone?'

'I have.' Sam grins.

Levi winks. 'Good luck to you, man. Come

74

and see me in Friesland some day.' He turns at the door. 'By the way, I liked your music.' He nods, suddenly serious. 'Yeah, man. Very cool.'

⋆ ⋆ ⋆

Sam sings with the band every night, with Cat watching from behind the backstage curtain. They return to the funeral parlour to have sex on those floor tiles again, and once on top of the mahogany desk, scattering leaflets, knocking into a vase of lilies so that pollen flies everywhere, making him sneeze. When she's not working, they walk the watery edges of the city, the beaches and inlets. They sit on her favourite bench, gazing out at the ocean and talking, talking; they have a picnic at Absecon Bay, watching the fishermen catch bluefish, the arc of a bridge spanning the width of river in an elegant hooped line. He comes to appreciate the old painted clapboard houses and wide avenues of the wealthier areas, and to love the tawdry reality of the poorer ones with their laundromats, plus-size shops and barber salons with *Lowest Prices in South Jersey* plastered across nearly every window.

When Cat is at work, he's got into the habit of sitting on his bunk with his guitar, composing songs. Every one of them inspired by her. He thinks of her face while his fingers move across the fretboard, how her features change depending on the time of day or her mood, so that sometimes her face is gentle, as he imagines a nun might look, and other times she seems lit from inside by a burning light, so radiantly, fiercely beautiful that it hurts him. He loves her crazy dress sense — jumbling colours like she's raided a dressing-up box — the fact that she's not afraid to be different. He loves that she's got a childish sense of humour, that when she laughs, she snorts. He loves that she finds joy in ordinary things. Then there's her unwavering moral compass — admittedly daunting, but in the end, central to who she is. He's never written love songs before, never felt the need. But these songs are clamouring for his attention, rising up in him almost ready-made. He doesn't share them with her, in case she finds them soppy, and because they're not good enough. Not yet. Not for her.

11

Cat, April 1983

Ray has been to the airport to collect a body. An American woman from AC who married an Englishman. She's to be buried at Our Lady Star of the Sea.

The woman has been embalmed in London and she's arrived snug in her coffin. It's a half-view casket of polished dark wood with brass fittings. The family want a public viewing at the service. Ray opens the panel, the oiled hinge releasing with a heavy clunk, and leans over to check that all is as it should be. He scrutinises her face intently. 'Nice work,' he admits. 'Very natural-looking.' He turns to me. 'Take a look, Catrin. A real professional job.'

The front door rings and he goes to answer it. I step up to the coffin. Ray's right. Whoever the embalmer was, he or she was an artist. The woman looks as though she's sleeping peacefully. What Ray didn't tell me was how beautiful she is, this dead woman. She's pale with neat features, long dark hair framing her face in glossy bangs, her small, shapely lips flushed ruby red. It looks as though she might open them to speak. I find myself leaning closer to listen for the sound of her breathing. She makes me think of fairy tales where a princess lies sleeping in a glass coffin, until the prince kisses her awake.

When Ray touches my shoulder, I jump.

'I need you for this funeral,' he says. 'We're supplying pall-bearers. You'll ride with me in the hearse, okay?'

'Oh, but I have it in the book that I get this weekend off,' I tell him. 'I have a . . . a friend here. He's . . . he's leaving soon.'

'Sorry, Cat.' He closes the viewing panel. 'Can't do without you. It's only a few hours on Saturday.'

My insides clench with frustration. 'But it's important, Ray,' I plead. '*He's* important.'

'Didn't I just know there was a man involved?' Ray sucks his teeth and looks sorrowful. 'Losing your head like a chicken.' He winks. 'Tell you what, child. You can leave straight after it's over.'

'Thank you.' I incline my chin towards the coffin. 'What's her name?'

'Elizabeth,' he says. 'Elizabeth Dunn. That was her married name. She was an O'Reilly originally.'

The O'Reillys are the nearest we get to aristocracy in this part of the world. They own the Atlantic and Liberty hotels.

Ray taps the coffin. 'Got to get this one right.'

★ ★ ★

'I have to work this weekend,' I tell Sam. 'It's the funeral of a woman who belongs to an influential family here. I'm sorry.'

'How long?'

'Just part of Saturday. I'll be free by the end of the afternoon.'

He holds me tightly, presses his mouth against my hair. 'I'll meet you when you've finished,' he says. 'I'm not singing at the club any more. They've found a new frontman.'

'Come to the Our Lady of the Sea, at about four o'clock?'

Sam nods. 'Was she very old, this woman?'

'No. She was young. And lovely. She was married as well.'

'Damn,' Sam says softly, wrapping his arms tighter around my waist.

★ ★ ★

It's raining on Saturday. One of those freak storms the Atlantic likes to toss around: squalls of bitter rain, winds that pounce like a tiger. Ray is determined that the weather won't ruin the glory of the occasion. He stands outside the hearse, immaculate in his tailcoat, overseeing the removal of the coffin, impervious to the water running down his dark skin. All six of us pall-bearers hover with black umbrellas, trying to keep the rain off the casket.

When the coffin is installed amongst banks of white roses at the front of the church, lid lifted, the mourners arrive through a scent of flowers powerful as bottles of smashed perfume. We stand quietly in our soaking clothes at the back, eyes lowered, waiting for the moment when we'll spring into action and cart the coffin out to the hole already dug in the wet ground.

I raise my chin a little, curious to spot the husband of Elizabeth Dunn. I'd imagined a prince — a big man with a head of fiery hair like a crown, someone imposing and full of authority — but the man I watch walking slowly down the aisle is slim, gentle-looking, with curling brown hair cut short. His round glasses are speckled with rain. He holds the hand of a small girl. She drags behind, stamping her feet, clutching a teddy to her chest. Throughout the service, I hear the wails of that child, rising to a peak during every eulogy. It gives me goose bumps over the ones I already have from the cold.

★ ★ ★

The lawn is slick with rain. We take it even slower than usual, the weight of the casket keeping us steady. Four men take over at the graveside, arranging the ropes that lower her into the shallow grave lined with fake grass.

I step back, allowing the family to have the front-row spots. The child kicks her father's shins. He leans down and gently holds her shoulders to try and stop her. She smacks her sodden teddy into his face, throws it against the coffin, dislodging a spray of roses. The other mourners frown and purse their lips. An elderly lady with a black veil jutting over her face tut-tuts. The father crouches down and tries to soothe his daughter, but she wriggles out of his grasp, yelling: 'I want my Mummy!'

Before I know it, I'm squatting down, looking into dark, angry eyes. 'Hi,' I say to the child. 'What's your name?'

She stops screaming, her mouth freezing into a

silent O. She stares at me, pressing against her father's legs. Her bottom lip trembles.

I take a deep breath. 'See if you can guess my name,' I say. 'I'll give you a clue if you like.'

She frowns and wipes a plump hand across her snotty nose. I pull out the clean hanky that Ray always makes us carry in our top pockets and offer it. She doesn't seem to understand what it's for, dangles it unused from her closed fist. She puts her head on one side. 'Are you Rumpelstiltskin?'

'What?'

'Rumpelstiltskin.' She repeats the long word carefully, stumbling over the syllables, her face serious.

'Um. No. I'm not. My name is an animal.'

'Dog.'

I smile. 'No. But it's an animal with a long tail and fur, and people keep them as pets.'

'A rat.'

This child says the weirdest things. 'Okay. Another clue. I chase rats, and dogs chase me.'

'Cat!' she shouts.

'Very clever.' I wink. 'Tell you what, why don't we go play a game just over there? Give your daddy some peace and quiet. We won't go out of his sight.'

She retreats into silence, fixing me with a long, appraising stare under wet spiked eyelashes. The kid could be a poker player. Time stretches, and I'm wondering if I've lost the match when she blinks and gives a solemn nod. I put out my hand. She takes it without hesitation.

It's stopped raining. We stand amongst the

dripping gravestones. 'What's your name?' I ask again.

'Grace.'

'That's a pretty name. How old are you?'

'Five and a half.' She gets a length of pink wool from her pocket. It's a tangled knot and she holds it towards me, and I understand that she wants me to unravel it. When I finish, she puts up her hands, stubby fingers splayed like starfish. 'Can you play cat's cradle?' she asks.

I am terrible at the game. I fumble between the strands of pink, plucking the wrong strings, dropping the ones I'm supposed to keep taut. But my clumsiness makes her laugh. 'No, silly!' she shouts. 'Not like that.'

'Hey,' I say. 'Did you hear about the actual cats who live inside the cradles?'

She gives me a glance both suspicious and curious.

I fumble around in my mind for words to weave a story. 'Inside every woollen cradle is an invisible cat. Each one the same colour as the wool. And they long for you to see them, so every time you pull the strings, the cat dances up and down waving its paws like this . . . ' I make a paddling action. She laughs. 'So, all these kitty-cats, Bob the blue one, Yasmin the yellow one . . . they're waving like crazy. But there was this one particular cat . . . Pete. Guess what colour he was?'

'Pete?' She bites her lip, then yells, 'Purple? Pink!'

'Yup. Smart girl. Pete the pink cat.' I glance towards the graveside, and see with relief that the

82

crowd is dispersing. Grace's father comes over and places a hand on his daughter's dark, springy hair. 'Thank you,' he says in an English accent. 'You're the first person to gain her trust since ... ' He pauses. 'I even heard her laughing.'

'We were having fun.'

'Daddy.' Grace pulls at his jacket. 'Daddy, I want her to tell me the rest of the story.'

'Not now. She has a job to do, darling.' She tugs harder at his sleeve and he bends down, listening to her whispering in his ear. 'No, Grace,' he tells her. 'She works here.' He straightens. 'This is a strange time for her — for both of us. And now, coming all the way over to Atlantic City, camping out in a hotel room, meeting relatives she hardly knows. We're stuck here for some time, unfortunately ... family duties, legal things. There are some complications. But really I need to get her home. Find some help. Try and get a new routine established.'

'Home?'

'London. Hampstead.' He glances towards his wife's grave. 'She wanted to be buried here. They all are. The O'Reilly clan.'

I can see Ray gesticulating to me from the other side of the churchyard. I'm guessing that Sam will be here any minute. My heart quickens at the thought of him.

I squat down. 'Goodbye, Grace.'

She drops her chin, angling away from me, rolling her body into the curve of her father, her thumb in her mouth. I feel something snap, the connection I shared with her breaking like a silk thread.

'She's tired.' He must have seen the disappointment on my face. He holds out his hand. 'Leo Dunn.'

'Catrin Goforth.' We shake. 'Or Cat, as your daughter knows me.'

'Cat,' he repeats. His fingers are surprisingly firm. 'We're staying at the Atlantic, Cat. If you're passing and you feel like calling in for a cup of tea. Room 242. I'm sure Grace would be happy to see you. She could do with a friend.' He gives a small smile. 'And maybe you could finish the story.'

I'm uncertain if this is that thing the English do when they say one thing and mean the opposite.

'I can see she likes you,' he adds, before he turns away.

I watch him swing his daughter up onto his hip. Her legs dangle below his knees. He staggers a little under her weight; she rests her head on his shoulder, tousled hair flopping over her face as her thumb goes back into her mouth.

12

Sam, April 1983

Sam presumes that the man in the black coat, spectacles misty with rain, is the one who's just lost his wife. There's a child, too. A chubby red-cheeked girl, leaning against her father's legs. She's motherless now. He doesn't know how Cat copes with such loss on a daily basis. The poor guy must be going through hell. While he, Sam, is the luckiest man in the world.

The rain has slowed to a drizzle. The priest hurries away, black robes flapping behind him. A straggling band of mourners leave the graveside, making their way towards the gate. The man and his child are last to leave. He's carrying her, her arms clasped tightly around his neck.

Relief fills Sam. He realises he was holding his breath, as if to avoid swallowing their grief. Churchyards make him uncomfortable. He doesn't like to be reminded of his own mortality, or those Sundays at home. He strides forward, marching over the sodden grass, calling to Cat. She looks up, a huge smile transforming her face. They kiss, a long, deep kiss that makes him want to laugh out loud with the knowledge of being alive with her. 'You're as wet as me.' She pats his sodden jacket, and then she's holding his hand, tugging him towards the church. 'Come on — I want to show you inside. And we can get out of the weather.'

He's not into churches — St Mary's put him off for life — but he'd sit in a cowshed, visit a sewer if it pleased her.

'I'm leaving soon,' he blurts out.

She stops and looks at him expectantly.

His throat is suddenly dry. 'Shall we . . . can we . . . I mean, I don't want this to end.' He licks his lips. 'I know we live either side of an ocean, and long-distance relationships are difficult, but . . .'

He sees a shudder go through her, and she leans against him, pressing her forehead hard into his shoulder. 'I don't want it to end either.'

Relieved, he touches her damp hair, takes her hand and raises it to his mouth. 'I'll need your phone number, then. I mean, if you're going to be my girlfriend. You've never given it to me.'

'Girlfriend?' She laughs. 'Somehow that sounds old-fashioned. Especially from you. But good. Really good.'

'Phone number?'

'Oh.' She's shaking her head. 'Our phone got disconnected.' She shrugs. 'It happens. Safer to write.'

'We'll do it the old-fashioned way then. Maybe that's better. I'll write first,' he says, 'because it'll take me a while to find somewhere permanent. I've got . . . stuff to sort out when I get back.' He walks faster, excited by his plans. 'But when I'm settled, then you could come and stay.'

She grins. 'You know I've always wanted to visit London, and now I've got an excuse.'

'Well then . . .' He's laughing. 'Give me your

address, and I'll keep it safe with my passport.'

She's dropped her chin to her chest. 'Hey.' He takes her salty cheeks between his palms, raising her face. 'What's the matter?'

'Nothing.' She smiles, eyes blurred. 'I'm happy. I've been feeling sick about you leaving — but now it feels like we really will see each other again.'

'Of course we will. We'll work it out. How about visiting in . . . say, a month?'

'I'll come whenever you invite me.' She blinks up at him. 'I've been saving for an air ticket for years — putting aside small amounts.'

They're inside the church now. Cat pulls Sam into one of the wooden pews. They sit next to each other, their clothes faintly steaming.

'Remind me — why did you want to show me this?' he asks.

'Whenever we move city and everything's unfamiliar,' she explains, 'I find a church.' She pats the wooden seat. 'It doesn't matter which city or town, churches are kinda the same. The smells. The hushed, echoey sounds. The slightly musty air. It's comforting.' She looks up at the arched ceiling. 'And they usually have heaters on in the winter. I discovered that when I was about eight.'

He blows out through pursed lips. 'It makes me ashamed,' he says. 'I took it for granted that I had a comfortable home with my own bedroom.' He rubs his eyes. 'I've lived such a stupidly privileged life. Boarding school. Oxford. A house in the country. We had peacocks on our lawn. It hurts to think of you as a little girl having to come to a church to feel safe and warm.'

'I feel safe now.' Cat touches his hand, and he curls his fingers around hers. 'Not warm, though.' She shivers, plucking at her damp clothes.

He puts his arm around her. 'Better?'

'Better.' She leans back, humming a run of notes. She's completely flat. He winces. He thinks she must be trying to hum a prayer or a hymn. But it doesn't sound quite right.

'Ouch!' He winces. 'Not exactly a songbird!'

She laughs. 'Hey, keep the compliments coming!'

'So put me out of my misery — what's the tune?' He grins.

'That's just it. I don't know. I'm trying to remember the lyrics,' she says. 'The one about getting on an airplane? You know the one I mean?'

'An airplane? Well . . . there's Al Green's 'The Letter'. 'Wooden Planes' by Art Garfunkel. 'Mississippi River'.' He's adding them up on his fingers. 'Jimi Hendrix!' he exclaims. ' 'Power to Love'.' He swings around to look at her. 'There's definitely airplanes in that one. Want more? Or choose a title, and I'll sing it.'

'Show-off.' She gives his arm a punch, grinning. 'And by the way, the one I was thinking of? I'm pretty sure it wasn't any of those.'

He sings a couple of bars from Al Green's 'The Letter' in a low voice, tapping the slow beat out on his knees. A great song. His chest swells, fat with happiness, and he changes vocal gear, singing properly. She joins in, loudly and badly.

88

A woman near the front turns and shushes them. Cat apologises, but they both have to stifle giggles.

They get up, hurrying along the aisle, hands clamped across their mouths. The act of suppressing hysteria makes his belly ache, and when they spill out of the church, their laughter bursts free.

It's stopped raining, sunshine setting the wet grass shimmering. They're going to write to each other, keep seeing each other, even with an ocean between them. They'll work the rest out as they go along. It'll be easy, he thinks, looking at Cat, still laughing, wiping her eyes, sunbeams in her honey hair. Together they can do anything. He thinks of the man he saw earlier in the graveyard, and how he's just sunk his hopes and dreams into a dank hole in the earth.

'The man you were talking to . . . ' He clears his throat. 'The man with the little girl. He's the husband, isn't he? Of the dead woman?'

She becomes serious. 'I looked after his daughter,' she says. 'She was pretty upset.' She shakes her head. 'Poor kid.'

'I wonder if she'll remember her mother later, when she grows up.'

'I don't know. Hope so. I'd feel bad for the mother if her child didn't remember who she was.' Cat slips her fingers into his and squeezes. 'I'm sorry. Is this making you think about your own mom?'

At first he doesn't know what she's talking about. 'No,' he says quickly. 'Look, let's not be sad. We've got so much to celebrate. Let's do something special tonight.' He bites his thumb-nail. 'I'll think of something.'

As they leave the churchyard, another song is forming in Sam's head, words and music rising inside him, inspiration bouncing off the tomb-stones, off the damp earth and the silvered watery world, from the feel of her hand in his. Another song for Cat.

13

Cat, April 1983

I meet Sam outside the Liberty Hotel. To my surprise, he leads me inside, through the plush gold and red reception up to the dark mahogany desk that runs along the back wall. 'What are you doing?' I whisper. He grins, squeezing my fingers. 'I'm booking us into a room.'

'Here? But we can't afford it.' I blink as I stare around. Everything is mirrored and shiny.

'I've got the cash. Ally's paid me.'

I can see how excited he is, how pleased with himself. He's doing this for me — for us. So I smile and try to look excited.

Sam signs the register and passes it over to me. I put my real name. I'm not going to pretend to be married. The receptionist widens her glossy mouth in our direction, and gestures towards a bellhop. He comes forward, bowing his head. 'Can I take your luggage, ma'am?'

He looks at my baggy checked trousers and worn-out Keds with a sneer, gesturing towards the floor by my feet with white-gloved hands, as if he can conjure up a pile of suitcases just by staring hard enough.

'We don't have any luggage,' Sam says, rescuing me. 'And if you give me the key, I think we can find the room ourselves.' He dips into his pocket and presses a couple of coins into the bellhop's hand. I can see that this is easy for him, normal.

We go up in a lift; it rises too fast, making my stomach lurch. We step out onto the patterned carpet of a long hallway. Sam finds our room with an exclamation of triumph, and flings open the door.

'Holy shit,' I whisper.

'Hey,' he laughs. 'We get a bed big enough for a whole family!'

The room floats before us: an expanse of cloudy carpet, and marooned in the middle, a round bed, ocean-liner-sized. The walls are flocked in silver, with the designs for playing cards in giant gold shapes; everywhere I look, I'm confronted by them: spades, clubs, hearts and diamonds. Gold drapes glisten across the floor-to-ceiling window. I walk across the carpet, feet sinking into the deep pile, and scrabble to find the opening in the drapes, but they won't pull. There's a button in the wall. I press it, and the drapes slide back with mechanical jerks, revealing the board-walk below, and beyond that the beach and the ocean. Sam pads after me to stand behind me, slipping his arms around my waist. The dark sea moves like the back of a whale, rolling and rising. I wish we were out there, running on the sand. The pit of my stomach plummets. Dad could be in the casino below, crouched over a roulette table.

'I should have told Mom I was going to stay out all night.'

He tightens his grip on my waist. 'I . . . I wanted to surprise you. But of course, if you need to leave . . .'

92

The situation is slipping away from us, slipping into something boggy and uncertain. 'No.' I turn to him. 'I'll stay. I'll just get up early. Go home before breakfast.'

He kisses me gratefully, and goes over to the minibar. He takes out a bottle of champagne and pops the cork. 'Here's to us.' He hands me a glass of bubbles, holding up his own. 'God, you gave me a hard time when I ran after you on the beach. Do you remember?' He laughs. 'I had no idea if you liked me or not.'

I want to tell him how much I liked him from the moment I saw him, how my world spun off its axis when he ran after me. But in a blink, everything has changed, and everything is wrong. I can't stop thinking about Dad: how hotel casinos have ruined his life, how his gambling has made me a prisoner. I take a gulp of the drink, put it down and begin to undo the buttons on my trousers; I need to feel Sam's skin against mine, to find the intimacy that's slipped away like Peter Pan's missing shadow. We're both undressing each other, pulling at buttons and sleeves, dragging awkward seams from the angles of our bodies. His mouth tastes of champagne. He's breathing heavily, fingers fumbling. His heart thuds through his chest. So loud, it vibrates inside my skin.

We tumble together into the giant bed. Silky sheets tangle around our legs, fat pillows spill off the edge as we roll from side to side. I sink my teeth into his skin, pull at his hair. I want to imprint myself on him. The sound of waves is a muted rush and sigh outside the glass.

93

Afterwards, we lie together, panting, our bodies blue-shadowed and mysterious, the open drapes letting in moonlight.

'You don't like it, do you?' he asks. 'The hotel room.'

'It's not that I don't like it — it's a relief not to worry about being discovered by Ray or Eunice. And these sheets . . . ' I run my fingers over them, crumpled now, but still silky. 'No carpet burns.'

'But . . . '

'To be honest, it's just . . . it's my dad. His grand gestures usually spell trouble. So I guess I'm kind of wary of them.'

'Oh God.' He sits up, clapping a hand to his forehead. 'How could I have been so stupid? You told me about him. I didn't think . . . '

'No.' I scrabble to sit up too. '*I'm* being stupid. I love being here with you. I love that you wanted to do something special for me.'

He touches my hair, pushing it back from my cheek. 'I never want to hurt you, Cat.'

I catch his fingers and kiss them. 'Thing is . . . being here . . . knowing my dad could be gambling downstairs . . . it's making me doubt everything. Our plans. I mean, how can I leave my parents and come to London? Who's gonna pay the rent?'

I hear the sharp intake of his breath. He pushes a hand through his hair. 'You . . . you said he'd been gambling for years, throughout your childhood,' he says carefully. 'So they must have managed before you had a job. You can't make them the reason you don't live your life,

94

Cat. You can't let a sense of duty stop you from being happy. Believe me, I know.'

I bite my lip. 'They're my parents.'

'They'll cope without you,' he says. 'If they have to, they will.'

'I hope so,' I whisper.

'There's a whole world out there,' he says. 'Not just London. So many places we could visit together. You have to set yourself free.' He gestures with his hand. 'Tell me. Where else would you like to go?'

'Apart from London?' I lie back in his arms. 'I've always wanted to visit the wild parts of the States. Somewhere like the Badlands. Go camping, maybe.'

'I was there, in the Badlands,' he says. 'Spent a couple of weeks alone, swimming in lakes, playing my guitar in the woods. And I saw a bear. A wild bear.' He pauses. 'It was incredible. She looked right at me with amber eyes. My heart stopped.'

'Wow. I'd love to have been there.'

He laughs. 'You're the first girl I've met who'd prefer to see a bear and sleep on the ground rather than in the comfort of a five-star bed.' He runs his fingers up and down my arm. 'I'd like to meet your parents before I leave,' he adds quietly. 'Think I should.'

'You saw how Mom was.'

'Yes, but I'm good with mothers.' He raises one eyebrow playfully. 'It's a skill I have. I'll win her around.'

I bite my nail. 'There's a reason my mom's like she is, why she wants me to be with a

Southern gentleman.' I twist the sheet between my fingers. 'The only impulsive, crazy thing she ever did was to run away with Dad against her father's wishes. But it meant she never saw her parents again. Never saw her brother. Because she took a risk on love, she's ended up disappointed, with no security, no chance of having a proper home, or being part of a community. And the man she sacrificed everything for is a liar who can't stay away from casinos. She was supposed to get married to a nice Southern boy who would have given her a good life.'

I stare out of the window at the moon, and it occurs to me that if I were to introduce Sam to Mom as a lawyer, all gussied up in a shirt and tie, his career prospects and his good manners would probably win her over. But I'm not going to do that. I want him to be the person he really is: that guy on stage in jeans and T-shirt.

'Ah.' He takes a big breath. 'Well, I get where she's coming from then, and under the circumstances I can see she wouldn't take to me straight away,' he says slowly. 'But . . . maybe in time, when she understands that we're serious about each other, and I'm not a bad person . . . maybe she'll relent.'

'Maybe,' I murmur.

'And meanwhile, I promise I'll never take you to an expensive hotel again.'

I laugh, relieved, exhausted. 'You were trying to do something nice. I know that. And I trust you. So you can spring anything you like on me. Just don't lie to me.' I look at him. 'My dad's lies have destroyed our family.' I swallow. 'Promise me, no lies between us. Not ever.'

'No lies,' he repeats, his voice subdued.

'Right — seeing as this is truth time, there's something else I need to tell you.' I take a deep breath. 'When you asked if there was something I wanted to do, that maybe I'm good at . . . there is. I love writing. I keep a diary, and I write short stories. I write about the people I cremate, the people behind the names on benches. I like imagining who they were. How their lives might have been.' It's the first time I've told anyone about my writing, but when I sneak a glance at him, he looks interested. 'I'm not aiming to be famous,' I tell him quickly. 'I just want to sit in a room making up stories.'

'A writer!' he exclaims, sitting up. 'The way you're always observing stuff — describing things you see as if you're trying to get to the truth of whatever it is. And you're such a good listener. It makes sense.' He grins. 'See, I knew there was something you were hiding under a bushel.'

'A bushel?' I roll my eyes.

I sit up too, and then we're kneeling on the bed, knees touching, and he takes my hands in his. 'Will you show me some of your stories? I'd really like to read them.' He squeezes my fingers. 'We should make a pact. If I leave my job and become a full-time singer-songwriter, then you have to promise to keep writing, get published. Oh Cat, this is so great, because we can be there for each other now.'

'Yes,' I tell him. 'I'd like that more than

97

anything.' I sit back on my heels. 'You haven't played me any of your own songs, though,' I remind him. 'You promised. Remember?'

'I don't have my guitar here,' he says. 'But I'm willing to go a cappella, if you don't object?'

'Go for it.'

He climbs out of bed and stands naked, lights from the boardwalk spangling him. He swallows, clears his throat, glances down for a moment. Then he looks right at me.

14

Sam, April 1983

He doesn't choose one of the love songs. None of those feels ready yet. Instead he sings something he wrote after he saw the bear. He stands, feet apart, more nervous than he can remember.

When he finishes, she doesn't move. He can't see her expression in the shadows. Nervously he climbs back into bed, trying to gauge her reaction. But as she puts her arms around him, squeezing him tightly, he discovers her cheeks are wet.

'You're crying!' he says. 'Was it that bad?'

'It was beautiful.' Her voice is choked with tears. 'You *have* to keep writing, keep singing.' She swallows hard. 'I believe in you, Sam.'

They lean back against the pillows, her head on his shoulder. He strokes her hair. Since they met, she's shared so much: telling him about her childhood, her father being a gambler, her desire to write. The truth is a key, he thinks guiltily. Without it, there's a door that will always stay shut.

'Damn.' She laughs. 'I've never cried so much in my life,' she says, wiping her eyes. 'And I've never been this happy.'

He kisses her shoulder, and turns his head to look through the hotel window at the moon, a huge yellow circle swimming in clouds. No stars tonight. Soon he'll be looking at the same moon in London. They only have two days left. The date of his flight encroaches like a shadow falling at dusk, inevitable and cold. He hasn't lied, he tells himself. He just hasn't told the exact truth. The fact is, his parents *are* dead. To him, they may as well be cold and buried in the ground.

He holds her tightly, her head heavy on his arm. *But what about Lucinda*, a voice in his head pipes up. *You haven't told her about your girlfriend at home.* Day by day, hour by hour, the glaring omission becomes more urgent and uncomfortable, the words to explain it stumbling around in his mind. But it's too late now. Too late to tell her the truth about Lucinda, his parents, any of it. *No lies between us*, she said. *Promise me.* He can't risk losing her. It's his mess, he tells himself, not hers; when he gets home, he'll face up to it.

He puts his nose into Cat's hair, inhaling her scent. He gets it now when people say their heart is bursting. He moves his hand to his chest as if to soothe the ache there.

'We'll go on camping trips together,' he murmurs. 'Climb mountains, explore forests.'

'Yes,' she says. 'And there'll be bears.'

'Lions.'

'Elephants,' she adds, yawning.

★ ★ ★

When morning breaks, he wakes to find her up and getting dressed. He hurries into his clothes

100

so that he can go with her. They slip out through the red reception onto the boardwalk. The deserted beach breathes its briny smells at them, washing away traces from the night before; the sea is pink and silver in the dawn. She wants to find a dolphin for him, and they stand by her favourite bench, gazing at the horizon. But there are no curving fins. 'Never mind,' he says. 'We'll see dolphins another day, maybe in a different ocean. And when you come to London, I'll show you the bench on Hampstead Heath. The one I told you about. We can sit on it and watch the kids flying kites on Parliament Hill. There's so much I want to show you, Cat. So many things we can do together.'

He walks her to the little clapboard house, watching her disappear through the screen door. Then he goes back to the hostel, crawling into his bunk, his skin sensitised under rumpled clothes, lips bruised from kissing. The smell of her on his fingers.

★　★　★

The last day arrives. The song isn't quite ready, he decides. He wants it to be perfect. He'll surprise her when she visits him. He has her address written down in three different places: on the end page of his notebook, on his guitar case in felt tip, and on a piece of paper folded into his wallet. But she's meeting him at the airport after work to say goodbye, and he's made up his mind: he's going to explain about his parents, about Lucinda. This is his last chance to tell her the truth before he leaves, before she comes to London. He needs to do it now, so the next part of their lives can start properly — clean and full of promise.

15

Cat, April 1983

Once, Sam and I knocked into the vase of lilies on the front desk, nearly sending the whole lot spinning to the floor. I let out a yell fit to wake every soul in the reefer, and grabbed it just in time. But we got away with it. This evening, he flies to London. Even now, he'll be packing his stuff, getting ready to leave. But instead of feeling desperate and unhappy, I'm excited, because after work, I'm going to the airport to kiss him goodbye, to sniff his hair and skin, to have one more hug. One more time in his arms. Until we meet in London. London! He said there was something important he needs to tell me. That he'd explain everything at the airport. And I wonder what it could be and if it has to do with being in London together. A plan, perhaps, for his music, or my writing?

★ ★ ★

I'm working the conveyor belt, overseeing a corpse moving smoothly into the roaring retort. When Ray taps me on the shoulder, I jump. I can't hear anything for the rumbling of air and fire. We watch as the cardboard box slides into place, and the doors close; then we walk away from the machine and he bends forward and

103

opens his mouth. 'Eunice wants to see you in her office,' is what comes out.

'What? Why?'

He gives me an exasperated look. 'She didn't see fit to tell me. Said it's urgent is all I know.' He puts his hands on his hips. 'So why you still standing here?'

I peel off my gloves, and he takes them from me wordlessly. My feet drag as I leave the heat of the crematorium, walking past the shadowy chapel, across the entrance lobby to the office. It was worth it, I tell myself. Whatever happens next, I can't regret it. I rap on the closed door, and turn the handle.

'Catrin,' Eunice says, looking up. 'Come on in.'

Eunice is a large woman, and her bosom and belly jiggle as she raises herself from her chair, straining to get upright. She nods towards her desk. 'Sit down. Your mom's on the phone.'

I stare at the ebony receiver lying on its side on the desk, and glance back at her.

'Your mom,' she repeats. 'She's on the line.'

I sink into the chair that clients usually use, the box of perfumed tissues placed just so by my elbow. Eunice walks around her desk, dropping a heavy hand onto my shoulder as she passes, and gives my bones a squeeze. 'Take as long as you like,' she murmurs.

I hear the door click as she leaves.

Maybe this time Mom's really ill. I pick up the receiver with the tips of my fingers. 'Mom? Are you okay?'

All I can hear is a muffled choking sound.

Then her voice, tearful, breaking. 'Catrin? Oh, I don't know what to do,' she wails. 'You have to come home. I don't know what to do . . . '

Fear chases up and down my spine. 'Mom, try and take a breath. Start from the beginning. Where are you?'

'I'm . . . I'm at a neighbour's house. She let me use her phone.'

A part of me relaxes. She's not in the hospital. I edge forward in my seat. 'What's the matter? What happened?'

'It's your father . . . He's . . . ' I can hear gulping, rustling, and gasps of breath.

'Dad? What's happened to him? Just tell me,' I almost shout, holding the phone hard to my ear.

'He's been arrested,' she whispers.

Shock hits me in the chest. 'Arrested?'

'For embezzlement. Joe came from the office to tell me. Oh Catrin!' She's crying again. 'I'm so afraid. Come home. Please. Come home now.'

★ ★ ★

I get off the jitney and jog through the streets, bag bumping my hip. My feet, heavy in my work shoes, hardly seem to move under me. I crash through the front door, calling for Mom. From the kitchen comes a low, wordless keening, as if a wounded animal has taken shelter.

She looks terrible. Undone. Her hair has escaped its chignon, her cheeks have collapsed. For a second I remember the dying bluefish, hooked by those fishermen at Absecon Bay. I root through the cupboard and find a bottle of

105

rum, collect a couple of glasses and pour. 'Sit down and drink this,' I tell her, settling at the table. 'Tell me slowly. Tell me everything.'

'All I know is what I told you.' She licks parched lips. 'Joe came over, said Arthur had been arrested. Three officers put him in cuffs and took him down to the precinct.' She slaps her hand against her forehead. 'Why would he steal from his work?'

'Mom,' I say quietly. 'He'll do anything to get money for gambling.'

'It's over, Catrin,' she says. 'I can't do this any more. I can't. I can't. I can't.' She breaks into sobs, clutching her skirts, swaying so violently I think she's going to fall. I get up and put my arms around her stooped shoulders.

'You're in shock. Let's get you into bed. I'll go to the pay-phone at the five-and-ten, call the county jail, see if I can find anything out.'

'You're a good girl,' she says, holding my cheeks between her palms. 'You're a good girl. But God help us now.' Her voice cracks. 'We're ruined.'

I get her into her nightclothes, give her a couple of sleeping pills. Her fingers tremble so much, she can't hold the water glass. I don't want to leave her alone in this state, so I sit on the bed, telling her that it will be all right, stroking her forehead, patting her fragile hand.

'You see, I was right to warn you . . . ' she murmurs.

I lean forward. 'What do you mean, Mom?'

'About that boy you were seeing. I don't want you to go through this . . . I don't want you to

106

know this . . . this humiliation . . .'

'Mom,' I say gently, firmly. 'I told you before, Sam's not Dad. He's on his way back to England tonight. But we're going to see each other again. He's gonna write me. I don't want you to worry about it, okay? I promise I know what I'm doing.'

She holds my gaze, and then sighs and nods. I pat her hand as it grips the edge of the sheet. When her eyes eventually close, I go down the stairs and onto the porch, closing the door behind me. Everything looks the same. Everything is different. I glance at my watch. Sam will be waiting in the departures lounge at the airport, looking through the crowd of changing faces, searching for me.

The payphone at the dime store has been vandalised, so I walk a block to find one that works. It rings for a long time; finally I manage to get through to someone on the desk. The voice is female, brisk and irritated. I fumble to press more money through the slot. She asks for Dad's first and last names, and date of birth. She verifies that he's been booked and is awaiting his arraignment. No visitors, she tells me when I ask. He's been assigned a public defender, and she gives me a fax number.

I click the greasy receiver back into its cradle, and the last of my quarters clatters inside the box. I think of Dad in some windowless room, his big body slumped over. Will they let him have a cigarette? Will anyone say a kind word? I look at my watch. Sam. I'm too late. I've missed him. My heart whimpers, dies in my chest like

107

roadkill. Overhead, a glittering speck leaves a vapour trail in the evening sky. I gaze up, straining my neck, wondering if he's there, staring down through the clouds. And the song I was trying to remember comes into my head — John Denver, 'Leaving on a Jet Plane'. I want so bad to tell him, to say, 'Guess what, I remembered,' to hear him laugh, singing it back to me: *Hold me like you'll never let me go.*

Maybe he didn't get on the flight. I have a crazy hope that I'll find him at home, waiting for me on the porch steps, guitar on his back. But then I remember. His visa's run out. The magic of the last weeks has gone, and now real life is falling hard and heavy on my shoulders. I feel sick at the thought of Dad in cuffs, being prosecuted, going to jail. The knowledge of my aloneness is clear and sharp.

I don't have a clue what to do. The unknown nightmare of what's to come snatches my breath away. How can I go to England now? I double up on the sidewalk, sickness in my throat. I start to walk I don't know where. Breaking into a run, I sprint as fast as I can, my head thrown back, arms pumping at my sides.

On the boardwalk, I stagger like a drunk towards our bench and collapse onto it; before me, the ocean moves in the dark, the same ocean I waded into that night, while Sam watched me from the shore. I tilt my head to look up at the sky, towards the airplanes criss-crossing the evening air with winking lights, so far away that I can't hear them roar.

16

Sam, April 1983

He waits till the very last call for boarding. After it comes, he keeps waiting, body rigid with nerves, until they're paging his name, and he has to run for it, dodging between people, leaping suitcases and trolleys. The cabin crew hurry him on as he goes through the boarding lounge onto the plane.

He keeps his head down, trying to ignore the annoyed glances of other passengers as the crew shut the door behind him. The plane is full, so it's easy to spot the one empty space, right in the middle of a row. After he's jammed his bag into an overhead locker and buckled himself in, he has an impulse to leap up and shout for them to stop the plane. He wants to get off, run back, find her. He begins to undo his belt, but like a coward he just sits there, staring straight ahead as the plane lifts from the ground.

He keeps seeing her slumped against a broken window, a bus skewed across the freeway, blood trickling from her forehead, obliterating that tiny birthmark she has above her eyebrow. He imagines ambulances. Blue lights. Sirens. Her pulse getting slower.

He refuses the tray of foil-wrapped food that an air hostess holds out, puts his headphones over his ears, and presses play on his Walkman.

Music enters him, blocking off the noise of the plane. Al Green's voice is like listening to an old friend bringing reason. He feels the fibres of his muscles release, the tension in his shoulders seeping away.

★ ★ ★

He thinks back to his old bedroom at home, his school suitcase lying empty, contents strewn across the floor. His window is open; outside, the long lawn is striped with summer brilliance. His mother kneels with a gardening fork in her hand, sunhat over her eyes, dogs sprawled nearby in the shade.

Carefully, he places the new album he bought from Woolies on the turntable, and twists the volume knob up loud. He's singing along with the Reverend Al Green, singing about love and happiness, imagining what it would be like to sound like that, what it would be like to stand on a stage and make people feel what he is feeling now.

He doesn't hear the knocking. And then his father is there, carrying fury in narrowed eyes and set jaw. He's bending over the record player and grabbing the arm, snatching the needle up. The shriek of it sliding across the grooves is terrible. The disc will be ruined.

'No good,' he's saying. 'Your school report. A disappointment.' His nostrils flare, and Sam notices black hair speckling the insides. 'Not good enough,' his father keeps repeating. 'Throwing away your opportunities. Dreaming your life away.'

The room is full of words; Sam puts his hands up as if he could bat them away. He waits, head bowed. His father is talking about the Great Plan: Oxbridge exams, going up to Oriel, following tradition, becoming a lawyer.

Sam looks at the red threads criss-crossing his father's cheeks, thin hair combed across the pink of his scalp. I don't want your life, he thinks. I don't want to be you.

His father comes very close. 'You're killing your mother,' he says quietly. 'She's sick with worry. She wants to see you make a man of yourself.'

He leaves the room, shutting the door with a click. Outside, one of the peacocks screams. Sam bows his head. Maybe he is a selfish little shit, he thinks. Maybe there is something wrong with him.

★ ★ ★

There's nothing wrong with him. There never was, except having a father who made him feel that being himself was a crime. Cat has helped him understand that. All his plans to give up law and be a musician seem simple when he's with her. He begins to compose a letter to her in his head. There must be a logical explanation for her not turning up. Something happened at work to delay her. Or her bus got stuck in a jam. She would have been so frustrated. He takes deep breaths. It will be all right. *I believe in you*, she said. He has a sharp need to confess the truth about his parents and Lucinda. If he can't tell her in person, then he'll explain in a letter.

★　★　★

He's stopped at Customs, waved over to a desk where two officers wait. He knows it's because of his long hair and earring, his scruffy sweatshirt. He forces himself to watch impassively while they dig their hands through his stuff, shaking out his washbag, unscrewing lids and sniffing at creams. They hand back his rucksack and guitar case with obvious disappointment, and he knows better than to make a comment. He heads out of the sliding doors into the bustle of the arrivals hall.

He joins the early-morning rush hour, standing on a packed Tube rushing through darkened tunnels. He's uncertain how Lucinda will greet him. When he first told her that he wanted to go to America, she told him he was being ridiculous. 'Come with me,' he pleaded. 'We can make it a road trip. Have an adventure.' But she wouldn't leave her shiny office in her Soho advertising company. 'Have you gone mad?' she said, after he'd told her he'd bought his ticket to New York. 'You're giving up an opportunity in one of the best law firms in London.'

'I'm sorry,' he said.

'You're risking losing me too,' she added. 'You should know that.'

'I have to do this.' He wanted her to understand. 'I'll call you every week.'

112

She refused to acknowledge him when he left for the airport, turning her face away from his kiss, the taxi rumbling below.

★ ★ ★

He stands outside his building and cranes his neck to look up. She knows he's due back. He opens the door and goes through the communal hallway, climbing three flights to the top floor. *The penthouse*, they used to joke. He buzzes once to give her some warning, then turns his key in the lock. It's a mezzanine flat, and the minimal open-plan kitchen and living room are clean and tidy. He heaves his heavy rucksack off his shoulder, puts his guitar case on the floor. As he straightens, he hears the creak of footsteps.

She stands halfway down the stairs, a small, upright figure. 'Jack,' she says. Her dark hair is immaculately styled, and she's dressed in a navy trouser suit with heels. She's never out of heels, the higher the better. He feels a lump in his throat. Only he knows how her diminutive stature bothers her — how she'll do anything to add height, balancing on precarious stilettos all day long, putting her hair up, even wearing hats.

She comes down the rest of the stairs, looking elegant and composed. But when she's close, he sees a tremor in her fingers as she fastens gold rings into her ears. She kisses his cheek, and he leans down to hug her, smelling her familiar Dior perfume. 'You look like a student,' she sighs, stepping away. 'And you need a shower.'

'Yeah. Twelve hours' travelling will do that.'

He gives her a rueful smile. He's thought hard about the words he'll use to explain to her about Cat. He wipes damp palms on his jeans, preparing himself, his heart thumping behind his ribs; but she's turned away from him, fiddling with the coffee machine. 'Have you got whatever it was out of your system?' she asks over her shoulder.

He starts. 'What do you mean?'

She turns back towards him. 'The stuff about your dad. I'm not saying it wasn't a shock at the time, but you're not a child. You have a job. Commitments. Me.' She takes a deep breath. 'Are you ready to get back to your real life, Jack? To be the man I fell in love with?' He suspects she's rehearsed this speech. It would be just like her to have it word perfect. 'I think I've been pretty patient,' she goes on. 'I'm not saying you don't deserve to have fun sometimes. You went straight from university into work. I get it. Maybe you've been working too hard. I suppose this trip to the States has been a kind of . . . sabbatical for you.'

He drops his gaze, staring at the ground. 'Lucinda . . . Lu . . . I'm not going back to work. This time away . . . it's been much more than having fun. It's made me realise that I can't commit myself to a career that makes me miserable.' He meets her eyes. 'I understand what I want to do with my life. And it's music.'

She touches her hair carefully, pushing a strand into place. 'Music? You're giving up everything you've worked towards for music? Everything *we've* worked towards? Just like that.

114

All our plans gone?'

'They were never really my plans,' he says as gently as he can. 'I was just trying to please people — do what was expected of me.'

'Please people?' she repeats in a cold voice. 'So it was all a sham, was it? You were just trying to *please* me when you asked me out at Oxford, when we moved into this place, when we talked about making a success of our lives?'

'No. Of course not. Lu . . . I'm sorry.' He goes towards her, but she holds up her hand like a traffic policeman. 'Don't. Don't touch me.' She shakes her head. 'I thought all that stuff about wanting to be a musician was just a reaction to your father — a way of getting back at him. I didn't think you meant it. What's happened to your ambition, your pride?' Her voice breaks, her mouth trembling. 'I thought you wanted to get to the top — be a partner in the firm.'

It's Lucinda who wants him to become a partner. But it seems petty to contradict her. He can't comfort her either. She doesn't want him to. He stands before her feeling helpless; he pushes up his sleeves, runs a hand through his hair.

Her eyes fix on his arm, the inked notes. She screws up her face in distaste. 'You've turned into a stranger.' She takes a step back, her chin tilted up.

'I never wanted to hurt you, Lu,' he says. 'I'm still me, but people change. And sometimes life . . . it just explodes under your feet. That's what it felt like when I found out about Dad. My whole perspective did a one-eighty.'

115

'*I* haven't changed. I'm the same person you met at Oxford.'

'I know,' he says gently. 'You've always been sure of who you are and what you want. I admire that in you. It's not the same for me, though. I feel as though I'm only just beginning to understand myself.'

She shakes her head. 'Then we're just not on the same page any more, are we?'

'The thing is . . . we have different values, different ideas about the future.' The truth of what he's saying gives him new strength. 'We were very young when we met.' He makes his voice gentle. 'I still care about you, Lucinda, but it's true, we don't understand each other any more and we don't want the same things.'

'It's over, then,' she says in a quiet voice. 'Isn't it?'

He nods. 'I'm sorry.' He gestures towards the kitchen. 'But this is your home. You stay. You can have the flat.' He's not going to tell her about Cat now. It would just hurt her more, and confuse the truth about them growing apart. 'I'll leave.'

Her mouth tightens. 'I'll send your things on. I suppose you'll go and stay with your precious sister or one of your dropout friends.'

He suspects that she's jealous of his closeness to Mattie. And she's always making snippy comments about Ben, not understanding that friendships rooted deep in childhood and shared memories can withstand the different choices you make as adults. But she's hurt, and he's not going to start a row. He ignores the jibe. 'I'll be

116

at Mattie's,' he says. 'If she'll have me.'

He picks up his bag. It doesn't feel heavy any more. Despite the sadness and guilt that's come with this ending, and the knowledge that he's hurt someone he used to love, a lightness has entered his bones.

17

Cat, May 1983

Still no letter from Sam. First I told myself that he was busy finding a place to stay, getting himself sorted. Then I worried that he'd interpreted my no-show at the airport as a message that we were over. But how could he? After the way we felt, the things we said? I don't mention his name to Mom — I don't want to hear her say *I told you so*. He doesn't know about Dad, about his trial. His not-knowing creates another distance between us, bigger than an ocean.

What if he's dead? What if he hasn't written because he's ill or been killed, and my whole life I'll never know the truth? He may as well have stepped off a cliff. He's gone as completely as that. And I miss him. I miss the curved line of his dark eyebrows, his bones, his skin, the fleshy knot of his beating heart. I miss his lopsided smile. His voice. His singing. I miss him holding me. The way he made me feel.

'I'll write to you when I'm on the plane,' he said. 'I'll post it as soon as I land.'

Maybe he hated the story I gave him; he's disappointed I'm not the writer he hoped I'd be.

Maybe it's to do with the thing he was going to tell me; maybe he'd changed his mind about seeing me again. No. I don't believe it. Dammit. I can't and I won't.

★ ★ ★

Mom does nothing all day. She gets dressed, but then sits and stares into space, drinking iced sweet tea from a Mason jar. I'm not much of a cook, but I can manage fried chicken. Mom nibbles at what's on her plate. She's thin. A Thanksgiving turkey's wishbone has more fat on it. She's changed since the day of Dad's arrest. She doesn't even water her geraniums; she just talks and talks about her life as a girl in South Carolina. She's started to use the names of her parents and brother with casual familiarity, as if her mom and dad are still alive and she's just stepped out of her childhood home and will be returning any moment.

'Did I tell you about the time I went picking wild plums?' she asks, twiddling the end of her hair ribbon between her fingers. 'Oh, I did love the taste of those plums. But they hung in a thicket where everyone said rattlesnakes lived. Daddy banned me from going into that thicket, but I disobeyed him. Well, my Lord, I nearly stepped on a sleeping rattler! Can you imagine? There it was, coiled in a circle under my raised shoe. Saw it just in time, those viper diamonds on its back. Had to stop myself screaming. Bit my lip so hard it bled. Put me off plum jelly for years.'

Mom won't discuss Dad or what's happened to him. She won't visit him either. He got five

119

years. On top of his jail sentence, he has a heavy fine, and must pay back every cent he took. It will take him a lifetime and more. We've been living off my wages and the stash of bills hidden at the back of my drawer that I'd been saving for a plane ticket to London. Our lease is up on the house soon; we can't afford to renew. I chew my food, half listening to Mom's chatter, her stories about warm peach cobblers and fireflies; tales of her white cat, Magnolia; descriptions of the moss-strewn cypress trees in the swamps. She doesn't understand — or won't understand — the situation we're in. I've decided to write to her brother, Daniel, tell him what's happened. She kept the letter he wrote her about their parents' deaths.

Thinking about writing to Daniel brings the pain of Sam's missing letter back. It's a physical hurt behind my ribs. I press a hand to my chest, as if I can push back the sorrow. I turn a sob into a cough, scrub my face on the edge of my shirt, dabbing at my eyes before I collect the dirty plates from the table and put them in the sink. I force myself to think about what I'll say to her brother. I won't tell Mom I'm writing him, not unless I get a reply.

Wiping my eyes, collecting myself with a little shake, I put a cup of coffee in front of her. She looks at me vaguely and smiles. 'Bless your heart, sweetie.' Sometimes I'm not even sure she knows who I am. She sits at the kitchen table for hours, completely still, not even playing a silent piano. There was ash in the sink. When I asked her what she'd burnt, she looked vague. 'Trash,' she said. 'Just some old trash.' Her fingers twitch constantly, as if she's striking a match. I worry she'll burn the house down while I'm at work. She wanders around before dawn like an antsy ghost. I've found her out on the porch a couple of times, first thing, sitting on Dad's broken-down chair, humming and watching the road.

18

Sam, June 1983

Something wet and spiky hits his face. He wakes with a shout, sitting up in the darkened spare room. His cheek is damp. His nephew stands at his bedside, grinning like a toothless demon, a loo brush in his fist.

Jesus. The little brat just whacked him in the face. Sam uses the edge of the sheet to wipe his cheek, not wanting to look at the specifics of what exactly he's removing. He pushes his legs out of the covers. He has no idea what time it is. Since arriving at his sister's weeks ago, he hasn't kept to any kind of routine. Most days he doesn't even know what date it is.

He stifles a yawn and blinks at the toddler. 'Watch out for the tickle monster!' He holds out his hands, wiggling his fingers. 'I'm coming to get you!'

River staggers away on chubby, uncertain legs, still clutching his weapon of choice, laughing.

Downstairs in the kitchen, Sam finds Mattie on her hands and knees picking up what looks like regurgitated food. The cat is on the table, tail in the air, stepping delicately around dirty plates and cups.

Mattie glances up at him, raising an eyebrow. 'At last, the prince awakes.'

'Your son just smashed me in the face with a

loo brush.' Sam grimaces. 'None too clean, either.'

'That's what you get for being a lazy sod. I've been awake since five this morning and I haven't sat down yet.' She hauls herself to her feet. 'You need to start helping.' She wipes her hands together. 'Otherwise it's bloody well time to move on.'

Sam drops into the nearest chair, slumping over the table. He picks up a blackened crust of toast and bites into it. 'I told you,' he says with his mouth full. 'I can't go anywhere until she replies. This is the return address I gave in my letters. I gave her your telephone number too.'

'It's been weeks, Jack.' She raises an eyebrow, correcting herself. 'Sam. She's not going to reply now.' She sits next to him. 'Look. I'm not saying this to be cruel, but someone has to tell you the truth. This girl, Cat, I know you've fallen for her. But I'm afraid she doesn't feel the same, or she would have written or called or something by now.'

Sam stops chewing, globs of marmalade on his lips, charcoal on his tongue, gritty and tasteless as coal dust. 'You don't understand. I *know* she felt the same. I know she did.' He drops his face into his hands, the musk of his unwashed body rising up. 'The thing that scares me is that I . . . I told her that I'd lied. When I wrote, I explained everything. About Dad, and how angry I was. How my parents weren't really dead. I explained that I was reinventing myself when I met her, that I'd renamed myself. I even told her about

Lucinda.' He looks at his sister. 'But what if I made a mistake, telling her all that in a letter?'

Mattie sighs. 'You did the right thing by explaining, even if you were an idiot to lie in the first place. It was good to tell her the truth. And if she can't handle it . . . ' She shrugs.

'She hates lies, Mattie. Her dad gambles, and she's lived with his lies all her life.'

'I know. You told me. About a million times.' She squeezes his fingers. 'What happened to your plans to work on your music?'

'Yes, but I've been waiting — '

'Stop waiting. Start doing. Stop this obsession with Hampstead Heath. God knows why you're schlepping across town to mope about there, wasting your time. It won't bring her back. Get on with your music. It will take your mind off her for a start. And what about your flat? You do own half of it. Have you discussed selling with Lucinda?'

'She can live in it, at least until she wants to move. I'm not going to force her out of her home. I'm the one who's let her down. It's the least I can do.'

She sighs. 'I suppose you're doing the decent thing, although I don't like to see you like this. It's a lot to give up, Sam. You've gone from being Mr and Mrs Perfect in your designer flat to being broke, alone and homeless.'

'Yeah,' he says, raising an eyebrow. 'Thanks for that, sis. You have a winning way with words.'

'Just saying.' She stands up. 'We're out of bread. I'm going to nip to the corner shop. Watch River for me.'

'I'll get it.' He starts to rise.

She puts her hand on his shoulder. 'There's a whole pile of Lego on the carpet next door. Why don't you teach your nephew how to build a flyover or something? I need some fresh air. Going out for a loaf of bread is about as good as it gets for me nowadays.'

The door slams. River is sitting on the rug next to the table, picking up bits of kibble from the cat's bowl and sticking them up his nose. He startles at the sound of the door, swivelling his head left and right. Realising that his mother has gone, his bottom lip begins to quiver. Sam slides off his chair onto the rug and sits cross-legged next to him. 'Don't cry, mate.'

Big, fat drops are dribbling down River's face.

'Want to play with Lego?'

River shakes his head.

Sam gets onto all fours. 'Look,' he says. 'I'm a horse. A gee-gee. Want a ride, River? Want to gallop round the house?'

River's nappy feels squishy against Sam's lower spine. Small, fat fingers tangle in his hair. He struggles to his feet, one hand under the child's bottom to avoid accidental dismounts, and then he's cantering through the rooms, bucking and whinnying, River digging his sharp little heels into his ribs like a rodeo rider.

After three laps around the downstairs, he collapses onto the sofa, panting, River sprawled across his stomach, hiccuping with mirth. In a matter of seconds, the toddler has closed his eyes, his lashes so extravagant they look as though they're stuck on with glue. Holding his breath, Sam slips out from under his nephew's sleepy weight.

He takes a small package of paper from his pocket — three pages covered in Cat's large writing, worn and creased with rereading and refolding: the story she pressed into his hand, telling him to read it when he was back in London. He almost knows it off by heart. She writes beautifully. He's studied it for clues as to why she doesn't reply to his letters, but he can't find any. The story isn't about them. It's about a woman called Cindy. A kind of modern fairy tale. He folds the pages again and slips them carefully into his pocket.

Mattie will be home in a minute. She was right, he admits to himself. Everything she said was right. He knows it in his bones. He can't stay hidden in his sister's spare room for ever. All those weeks with the covers pulled over his face, not helping Mattie or doing anything useful, just feeling sorry for himself, listening to sad love songs on his Walkman. It's anger that's building inside him now. He visualises Cat's wide cheeks, her gappy smile, her long, silky honey hair. And then he rubs his hands over his face so hard that it hurts, as if he could erase the image, wipe himself clean of her memory.

19

Cat, June 1983

I don't get further than the screen door before I'm aware of a difference in atmosphere. The house feels alive. And there's a strong smell of tobacco. For a second, I think Dad's home. But I find a stranger in the kitchen, he and Mom deep in conversation. He's silver-haired, with a generous moustache, sitting at our table looking quite at home, one ankle balanced on his other knee like a much younger man, a cigar between his fingers. I'm pretty certain he doesn't come from this neighbourhood, not in that tailored linen suit and those fancy brogues.

'Mom?'

She turns to me, and the animation in her face makes me catch my breath. I haven't seen her look like this for years. Maybe not ever.

'Why, there she is!' she exclaims, getting up and coming over to me. 'My daughter, Catrin.'

I stand, awkward, confused, while the silver-haired man appraises me thoughtfully, nodding as if he's delighted by what he sees.

'Catrin, say hello to your uncle. This is my brother, Daniel.'

'Daniel?' I shake my head. 'Holy shit. You came.'

'Soon as I got your letter.' He climbs to his feet, extends his hand to take mine. 'I've been

127

waiting for this. Knew Lydia would need us eventually. That man — excuse me, I know he's your daddy — he was always gonna end up in the gutter.' His grip is warm and firm. 'No gentleman runs off into the night with his bride-to-be. No, ma'am. Broke our mother's heart.' He kisses the back of my hand and releases me.

'Now, Daniel, don't you say another word, or I'll start crying again.' Mom flutters her hands like two broken wings.

'Don't fret, Lydia.' Daniel pats her arm. He turns to me and clears his throat. His eyes are the exact same colour as Mom's. 'I've come to tell you that you have a home with me back in South Carolina. My wife died three years ago and I live alone. We never were blessed with children. I'd be happy and proud to have you both come live with me.'

Mom sits down, skirts settling in folds. She dabs at the corners of her eyes with a hanky rustled up from a pocket. 'Think of it! I'm going home,' she murmurs. 'After all these years.'

'What about Dad?' Things are moving so fast, I feel dizzy. I drop into a chair next to her.

She recoils at the mention of him. 'You know I can't visit him in that place. I won't.' A note of hysteria has entered her voice.

'There, there, darlin'. Nobody's gonna make you.' Daniel pats her arm again. He looks at me, concern etched into his elegant, aged face. 'No lady should have to enter a penitentiary.'

'Why did you never come before?' I ask him. 'All this time. Not a word.'

'It's a sad waste of years, Catrin.' He inclines his head, closes his eyes briefly. 'After Lydia ran off, our daddy wouldn't have her name spoken in the house. Forbade us from mentioning her again. But now that he's dead, God rest his soul, and your daddy incarcerated, we can be a family again.'

'I don't understand.' I lean across and whisper to Mom. 'Are you leaving Dad?'

She gives a short, high-pitched laugh. 'I stood by him our whole marriage. Lord knows it was hard. He broke my heart a long time ago. Now,' she lifts her large eyes to the ceiling, 'I have nothing left to give him.'

'But he'll be counting on you being here when he gets out.'

She presses her lips together, narrows her eyes. 'I can't be his wife any longer.' The muscles in her neck pull tight. 'I made a mistake, Catrin. All those years ago. I should have listened to my daddy. He knew better. Always did.'

We have supper together. The first meal Mom's cooked since Dad's arrest: baked sweet potatoes and fried catfish. As we eat, we snatch stunned glances at each other. Mom and her brother talk about people I've never heard of, pull out old memories, examining them. Mom breaks down in tears, and next minute she's laughing. Daniel tells us about his house and garden, the magnolia trees outside the veranda, a pond full of snapping turtles. He says there's a grand piano waiting for Mom in the parlour. Explains what bedrooms he plans each of us to have. Mom listens with shining eyes.

'Oh, you'll love it there, Cat,' she tells me. 'The South is in your blood.'

* * *

Uncle Daniel is staying in my room, tidied in a hurry. I'm on the couch. I can't sleep for thinking about the evening — about how different Mom was with her brother — and the planned move to South Carolina. I fidget on the narrow cushions, rearranging the pillow under my cheek, thinking of Dad, and how he doesn't know his marriage is over. The one time I visited, he seemed reduced by his surroundings, older and smaller than I'd remembered. I don't want to have to tell him about Mom, but I don't have a choice. He needs to know. I don't blame her. He betrayed her; lied to her every day. She lost respect for him — there's no hope for love after that. I curl around my sadness, hugging it close. There's no denying, though, that Daniel's offer is the best thing that could have happened. It's like I can breathe again.

* * *

It's barely past dawn when I sit up on the lumpy cushions, heart racing. The idea came to me at a slant. Or maybe Frank whispered it while I was sleeping. *Come on, Cat, you know South Carolina isn't your destiny. If I'm not mistaken, there's another place calling your name. You've been dreaming of going as long as I can remember, and now you've a reason. Find a*

130

way, Cat. Find Sam. You know you can if you want to. Get to London. Get to Hampstead. Leo Dunn lives there, remember? The widower from the funeral. Isn't that where Sam lives too? There's the bench on the Heath he told you about — find it, and you'll find him. There's nothing to stop you any more.

I stumble up, pulling on my clothes from the night before, panic making me gasp, because I have no idea if I'm in time to catch Leo Dunn and his daughter, Grace, before they leave Atlantic City.

20

Sam, June 1983

Cat, my love,

I'm sitting on the bench on Hampstead Heath I told you about. Being here makes me feel closer to you, and I wonder if you might even read this on your bench on the boardwalk. Can you feel me sitting beside you? I haven't given up hoping that you'll forgive me for lying about my parents, and Lucinda. Don't worry, I'm not going to keep giving excuses like a broken record — I've said it all in my other letters. It's over with Lucinda. The writing was on the wall months before I even met you.

I love you, Cat. That's what's really important, isn't it? Because I think you love me too. We had so many plans and dreams, and I still want to share them with you. Just write back, my love. Even if you're angry. Please. This silence is unbearable. The truth is you've unlocked something inside me. When I'm with you, I'm the best of myself. And the music — because of you, the songs keep flowing. Every one of them about you. For you. You are my touchstone, my soul. And I want to do the same for you. I want to support your plans, help you make them a reality. I loved your story. It gave me a shiver down my spine reading your words. You're that rare thing — a real story-teller.

I'm enclosing a song for you. I wrote it in Atlantic City, but didn't have the guts to show you. It's called 'Ocean Blue', and it says exactly what I feel. I hope I can sing it to you soon.

First time I saw you,
Beside the ocean blue,
I just knew you were
Someone to be close to.

I stood in the dark
While you splashed in the sea.
You always were braver than me.
But darling, remember us
Kissing slow on the Avenue,
Talking 'bout our past.
God, I wanted it to last.

I can do what it takes, babe,
I can be me,
But only with you, only with you.
Yeah, I can be me, but only with you.
Always for ever in our ocean blue.

It's your smile that makes me brave,
Your voice that holds me close,
Whispering all I am, all I need to do.
And those dreams, baby,
I want to share them with you.

133

'Cause it's not just me alone,
It's the sweetness of two.
When I'm with you,
I'm always at home.
So stay with me, lay with me,
Sweet girl of mine, with breath like the
  sea.

I can do what it takes, babe,
I can be me,
But only with you, baby, only with you.
Yeah, we can be us, but only with you.
Always together in our ocean blue.
Always for ever, in our ocean blue, blue,
  blue.

Sam slips the envelope into the first postbox he finds on his way back to south London. He stops off to buy supper ingredients in Mattie's local supermarket: fresh tomatoes, pungent basil, and a good bottle of Merlot. Mattie and River are out for the day and Sam wants to have the meal ready before they're back. He hums the tune for 'Ocean Blue' as he queues at the checkout, buoyant with hope. He wishes he could play it for her, but including the lyrics in the letter was his best effort yet at explaining his feelings. She'll reply this time. He's sure of it.

In the high street, carrier bags straining from both hands, he notices a hearse crawl past. He glimpses the coffin inside, a wreath of purple and white flowers on the side that says MUM in capital letters.

Suddenly he's swaying, his mind loud as a

clanging bell. The funeral home! He should have rung the funeral home. Why didn't he think of it before? Urgency ignites, firing through his muscles. He's running, his feet smacking the pavement hard at every stride.

He dashes into the hallway, grabbing up Mattie's phone to dial international directory enquiries. But then he stops with a shock. What's the name? He can picture it clearly: the yellow-painted clapboard, the shuttered windows. The fir tree standing sentinel at the bottom of the path. He wipes his hand over his brow, balls it into a fist and thumps his forehead. Think. Think. There was a colour, he seems to remember. A colour in the name. Blue. Red. He sees the tree again, silhouetted against the street light, feels Cat's hand in his, glimpses her smile over her shoulder as they mounted the steps to the door. The sign was there, next to the entrance. It comes to him suddenly: *Greenacres*.

The phone rings and rings. A man's voice answers. 'Greenacres Funeral Home.'

'Hello,' Sam shouts down the crackly line. 'Can I speak to Cat? Catrin Goforth?' He pauses. 'It's . . . it's urgent.'

There's silence, and he hears the echo of time and space rushing to meet him. He sits down hard on the edge of a chair, gripping the receiver. 'Hello?' he repeats. 'Did you hear me?'

'Catrin's not here,' the voice tells him, slow words dropping through the wire.

'When will she be back? Can you tell her I called — '

135

'She's left,' the voice cuts in. 'She doesn't work here any more.'

'What do you mean?' His racing heart stutters in his chest. 'Where can I reach her?'

'I can't help you with that, I'm afraid.'

'Wait!' he yells. 'Just tell me. Is she working in another funeral parlour in Atlantic City?'

There's an audible sigh. 'To my knowledge, she's no longer in Atlantic City.'

'What? Where's she gone?'

The line is dead. Sam lets the receiver drop; it falls, dangling by its curling cord.

★ ★ ★

Sam serves up pasta with tomato sauce onto three plates. He's amazed that he can stand, let alone make a meal. Since the phone call, he feels strung out, and at the same time numb and strangely detached. She's gone. He'll never see her again.

River is in bed, and Mattie sits with bare feet up on another chair, a large glass of red wine in her hand. Luke, back from the City — from whatever mysterious job he has there — is slumped opposite his wife, his tie loosened around his neck, sleeves pushed to the elbow.

Mattie rolls a cigarette so meagre it's hardly fatter than a blade of grass. She blows out a long stream of smoke. 'God, this is the best time of the day.'

'I wanted to thank you,' Sam tells them. 'Both of you. I know I've outstayed my welcome and been a terrible guest.'

136

'Oh, shut up!' Mattie puts her head on one side and pouts. 'You know you can stay as long as you like. I didn't mean what I said before.' Then she looks at him hard. 'Has something happened? You've been very quiet since I got back.'

'Nothing's happened.' Sam prods at his pasta with his fork. 'I've just realised I've been selfish, that's all. Selfish and stupid. Moping over . . .' he struggles to say her name, 'over Cat. I need to pull myself together. I've made a decision to focus on my music, so I need to get on with it. I'll stay with Ben while I figure out how to get a singing career started.'

'Well, that's good news, Jack,' Luke says. Then he pauses, frowning theatrically, 'Sorry, you're Sam now, aren't you? Or maybe there's another name you've decided on? I can't keep up.'

'Luke!' Mattie says sharply. 'Leave it.'

Sam puts his fork down and looks at his brother-in-law. 'It's not that hard to understand,' he says. 'I've changed my name. People do it all the time.'

'It's ridiculous.' Luke lifts his lip in a sneer. 'Mattie thinks so too. She's known you as Jack all her life. She just doesn't want to tell you the truth because you're so bloody fragile right now. Apparently.'

Mattie glares at him and shakes her head. 'Ignore him. My real worry is what's going on with you and our parents. Can't you forgive them?' She places her fingers together as if she's measuring them against each other, and leans forward. 'Dad and Mum are human too. They made mistakes — '

137

'Mistakes!' Sam sits back in his chair, pushing himself away from the table so the legs scrape against the floor. 'I wouldn't call any of it a *mistake*. He knew perfectly well what he was doing. It went on for years. A fucking lifetime of deceit. The lies he told. He's . . . he's a psychopath, and a hypocrite. And all the time . . . God!' His jaw grinds against itself. 'I'm glad you can forgive them.' He swallows. 'But it's a mystery to me how you've managed it. Maybe it's the yoga. Or being a mother. Or just being a better person than me.'

He catches Mattie and Luke giving each other glances under raised eyebrows. He ignores them, sloshes more wine into all their glasses with unsteady fingers. A sudden thought comes to him and he puts the bottle down with a thud. 'You haven't seen him, have you?' he asks.

'Who? Dad?'

Sam makes a dismissive sweeping gesture with his hand. 'No. Him. George, or whatever he's called.'

'I haven't seen him since that day, no.' Mattie places her arms on the table and pillows her head there. Her voice is quiet. 'Your anger is exhausting. I think I liked it better when you were moping over that girl.'

Sam arranges his fork and spoon neatly on his red-smeared plate and gets up from the table. 'I've been stupid about a lot of things — especially Cat. And I regret hurting Lucinda. But what happened with Dad is different. It changed everything. I've burnt my bridges with Lucinda and the law firm — not that I want my old life back. I need to go forwards, make things happen with my music.'

Mattie nods. 'At least think about contacting Mum. She's a victim in this as much as the rest of us.'

He sighs, relenting.

She comes around the table and puts her arms around his waist. He rests his chin on her head. 'Don't worry about Cat,' she says. 'Or Lucinda. You two were never really right for each other. Plenty more girls out there. Especially if you're a rock god.' She steps back and grins, a quick Mattie flash of wickedness.

He nods. But his mind isn't focused on what she's saying any more. He's trying not to remember a dark beach in Atlantic City, Cat close beside him, their arms entwined, ankles tethered, their hearts thundering with the same rhythm as they flew across the sand into the night, running as if they were one person.

Part Two

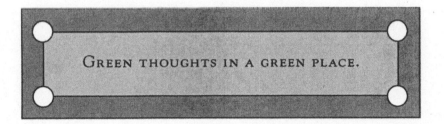

GREEN THOUGHTS IN A GREEN PLACE.

21

Cat, February 1984

These days I wake in a white Gothic house on a tree-lined London street. If I turn right out of the house and walk up the hill, within ten minutes I'm in the open spaces of the Heath, and it's like Sam said, a kind of wild park with woods and lakes. I found the bench. It took a while. I went to every single one, reading the inscriptions engraved in the wood. Ever since I found it, I've gone there each day, hoping to see him. I left a note once. When I went back, it had gone, but someone could have taken it, or the wind, or the rain. I'm not giving up. One day he'll come.

Leo's house is tall and narrow, with battlements and fairy-tale windows. The rooms have working fireplaces and old-fashioned mouldings like piped frosting. There are paintings hanging on the walls, modernist swirls of thick paint, and everywhere bookcases are jammed with novels. My footsteps padding across oak boards sound as if I'm walking across the shiny surface of my own dreams.

The dream stops when I knock on Grace's door to get her up for school. I never know what I'll find: sometimes she's buried inside her covers, rolled up in her blankets like a small hibernating bear, refusing to come out; or she's already buttoned skew-whiff into the wrong clothes, down in the kitchen helping herself to a breakfast of chocolate cookies and ice cream. This morning she was naked, drawing over her wall with felt-tip pen.

I have a few hours during the day when I can breathe easy, knowing she's safe at school. My duties are light: a bit of housework, nothing too strenuous, because a cleaner comes once a week. I shop for food. I bundle clothes into the washer in the utility room next to the big basement kitchen. No more dragging bags to the laundromat. There's even a dryer for wet days, a line in the garden for sunny ones. Once I'm through with my chores, I'm free. Leo says I can read any of the books in the house, and he's given me a list of museums and galleries he says I should visit. Often I sit in a café writing stories. Every day I go to Sam's bench with a book. It's kind of secluded because a hawthorn tree grows right behind it, but it's on the top of a hill with a long view of the Heath and the distant city. Sitting bent over my book, I glance up each time a shadow falls, my heart singing with expectation. But it's never him.

★ ★ ★

Grace's primary school is fifteen minutes away on foot.

Today, halfway down the hill, she drops onto the sidewalk, hunching into a ball. 'Come on, Grace,' I say. 'We're gonna be late.' I squat next to her. 'Gracie, please get up.'

144

'That's not my name!' She twists her head to peer at me with an angry expression.

'Okay. I'm sorry.' I sit down on the sidewalk next to her and start to hum. 'Once,' I say, slowly and casually, 'there was a doodlebug who thought he was a butterfly.'

'What's a doodlebug?' Her voice is muffled, her mouth against her knees.

'One of those insects with an armoured shell on top. Tiny. Grey. They can roll right up into a ball, just like you're doing.'

She uncurls herself and sits up, interested, despite herself.

'Let's walk awhile and I'll tell the story,' I say, getting to my feet and giving her my hand. Reluctantly she puts her fingers inside mine. 'Well, he kept on trying to fly. He'd launch himself off the top of high things, like tree branches and park benches . . . ' I keep talking. We're making headway now. The school gates are just around the corner.

★　★　★

Her room is large and pretty: a rocking horse by the window, shelves stuffed with plushies, and a giant doll's house. Everything a kid could want. After dropping her at school, I settle on the floor with a bowl of soapy water and begin to rub at the marks with a damp cloth. She's drawn stick people, but they're missing arms and legs. Blood pours from cracks in their heads. Their mouths are open in silent screams.

Whenever anything like this happens, Leo

145

always tells me, 'Give her time. She's still grieving.'

I got a book out of the library on how to help bereaved children, and it said to keep everything as normal as possible: familiar routines are essential; no big changes. I have no experience with children, let alone one who's lost her mother. It's a miracle Leo agreed to take me on. It was Grace who made the decision really. When I arrived at their hotel first thing in the morning, Leo asked me to wait outside in the corridor while he talked to his daughter. When he opened the door, he told me she'd like me to be her new au pair. They were leaving that day. I'd only just caught them. Eunice gave me a reference. And that was that.

On the way over on the plane a few days later, the hum of the jet engines under my feet, I was excited about finding Sam. I'd convinced myself there was bound to be an explanation as to why he never wrote: all I needed was to find him, and we'd straighten things out and carry on from where we left off. When he didn't show up on the bench, I went through the phone book, flicking tissue-thin pages to the letter S, eager to hear his voice, his surprise when I told him where I was.

'Wrong number,' I was informed each time. 'No one of that name here.'

I keep hoping to see him on the Underground train or sitting opposite me on a bus, standing outside a shop, walking along the sidewalk. I scan crowds, looking for his dark head. I didn't realise how big London is; how it's split by the river into north and south; how it can take hours to get from one part to the other.

I thought he lived in Hampstead, but I don't have an address. I don't know what his sister Mattie's second name is, or how his parents died. He mentioned he went to Oxford University. But when I called up, I found it's made up of different colleges. I've tried each one. None has a record of a student called Sam Sage.

* * *

Where are you, Sam? I remember how you sounded up on the stage at Ally's, the way my stomach dropped and lurched during your performance. Most of all, I remember how you made me feel when we were together: your fingers and mouth and tongue lit up my body. I was home at last.

I sit on your bench every day, waiting for you. I didn't make you up. You were flesh and blood in my arms. I remember the smell of your skin. The feel of your lips on mine. I miss you.

* * *

Mom writes me on paper scented with rose water, telling me of her reclaimed life in the South. She never mentions Dad. His letters are infrequent, shorter. He seems convinced he'll win Mom back as soon as he's out.

No chance, my brother's voice sighs. *She needs him like a mule needs a steering wheel.*

Frank. Since living in London, I hear him less

and less. When I do, his words are a faint echo, as if they're coming across miles of ocean, inside the whip of an Atlantic wind.

★ ★ ★

There are cliques at the school gates. At the top of the pack are mothers, and then nannies. The odd father loiters on his own, uncomfortable and uncertain. Au pairs are bottom of the pecking order. I guess I fall into that category. Dougie is the only male in the playground today, and the only 'manny' in the school. He's wearing a trilby hat and long scarf. He waves when he sees me. 'Thank God you're here,' he says, kissing my cheeks with cold lips. 'I smiled at one of the mums and they closed ranks in military formation. Honestly, you'd think I'd flashed my ding-dong at them, not my teeth.'

'Ding-dong?'

'Quaint term for penis,' he tells me. 'Less sexual than cock. Less offensive than fuckpole. Cuter than knob.' He adjusts the flowing tail of his scarf and tosses his head. 'Tallywacker would have been a more flamboyant choice, I admit.'

'Tallywacker?' I laugh.

'I know.' He grins. 'Isn't it a lovely euphemism?'

Just then, the bell rings, and a percussion of clattering footsteps, banging doors and chil-dren's voices fills the air. The two little girls that Dougie looks after rush towards him, pale blonde plaits flying behind them. They land in his arms in a whirlwind of satchels, knobbly

148

knees, clutched artwork and empty lunch boxes. He arranges confusion into order, answering breathy demands and wiping runny noses. They each hold one of his hands. 'Right, we're off,' he says. Then, looking around, 'No Grace?'

I'm straining my gaze towards the infants' entrance, searching for her dark curls, her green coat. I have a familiar sinking feeling. 'I'd better go look. See you tomorrow.'

'We'll get a date for coffee soon,' he calls over his shoulder. 'We need a gossip.'

I find Grace just inside the entrance. She's there with her teacher, a plump woman with oversized pink-framed glasses. Miss Fisher bends down and puts her hand on Grace's back. 'Sit quietly over there, Grace. I just need a quick word with . . . '

'Catrin,' I remind her.

She leans close enough that when she breathes out, I taste the leftover cheesy tang of her lunch. 'I'm afraid Grace bit another child today,' she says in hushed tones. 'Luckily her teeth didn't break the skin, but she's left a nasty bruise.' She glances over at Grace, sitting on a chair by the door, swinging her legs. 'We can't keep making excuses for her. It's just one thing after another. We had to punish her.'

'How?' I ask angrily. 'How did you punish her? She's only six.'

'She spent a lesson on the naughty step. Excluding children is often enough. She needs to know right from wrong.'

I stand taller. 'She doesn't need to be punished. She needs help. She's just lost her

149

mom.' I glance at Grace to make sure she can't hear. 'It's hard for her to understand what's happened. Acting out is her way of expressing it.'

I turn my back on the teacher. 'Hey, let's go, doodlebug. There's ice cream for dessert. You can put sprinkles on too.'

★ ★ ★

At home, I grill her favourite fish fingers, only burning them a bit. When she's finished eating, I sit beside her. 'Grace,' I begin cautiously. 'Why did you bite someone today? Miss Fisher told me.'

She rubs her finger into the last swirl of ketchup and licks it. She shrugs.

'Did they upset you?'

She shrugs again, not looking at me. 'Can I get down?'

'You mustn't hurt other people.' I place my hand over hers gently. 'Even if they make you cross.' Her fingers are hot and sticky. 'I know life's difficult right now. But things will get better, sweetheart. I promise.'

She blinks, pulling away. 'Can I get down now?'

I sigh. 'Wipe your hands first.' I give her a damp dishrag. Expressionless, she rubs it between her palms, then clambers off her chair and walks out of the kitchen. With a hollow feeling in my chest I listen to the thump, thump of her feet as she climbs the stairs to the next floor.

Framed photographs of Elizabeth are propped

150

on dressers and sideboards; they hang from walls, sit on mantelpieces. Wherever I look, she's there gazing back at me. In private moments, I've picked one up and held it close, as if Elizabeth might whisper words of advice. I remember her in her coffin. The woman in the pictures is animated, smiling, with her dark eyes wide open. She'd been an actress before she married Leo. She has the radiant look of a star.

I dry my soapy hands on a towel, and glance at the clock on the wall. I'll make a start on Leo's supper, have it ready for when he gets back from the hospital. I'm teaching myself how to make English food from cookery books stacked on the shelves next to the oven, bizarre-sounding things like shepherd's pie and liver and bacon, recipes earmarked, stained with splashes, and scribbled on in Elizabeth's handwriting. I try and follow the instructions, but somehow I over-salt dishes. Onions blacken in frying pans. Water boils dry. But Leo keeps a sense of humour, says if he'd wanted a cook, he would have employed one.

This is not how I imagined life in London when Sam invited me to stay. I wonder where he is now; if he's even here, in this sprawling city. From my bedroom window, I have a glimpse of distant rooftops and tower blocks. Sam could be in one of those buildings. I could walk past his front door, and never know it.

22

Sam, February 1984

Sam's bed at Ben's place is a broken-down settee covered in old rugs. Most evenings, the air is thick with nicotine and the sweet stink of spliffs. Loud punk music plays on the stereo. Sam can't stop himself from imagining Lucinda's horror if she saw this place, her poor opinion of him plummeting even lower.

After another rowdy party, he wakes from an uneasy sleep and finds that he's curled uncomfortably on the sofa, a motheaten rug draped over his shoulders, the ancient fabric stained with alcoholic spillages, cigarette ash and God knows what else. He must have passed out at some point in the evening. He turns onto his back, rubbing his calf muscles. He's too cold to go back to sleep. He wraps the blanket closer and stares up towards the ceiling, remembering.

★ ★ ★

It was his mother's birthday. He and Lucinda, Mattie, Luke and River were all at his parents' house, sitting around the table. There was an iced cake with candles, and cucumber sandwiches. He was accepting a slice of Victoria sponge when the doorbell rang. The dogs barked.

152

Everyone looked at everyone else. 'My goodness, who can that be?' his mother asked.

'I'll go.' Sam put his plate down.

He opened the front door to a tall young man about the same age as himself, eyes glittering with some unspoken, deeply felt emotion. He was a hefty, rugby-playing type, red-haired; meaty hands dangled at his sides, clenching and unclenching. Sam wondered if he was unhinged, even dangerous. He tightened his grip on the doorknob. 'Yes?' he said warily. 'Can I help you?'

The man kept on staring with that intense gaze. His broad freckled face flushed. 'Are you Jack?'

Sam frowned, leaning back. 'Who are you?'

The man took a great shuddering breath. 'I'm George,' he said. 'Your brother.'

* * *

His father came to see what was happening. Then George was jabbing his finger and shouting that he'd followed him home, explaining in a garbled rush that he'd spent the previous day crouching in the rhododendron bushes observing his father's double life. 'Peacocks,' he shouted. 'Bloody peacocks on your lawn. You live in a mansion with your other children. What about me and Mum? Weren't we worth this?' His voice became hysterical as he told them that he'd returned to London and found out that his mother had known all along about the other family: a wife, children. His half-siblings, for

153

God's sake! He started to cry. 'I'm the bastard, though, aren't I?'

Instinctively, Sam moved to his mother to protect her, but he understood at once by the look on her face. 'You knew?'

Eventually their father persuaded George to leave, bundling him into the Daimler. Their mother, sitting before her crumbling birthday cake, lit a cigarette with trembling fingers. 'I'm sorry,' she sobbed. 'I thought it was better for you not to know.' Mattie comforted her, but all Sam could think of was the hollow sham of his life, the assumption that he would do his duty, the obligations put upon his shoulders, his miserable school days, a career he didn't want.

His father had been living with George and Maureen, his ex-secretary, from Monday evenings to Friday mornings, before returning to the country to be with his official wife and three other children. He'd split his time between the two families during the holidays, keeping the charade going for over twenty years. It made it easier for him, Sam supposed bitterly, that both women accepted the situation. But none of the children, or relatives, or friends, or work colleagues had had a clue. He'd been a conjuror of lives, juggling names and places and dates without a slip. Until now.

* * *

He must have fallen asleep again, because he wakes to a trickle of light through fabric draped over a grubby window. He can see his breath,

154

smoky in the cold air. He's fully dressed, apart from his shoes. He fishes them out from under a chair and pads into the kitchen, finding Ben at the table drinking from a tin mug.

'Hey,' Ben says in a raspy voice. 'Tea?'

'Thanks.'

Ben sniffs the milk bottle before sloshing some into a cup. 'Listen, we need another guitar in Slaughter,' he says. 'How about joining the band?'

'I'm not really into punk.' Sam accepts the grubby mug full of hot liquid. 'Thanks for the offer, but I'm going to stick to my own music. I've got some songs ready.'

'Just you and your guitar?'

He nods. 'I'm going to try open-mic nights, local pubs. Try and get some momentum going.'

Ben makes a noise through his teeth. 'You'd better get down to the dole office then.' He puts his feet on the table.

Sam shakes his head. 'I'll get a part-time job to keep me ticking over. Anything will do. Barman or waiter.' He takes a sip of tea and grimaces at the taste of curdled milk.

It feels like an age ago that he was kneeling on a bed with Cat's hands clasped in his. *I believe in you.* Her tears wet on his cheek. He has a stab of pain in his chest. Missing her comes in waves, when he's least expecting it. He grips the edge of the sink, staring out into the rainy Brixton street. He's miles away from Hampstead here. He doesn't go to the Heath any more. There's no point. He'll never show her the bench, sit with her there, watching kites dancing above the hill.

155

But he has his songs, and the task of getting them into the world, finding a way to make people listen. He and Cat only had three weeks together. He's got a lifetime of making music before him.

23

Cat, August 1985

I've stopped going to the bench to wait for him. He's not going to come. Something has died inside me, but I'm not going to die with it. I'm in a city I always wanted to visit, so what can I do but try and make the most of it?

On our days off, Dougie takes me to his favourite places: the Victorian hothouses at Kew, where we climb spiral staircases in jungle heat, and Portobello Market, browsing for old records and chipped china, vintage scarves and ropes of beads. Weekends we ride the Tube to Knightsbridge, waltzing past men in dark glasses guarding shop entrances. Dougie stalks around with his nose in the air, picking out clothes for me to try. The clothes don't even have price tags. A look-don't-buy situation. He has an amazing skill for knowing what looks good with what; he says he wants to work on a fashion magazine. In Soho, we sit on high stools to drink espressos in an Italian coffee bar, men arguing and waving their arms while a football match plays across a screen.

I've missed swimming in the Atlantic. The cool, reedy water of Hampstead Ponds couldn't be more different; it's grittier and heavier than any water I've been in, strands of slimy weed waiting to catch in toes and fingers, the silt on

157

the bottom stirring up muddy clouds. I go to the Ladies' Pond, enclosed by thick foliage, where some women strip off and swim naked. It's not the wide expanses of the Atlantic — it's contained, intimate — but when I summon up the courage to swim without my bathing suit, I feel a rush of freedom. The water is noisy with ducks and coots. Sodden feathers stick to my skin when I pull myself out. Elderly ladies do backstroke, staring into the sky.

★ ★ ★

They're calling it a heatwave on the news. Long, dusty days and sultry, sticky nights have turned London into an unrecognisable city. Windows stay propped open, letting out snatches of conversation, the rattle of meals being prepared, the blare of radios; people walk more slowly, smile more often. Ice-cream vans traverse the streets, trailing mechanical chimes.

It's too hot to go into town. Dougie and I are on the Heath, and although it's Saturday, we have the girls with us — all our charges. I'm glad to see Grace with other children. Dougie's two are sweethearts, allowing her to join their games. We've had a swim in the crowded Mixed Pond. I stayed close to Grace as she spluttered her way round.

We find a bench to eat our picnic on. Not Sam's bench. I don't want to share that with anyone, not even Dougie. Grace is playing with the others, the three of them squatting together in the shade of a nearby tree.

Dougie and I spread out a rug, lying flat with eyes shut against the glare, the lilting murmur of the girls' voices reassuringly close.

I yawn, covering my mouth, suppressing another one. 'Sorry. Grace had nightmares again last night.'

'Do you know what they're about?'

'She can't explain. But sometimes she shouts 'Mummy'. I guess she's just still really missing her mom.'

'Poor kid. Doesn't Leo get up for her?'

'Sometimes, but he has an early start and people's eyes to fix. I'm fine about losing a little sleep.'

'How are you getting on with him?' he asks.

'Good. He's great.'

'You know the premise, though, don't you?'

'What do you mean?'

'Widower and young nanny . . . you're kind of obliged to get together.'

'Jeez, Dougie — this isn't *Jane Eyre!*' I feel for his wrist and give it a playful slap. 'Leo's not like that. He's private and respectful. I like him a lot — he's easy to talk to, and he's read loads of the same novels I have. He treats me like an equal, makes me feel at home.'

'Sounds like you have a connection.'

'Guess I'm lucky.' I smile to myself, remembering how he makes a joke of my cooking, telling me that I should be up for a Michelin star, or that Carrier himself will be wanting my recipes. He never gets mad about it. 'I couldn't have chosen a nicer employer. He *is* attractive, in that quiet, English way, but . . . '

159

'He's not your type?'

'I don't think I have a type.'

'Okay then, if it's not him, who is it that you're pining for? Because I get the feeling there's a man somewhere. Someone you don't talk about. Even to me. Which, by the way, is a crime.'

My eyes snap open in shock. 'What?'

He looks smug. 'Thought so.'

'Are you psychic or something?'

He laughs. 'Not much gets past me, hen.' He makes a woo-woo face at me, like a ghost. 'I'm the seventh son of a seventh son. So naturally I have magic powers.'

'Sure you do.' I raise an eyebrow. 'But . . . yeah, you're right, there was someone . . . '

'Ah ha!' Dougie exclaims. 'Who?'

'I met him in Atlantic City. He was English. But after he left, I never heard from him again. He's here, I think. Somewhere in London. But I have no way of getting in touch with him. I tried the telephone directory. He doesn't seem to exist.' I stare up into the glare, and it's as though I see Sam there in the brilliance, the silhouette of him walking away with his guitar slung across his back.

'So you followed him across an ocean. How romantic,' Dougie sighs.

I nudge his arm with mine in acknowledgement; our skin, tacky with suntan oil, makes a tiny kissing noise. 'Only it wasn't romantic. It was stupid,' I admit. 'Turns out I didn't really know anything about him. When we were together I thought I'd found 'the one', you know. I thought we had a future together. He invited

160

me to London. He even read bench inscriptions, like me. He said there was a bench here on the Heath with an inscription he loved.' I swallow. 'I found the bench. I went there every day, but he never came.'

'And he didn't even tell you what he did for a living?'

'He was a lawyer. But he was about to leave his firm. Really, he's a singer. He's talented. Writes his own stuff.'

'Ooh.' Dougie raises himself on his elbow. I feel the darkness of his shadow falling across my face. 'Would I have heard of him?'

I turn my head from side to side against the picnic rug. 'Uh uh.'

'Shame.' He settles himself on his back again. 'Well, my advice is, find yourself another man. Plenty in this city. I'll help.'

I lick my lips. 'Maybe. But not just yet. I want to focus on Grace. She's so unhappy. She needs all my attention.'

There's a sudden wail. A child is crying. Instantly, Dougie and I sit up. 'Lily? Phoebe?' Dougie says. And then, in a sharper voice, 'Where's Grace?'

I stagger to my feet, swivelling my head, straining to see through the dazzle of picnickers, dogs, children in bright swim-suits. Dougie is examining Lily's thin arm, the red welt rising against pale skin. 'She bit me and then ran off,' Lily sobs, as Dougie scoops her into a hug.

'Where did she go?' I shade my eyes with my hand. 'Which direction?'

Phoebe points up the hill towards the woods. I

look for a small, plump figure marching away, expecting to glimpse untidy dark curls, a yellow T-shirt over a blue costume. I can't see her. She can't have got far, but my heart crashes inside my ribs as I take off up the hill at a jog, stopping to ask people if they've seen a little girl. A girl in yellow and blue? They shake their heads. Mothers clasp their own children tighter, giving me pitying looks.

The heat is oppressive. There's a sting of salt in my eyes. Tears or sweat or both, because now I'm scared. I'm stumbling barefoot over the rough grass of the hill, making my way around families sprawled on picnic rugs, couples stretched on towels. I enter the woods. Two lovers lie in each other's arms on the ground, half hidden in long grass, oblivious to my footsteps trampling close. I shout her name. 'Grace! Grace!'

The Heath is huge. How am I going to find her? The churning fear in my belly is getting worse. I retrace my steps, going downhill, still calling. My throat is sore from shouting. When I get closer to our spot, Dougie shakes his head.

'She's not back?' I'm sick with disappointment. 'Should I call the police? Her dad?'

'Don't panic yet,' he says. 'Come on, let's all of us look.'

We make a plan. I'll go and check the pond, in case she went back to it; and if she's not there, I'll look up the hill one more time. Dougie and the girls will go to the house, in case she went home. I have thorns in the soles of my feet. I don't have time to deal with them; I just pull my sandals on. She has to be all right, I tell myself, scanning the landscape.

The Mixed Pond is busy with bathers. I ask the girl on the gate if she's seen a small child, and she shakes her head. 'But it's been hectic. I suppose she could have slipped past . . .'

I stare out over the dark water, the bobbing heads and laughing mouths. I'm terrified I'll see her floating face down. She's not a strong swimmer. People are kind, once they understand. There's a search. Nobody has seen her in or out of the water. 'She's not here,' the girl tells me, her voice full of sympathy.

I nod, my chest tight. I need to stick to the plan. I hurry back up the slope again where she was last seen, shouting her name. In the woods, the lovers have gone. There's a small figure sitting on the ground under a tree.

'Grace!' I sink onto my haunches next to her. 'Thank God you're all right!'

I pull her into my arms. She lies against me, heavy and inert. I rock her in my lap, murmuring her name, my lips in her hair. She starts to cry: shoulder-shuddering gulps that come from deep in her belly.

'Sweetheart,' I manage. 'You're okay. I've got you.'

Her arms slide around my neck, and she presses her hot cheek against mine. We sit in the glade, clutching each other. Her cries make my heart ache. When she stops, I find a tissue in my pocket to wipe her face, blow her nose. I kiss her hot forehead. We manage shaky smiles. 'Come on,' I say, helping her up. 'We have to tell the

163

others you're okay.'

As we make our way down the hill, I turn to her. 'Grace, please don't run off like that again,' I say quietly. 'Anything could have happened.' I keep walking. 'You scared me to death. And it was naughty to bite Lily. You hurt her arm — and you hurt her feelings. Never do it again, promise?'

She jerks to a stop, snatching her hand away, her tear-streaked face reddening. 'You're not my mum. You can't tell me what to do.'

I look at her small, quivering body. She's confused by my role in her life. 'Your dad's asked me to look after you, though,' I say firmly. 'So you still need to follow some rules. Now,' I give her an encouraging smile, 'let's go home.' I hold out my hand again. 'You need a bath, young lady. Looks like you've been rolling in dirt.'

I breathe a sigh of relief when she puts her fingers inside mine.

★   ★   ★

After Grace has had a bath, she slides in between her sheets meekly. 'Will you tell me a story?' she mumbles, thumb in her mouth. I pick up one of her many picture books, but she shakes her head. 'You tell it.'

'If you close your eyes. And promise to go to sleep.' I smooth tangles of damp hair back from her forehead.

She nods, eyelids closing obediently. Her chubby hands rest on the sheet, linked like a thoughtful grown-up's. A painful warmth swells

164

in my chest. I lean down to kiss her flushed cheek. Seems that love has sneaked up on me when I wasn't looking. She opens her eyes, then closes them again.

I begin to tell her a story, about a little boy who's afraid of the sea, even though he lives right on the coast, and how when a whale washes up on a beach, he saves her by his quick wits and his ability to get the whole village working together. 'And do you know,' I finish, 'that little boy learnt to swim right after that. And he was never afraid of the water again, because he knew his friend the whale was somewhere close.'

Making up stories for Grace is a way of connecting with her. I'm going to think of more ideas, especially ones to make her laugh. I leave her lying with her mouth open, wet, wrinkled thumb slipping onto her chin, a string of saliva shining on her lip. Her breathing is slow and steady. She gives a whimper in her sleep and turns onto her side, facing away from me. I tiptoe out of the room, closing the door.

★   ★   ★

While I wait in my room for Leo to return, I open my diary and scribble across the page. As I describe the afternoon, how Grace went missing, and how empty and afraid I felt, it hits me that love comes with responsibility, and I don't know if I'm the right person to care for her. I'm not a mom, or a qualified nanny. What if I'm messing up her childhood, doing everything wrong?

I raise my head, listening to Leo opening the

front door downstairs. He changes out of his suit before going to find his meal in the kitchen. When I go down, he's sitting at the table with a glass of wine. We smile at each other as he brings his plate to the sink. 'Sorry I missed her bedtime again,' he says. 'Did you have a nice day?'

I clear my throat. 'About that. I need to talk to you.'

'Of course.' He nods towards an empty chair. As I take my seat and he slides into his, I notice how tired he looks. He works such long hours. I can't imagine how nerve-racking it must be to operate on people's eyes.

'Everything all right?' He's making an effort to sound cheerful. I notice his gaze shift past my head to the photographs on the dresser. Elizabeth smiling her brilliant smile.

I look down, pressing one finger against the grain of the wood. 'I'm worried about Grace,' I tell him. 'I'm trying hard to get through to her, but . . . but I'm not managing. She bit a child at school, and she did it again to Lily today. Then she just ran off. I couldn't find her. I thought . . . I thought I'd lost her.' I glance up and catch the bleak expression on his face. 'I'm sorry.' I push on, determined to say what needs to be said. 'I don't think I'm the right person. Maybe you need a trained nanny. Someone who knows what they're doing.'

He sits for a moment, his hands slack around the glass in front of him. Then he takes a long in-breath, exhaling slowly. 'I need to tell you something.' He looks at me, his blue eyes misty behind his glasses. 'Elizabeth died here, in this house. She tripped and fell down the stairs.'

I gasp, sitting rigid in my chair.

'It was just Elizabeth and Grace at home. So it was Grace who . . . who found her lying at the foot of the stairs,' he continues in a low voice. 'She had been playing in her room and then . . . she must have heard the scream. She was alone with her mum's body for hours, trying to wake her. The whole experience . . . well, you can imagine the effect on her. It's why she's confused. Frightened. Angry. I've arranged for her to see a grief counsellor. But she needs you, Cat. She trusts you. If you leave now, it'll be another loss. And . . . and I don't think she could cope.'

I imagine Grace alone with the broken body of her mother. The thought fills me with horror. No wonder she's having nightmares.

Leo reaches across and brushes my forearm lightly. 'Please don't go.' He withdraws his hand. 'Not unless you're miserable with us.' He leaves his hand lying on the table, fingers splayed, those intelligent fingers that negotiate the intricate workings of eyes. 'I'm not a risk-taker, Cat. I'm someone who thinks things through carefully. And I promise you, I know what I'm doing when I say that you're the only person I want looking after my daughter.'

I swallow, staring down at my lap. His words make me glow.

'If there's anything I can do to make things more comfortable . . . anything you need in your room . . . '

'No,' I say. 'I love my room. This house.' I

swallow. 'I just . . . want to do the right thing . . . ' I remember the book about grieving children, how it's essential not to make any big changes. 'I don't want to leave.'

'Then you'll stay?' He looks relieved. 'I know you care about her. I couldn't ask for anything else.'

★ ★ ★

In my room, I throw open the windows, wide as they'll go, and stand in my bra and pants, hungry for a breeze, looking over the darkening garden towards the Heath. Below me, there's a murmur of voices coming from neighbouring gardens, the chink and clatter of barbecued meals being eaten.

The thought of Sam is inside my head, but I can't quite picture his features any more, can't recall the exact smell of his skin. It was because I was thinking of him that I wasn't focused on Grace. She could have been kidnapped, hurt, lost. And it would have been my fault. Sam's gone. What I have is Grace, who needs me, and Leo, who's becoming a friend as well as my employer. I have a home in this house, and I have my writing. These are the things to cherish, to look after. To fight for. I close my eyes, and from the garden comes a soft breeze at last, the sweet kiss of air on my skin.

24

Sam, August 1985

Sam barges shoulder first through the swing doors, out of the steamy kitchen into the busy dining room, balancing a tray of plates on one arm. The chef — a bucolic Irishman who resembles a prizefighter — is in a particularly filthy mood this evening, and Sam doesn't fancy his chances if he messes up the orders. He needs to concentrate.

He places the plates carefully in front of the right customers, before whisking out his notepad and pen and hovering over the next table: a grey-haired couple who have been prevaricating over the menu for ages. He stands waiting for their order.

There's a tune in his head that he can't quite catch. An idea he had for a song called 'Cindy', based on Cat's short story, the tattered pages of which are locked away in a drawer along with the songs he wrote about her in Atlantic City. He's still living at Ben's. He's inherited a room from someone who moved out. But they're going to be evicted in a matter of months. 'No worries,' Ben said. 'There's a squat in Peckham with space.' But Sam can't face the unwashed crockery in the sink and the beer cans under the sofa, the endless uninvited guests. He needs space and quiet to work.

169

'Did you get that?' The man at the table frowns up at him.

Sam blinks. 'Um . . . ' He glances at his blank notebook. 'Could you verify one more time?'

The man makes a tutting noise, shaking his head at his wife. 'Thought the service here was supposed to be good.'

She looks aggrieved. 'Should be, for the price.'

The man repeats their order in a sarcastic tone.

'Thank you, sir.' Sam snaps the notebook shut and hurries back to the kitchen. It's humiliating having to be polite to rude people. But it's the only thing paying his way right now. It's a struggle to get pubs and clubs to book him when he's using a payphone at the end of the street. He can't see how he'll ever make a living out of his music. In his head, he hears his father speaking the words that arrived in a letter after Sam left the law firm. *You are a disgrace and a disappointment. You are no son of mine.*

★ ★ ★

It's gone ten o'clock on a Thursday evening. Polite applause tails away as the audience rush to the bar to get their orders in. He's dismantling the mic when a dark, bone-thin man approaches, a cigarette in the corner of his mouth, eyes narrowed against the smoke. 'I liked your set. You've got potential,' he says. 'Can I get you a drink?'

The man introduces himself as he puts two

170

beers on the table. 'Marcus White. I know who you are,' he says when Sam opens his mouth. 'You don't have a manager, I presume,' he continues. 'No agent?'

Sam shakes his head. 'I've been writing my own stuff, playing pubs and clubs for a while, but I can't seem to get a break.' He takes a sip of his drink. 'I've sent off demo tapes. Never heard anything back.'

'You've got a great voice,' Marcus says. 'And your music's got something. But it's all about bands now.' He drums his fingers on the table. 'I manage a few acts, and I'd like to help. How would you feel about fronting a band? With your looks and your sound, I think we could put something together that would be right on the money.'

Sam wipes the froth from his top lip. 'A band? I'm not sure . . . '

'You'd be a natural frontman.'

'Would it work with my music, though? My songs are written to be performed as solo acoustics.'

Marcus makes an impatient gesture. 'You want to play in dumps like this for ever? I promise you, man, you won't regret it.' He grins and rubs his finger and thumb together.

This is the first opportunity that's come Sam's way in two years, and Marcus is the only person since Cat to properly listen to his music. But still, doubt pulls at him.

'I don't know,' he says. 'Can I think it over?'

'Sure,' Marcus says. 'Come see me in my office. Here's my card. Don't wait too long.'

171

Three days later, Sam finds the address on Shaftesbury Avenue. The reception is plush, and the girl behind the desk tells him to wait. There are framed gold discs on the walls, photographs of Marcus shaking hands with Malcolm McLaren, Stevie Wonder, Princess Diana. Sam blinks at names of top bands. He didn't expect this.

When he's called into the office, Marcus looks up from a wide desk. 'Sam Sage.' He opens his arms. 'My new frontman.'

Sam clears his throat, sinking into the chair opposite. 'I'm really interested, Marcus, and grateful for the opportunity, only . . . I need some reassurance that I'd have artistic control.'

'Obviously there'll have to be some changes,' Marcus says impatiently. 'We'll be resetting the music for a band — a five-piece probably. But the bigger sound will give your songs more impact.' He drums his fingers on his desk. 'Look, you'll be frontman, and you'll get writing credits and royalties. We can work out the finer details in the contract.'

It's not the answer he wanted, but Sam thinks of recent gigs in half-filled pubs where chatter obliterated his singing. If he wants people to hear his music, this is his best chance. After all, it's his material. If he can work with the right producer, be at the centre, he'll keep creative control.

He reaches across, offering his hand. Marcus takes it. 'I'll have my lawyers draw up the paperwork.'

'Any thoughts on a name for this new band?' Sam asks.

'Something easy to say and easy to remember,' Marcus says. 'Could be anything, really. I mean, think of the Beatles. Who would have thought of calling a band after an insect?' He lights a cigarette. 'They took inspiration from Buddy Holly's group, the Crickets. Changed the spelling to incorporate the idea of beat music.' He grins. 'Lennon's idea, obviously.' The phone on his desk lights up, and he waves a hand at Sam, 'You'll be hearing from us.'

*   *   *

There are four of them in the Lambs so far: Sam on vocals and rhythm guitar, Rick on lead guitar, Susie on keyboard and backing vocals and Jonny on bass. They're just missing a drummer. Marcus has found them a room in Streatham to practise in.

It's a hot afternoon, and they're holding auditions for the drummer. They've seen four hopefuls already, but none of them is right. Just as Sam's wondering where the fifth person has got to, the silhouette of a tall man appears in the open doorway.

Sam squints into the sunlight, and puts a hand over his eyes. 'Can't see a thing, mate,' he tells the tall man. 'Come in,' he says. 'Drum kit's over here.'

As the man steps out of light into shadow, his cloak of invisibility slips away. Sam's already reaching through space to greet the newcomer

173

with a handshake. Except he's not a newcomer. Before Sam can retract his hand, George grabs it between both of his.

'Jack?' he's saying, grinning. 'You're in this band? I can't believe it!' His damp fingers radiate heat. He squeezes, and Sam feels the bones in his hand rotate.

He remembers George standing on the doorstep: *I'm your brother*. Sam pulls away. 'How did you find me? What do you want?'

'I've come for the audition.' George shakes his head. 'It just said it was for a band . . . I mean, I didn't know you were going to be here . . . '

A bead of sweat trickles down Sam's spine. 'Cut the bullshit,' he snaps.

George's large, florid face glows; he takes a hanky from his back pocket and wipes his brow. 'It's true. I'm a drummer,' he says slowly.

'All right then.' Sam nods towards the Yamaha kit at the back of the room. 'Prove it.'

George goes across to the drums. He rearranges the seat, concentration creasing his face. He gives the cymbals a couple of hits.

'You know him?' Marcus asks, curiously. 'Why did he call you Jack?'

'I changed my name. He's my half-brother,' says Sam.

Then any conversation is impossible, as George, his sleeves jammed to his elbows, begins. He starts with a whisper of roll over the snare, leaning low, and then he's bolt upright and his sticks are moving, his foot pumping, driving a complex beat into a heart-thumping rhythm. His mouth is pursed; his head nods. His

174

huge body has taken on a kind of grace as he stretches over the drums. He tosses his sticks in the air and catches them in one fluid movement to come down on the rack toms with a sound like thunder. When he finishes, head bowed and chest heaving, there's a moment of ringing silence before the rest of the band applaud.

Marcus says, 'He hit the shit out of those drums. Why didn't you tell me about him? We've found our missing drummer, right?'

George looks sheepish as the others continue to clap and whistle through their teeth. He takes off his shirt, balling it up to wipe his glistening face, then reaches into his bag and pulls out a clean one.

⋆ ⋆ ⋆

'So . . . I've got the gig?' George asks. They're walking through an alley, taking a shortcut to the high street.

'We're playing Dingwalls in under three weeks,' Sam says. 'I won't find anyone as good as you before that.'

George lights a cigarette and takes a deep drag.

'I can't believe it's a coincidence you're here,' Sam says, squinting through the drifting smoke. 'What do you really want?'

'I told you,' George says wearily. 'I wanted the job. I saw the advert in *Melody Maker*.'

Sam still feels as though George has somehow tricked him. The shock of seeing him hasn't left his body. 'If that's the case, then we're stuck with each other,' he says. 'Until I can find a drummer to replace you.'

George scratches his scalp roughly. 'It was traumatic for me too, you know,' he blurts out. 'You're not the only walking wounded.'

'Look, don't start. My mother's *married* to my father. You shouldn't even exist.'

'Yeah, but I do.' George stops and glares at Sam. 'So you'd better get used to it.' He drops the cigarette onto the path, grinding it underfoot.

'You know, it's pretty bloody ironic finding out about you,' Sam says. 'For as long as I can remember, my father's gone on about me doing my duty as the only son.' He scuffs his boot along some loose stones. 'Turns out that was a bit of a joke.'

'Our father,' George corrects.

'What?'

'He's my father too.'

'*Our* father.' Sam scowls. 'But I don't suppose you were made to carry the family name like it was the fucking Olympic torch.'

'I don't have the family name,' George says, his voice gruff. 'Dad never married Mum.'

Sam stares at him. George's familiarity with his father makes him feel disorientated. He has an overwhelming need to punish this stranger, this big lout standing here cluttering up his life. He curls his lip. 'Don't whine about it. You've had all the privileges, and none of the crap I've had to put up with.'

'Privileges?' George snorts. 'You were the one with peacocks on your lawn, mate. You got to go to a posh boarding school. Then Oxford University, wasn't it? I'm a bastard, remember? I went to the local state school.'

'I would have given anything to be at an ordinary school.'

'God, you're a spoilt brat.' George spits the words.

'Is this what you really came for?' Sam rubs his chin, angry and tired. 'To insult me?'

'Don't be ridiculous.' George prods him in the chest with his finger. 'You're the one moaning about having a silver spoon in your mouth.'

'You came to my house and made my mother cry,' Sam says. 'Ruined her birthday. Upset my sister.' His fingers curl into fists.

'What, you think my mum hasn't cried too? You're a typical upper-class wanker, aren't you? Poor little rich boy.'

'At least my mother didn't throw herself at someone else's husband,' Sam says, scrabbling for words to hurt. 'At least she's not a . . . a slut.'

'Don't talk about my mother like that!' George pushes him, the force making him stagger backwards.

Sam recovers his balance and pushes George back. The thud of his palms on George's chest feels good. All the rage inside — fury with his father, disappointment with his music, the loss of Cat — comes crashing through him, and his fist swings. The impact of knuckle and bone is shocking. His arm jars into his shoulder as his hand makes contact with George's jaw.

George's head whips back. The blow, satisfying for a second, leaves Sam's knuckles smarting, and a taste of remorse in his mouth. But there's no time to apologise, because George is already charging at him with a roar, rugby-tackling him around the waist, skull thumping into Sam's solar plexus.

They're on the ground, pummelling at each other. George is stronger, bigger, heavier. He pins Sam down and sits astride his chest, a weight cutting off his breath, shouting into his face, spit spraying. 'Apologise. You bastard.'

But Sam no longer has any intention of apologising. He's powered by adrenalin, a red rage making him almost elated. He writhes out of George's grasp, twisting his hips to the side. George flails back, and scrambles clumsily to his feet. Sam hasn't time to get up off the ground before George comes back at him with furious intent, eyes glittering; instinctively, Sam covers his head and sticks out a foot. He feels a jolt as it catches George's ankle, hears the thump of George going down, the vibration trembling through the ground. When he looks up, George lies still as a fallen tree.

Sam gets onto all fours, touching his swollen lip with his tongue, tasting blood. He spits onto the ground and staggers up, breath tearing out of him. 'Fuck,' he pants. 'It's over. Get up.' He holds out his hand to George. But George doesn't move. He's sprawled face down.

'George? Come on. This isn't funny.' Sam kneels and prods his shoulder. George is still motionless. With a shudder of fear, Sam rolls him over. He gasps. Blood gushes from a gash across George's forehead. The left side of his face is obliterated, smeared in sticky red. 'My God! George? Talk to me. Can you move?'

George groans and sits up slowly, clutching his face. Bright blood seeps through his trembling fingers.

'We need to stop the bleeding.' Sam roots around in George's bag and pulls out his rolled-up shirt. Bunching it, he dabs at the blood. His efforts reveal a jagged tear that runs across George's eyebrow and through his left eyelid. He sees a glimpse of white — bone or muscle — and his stomach turns.

George moans. 'I can't see . . . '

'Okay, mate.' Sam tries to keep his voice steady. 'You're going to be fine. We need to get you to hospital.' He looks around at the empty alley. He can hear a rush of tyres coming from the high street up ahead. Black cab, he thinks. Or he'll flag down a passing motorist.

*   *   *

Sam waits all night in a hospital corridor, slumped on a chair with George's bag clutched to his chest. George had an emergency operation shortly after they came in. 'You should go home,' a nurse tells him. 'You won't be able to see him until tomorrow.' But Sam refuses to go anywhere; not until he knows that George is all right. He sits cradling his right fist. It throbs, blue-green, a reminder of the blow he struck. It's his fault, he thinks. He started it.

It's late morning when he finds George's ward. A small group of people stand around his

179

bedside, one of them with a clip-board. A man in a white coat, who appears to be in charge, is talking to George; when Sam gets to the bed, the doctor glances up with a tired expression, and gives a small distracted nod before turning away, the group hurrying to follow him. Sam watches the retreating figure with his entourage trailing behind. There was something about the doctor's face, with its round glasses, its pleasant, boyish features. Sam has an odd feeling that he's seen him before, somewhere else: in another life, it feels like.

'That was my surgeon,' George says. 'Saved my eye. He says I'm going to have a spectacular scar.' A bandage obscures the left side of his face. His usually ruddy skin is greyish, and there's a bruise on his chin. He smiles weakly.

'I'm sorry,' Sam says. 'Fuck. I'm so sorry.'

'It was an accident,' George says. His gaze falls on Sam's split lip and colourful right hand. 'Bet that hurts.'

'Yeah. Like hell.' Sam grins.

'Remind me to teach you how to throw a proper punch,' George says.

Sam raises one eyebrow. 'If that wasn't a proper punch, then what's that big black mark on your chin?'

George laughs and then winces, putting a tentative hand up to the bandage.

Sam holds up the plastic bag he's carrying, 'A few things from the shop.' He puts a collection of fruit, copies of music magazines and a bunch of flowers on the bedside table.

'You two have been in the wars,' a nurse says

180

as she checks George's temperature. 'I'll pop these in a vase, shall I?'

Sam sits next to the bed. Glimpsing the parts of George's face not obscured by bandage, it's impossible not to notice details that remind Sam of himself and his sisters. They share the same oval eyes, heavy lids making a wide space between eyelash and eyebrow. There's a familiarity when George speaks, the way he shows his top teeth when he smiles. This hulking man with the body of a wrestler and his shock of red hair — this stranger — shares blood with Sam, fifty per cent of his DNA. And he shares the same pain of betrayal.

Sam feels a prickle of shame. Mattie's always telling him he's too hot-headed. He sighs. 'Look, I'm sorry about the things I said.' He rubs his temples. 'I've been taking it out on you. And none of it is your fault.'

'It's all right.' George looks embarrassed. 'I get it. I turned up on your doorstep and wrecked your life.'

'No,' Sam corrects him. 'You didn't wreck it. Our father did.' He clasps his hands together. 'But we're not going to let him ruin things for us, right? I'm glad you showed up for the audition. Glad you can be part of the Lambs.' And as he says the words, he realises that he means them.

George beams. 'I always wanted an older brother.'

His happiness is infectious. Sam grins. There's strength and solidarity in having a brother; it promises a different kind of friendship and warmth from the kind he already shares with his sisters. He nods his head. 'Brothers. Odd. But true.'

'I expect you wanted one really,' George is saying. 'You just didn't know it.'

'Nope. Never occurred to me. Had my hands full with two sisters.' Sam laughs. 'Well, now they're your sisters as well — I'm not outnumbered any more. They're strong characters, I warn you.' He puts his hand on George's arm. 'Welcome to the family.'

Both men blink furiously, then look away as the nurse reappears with the flowers arranged in a vase. 'There,' she says. 'Don't they look nice?'

★ ★ ★

It's only later, when Sam's back in Brixton, that he remembers where he's seen George's surgeon before. The realisation makes him gasp. He sits down heavily on the ramshackle sofa, reliving a stormy day in Atlantic City, a funeral in a graveyard. He can smell the soft green of the rain, the muskiness of the yew tree. He watched Cat and the man speaking in hushed voices between the gravestones. A man in round glasses who'd just lost his wife. He doesn't remember Cat saying he was English. But George's surgeon was the same person, Sam is sure of it. What are the chances? he thinks. The coincidence opens a sudden temptation to hope — because if he can brush past the same stranger twice in his life, in different places, under different circumstances, then maybe he could bump into Cat again.

182

He gets up, angry with himself. Jesus! Anyone would think it was him who'd got the head injury. Her silence all those months ago was a clear message. He mustn't turn into one of those pathetic people who only want what they can't have.

25

Cat, October 1985

The roller rink is loud with pop music, clattering wheels and the crash of skaters as they stop themselves by slamming into the side. I watch beginners tumble onto their bottoms with a shout. It looks painful. And fun.

Leo and I step tentatively onto the busy rink. Immediately my knees and ankles slide away from me. Leo, his face pinched with anxiety, is hanging onto the side with white knuckles, but Grace pushes off into the centre, arms out to balance, a grin on her face.

'Come on, Daddy!' She staggers, but regains her balance.

Leo looks at me, hooks his glasses up his nose with one finger, and shrugs. 'Right. I'm going for it. Pray for me.'

And he's off, tottering and slipping through the whirl of skaters towards his daughter. He's doing this for Grace, her single wish for her eighth birthday treat. She's grown in the last few months; her legs, once sturdy and plump, are now thin, with out-of-proportion knobbly knees.

I take a breath and let myself slide forward. Holy shit, I'm skating! Someone rushes past me at speed, and I wobble, windmilling my arms. But I remain upright, reaching the other two with a laugh of triumph.

Grace is holding her father's hand, and she grabs mine so that she's between us. We giggle and flounder and nearly fall, but somehow our little chain of three remains upright. Madonna is entreating us to get 'Into the Groove'. I'm seduced by the repetitive circles we're making together. Round and round we go with the thumping disco beat and skaters whizzing past. And it occurs to me, anyone looking at us would presume we're a happy family.

Grace lets go of both of us and pushes ahead. 'Careful!' Leo begs, and I feel his fingers closing around mine. He gives me an apologetic glance. 'Do you mind? Not sure if I can stay upright.'

I shake my head. His hand is warm and dry. I clasp him tighter. Grace glances at us over her shoulder.

'Look at her! She's getting pretty confident,' I say.

'Yes, it's wonderful to see,' he says. And then he yelps in horror.

Grace is down. She's flat on her face. I let go of Leo and drop to one knee to check that she's unhurt.

'Grace?' He's calling from behind me, anxiously. 'Is she hurt?' he asks.

'Don't worry,' I tell him. 'She's fine.'

She takes my outstretched hand, and together we stagger back to our feet, giggling. Her knees and palms must be stinging like crazy, but she doesn't cry or complain. 'Brave girl.' I smile at her.

Leo's at the side again, and there's a hint of desperation in the way he's hanging on. He gives me an embarrassed smile. 'How about some lunch?' he calls.

★   ★   ★

There's a café at the rink, and that's where Grace wants to eat. Inside the plastic-bright interior, we gorge ourselves on greasy burgers and salty fries and drink too much fizzy stuff. It reminds me of being in Atlantic City. 'You Spin Me Round' blares out of the speakers.

Grace sits between us, cheeks flushed and eyes too bright. Sugar rush, I think. She's wound up tightly with all the excitement, and there's the symbolism of the date, too. Elizabeth and Leo were married on Grace's birthday: the fifteenth of October. I glance at Leo to see if he's struggling with conflicting emotions, but if he is, he's doing a really great job at covering it up. He's a good dad. I finish my drink, glancing at the two of them either side of me. My life with Leo and Grace is something I could never have imagined, but it feels like this is where I'm supposed to be.

★   ★   ★

There's a letter for me on the hall table. We were in a rush to leave the house after breakfast, and the only mail we opened was cards for Grace.

I leave my letter where it is. It's time for Grace to open her presents. Mine is a diary. She's seen me writing in one, and asked for one of her own. I've got her a purple beauty with silver lock and

186

key. She flings her arms around my neck. 'I love it! Thanks, Cat!'

'You're welcome, bug. Happy birthday.'

She's warm and solid in my arms. I inhale strawberry shampoo and milky skin. We've come a long way since those early days. Her memories of her mom's death seem to have faded. The nightmares have stopped. She's a happy, lively child.

She holds the diary against her cheek. 'What shall I write in it?'

'The truth.'

'The truth?'

'Yeah, about how you feel, and maybe what you did during the day. But most important is putting down your feelings, because a diary is like the best secret friend you can have. It will always be there for you, and it'll never judge you, or tell anyone else your thoughts.'

She smiles. Then she's turning away, ripping the paper off another present.

★ ★ ★

It's hours later — after Grace is in bed — that I allow myself to go to my room and open the envelope addressed to me.

Kit-Cat,

I'm a free man. A changed man. I know I caused you and your mom pain, and for that I am truly sorry. I received help in jail for my gambling from a Christian group, and I intend to stay away from casinos and

187

nearer the Lord. That means I can no longer live in Atlantic City. I must find somewhere far away from temptation — Utah or Tennessee maybe, even Alaska. Don't worry about me. I'm a strong man. I could be useful somewhere. I hope your mom will forgive me in time if I prove myself to her. She always was and always will be the love of my life. I'm glad that you have a job and a home in London. Perhaps one day I can visit with you there.

Dad

PS Will forward my address when I've settled somewhere.

I hold the letter in my hand. His loneliness seeps out of the paper, out of the inky scrawl of his handwriting. He's on his own, and he's starting over. He's never had to take care of himself.

I get up and look through my window at the view I've come to love, and wonder if I should give up my job and go home to take care of him.

There's a quiet knock on the door; Leo puts his head round. 'Just wanted to say thank you for today,' he begins, smiling; then he sees my face and the letter in my hands. 'Are you all right? Not bad news, I hope?'

I raise my shoulders, let them fall. 'My dad. I told you he was in prison for embezzlement? Well, he's out. He says he's going to stay away from gambling, move state, start again.' I sigh. 'But he's old. I don't know if he'll manage . . . especially without my mom.'

Leo comes into the room. 'You want to go back to the States?'

'Not really. But maybe I should.'

Leo tilts his head to one side. 'If he's not asking you to come home, then perhaps this is something he needs to do for himself.'

'Yeah, he kind of said that, I suppose.'

Leo rubs his chin, and sighs. 'Look, I don't want to persuade you to stay if you need to go to him. We'll organise cover for while you're gone.' He swallows. 'We'll miss you, of course.' He comes closer. 'I'll miss you.' His voice is soft.

'I need to think about it,' I say, biting my fingernail.

'The other possibility,' he says gently, putting his hand on mine, 'is for your father to come here. We've got a spare room. He could stay for a while.'

I stare at him in amazement. 'You mean that? Really?'

He laughs at my expression. 'Cat, you're family now. Of course I mean it.'

'Thank you.' I can hardly speak; a hard lump blocks my throat.

'It's the least I can do. The main reason that Grace is happier is you. Neither of us can imagine life without you.'

We look at each other inside a space that hums with the unspoken. Then we both move at the same time, stepping close. As he dips his head, I shut my eyes and part my lips. But the feel of his mouth doesn't come. Our noses clash as he takes an abrupt step back. 'Oh God, we can't do this,' he blurts out. 'I'm so sorry.'

My pulse jumps at my throat. 'We . . . we can't?'

'It's not right. I feel as if I'm . . . taking advantage.' He touches my cheek with the backs of his fingers. They tremble against my skin. 'You mean so much to me. I don't want to do anything to spoil what we have.'

I open my mouth, but he's already speaking again.

'Please forgive me. Can we . . . can we pretend it didn't happen?' His face is pink.

I give myself a second, gazing down at my feet. Then I manage to meet his eyes and nod.

He looks relieved. 'I nearly forgot,' he says in a newly bright voice, holding up the book in his hand. 'If you haven't already read it, I thought you might like this, Scott Fitzgerald's *Tender Is the Night*. It's my favourite novel.'

I take the battered paperback.

'Goodnight, Cat,' he says softly.

The door closes behind him. I follow, but stop with my hand resting on the handle. I have to respect what he said. Then I remember: it's his wedding anniversary today. No wonder kissing me didn't feel right to him.

In bed, I look up at the moonlight making patterns on the ceiling and know that Dad won't come and visit. He's too proud. But I'm overwhelmed by Leo's generosity, his kindness.

I'm staying. Relief fills me. This house is my home. And I feel as if I'm making progress: with Grace, and with my writing. I have a collection of children's stories now. After I read them to Grace, she tells me what she liked best, and what she didn't like. It's a kind of game we play together. With her help, I think I'm becoming a proper writer.

I can't sleep. I can't stop thinking about Leo, wondering what it would have felt like to kiss him. Because I wanted to. I still do. He's the first man I've wanted to kiss since Sam. I switch on my bedside light and open the novel he lent me. The pages are soft from use, well thumbed, much loved. I press my own fingers over the curled edges, reliving the seconds before the almost-kiss, the way the air between us tightened, my insides hollow with longing. And I think of the look on his face, the sound of his breath catching in his throat. He wanted me as much as I wanted him.

★ ★ ★

There's been a massacre in Grace's room. I stand at the threshold in the brilliance of morning light, my hands clamped over my mouth. Her dolls are lying on the carpet, slaughtered, ruined. She's hacked off their hair, torn off their limbs, gouged out their eyes with a pair of scissors: the murder weapon in plain sight, stolen from her father's desk.

She sits up in bed, rubbing her face. Her dark hair is a wild mop, her cheeks rosy from sleep.

'Grace . . . what . . . what have you done to all your lovely dolls?'

She lets her gaze drift to the floor. 'I'm too old for dolls now.'

I kneel down, fingering tufts of shorn acrylic

hair, the colours mixed together like the remains on a hairdresser's floor. I skim over the torn plastic of their sightless, still-smiling faces. 'But some of them are nearly new — we could have given them to someone else, or just put them on a shelf.' I turn up my palms helplessly. 'You're not really too old for dolls.'

'I hate them,' she says, pulling the covers over her head. 'And . . . and I heard you . . . I heard you talking to Daddy last night.' Her voice is muffled.

I sit on the bed and place a hand on her motionless shoulder. 'What did you hear, Grace?'

She stays hidden under the sheet. There's a long pause before she speaks. 'You're going away.'

Shock hits, then guilt. 'No.' I swallow. 'I'm not going anywhere.'

'I know . . . I know why you don't want to stay. It's because I'm bad.'

'Grace, listen to me, I'm staying right here.'

There is silence from under the covers. I can't pull them back. I have to let her make the decision to come out.

'I don't want you to worry about that, okay?' I say.

A ripple of fabric. Her shoulder moving. But she doesn't reappear.

'Shall I tell you a story?' I ask. I decide to take her lack of response as a yes. 'Once upon a time,' I say, 'there was a little girl who stayed in bed all the time, not because she wanted to, but because her legs didn't work properly. She wished and

192

wished that she could leave her room, and to pass the time she used to look out of her window and imagine flying to exciting places. Her favourite toy was a little china horse she kept on her dresser; he was snowy white with a long mane and tail.' Still Grace remains hidden. I keep talking. 'One night, she woke up with something soft nuzzling her shoulder. To her surprise, it was a horse, a great big white horse with a long mane and tail, standing right there in her bedroom, snorting and stamping his feet, and leaning down to push at her gently with his velvety muzzle.'

I feel a twitch of interest. 'Her toy horse came to life?'

'He sure did.'

I continue the story, and slowly, slowly she emerges from under her sheet: forehead, nose, and mouth. She puts out her hand, and I take it. We grip each other tight. Her dark eyes fix on my face. Unblinking, she watches me speak, following the story like a lifeline thrown between us.

26

Sam, October 1985

His mother is already settled at a corner table in the Fortnum & Mason tearoom, where they meet once a month. Dressed in a tweed two-piece suit, a string of pearls around her neck, she holds herself like a duchess. Sam smiles, knowing she'd rather be in an old skirt covered in dog hair, rooting around in the flower beds at home. He straightens his shoulders as he weaves through the tables towards her; he needs to break it to her that he's living with George now.

'Mum,' he says, kissing her before sinking into the seat across the white linen tablecloth. 'Have you ordered?'

'Cream tea for both of us,' she says, lighting a cigarette. 'Are you still living in that dreadful place . . . what do you call it? The squat?'

This is his cue, earlier than he expected. He shakes his head. 'I've moved out. Now that I'm in the band, things are looking up.' He glances at her. 'I'm sharing a flat in Balham with another band member. And . . . it's George.'

'George?'

'Yes.' Sam swallows. 'I wanted to find the right time to tell you,' he says gently. 'George . . . as in Dad's other son.' He tries to assess her expression. 'He's my flatmate. He's a really talented drummer.'

At that moment, the waiter arrives with their tea. They wait while he arranges the cups and plates in front of them with long-winded ceremony. When he's gone, she picks up the teapot. 'You're friends now?'

'Turns out he's a good guy.' Sam touches her hand. 'Do you mind?'

She shakes her head. 'No, darling. He's your half-brother. If any good can come out of all of this, then I'm glad.'

'That's generous of you, Mum.' He watches her bite into a scone. 'But I still can't understand why you let Dad get away with it.' He looks at the cream on his plate and feels nauseous. 'All those years he was cheating on you. Why didn't you leave him?'

She dabs at her mouth with a napkin. 'It suited me.'

Sam looks at her in surprise.

She puts a hand over his and squeezes. 'I never really liked the physical side of marriage. It was the home I was interested in, the security and companionship. And you children, of course. I turned a blind eye to the other woman because . . . well, because the arrangement let me live my life the way I wanted.'

'The arrangement?' Anger coils in his belly. 'Didn't you think about us? You knew how unhappy I was at school.' He pauses, trying to control the swell of his fury. 'Why didn't you protect me? Say something to Dad? Tell him to leave me alone?'

She picks up a spoon and stirs her tea. 'I knew you didn't like school. But lots of children don't.

195

Sometimes things that are good for us can be unpleasant. Your father only wanted the best for you; for you to be successful.'

'On his terms.'

She frowns. 'Those were the only ones he knew.'

Sam sighs. He'll never really be able to talk to her about this. She's had the same kind of upbringing as his father: nannies, boarding school, choices made under the jurisdiction of tradition, and no discussion of anything personal, ever. She loves him, but she's always been happiest with her dogs and her garden. He notices that her lipstick has seeped into the lines around her mouth. He sits back in his chair, rubs at his nose.

'Your father's mellowed a little since he first heard about your change of career,' she says. 'If you could bring yourself to come and see him . . .'

At the thought of his father, his stomach cramps and twists. 'I don't know.'

He's aware of someone hovering over him. He glances up. 'Jack?' Lucinda stares down: a less angular, softer version of Lucinda, in a floaty dress. It's a shock to see her, and with another shock he realises that under the flowing folds of her dress, she's pregnant.

'How are you?' she's asking. 'And you, Mrs Winterson, how nice to see you.'

'You look wonderful,' he says, truthfully.

She gives a rueful smile. 'I'm due in two months. Harry and I are living in Kensington. Harry Chivers. He's a barrister.' A large

196

diamond glints on her ring finger.

'You're married.' He's filled with a rush of affection for her. 'That's great, Lu.'

'And you? Is there another Mrs Winterson?'

He shakes his head. 'There's only one.' He gestures towards his mother.

'How did the whole music idea work out?' She tilts her head to the side. 'Are you a singer now?'

He's relieved that he can give her a positive reply. 'I'm in a band called the Lambs. You won't have heard of it. But we're playing my music.'

'A band?' She says the word as if it's faintly amusing. 'I hope it was worth giving up your career for, Jack, I really do.' She looks at her watch. 'Must dash. Meeting my sister-in-law.' He stands and stoops so they can brush each other's cheeks with air kisses. She feels like a stranger, and it makes him feel sad and relieved at the same time.

As she winds her way through the tables — a tiny, upright figure — waiters bow deferentially.

'Goodness, that was more interrogation than conversation,' his mother says.

He manages a laugh. But his hands are shaking as he calls for the bill. The last time he saw Lucinda, he was still under the illusion that he and Cat had a future together. 'She is, as they say, a force of nature.' He puts some coins onto the saucer for a tip. 'But I'm glad things have worked out for her. Now, this is our time, Mum. What would you like to do next? Have a look at what's on across the road at the Royal Academy?'

She wrinkles her nose. 'Actually, my feet are

killing me. I think I'll get the early train home. My boys will be wondering where I am.'

Sam knows she means the dogs.

★ ★ ★

He watches as her taxi pulls away, then turns, pushing a hand through his hair. He startles for a second as he catches a glimpse of himself in a shop window. Beyond his reflection, there's a banked-up display of books. He looks closer. They're children's books, with bright covers and pictures of animals and cartoon kids with oversized heads. He goes into the shop and, ignoring all the best-sellers and tables full of special offers, heads straight for the G section, running his fingers over different-coloured spines, searching for her name: Catrin Goforth. It's not there. It never is. He always checks whenever he comes across a bookshop. Disappointment plucks at him. Unwilling to give up, he approaches the assistant at the desk and asks if he's heard of an American author by that name, but the young man shakes his head.

★ ★ ★

Since George joined as their drummer, the band have laid down some of the best tracks in a recording studio. The resulting promo tapes are with record companies now. They're waiting for responses. And Marcus has been busy fixing up gigs all over the country. The band pile into an

198

old Transit and travel from one venue to the next.

Sam finds inspiration for new stuff by walking the streets of whichever city he's in, watching the people around him, letting his mind drift. On a park bench in a garden square eating his lunchtime sandwich, with pigeons pecking hopefully at his feet, he is jolted back in time to that bench in Atlantic City, Cat reading the inscription to him. It was the first thing they shared, their passion for words on benches. He puts his sandwich down, his appetite gone.

For the rest of that afternoon, he hunts down benches, looking for lines to give him ideas for lyrics. *Lost now but loved for ever. Beloved granny and grandad. The dancer is gone, but the dance lives on.* Some are mundane, some funny, some beautiful. And he reminds himself that whatever the words say, they are always a testament to love. The love he and Cat shared was just a spark really, the bright beginning of something that never had a chance to grow. But it will live inside him for ever, as first loves do. And he'll always be grateful to her for giving him those feelings, and for helping him have the strength to change his life.

★　★　★

The mechanical noise of the doorbell shrieks through the flat. It's late morning and the remains of breakfast are spread over the kitchen table. George answers, and Marcus stalks into the sitting room, running his hands through his hair. He fumbles in his pocket and pulls out a packet of Player's, taps one out and lights it. Sam and George wait as he blows out a long stream of smoke.

'Island called,' he says at last. 'They want to meet you.'

'Fuck,' George says. 'Fuckety fuck!' He grabs Sam's hand and squeezes, his other on Sam's shoulder like a big warm paw. 'This is it, mate. This is it!'

'Yep.' Marcus takes another deep drag. 'I wanted to tell you in person. Call the others. We've got a meeting tomorrow afternoon at their offices. Time to get your shit together.'

Sam embraces George. George embraces Sam, nearly breaking his ribs.

* ★ ★

Island have offered the Lambs a deal. They'll be cutting their first album in a London studio, working with the material that the record company have already heard. But the men in suits want a love song to be the first single. Something heart-wrenching. Can they write one in time?

'Of course,' Marcus assures them smoothly. 'No problem. Sam will come up with something.'

'Can't we use one of my other songs?' Sam says afterwards. 'There's a few that are written in a minor key — what about 'Cindy'?'

'A sad ballad won't cut it,' Marcus snaps. 'They're asking for a love song.'

Sam shakes his head. 'I don't know if I can.'

'Haven't you ever been in love?' Marcus asks him impatiently.

The band are gathered in the local pub to celebrate the deal, Sam and Marcus alone in a corner. Before Sam can reply, Marcus is talking again, tapping his foot nervously. 'For fuck's sake, you can't be a writer if you've never had your heart broken.'

Sam looks away, digging his fingernails into his palms. 'I don't know . . . I don't know if I can do this.'

'You haven't got a choice,' Marcus says, his face hard. 'This is the golden opportunity. You need to come up with a single. A cracking love song.'

Sam thinks of those songs he wrote in Atlantic City years ago, his songs for Cat. He scribbled them down and then shoved them into envelopes, put them under his clothes in a drawer, out of sight. He wonders if he could bear to listen to them again, play their chords, work on them with the band. Has enough time passed to make that possible?

27

Cat, February 1986

Leo's away for the weekend at a conference in Switzerland. 'Not that I needed to go for the weather, did I?' he laughed on the phone last night. Snow has been falling for days, turning the garden into a tiered white wedding cake. When the sun comes out, everything glistens and sparkles. He'd rung to say goodnight to Grace, but we ended up talking for over an hour. As soon as I put the phone down, I missed him.

When the post comes on Saturday morning, I hurry to pick it up. I sent some of my short stories off to a literary agent weeks ago. There's a large brown envelope addressed to me. I open it with a thumping heart, disappointment sliding through me like ice water as I pull out my returned manuscript. There's a short rejection note: they advise me not to submit handwritten work, but there's no feedback about the content. They must have hated it.

There's no time to let myself get depressed. Grace has been given the starring role in her ballet school's end-of-term show. She came home, cheeks glowing, handing me a sketch of an outfit that I'm supposed to somehow magic up from my non-existent sewing kit. Grace is beyond thrilled. I can't let her down. There's a sewing machine in the cupboard under the stairs that must have belonged to Elizabeth, and I set about teaching myself how to use it.

'Come here, bug,' I tell Grace. 'Let's try this on you for size.'

Obediently she strips down to her knickers and vest and stands still to let the half-made dress fall over her outstretched arms and head. I kneel beside her, pins at the ready, and sigh in frustration. I've got the waist measurements totally wrong. It billows around her. Grace sticks out her belly and laughs.

'Holy moly! We could fit three of you into this,' I say, beginning to gather it tighter. 'Or turn it into a sail for a boat.' I fix the pleats into place with dozens of pins.

'Nancy's mum is paying someone else to make her costume.'

'Is Nancy's mum as hopeless as me at sewing, then?'

Grace shrugs. 'She's just really busy.'

'What does she do?'

'Something to do with books, I think. She's always rushing to meetings.' Grace thinks for a moment. 'They *do* have a lot of books at their house. Even more than us.'

Grace and Nancy have become best friends. They met at Miss Miller's dance class. I love how Grace relishes talking about her new friend, slipping her name into conversations whenever she can.

When I've finished, she steps out of the bristling fabric. 'Careful of the pins,' I remind her.

She sits at one side of the table in the sitting

room doing her math homework, while I sit at the other attempting to take the waist in. The thread snarls under the little silver foot and breaks every five minutes. 'Ouch.' I suck my punctured finger. Grace twirls her pencil, adding up numbers. The machine rattles and hums. Outside the window, snow falls.

When she tries the dress on again, Grace runs out of the room to look at herself in the full-length mirror in Leo's bedroom. I hold my breath, listening to her feet on the stairs, wondering if she'll notice the imperfections: the wonky hem and crooked seams. But when she comes back, she flings open the door — 'Ta da!' — and twirls around the room, dropping into a low curtsey before me. 'Princess Grace thanks you for your work,' she says, her face shining.

'If you're a princess, what am I?'

'A humble peasant woman, of course.'

I raise my eyebrows. 'Really? Well, this humble peasant woman needs you to get your royal bottom into bed before your dad gets home, so,' I make a grab for her, 'scoot!'

She dodges me, and runs giggling for the door.

'You've got five minutes to get into your PJs!' I yell after her.

* * *

She's settled against her pillows, and I curl up next to her. 'Will you tell me a story?' she asks. Although she's old enough to read to herself, we've continued our habit of made-up bedtime tales. She has her thumb in her mouth and a

204

faraway look in her eyes as I invent the next adventure of the little girl we've called Sally and her china horse.

As I finish, Leo steps into the room, bringing the chill of the outside with him. He's got a dusting of snow on his coat, and his cheeks are flushed. He kisses Grace, who murmurs sleepily and closes her eyes.

'I was listening outside the door,' he says quietly. 'You've got a talent. Why don't you write them down?'

'I've got notebooks filled with them.' I smile. 'Are you hungry?'

'I ate on the plane. But I've brought presents.' He takes my hand, and I realise how natural it feels to join our fingers. He leads me downstairs. There are packages on the hall table. 'Grace can open hers tomorrow,' he says. 'But this one's for you.' He gestures towards the largest parcel, unable to contain his enthusiasm.

'It's too big for chocolate,' I say, touching the brown paper, drawing out the moment by teasing him. 'A large cuckoo clock?'

He rolls his eyes. 'Don't keep me in suspense!'

I untie the string, unwrapping the paper. Inside is a small portable typewriter in a leather case. I gasp, genuinely surprised.

'I think it's time you got professional,' he's saying. 'Send off some of your stories to magazines or publishers. They're good enough.'

'I don't think they are,' I say. 'I just got a rejection note from an agent.'

'Nothing worthwhile is ever easy,' he says. 'You can't give up at the first hurdle.'

205

'I think they *were* put off by it being handwritten . . . '

'Exactly. Now you can change that.'

I take the machine out of the case and run my fingers over the neat rows of keys. 'I want to use it right now,' I tell him. 'Hope it's easier than a sewing machine!'

'You've no idea how lovely it is to come home and find you telling Grace a story.' He's standing right beside me, so close his breath warms my cheek. 'You've brought joy back into this house, Cat.'

I turn, wrapping my arms around his neck. 'Thank you,' I whisper. 'For the typewriter.' I pause. 'For everything.'

I can feel his heart thudding through his ribcage. But he clears his throat and steps away from my embrace. 'I've got a good bottle of Chablis in the fridge,' he says. 'Let's toast your new venture in the literary world.'

As we sit in the kitchen and clink glasses, my gaze catches Elizabeth's brilliant smile. 'I think Grace is growing to look a lot like her mom,' I say.

'Thank God it's only Elizabeth's looks she's inherited.' A hardness has entered his voice.

I put my drink down. 'What do you mean?'

'I keep these photographs out for Grace.' He gestures at the gleaming frames. 'If it was up to me, I wouldn't have a single picture of her anywhere.'

I hold my breath, waiting for him to continue.

He takes his glasses off, squeezing the bridge of his nose. 'Our relationship was a failure. But I don't want Grace to know that; she deserves to think the best of her mother.' He swallows a gulp of wine. 'Elizabeth was trying to be an actress when we met. She'd failed in America, so she thought she'd try London instead. She didn't actually have any talent, just the looks. But I was dazzled by her.' He gives a short, humourless laugh. 'She was vivacious when she wanted something. Someone.' He puts his glasses back on. 'She fell for this house, the romance of me being a surgeon. Because of the house, she thought I was wealthier than I am. I inherited this place, otherwise it would be completely beyond my means.' He's staring at the table. 'I suppose marrying me was a way out of a failed career. I don't think she could face going back to the States.' He pauses. 'I disappointed her. Her life here disappointed her. It wasn't glamorous enough. She started drinking.' He looks up at me. 'She was selfish and spoilt. I know that sounds harsh, but it's the truth. I'm pretty certain she was seeing someone else. There were . . . signs. But at the time, I stuck my head in the sand. What if she'd wanted custody of Grace, taken her back to the States?'

My head is full of his words — this new information clamouring for attention, spilling over the bounds of my ability to process it, contain it — but now I understand the reason for his expression when he thinks he's unobserved: this is the pain he carries all the time.

'When she fell down the stairs.' The hardness is back in his voice. 'She'd been drinking.'

207

'Oh,' I say. 'God. I'm sorry.'

'I should have told you. But it was shameful. The whole situation. I couldn't bring myself to talk about it with anyone.' He touches my hand. Those long, clever fingers of his, the coolness of them against my skin. Without thinking, I take them and kiss them, one by one.

'Cat,' he whispers.

We stand up and he slips his hands around my waist. Then we're leaning against each other, the thump of our hearts synchronising. This man is dear to me — his voice, his smell, the way he moves; he makes me feel safe. We find each other's lips, and this time he doesn't pull away. The kiss is sweet and gentle. His fingers move up my spine, making me shiver. He squeezes me tight to his chest. We are kissing in earnest now, our breath coming fast.

We both break away at the same time, faces flushed. My own thoughts are mirrored in his questioning gaze. 'If we take this step . . .' his voice trembles, 'it's huge.'

I consider what's at stake: it's the first time I've felt part of a proper family, known real security. But is it enough to stop us, when I want him too? When I'm hungry for intimacy, for affection? I falter, watching confusion play over his features, doubt pulling at his mouth.

'Let's give it a bit more time,' he's saying. 'Let's think about it. We . . . we need to be sensible.'

His words make me smile, because you can't be sensible about love. It either is or it isn't; there's no reasoning with it. But it's just like Leo to be cautious, to use his mind to try and control something that's uncontrollable.

My pulse slows, and I take his hand in mine and squeeze. 'Okay,' I tell him. 'Let's be sensible. For now.'

He exhales loudly, shaking his head. 'You have no idea the control I'm using at this moment. I should get a medal.'

We smile at each other and step away, keeping eye contact, until only our fingertips hold on. Then we let go.

28

Sam, June 1986

Sunset casts a flattering glow over the first guests, making them shimmer as they accept flutes of champagne from waiters dressed in togas. A jazz band is playing, the singer giving throaty renditions of Ella classics. The party's being held on a roof terrace. There are plastic flamingos and gold palm trees, reminding Sam of Atlantic City. He leans against a wall, at the edge of the action. He can smell the fumes from the gritty street far below.

A redhead with skin like double cream is in the middle of the dance floor. Nobody else is dancing except her; she moves slowly, undulating her hips, twisting her arms. With her colouring and curves, she should have been painted by one of the Impressionists, he thinks, Degas or Matisse.

'Oh, I love Matisse,' she says, when he tells her. 'I get sick of all those art snobs saying it's not proper art if it's pretty.'

She looks up at him under dark lashes when he asks her name. 'Daisy. Daisy Armstrong.' She smiles, 'I know exactly who *you* are, Sam Sage. I love your new single, 'Ocean Blue'. Really gets me, you know, right here.' She presses her chest. 'I'm a total romantic.'

She is so knowingly coquettish that Sam finds

it entrancing. Her glances and pouts are performed with the grace of a dancer, her timing skilful as a chess player, and he appreciates the fact that she doesn't take herself too seriously.

She doesn't capitulate to his advances at once. It takes a conversation on the merits of different Impressionists and two cocktails before she agrees to leave and have dinner with him.

★ ★ ★

They go to a Japanese restaurant. Kneeling at the low table, she says, 'I didn't want to burst your bubble before, but Matisse is technically thought of as a Fauvist rather than an Impressionist. I thought you should know. For future reference.'

'Oh, what's the difference?' he asks.

'Mainly colour. Matisse used a brighter, bolder palette.'

He groans, 'So my chat-up line did nothing but expose my lack of knowledge?'

'It was sweet.' She leans forward conspiratorially, 'Actually, I was all yours before you said a word.'

He swallows hard. 'You mean there was nothing I could have said to put you off?'

She tilts her head to one side. 'Maybe if you'd compared me to a Renoir.'

'What's wrong with a Renoir?'

'Cellulite.' She winks. 'Lots of cellulite. The man was crazy for it.'

He laughs. 'What do you do, Daisy Armstrong, when you're not giving art history lessons?'

'I sing,' she tells him, waving her chopsticks. 'And model. But really I want to be a star. It's all I've ever wanted, since I was a little girl.'

'I think you're made to be a star,' he says, looking at her huge green eyes, the tumbling curls spilling over her naked shoulders.

'But nobody's giving me my big break,' she sighs. 'This business is tough.'

'I played the pub circuit for a couple of years before the Lambs,' he says. 'It felt as though I was banging my head against a brick wall.' He puts a piece of sushi in his mouth, the horseradish making his eyes smart. 'I'd like to hear you sing.'

'Really?' She unfolds herself from the low seat. She's kicked off her heels, and her long split dress trails on the floor. She grins down at him and his heart lurches. 'How about now?'

He waits in breathless anticipation. She opens her mouth and belts out a Whitney Houston song. She warbles and riffs, not quite hitting those tricky high notes, her voice swallowed by vibrato. The other diners turn and stare in amazement.

When she finishes, most of them clap, including Sam.

Daisy bows and flicks her hair, then sinks back onto her knees and leans across the table. She's practically purring. 'Well?'

Sam nods, 'Um. Amazing. Really . . . breath-taking.'

The girl can't sing. But my God, he thinks, she's got guts.

There have been other girls since Cat, but

212

none has intrigued him like Daisy, and he supposes part of the attraction is that they're so different. If Daisy's like looking at a gorgeous painting, a kind of clever and intriguing artifice, then Cat's the subject, the real thing, with nothing hidden. But he wasn't able to live up to her high standards. With her truth and her unwavering need to do the right thing, she obviously found him wanting. With Daisy, though, he thinks, he can just be himself. A bit selfish, a bit shit — in other words, a normal human being.

* * *

He takes Daisy back to the flat. They don't bother with the pretence of coffee. They're already removing each other's clothes as he flings the door to his room open. He kisses her bare shoulder near her heart tattoo, buries his face in her hot neck, inhaling the patchouli she wears, the musky aroma of her skin.

She giggles, pulling his face down to meet hers, her lips parting for him. 'Fuck me,' she whispers.

Afterwards, she falls asleep, curled on her side, one hand by her cheek, snuffling gently. Sam gazes down, wondering at the vibrant lustre of her hair, the fullness of her lips. He touches one of her red corkscrew curls, threads it through his fingers, pulling it straight and watching it bounce back. She's not just gorgeous, she's smart and funny and brave. Hope flares in his chest that this woman could be the one to erase his

213

memories of Cat, give him another chance at love.

'Ocean Blue' is a huge hit; it's had the number one spot for weeks. And there are other songs he wrote for Cat on the album. When he sings them, his voice is raw with emotion. Every word, every note takes him back to her, scrapes out the void of missing her all over again. He was afraid that he'd never get over her if these songs were a success, that he'd be committed to singing them for the rest of his career. His worst fears have come true. It's the music he wrote for her that's propelled them into the big time, but Cat herself is lost to him for ever.

Sam rolls close to Daisy, breathing in the unfamiliar scent of her skin, the salty tang of sex. He puts his arm around her waist and pulls her in, fitting his body to the shape of hers. She murmurs and sighs.

July 1986

George and Sam are watching the Wimbledon men's final. Daisy slips onto the sofa between the two men. 'Becker's pretty cute,' she says.

She's in a pair of cut-off denim shorts, her creamy legs smooth, her toes painted scarlet. Her knee presses against Sam's thigh, a distraction from the brilliance of the game, as a ball flies over the net in a flash of yellow.

'Whoa! Becker's thrashing him,' George says. 'No way is Lendl coming back from this.'

'Oh, I can't watch,' Daisy says, putting her

214

hand over her eyes. 'I hate it when people lose. I always feel sorry for them.'

'Don't waste your pity,' George says. 'These guys are sportsmen. They're tough as nails.'

'No.' Daisy squints through a gap in her fingers. 'It's awful. Look at his face. He's going to cry.' She gets up and pads into the kitchen. 'Tell me when it's over,' she calls.

George smiles at Sam. 'You've got yourself the sweetest girlfriend, as well as the sexiest.' He thumps Sam's arm. 'You're a lucky bastard.'

'Yeah, I know.' Sam shrugs.

'Hey, Daisy,' George yells. 'Brace yourself — Becker's about to win Wimbledon!'

'You cannot be serious!' she calls, doing a bad McEnroe impression.

A memory from his first date with Cat comes back to Sam in a rush.

'You okay?' George glances at him.

Sam nods, as Lendl's ball fails to clear the net.

George leaps to his feet, cheering. Daisy is back with a tray. She's made Pimm's in a jug filled with ice, decorated with sprigs of mint and slices of cucumber. She sets it down carefully, giving them a spectacular view of her cleavage, and then stands up to pour them all a glass. 'Cheers, Daisy,' George says.

On the TV, Becker is raising his arms in jubilation.

Sam holds his glass, the sides cold and slippery with condensation. 'Thanks, baby,' he says, raising it to Daisy. 'You're the best.'

He finds himself saying things like that: you're the best; you're the sweetest; I love the way you

215

do that; I love your laugh, your eyes, your smile. But he knows Daisy is waiting for him to tell her that he loves *her*. Only he can't. Sometimes he feels as though he's going to say it, but then she'll do something that only a few weeks ago seemed adorable or clever but now feels too knowing. To make up for the lack of words, he leans across and kisses her on the mouth. She kisses him back, immediately warm and generous, her lips full of forgiveness.

'Hey, you two,' George says. 'Get a room, can't you? Have pity on the single man.'

They break off, laughing. Daisy ruffles George's hair, and suddenly it feels so easy that Sam thinks those elusive words might be sayable after all. Soon, he thinks, when the moment is right.

29

Cat, July 1987

Whitney Houston's 'I Wanna Dance With Somebody' plays in every shop and café that I go into. The song drives me crazy. It's impossible to shake off, and I find myself humming it before I've realised.

'We're getting you a new outfit,' Dougie says, marching me through Covent Garden. It's like our old Knightsbridge game, but this time we're in the business of buying. At least, I am. Dougie seems to get most of his clothes for free, or with a fat discount, since he started his new job as junior fashion assistant at *Harpers & Queen*. 'You need something without polka dots for a change,' he's saying. 'And you never show those legs of yours off. You won't be young for ever, you know.'

'You're sounding disturbingly like my mom,' I mutter, as he thrusts items of clothing at me through the changing-room curtain. He tells me that I look a bit like someone called Tatjana Patitz, and that when he was on a shoot with her the other day, he noticed her knees didn't even wrinkle in that place just above the bone and before the thigh where everyone else's knees do. They are the legs of a goddess.

I step outside the booth and twirl before him. He claps his hands together. 'Just needs a narrow belt to set it off.'

'But where am I supposed to wear this?' I ask, as he threads a belt around my waist. 'I never go anywhere.'

'Exactly. With the right outfit, you might change that.'

I'm looking at myself in the mirror, uncertain of the new me. Maybe this girl could sign a publishing contract, live her dreams. Except I picked up another package from the doormat this morning, my typed stories returned from a different agent with a rejection note. Reading the brief lines, I felt very far from achieving my dreams.

Dougie's holding up a white blouse against me. He stops for a moment and sighs. 'I love this song. So romantic.'

It's him. I know before I can voice it in my head. Before I can bring his name to my tongue. The music goes right to the core of me, enters me like a drug, spinning me back to my bench on the boardwalk; shivering in his arms on the beach; the itchy tiles at the funeral home, his body over mine, inside mine; his smell, his breath, his voice. Him on the stage at Ally's, looking at me in the wings and winking. *This one's for Cat.*

'Are you all right, hen?' Dougie's saying. 'Here, sit down. You look like you've seen a ghost.'

I'm in a chair, head between my knees, blood hammering at the walls of my skull, blood leaping out of my heart. I am drowning in memories. I struggle to the surface, put my hands over my eyes. 'It's him,' I whisper. 'It's

218

Sam. The man I told you about . . . '

'What? Where?'

The song is ending now, the chorus washing away, and I want to run after it, drag it back. I want to hear his voice again. 'Sam Sage. The man I met in Atlantic City. That was him. Singing that song.'

'No! He's all over MTV. He's a star, darling.' He pouts. 'You said he wasn't famous.'

'He wasn't. Not then.'

Dougie bends down and raises my chin to look into my face. 'Well, now you'll be able to find him, right? He's in that band, the Lambs.'

I break free of his grip and glance away. 'No. No. It's over between us. He never wrote. Never contacted me. He had the chance, and he didn't . . . he didn't want to see me again.' I swallow. 'Anyhow, it was years ago. There's no way I'm going to try and contact him now like . . . like some deluded fan. What would I say? Hey, remember me? Can you imagine if he didn't?'

Dougie sucks in his breath and looks at me disapprovingly. 'If an old lover of mine made it big, I'd make damn sure they did remember me.'

'I'm not like you, Dougie,' I say quietly, looking down at my exposed legs under the short skirt. 'I'm not gonna buy these things. I feel kind of sick. I want to go home.'

'Well, I'm going to buy them for you. One of these days, you'll want to look like someone other than a nanny.' He holds up his hands. 'You can thank me later.'

★ ★ ★

219

Hearing Sam's voice has broken something inside me, untethered me, made me restless and heartbroken and angry. I don't understand my feelings. I didn't think it would hurt this bad. The comforting ritual of my days has been upended by one song. One song.

I want it to be about me. I push the idea away. Impossible. Ego-driven. After all, it's years and years later. He'll have new loves to write about.

Soon as I can, I buy the album, smuggle it into the house and shut myself in my room. I read and reread the lyrics printed on the inside of the CD. And I'm totally confused, because 'Ocean Blue' does seem to be about me. But if he felt those things, why the hell didn't he write? I sit staring into space, listening to his voice, pressing play over and over. I'm going to wear the CD out soon, and however many times I hear it, it won't answer my questions. But whatever reason he had for walking away, the song's a reminder of our time, and it makes me feel better knowing I didn't imagine it.

November 1987

Grace is doing her homework upstairs. Leo is late home. He has a game of squash on a Wednesday, but he's usually back by eight o'clock. His food is congealing under tin foil in a warm oven. The radio is on in the background, and as I shake out kibble for the cat we've recently acquired — a bossy stray that in truth has acquired us — a news bulletin comes on.

220

There's been a fire at King's Cross underground station. Multiple casualties, the newsreader is saying.

I stand still, my fingers pressed over my mouth. Leo always rings to tell me if he's delayed. There's been no word from him. He plays squash in a sports hall in King's Cross. It's the station he'll use to get the Northern Line to Hampstead. Fear skims my skin with ice.

I go upstairs and find the CD player turned up loud, and Grace singing along to 'Walk Like an Egyptian', doing the walking dance around the room, chin jutting in and out, arms bent. She sees me and sings louder, her cheeks flushed: '*Slide your feet up the street.*' She gestures for me to join in.

I can't let her see my fear. I manage a few steps, stretching my lips into a smile. The song ends, and I switch off the machine with shaking fingers. 'Time for bed,' I tell her.

I try to appear normal as I kiss her goodnight. She doesn't ask where her father is. She's used to him missing her bedtime.

The cat jumps onto her bed, purring. I go to pick him up.

'Oh, let him stay,' she says.

She's got one hand on his furry belly, her thumb in her mouth. I want her to have all the comfort she can.

'Just for tonight,' I say. 'You two do look pretty cute together.'

She grins and rolls her eyes, lifting up her arms for a hug. 'Can I read for a bit?' She reads my stories for herself now. Her enthusiasm makes me determined not to give up. She smiles. 'I want to know what happens at the end.'

'Fifteen minutes.' I squeeze her tight. 'School tomorrow.'

★ ★ ★

I close the sitting room door and turn the TV on, keeping the sound low. I sit on the edge of the sofa, hunched over, staring at the screen. There's footage of injured people being brought out of the station by firemen in gas masks and yellow helmets. Bodies on stretchers covered in red blankets. Could one of them be Leo? My stomach churns. A woman is interviewed. She talks of smoke, a ball of fire, panic, a desperate rush to safety. There are tears in her eyes. An emergency number appears on the screen, and I scribble it down.

When I eventually get through, a voice on the other end tells me which hospitals the injured and dead are being taken to. I pace the room. I'm too scared to ring the hospitals. I can't face the worst — can't face someone telling me he's dead. I feel sick. I might have lost him. We've been holding back out of fear, and I realise how stupid we've been. We've been doing a kind of dance around each other for months, careful not to touch each other, careful to be careful. What was the point? Life is short. Too short to be sensible. I wish he was here right now so that I could show him how much I care for him, how much I want him. I dig my fingernails into my palms. 'Please let him be okay,' I say aloud.

'Please.' And I'm not sure who I'm begging a favour from, what god or deity or element of fate I'm making bargains with in my head.

When the news finishes, the adverts continue as if nothing has happened. I switch the TV off.

★　★　★

I wake up, confused, my mouth stale. The room is dark. But there's movement inside the darkness, an acrid stink of smoke.

'Leo?' I gasp.

'Cat? You gave me a fright.' His voice is hoarse. 'What are you doing on the sofa?'

Light floods the room, making me blink. He's put a lamp on. He's soot-smudged, his clothes filthy. His glasses are greasy, his face hollowed out with exhaustion.

'The fire. You were in the fire.' A sob breaks through me.

He sinks onto the sofa next to me, nodding. He takes off his glasses to clean them with the hem of his shirt. I put my arms around him, or perhaps it's the other way round. I'm not sure how it happens, but we're holding each other tightly, not letting go. A shudder goes through him. I clasp him closer, as close as I can. 'I thought you were dead,' I sob.

'I'm sorry. I didn't have time to call,' he says. 'I got there after it'd happened — the fire ball in the ticket hall. I just missed it. But the injured . . . they were everywhere.' He stops, takes a gulp of air. 'It was carnage. I've never seen anything like it. I had to stay and help. I wasn't thinking

223

about you and what you'd think. I'm sorry.'

'No.' I wipe my nose with the edge of my sleeve. 'I'm just . . . I'm happy you're not hurt.'

'Cat,' he says softly. 'Darling.'

Then his mouth is over mine. His lips taste of charcoal. He is trembling. I put my hands either side of his face and hold him steady, our mouths pressed together. His glasses tumble from his lap with a quiet clatter.

★ ★ ★

In his bedroom, he switches off the light as we tug at each other's clothes. The last man I slept with was Sam. Leo's body feels different — his bones narrower, his muscles more sinewy. The differences are disorientating. I force the thought of Sam out of my head as Leo touches my breasts, as he lowers me gently onto the bed. His mouth is moving over mine. I inhale the bitter stink of smoke, the acrid remains of the fire in his hair, on his skin. I hold him tighter, knowing how close I came to losing him. His fingers are skilful. He makes me come quickly, a flare of hot brilliance bursting through me. 'Sorry,' I murmur into his neck. 'I didn't do enough for you . . . '

'I loved giving you pleasure,' he says. 'I've been dreaming of this for a long time.' He sniffs his arm. 'God, I smell of ash, don't I? Sorry. I'll have a quick shower.' He sits up. 'Don't go anywhere.'

I kiss him gratefully, and lie back in his bed, missing him, listening sleepily to the distant sound of running water. When he climbs in next to me, lemony and clean, his hair damp, I fall asleep in his arms, exhausted, and at peace.

★ ★ ★

Leo is snoring. It's still dark outside. I check the digital clock on the bedside table. Six o'clock. I push back the covers quietly and sit up, my bare skin prickling with cold. Leo stirs and wakes. 'Where are you going?'

'I should go back to my room. If Grace wakes early . . .'

He sits up, rubbing his eyes. 'I don't want you to go.'

'But I should.' I smile, and slip my feet onto the floor.

He catches hold of my hand. 'Wait,' he says, his voice urgent. 'This isn't how I want it to be, Cat. I don't want to hide this. Not from Grace. Not from anyone.'

I turn, squinting through the dimness at him.

He switches on his reading light; a pool of light floods his face. 'This might seem . . . sudden. But I think you know what you mean to me now. I can't imagine my life without you.' He pauses, fumbles on his table and finds his glasses. He puts them on. 'I need you, Cat. We both do. Would you . . . would you consider marrying me?'

I stare at him.

'We already live together,' he says earnestly. 'And I think, with Grace, we should make our relationship clear, official. No confusion. I'd like to make you happy, Cat.' His voice is low, our faces nearly touching. 'I'd like to have that chance.'

'I just . . . It's so unexpected. I need to think.'

'Of course.' We sit back, gazing at each other. He looks as stunned as I feel. 'Thank you for last night,' he says, kissing my cheek.

'Leo.' I smile. 'You don't have to thank me. I've wanted this for as long as you have.'

The winter morning is dark behind the curtains, just a faint wash of yellow beginning to erase an inky sky. I gather my clothes up in a bundle and hold them to me as I leave the room. I can feel his eyes on me, know that he's looking at the curve of my spine, the dip it makes before my bottom, the roundness of my buttocks. And I walk slowly, his gaze like a torch at my back, illuminating me.

★   ★   ★

It doesn't take me long. Two days later, I've made up my mind. I trust Leo not to break my heart. 'I'll marry you, Leo Dunn,' I tell him. 'As long as Grace is okay with it.'

He kisses my nose and says, 'Thank you, my darling.'

★   ★   ★

She's back from school, eating an apple in front of the TV. 'Hey, bug. Can you turn that off for a moment,' I say. 'I've got something important to ask you.'

She turns the dial, and the only sound is the

226

crunching of apple in her mouth. She swallows. 'What?'

I take a deep breath, my heart hammering between my ears. 'Your dad . . . he's asked . . . ' I bite my lip. 'Grace, your dad's asked me to marry him, and I wanted to check with you if — '

I don't have a chance to finish my question. She's hugging me around the ribs, her thin arms squeezing the air out of my lungs. She's got so tall lately, her head nearly level with my shoulders.

'Yes,' she's saying, 'Yes, please!'

We're both laughing and crying. 'Wow,' I tell her, holding out my still-shaking hands. 'That was the scariest thing I've ever done!'

'Let's tell him now,' she says. 'You can phone him.'

And as she drags me over to the door, I realise that I'm going to be her mom for real, and the three of us can start over as a proper family.

Part Three

WILL OUR MARRIAGE BE LIKE THIS PARK?
CHANGING THROUGH THE SEASONS,
MAYBE MUDDY IN PARTS,
OH, BUT FULL OF LIFE.

30

Sam, March 1988

Two crazy years. Behind him, endless miles of tarmac, white lines running together, leading to the next gig. Towns and cities where he had to be reminded where he was before he stepped onto the stage to greet the crowd. *Hello, Birmingham . . . Cambridge . . . Reading . . . Leeds.* Hours that dragged like sulky children while he languished in anonymous hotel rooms, or on the plush tour bus. No more fighting for knee space with a couple of Fender amps and a telecaster. He wouldn't say it to anyone, but he missed being squashed together elbow to elbow. There seemed to be more jokes in the rattling Transit van, more laughter.

It was harder than he'd ever imagined to keep singing night after night, the strength it took, the stamina. The sheer weight of oxygen moving through his body was like being an athlete, a long-distance runner. So he did what was expected of him: took a hit when his bones ached and his mind felt numb.

And then, the following year, America. The USA tour was a whole different circus. More miles to cover, more venues to play, coast to coast. Their new single made it high in the *Billboard* charts, and the States opened to them as if they'd pressed a magic button. Sometimes, standing on a stage in some American city, he'd wonder if Cat was in the audience.

★   ★   ★

He's exhausted. He's forgotten what it's like to stay in one place, to sleep in his own bed. He's anxious to get back to writing for the next album. It took years to create the music for the first one; he put his whole life into that record. But now he has to get something ready for recording and pressing in a matter of months. The thought is terrifying.

They'll be working with Lucas Jones again. Lucas transformed their original material for the first album, nudging them into something more commercial. The changes didn't sit well with Sam. But every time he began to debate the way the album was shaping up, Marcus would take him to one side. 'Lucas knows what he's doing. You've signed a contract. Let it go. Enjoy the process.'

May 1988

Daisy leans over Sam's bare chest, propping herself on her forearms. Her breasts are squashed against him in a distracting fashion. But he can tell from her expression that he needs to concentrate on what she's saying. 'Can I sing on the next album?' She pouts. 'You promised.'

'I didn't promise, babe.' He clears his throat.

232

'Sorry. But I don't think your voice is . . . right.'

'But you said I was made to be a star. I thought you'd make it happen for me. You could if you wanted to.'

'Daisy,' he sighs. 'We talked about this before. You need to do some work on your voice. Maybe take singing lessons. I'll pay.'

She frowns and shifts her weight, her elbows digging into his ribs. 'Are you writing songs about us? About me? For the new album?'

'I'm struggling to write anything at the moment,' he says. 'I need to come up with something different. Something more upbeat. Not love songs this time.'

She tilts her head to one side, narrowing her eyes. 'That's not fair. I've been waiting my turn.'

'Your turn?'

'Yes — *she* got her songs, didn't she? The mystery woman. Whoever the hell she was you wrote those songs about. All those romantic ones.'

His body tenses, his skin suddenly hot. He's aware of the weight of her pressing down on him, restricting his breath. He shifts so that she slips to one side, under his arm. 'Daisy, I don't want to talk about this.'

'So you admit she exists — that they're about her? Not me?'

'Yeah, they're about someone I met in America. I haven't seen her for years. It's over. Long over.' He scratches his chin. 'Look. I need to get up . . . things to do.'

He rolls away and pushes his feet to the floor.

'But you must have still been thinking of her

when we met,' she persists, 'if you wrote them just before . . .'

'No. I wrote them a long time ago, then put them away in a drawer. I only got them out to work on because I knew . . . I knew they had something I needed.'

'Well, she'd better not make an appearance now.' He hears Daisy's sulky voice at his back. 'She'll have me to contend with.'

He stands up in one quick movement and grabs his shirt and jeans, tugging them on. 'Don't be ridiculous, Daisy.' He looks down at her, luscious and creamy as a Botticelli angel. 'I told you, I haven't seen her for years. It's pointless to get jealous of someone in my past.'

'I can't help it,' she wails. 'I can't even listen to the songs. They make me so mad. I can't stand that you've written them about someone else. They're so beautiful . . . Why can't you write something like that about me?'

He shoves his feet into his trainers, and paces up and down beside the bed. Her words have released a darkness, and he presses the heels of his hands into his eyes, making the insides of his lids flare with colour. 'Please don't go on about this. I can't write a song to order . . . You know that isn't how it works.'

'Baby.' Tears glisten in her eyes. 'I'm sorry, okay? I'm so crazy about you. It makes me lose my mind sometimes. Come back to bed . . . '

He knows he should sit down, hold her in his arms, reassure her with gentle words and kisses, but there's a knot in his throat stopping speech. He closes his eyes against a sudden sickening

234

lurch of vertigo. He can't go to Daisy. He doesn't even want to touch her. He strides out of the room, grabs his jacket and leaves the flat, ignoring her yells for him to come back.

June 1988

The one scheduled break from studio time is for the Lambs to play a concert at Wembley Stadium held in honour of Nelson Mandela. They are one of many bands and singers booked for the event. Eleven hours of music has been planned, to be televised around the world: two stages, seventy-five thousand people in the audience.

A breeze blows across the packed stadium, but the heat from the crowd rises like mist from a river. The sound of their collective breathing makes the hairs rise on Sam's arms. He's never played a crowd so huge. Adrenalin hums through him, pulsing in his twitching fingers and trembling legs. Big names have already taken to the stage, including Al Green himself.

Backstage, as well as the roadies and security, there's a crowd of hangers-on and performers drinking and smoking and watching front of house through gaps in the fluttering banners. Daisy is one of them, in a purple leather catsuit, her plastic identity tag swinging around her navel. She won't stop going on about singing backing vocals. He remembers Cat trying to hum a song about aeroplanes. She knew she couldn't sing; she laughed about it. That big, wicked laugh that rumbled up from her belly.

Jesus. He runs his fingers over his scalp. He's got to focus. He's about to step onto the biggest stage of his life. So why does he want to crawl into a hole and cry? He can't tell anyone how he feels: the treacly blackness that consumes him, dragging him down and down until he thinks he'll never scrabble back to the surface. Only a hit of chemicals lifts the weight of exhaustion that exists inside him. He remembers how George once called him a spoilt brat; if he starts whining about how miserable success is making him, the insult would be justified. He has to keep going. One step at a time. One song at a time.

'Right, we're up next!' He makes an effort to sound upbeat. The whole band depends on him for their energy.

They're on. Arranged on stage, they're dwarfed by the massive set. Behind them, a picture of Mandela's face rears big as a house. Huge banners with African drawings rustle in the breeze. Beyond the lights, Sam stares out at a rippling landscape of heads and waving arms. Fear swallows him whole. Then he hears the click of George's sticks, a metronome reminding him of his heartbeat, and he grabs the mic and twists it off the stand. The crowd roars its appreciation. His ribs expand, his throat opens and his voice takes flight. He leaps down onto the lower stage and thrusts his arm into the air. Thousands of arms follow, thousands of voices echoing his.

31

Cat, June 1988

I look in the mirror, brushing my hair back from my face, applying mascara. We're having a registry office wedding, and then a small reception in a restaurant nearby. I'm wearing a silk dress in dove grey that Dougie picked out. It's not my style, but he was adamant that I should develop a more sophisticated look now I'm to be a married woman.

He's giving me away, as Dad isn't here.

I lean forward and slide a pair of pearl drops through my ear lobes. I don't look like me at all. Maybe that's good.

I go down the stairs — the same ones Elizabeth fell down — and I'm blinded for a second by sunshine streaming through the glass over the front door. I stumble, lost inside that liquid gold, and clutch the banister tightly, my breath caught in my throat.

Sounds from the TV reach me. I follow the noise and find Grace lying on her tummy on the floor, the cat, which she's named Fat Mog, stretched out next to her, tail twitching. On screen there's a band singing in front of a huge crowd. 'What are you watching?' I ask.

'It's a pop festival,' she tells me. 'They're trying to make South Africa free. Wet Wet Wet were on. And it's that man's birthday — you

237

know, the man in prison there.'

'Nelson Mandela?'

'Yup.' She sits up and scoops the cat into her lap. 'That's him.'

'Well, sweetheart, I'm sorry, but we have to switch it off now. We don't want to be late for Dad.'

The tabby struggles out of her arms and stalks off, tail in the air. Grace doesn't seem to notice; she's looking at me with an anxious expression. 'Cat . . . you know you're marrying Dad? But I can't . . . I can't call you Mum, because,' her lips tremble, 'because I already have a real mum, even if she's dead.' To my horror, tears spill from her eyes, rolling down her cheeks.

I stare at her, stunned by her words. She thinks she's betraying her mom by accepting me as her stepmom? 'Hey, don't cry, sweetheart.' I crouch to wipe her tears away. 'I'll never replace your real mom. I know that.'

She nods gratefully, and presses her face against me, sniffing.

'Listen, bug, you can call me whatever you like,' I tell her. 'Stinky Pants or Big Ears . . . '

She laughs.

'That's better! But seriously, Grace, don't worry. Of course, if you ever change your mind, I'd be thrilled to hear you call me Mom. But if it doesn't feel right, that's okay too.'

On screen, Lenny Henry is doing a Michael Jackson impersonation.

'Cab's due in five minutes,' I say, standing to look at my watch. I nod at the set. 'You'd better turn that off now. Go get your dress on.'

238

Upstairs, I knock on the spare-room door. Daniel and Mom have flown over for the wedding, and Daniel has gone ahead with Leo to the registry office. Mom looks up. 'My goodness . . . ' She dabs the corners of her eyes with a lace hanky. 'You look real beautiful, Catrin.' She takes my hands in hers and squeezes. 'I'm happy for you. He's a gentleman. I can rest easy knowing this one will take care of you. And the little girl seems nice. But of course, you can have your own baby now.'

I let go of her hands. I think of Grace's tearful face. *I can't call you Mum.* 'We haven't discussed that, Mom.'

Mom rolls her eyes. 'You're not so young any more. Let me tell you, the years pass mighty fast. Leo can provide for you. He's a top surgeon. There's no need to be cautious about,' she lowers her voice, 'money.'

'It's not money I was thinking about.'

But she's still speaking. 'Lucky that your relationship with that young drifter never came to anything,' she says. 'You wouldn't be living in a house like this, I'm sure.'

I frown. 'I don't want to talk about that, Mom.'

She leans towards me, the scent of roses overpowering, and touches my arm. 'Though actually, luck didn't come into it. I was looking out for you. A mother always knows what's best for her child.'

A prickle of cold runs across my skin. 'What? What are you talking about?'

The sharpness of my voice makes her take a step back. 'Oh, nothing. Forget I said anything.'

239

'No.' I make an effort to calm my voice. 'No. Tell me, Mom. Please.'

'His letters,' she says, keeping her eyes on my reaction.

'Letters?' The word crashes through my head like a runaway steer. I stare at her. 'He didn't write any . . .'

She looks wary now. She nods. 'Well, yes, he did. A few, anyways.'

'A few?' The room tilts. 'Wait. How did you know they were from him?'

'You said he'd be writing. They had an English postmark.' Her voice is almost confiding.

'He wrote me letters?' I feel sick. 'He wrote to me and you . . . what? What did you do with them?'

She's wary again. She pats at her hair. 'I burnt them.'

'No.' A small sob breaks free from my throat. 'How could you do that? It wasn't your right. It wasn't your right to do that.'

'He was no good.' She puts her chin in the air. 'I could see it, even if you couldn't.' She reaches out her hand to me, and I flinch back from it. 'You were blinded by his charm, Catrin. I don't blame you.'

'What did he say in his letters?'

'Oh, I don't rightly remember . . .'

'You must remember something. Tell me. You owe me that.'

'Well. My goodness. I guess it was the usual sort of thing. Promises. Talk about love. And I do recall he sent some kind of poem. About the ocean.'

240

A strangled wail punctures the air. The noise is coming from me. I sink onto the bed and lean forward onto my knees. *Sam!* Inside, I'm crying his name.

Mom is still talking. A white noise crackles around my head. I put my hands onto the bedspread either side of me to feel the texture, pinching a fold hard between my fingers. I'm fighting to make sense of what she's telling me. Sam wrote to me. He didn't forget me. He kept his promise.

But it's too late.

I stare up at her. Her words resolve themselves out of the crackling. 'Now, Catrin, don't go making a scene. It was for the best.' She puts a hand to her throat. 'Lordy, I don't understand you — it was so long ago.' She looks hurt. There's a prim ghtness to her lips. 'You're getting married to o,' she says, as if I've forgotten.

Vhat would she say if I told her that the poem ead is now a hit song played on the radio? 's no point. None of it matters any more.

 too late. The words thunder through me nd over. Too late. Too late.

ve a sudden urge to get up and run — run par and out of the house. And go where? I thiWhere can I go?

 Grace is in the room, bouncing with excient. 'Taxi's outside.' Her cheeks are flushShe's wearing a dress in the same dove grey mine, with a pink sash around her waist. I gup on shaky legs. 'Thank you, bug,' I tell her. et's go. We don't want to keep Daddy waitin, do we?'

I don't look at my mother as Grace slips her hand into mine.

★ ★ ★

I won't remember the details of my marriage vows later. Everything is a blur. As I stand next to Leo in front of the registrar with my posy of daisies, I feel like I'm coming down with flu. I'm dizzy enough that I think I might faint right there. I squeeze the stalks of the flowers hard, my knuckles flaring white. 'You look beautiful,' Leo mouths. The registrar, a woman in a dark suit, is speaking. I tell myself to breathe, focus. Repeat her words. Smile.

Afterwards, my lips must feel cold to Leo, but he's smiling and laughing, his arm around my waist. Grace throws handfuls of confetti when we are outside on the steps. I blink in the hazy sunshine, ducking under the shower of paper.

It takes a long time to get to the restaurant. Our cab is stuck in a jam. The others are following behind in a different taxi. Our c nudges along at a stop-start pace. Music dri out of the cabbie's radio. Applause, and th another song. 'There's a concert in honou Mandela, apparently,' Leo tells me. 'I think being broadcast live.'

Our driver nods. 'Terrible traffic all day. I't know why we got to interfere with what's ing on in another country. They can sort then lves out, can't they?'

Leo raises his eyebrows at me. I rais mine back.

A new song begins, and my heart jumps. *First time I saw you, beside the ocean blue* . . . The audience roar in appreciation. His voice floats over the airwaves, soft and intimate. *Remember us kissing slow on the Avenue* . . . My body is cold, then hot, my pulse leaping under my skin.

I lurch forward. 'Turn it off,' I tell the driver. 'Please.' Sliding the partition window shut with trembling fingers, I sit back, hoping Leo can't hear the thunder of my heart, sense the shock ricocheting through my body.

'I don't mind having you all to myself for longer,' he's saying. He runs his fingers through my hair, picking out bits of coloured confetti: yellow, pink and white in the palm of his hand. 'You are happy, aren't you, darling?'

'Of course,' I say. 'Of course I am.'

32

Sam, December 1989

Amongst flailing limbs, and bodies whirling under purple strobe lights, a woman walks around in a gold bikini with a python coiled around her neck. The New Year's Eve party has reached the point of fracture, helped along by the legendary cocktail of drugs available at Decker Grant's West Berlin mansion.

A girl appears by Sam's side. He squints at her. Her dilated pupils pulse. Shining silver hair swings around her cheeks. Her top is slashed to the waist at the front. 'I was in your last video. In the open-top car?' she says. 'St Lucia?'

'Right. Yeah. I knew that.'

The party whirls past them in a pleasant slip-sliding sensation. She's touching his arm, rubbing at his bicep. He clenches it, and she giggles. 'Wanna go to your room?' she murmurs.

He's certain he's never seen her before. He reaches out an unsteady hand and, with great concentration, touches her silver hair to see what it feels like. It looks like something hanging on a Christmas tree.

The girl is yanked away. Her eyes widen. And she's gone.

'I'll kill her if she touches you again,' Daisy slurs, scowling at him.

Sam finds he has threads of silver clutched

between his fingers. He raises his shoulders, lets them fall. He lacks the words or the energy to explain. It just happened. Like rain. Like . . . like . . . He frowns, confused. He can't remember what word he's looking for, or why he's looking for it. He staggers away. He needs more alcohol, more lines of coke. The party is spiralling downwards, and he's going with it.

Just a few streets away, there are shovels unpicking stones, pickaxes razing the Berlin Wall to the ground. Sam wanted to go and see it, but Daisy was horrified by the suggestion. 'No way,' she said. 'What if there's a stampede? It could be dangerous.'

The top floor of Grant's modern house is a giant glass box, built in such a way that it protrudes vertiginously over the limits of the lower floors, so that Sam sees the pavement swinging far below. Twisting his head left and right gives him a panoramic view of the city, and tilting his head back, he's stargazing. Standing inside plate glass, amongst a crowd in designer clothes, with champagne glasses raised, he and Daisy toast the start of a new decade, while the freezing night sky turns into a battleground of pyrotechnics.

Daisy's lips find his own. 'Love you, babe,' she slurs.

He slides the strap of her red dress back onto her shoulder. 'Happy New Year,' he says, but the words are dead in his mouth. The glass box reels around him, and he stumbles back, stepping on someone's foot, spilling someone's drink. Above his head, the air explodes with colour. He closes his eyes against the confusion, and somehow, he is not on his feet any more, but tumbling through space, silent and earthbound, like a dud firework.

January 1990

Early next morning, the first of 1990, Sam leaves Daisy sleeping on black silk sheets while he and George cross from West into East Berlin. There's a long line of people waiting to come in the opposite direction. Much of the wall still stands, the stones covered in new graffiti, but huge chunks have been demolished, as if a giant creature has been snacking on concrete. Sam bends down and picks up a handful of rubble, examines its pinkish colour. He slips it into his pocket. Dazed-looking border guards huddle in groups, smoking, their guns slung over their shoulders. The ground is littered with the frazzled remains of fireworks and torn streamers, and here and there, an abandoned shoe or piece of clothing.

The air is flecked with white. Sam looks up, letting petals of sleet land on his face. The cold wetness is a relief. There's a thumping bass slamming against the back of his eye sockets. He touches his temple, and finds he has a bruise there.

A new year. A new era. He wants this first day to be the start of something good, something different. The Lambs have topped the charts again and again. But the music they make isn't what Sam set out to do. It's time he faced up to it — did something about it. And then there's Daisy. He sighs.

George plucks at his arm, pointing out a photographer taking photos of the wall. 'Let's go before he recognises us.'

The two men find a café. It's packed with people who've probably been up all night. They squeeze onto the end of a crowded table and order two black coffees, delivered after a long wait by an unsmiling girl.

'Here's mud in your eye,' says George, raising his glass cup. 'Talking of which, that's some shiner.' He wrinkles his forehead. 'Wild party. Shame you didn't come with us to see the Brandenburg Gate.'

'Yeah, I was gutted to miss it.' Sam takes a swig of burning, bitter liquid.

'It was insane,' George says. 'Everyone standing on the wall. This jubilation in the air.'

'But think of what they lost for all those years,' Sam says. 'What they suffered.'

'Exactly.' George nods. 'Maybe grist for a song?'

Sam runs his tongue around the burnt interior of his mouth. 'But that kind of political idea doesn't work for what we do, does it? It's not what people buy a Lambs album for.'

George says nothing. Heaps some sugar into his cup.

'And let's face it, that's all anyone wants from us,' Sam continues. 'The same commercial sound. I have this longing to write something more . . . I don't know . . . interesting.' He rubs his face hard. 'Does that sound crazy?'

'No.' George wrinkles his eyebrows. 'I know you're frustrated at the moment.'

'Hell, listen to me moaning!' Sam grimaces. 'Guess it's not such a bad place to be, if I let myself get some perspective on it.' He touches his brother's arm, making an effort to smile. 'We've had some amazing years. Been to incredible places and met extraordinary people. Made some serious dosh. Two platinum albums in a row. No one can argue with that.'

'How are you so bloody optimistic with a hangover?' George asks. 'It really pisses me off.'

Sam grins. 'That was my aim.'

Sometimes acting himself is easier than being himself, and he understands why Daisy does it, why her whole life is a pretence.

Outside the café, George points out a brand-new advert for a fizzy drink. 'It's started already.' He scowls. 'The slide into capitalism.'

The advert yells its redness into the hushed grey of the winter morning. *Drink me, and you will be happy.*

'Like a fucked-up Alice in Wonderland,' George says.

They turn away from it.

'Want to explore a bit?' he asks. 'Get a train into the countryside? See the real East Berlin?'

Sam thinks of Daisy waiting for him at Decker Grant's place. He shrugs. 'Why not?'

★ ★ ★

At the station, they take the first train into the countryside, travelling past vast fields hidden

248

under snow. They get out at an unpronounceable village, and wander through quiet streets. There's no sign that this day is different from any other. Nobody looks at the two men: George, broad-shouldered and red-haired, wrapped in his tweed overcoat; Sam in his battered leather jacket, collar up, cap over his tangled hair. He feels invisible for the first time in a long while.

They stop at a kiosk selling chips. As they wander off, clutching greasy packages, George pops a chip in his mouth. 'Listen, mate,' he says, gasping at the heat. 'I wanted to get you on your own, because . . . I'm worried about you.'

'Me?' Sam watches a small car go by. The engine sounds like a lawnmower.

'Yeah. Seems to me that you've been pushing it too hard for a while now. Working all night, taking maybe just a few too many hits of coke to see you through.'

Sam rubs his nose. 'What are you saying? I'm not an addict, George. For fuck's sake, we're under pressure to get this album finished.'

'But it's not just the album, is it? You seem . . . I don't know. Wired. Depressed.' George touches his shoulder. 'I haven't seen you laugh — really laugh — in a long time.'

Sam shakes George's hand away. 'Look, just leave it, all right? I use some chemical help sometimes. So what? Who doesn't? I don't need you being all censorious.'

'Hey, take it easy.' George's voice is careful. 'I'm not nagging, but I thought we could talk.'

'I just . . . I don't need this now, okay?' To his horror, Sam feels tears stinging his eyes.

249

Before he embarrasses himself completely, he strides away, dragging his sleeve across his face. What's wrong with him? His heart aches. George's words hurt because they're true. He stops beside a house, and a flash of yellow through the window makes him turn to look. A canary in a cage. Such a tiny creature, all alone, singing. A memory of a white church comes back to him, Cat's leg pressing against his as she tries to hum the aeroplane tune.

Suddenly he realises what it was — the song she was trying to remember. He begins to hum the familiar tune, the lyrics in his head conjuring up an image of a man standing by a door, packed bags at his feet. A sleeping woman stretched out in bed, early morning light soft on her face. He imagines the roar of a jet across a sky. And he sings out loud, the words making him ache.

His cheeks are wet, tears making a ticklish path along the side of his nose. She was the most real person in his life. Being with her in Atlantic City was the last time he was himself, the last time he was whole. He feels weird, constricted, as if someone has their hands at his neck, squeezing. He opens his mouth, but no words form. Instead, there's a choking sound.

'Mate.' George is there, plucking at the sleeve of his jacket. 'Come on. Come away.'

'I'm a fake,' Sam whispers.

'I think you're burnt out.' George's voice is slow and careful. 'It's understandable. It's been a non-stop ride. Maybe you need a proper break. Some help . . . you know?'

' 'Leaving on a Jet Plane'.' Sam wipes his face with his fingers. 'Fuck.' He gives a short laugh. 'John Denver. Only took me seven years.'

'What?' George sounds concerned.

'Nothing.' He squeezes his eyes shut. They walk on in silence, just the sound of their boots creaking through the snow. 'It's over,' he says, 'with Daisy. I can't do it any more.'

'It's got kind of toxic between you two. So yeah, maybe for the best.'

'I'm sorry I snapped,' Sam says, leaning against George's bulk. George pats his arm silently.

They stand on the cold station platform, waiting for the train to Berlin. Sam thinks about Daisy. He doesn't want to hurt her, but there's no avoiding this. He stamps his feet and blows on his hands. The sensation of the icy air is a relief, the way it scours his throat, stings his lungs like salt water.

33

Cat, January 1990

'Morning, sleepyhead.'

I surface, mumbling remnants from already forgotten dreams. I am reluctant to leave the warm darkness behind. Wherever I was, I wanted to stay longer.

I open my eyes. Leo is leaning on one elbow, smiling down at me with that quizzical look of his, although I know that without his glasses, I'm just a blur. He kisses my mouth. Then he lies down again and puts his arm around me, his nose nuzzling my neck. 'I've been thinking . . . I'd like to have another child, Catrin,' he says in a voice that trembles with anticipation. 'A baby. With you.' He squeezes my ribs. 'What do you say?'

'A baby?' I blink up at the ceiling.

'New year. New decade. It couldn't be a better time to make a new member of the family.' His voice smiles.

My hands move to my belly, excitement catching like a spark. 'A baby,' I repeat, getting used to the idea.

'I've always wanted a son,' he says.

'To be honest, I've never thought much about having children,' I tell him. 'But that's because I've never been in a situation where I could have one.'

252

I can feel him waiting for me to give him an answer. I'm a married woman, secure, settled. Having a baby is suddenly not just possible, I realise, it's expected.

'Yes . . . yes . . . I'd like to have a child,' I say slowly. 'With you.' I feel for his hand and slide my fingers through his.

He squeezes my hand, then he's up on his elbow again. He turns to find his spectacles on the bedside table and puts them on, his blue eyes bright with excitement. 'I'm so happy, darling.'

I smile up at him. 'Do you think Grace will be okay? Do you think she wants a sibling?'

'She'll be thrilled at the idea.'

I sit up, pulling the sheet around me. 'Let's talk to her. She should feel included.'

Leo nods. 'Good idea. Why don't you mention it to her casually this morning, so that she doesn't feel under pressure to give the right answer.'

'This morning?'

He shrugs. 'Why wait?'

I grin. 'I'll try and find the right moment.' I glance at the bed-side clock. 'I'll go down and make sure she's eating breakfast.'

'I've invited David and Lucy for supper this Saturday, by the way,' he says. 'That's all right with you, isn't it? I told them they could take us as they find us. Don't go to any trouble — they can eat with us in the kitchen. Whatever's easy.'

My cooking is almost edible nowadays. Leo's even dropped the cordon bleu jokes, but he never puts any pressure on me to come up with dinner-party dishes. He slides his feet onto the carpet and reaches for his dressing gown.

David's one of his colleagues from work, and a fellow golf enthusiast. Lucy, his wife, is also a doctor. They've welcomed me as Leo's wife. When I'm alone with her, Lucy bemoans the loss of her husband to the golf course. I don't want to join in and gripe about Leo's long working hours, his weekend absences, but it's true I didn't expect to be alone so much after we married. It's okay to sacrifice romance, though, I tell myself, if it's for a different kind of love — something grown-up, secure and kind.

Leo hums, searching in his drawer for a pair of clean boxers. If he's not away lecturing, or at a conference, his routine is the same every morning: a shower, before dressing in a dark suit and tie; then coffee and cereal, ten minutes looking at the headlines in the *Guardian*, and off to get the Tube to Moorfields Eye Hospital. On a Wednesday, he has a different Tube journey to a private hospital, with squash after work. Saturdays are reserved for golf. He is a creature of routine. But after living with my erratic father, I can only see it as a good thing.

'What are your plans for later?' he asks. 'Anything fun?'

'I'm about to start on the second draft of my children's book.' I hand him his tie. 'The one about young teenagers going back in time and solving crimes.'

'Ah, yes. A novel instead of short stories?'

'I didn't have much luck with the short stories, did I?' I attempt a carefree laugh. The pile of rejections I received after sending them off was crushing. 'Maybe a novel will be easier to get published,' I say. 'It's giving me time to get to know my characters better, build up their world.'

'Well, I'm glad you're keeping busy, darling.' He's heading for the door. 'You can tell me more about it this evening.' He's already thinking about his list of patients and the operations lined up. Then he stops and turns back. 'And maybe we can make a start on the other thing we discussed?'

'What thing?'

'The baby thing,' he says. He raises one eyebrow. 'We can have fun trying, anyway.'

I throw the pillow I'm holding at him and he ducks, laughing.

* * *

Grace is in the kitchen, dressed in her school uniform. She's leaning into the fridge when I come in, and she replaces a carton of orange juice on the shelf and shuts the door. 'Morning, Cat.'

I wish she'd call me Mum. I'd hoped after the marriage, she would. But that was before she told me it would make her feel disloyal to Elizabeth.

'Morning, bug. Have you eaten enough breakfast? Want me to make waffles?'

She shakes her head. 'No time. I had a bowl of cereal. Nancy's mum's picking me up again this morning.'

'Hey, guess what, I'm nearly ready for you to read my book,' I tell her. 'The kids who

255

time-travel and become detectives in other eras? I've covered them going back to Roman, Elizabethan and Victorian times.'

'Oh, that's exciting.' Grace smiles. 'I can't wait.'

'Great,' I tell her. 'In fact, I'm relying on you. It's for your age group, so I need you to be very honest with me; no holding back to save my feelings.'

'I'll do my best.' She swings her backpack onto her shoulder. 'Any title yet?'

'Maybe *The Time-Jumpers?*'

She screws up her face, thinking. 'Yes. I like it. Or *The Time-Jumping Detectives?*'

'Nice. Thanks.' I clear my throat. 'Grace, listen, there's something I wanted to run by you . . . Your dad and I were wondering about the possibility of having . . . having a baby.' I swallow. 'How would you feel if — '

She gasps. 'A brother or sister?'

I nod, watching her face for any ambiguity, but it's shining with joy. 'I'd like a sister more than anything,' she says quickly. 'A baby sister would be amazing.'

'Well, I can't promise to get the sex right,' I tell her, smiling. 'It might have to be a baby brother.'

She shrugs. 'That would be cool too.' Then she grins. 'When? When would you have a baby?'

'When? Well . . . I don't know. Let's see, it takes nine months for a pregnancy to come to term, and it can take a bit of time to conceive.' I glance at her to check she's not embarrassed. 'But I suppose there *could* be a baby before the end of the year.'

She claps her hands. 'If it's a girl, can we call her Sally?'

There's a discreet beep of a car horn outside. Grace kisses my cheek and heads for the door.

'Bye, sweetheart,' I call after her.

★ ★ ★

Her bedroom has been repainted cream. Gone are all the babyish toys. A big framed photo of Elizabeth sits on her nightstand. Her dressing table is loaded with fashion jewellery. Madonna pouts from posters stuck to the wall, alongside posters of dancers caught by the camera, leaping and twirling.

I gather up her dirty clothes from the linen basket in the corner, and find the cat curled under her desk in a patch of sunlight. I lean down to tickle his soft belly, and he purrs, arching his back. 'Hey, you.' He's getting old. He looks like a walking doormat; even his whiskers are crinkled and lopsided. But Grace adores him. Her diary is lying next to her bed. She's kept up writing in it since I gave her that first one. She never bothers to lock it. She trusts me.

★ ★ ★

Unsurprisingly, given the temperature, the Ladies' Pond is nearly empty. Only a few hardy swimmers are cutting their way through the dark water. I get in quickly with a gasp, and keep moving through the freezing, grainy push of the pond. I think about a baby growing inside me, a creature curled in its own watery world: limb buds sprouting, the ripple of a turning spine, the kick of hands and heels against the drum of my belly. I love Grace like my own, but love isn't finite. There's so much more I can give — an overflowing of feeling. And Leo and I can provide a baby with a proper home, with all the security I never had.

Towelled off, and dressed in warm clothes, a hat pulled over my wet hair, I hurry back to the house. A baby! Thinking about Grace's shining face makes me smile through my chattering teeth. She'll make a wonderful big sister. I'll tell Leo that we can start practising in earnest.

34

Sam, March 1990

Mattie picks him up from the Priory. He slings his bag into the boot of her car, and slides into the passenger seat, snapping his seat belt. As they drive through the gates onto the road, he spots a couple of paparazzi lurking on the pavement and keeps his face turned away from their long lenses.

'You look better,' Mattie says, dumping the clutch. 'Like yourself again.'

'I didn't realise how bad it had got,' he tells her. 'I was in a bleak place. And George was right. I was taking too many drugs.'

'You're not alone in that, kid. Not in the music business,' she says, glancing in the mirror at the photographers and pulling away with a crashing of gears and sudden skid of tyres.

'Slow down, James Bond,' he says, grabbing the door handle.

She makes a face at him. They pass teenagers in uniform walking home from school. Sam turns his head to watch them, absorbing the ordinariness of the scene — the way life keeps going with its rhythms and routines. It makes him want to start writing again, to begin a new song.

With nobody on their tail, Mattie sticks to the twenty-mile-an-hour limit in Richmond Park.

Sam lets go of the handle. Winding down the passenger window, he sees a herd of deer grazing close to the road. A young stag lifts his head, regarding the car with watchful eyes.

'River's excited to see you,' Mattie's saying.

'Great.' There's so much to do, to change. He made decisions while he was recovering from his burnout. He's had time to think. But now he'll have to act on those decisions, talk to the suits at Island, to Marcus, to George and the rest of the band. It feels overwhelming. He takes a big lungful of fresh air before he closes the window. They've pulled onto a main road, leaving the park behind. London traffic crowds in from every side. An impatient horn sounds behind them, and Mattie swears under her breath as she negotiates a junction.

'George is coming for supper tonight,' she says, slamming her foot down and accelerating straight ahead.

'Great,' Sam repeats as the back of his skull hits the headrest. And so it begins, he thinks. He is thirty-four years old. This is his second chance.

★ ★ ★

River is in bed at last. Luke is pouring the wine. Sam's staying in their spare room until he feels up to returning to his place in Islington: a tall Georgian terraced house, fresh from renovation and refurbishment, with a recording studio in the basement and a marble bathroom for every bedroom. Since acquiring it, he's hardly spent any time there; when he did, the tasteful rooms felt like a deserted hotel, and he wandered through them, restless and lonely, calling up friends and acquaintances to come over and fill the space. He realises now that he much prefers Mattie's place to his own. He likes River's toys strewn over the floor, the jumble of shoes spilling from the rack in the hall. He looks around him at wooden kitchen surfaces crowded with jars of pulses and stained cookery books, a vase of fresh tulips on the table, and feels his shoulders relax.

Luke offers him wine. Sam shakes his head. 'I'll stick to a soft drink, thanks.' Mattie puts an iced soda and lime in his hand. The doorbell goes, and she's off to answer it, trailing a thin line of smoke from the rollie between her fingers.

Sam is expecting George to appear, but instead there's the sound of raised voices. Both female. Luke cocks an eyebrow. 'Sounds like trouble.'

Sam frowns, recognising the other voice.

Daisy, tearful and drunk, sways on the doorstep. 'Babe,' she slurs when she sees Sam. 'I miss you.'

'Daisy,' Sam says, taking her arm as she lurches sideways. 'What are you doing here? I thought you were seeing someone?'

She makes an angry sound in the back of her throat. 'He was just a rebound, a . . . what do you call it . . . consolation fuck. Not you, babe. He couldn't be you.'

'Daisy,' he sighs. 'Look, you'd better come in and have a black coffee. Then I'm putting you in

261

a cab home.' He gives Mattie an apologetic glance. She rolls her eyes.

Daisy slumps at the table, red hair straggling around flushed cheeks. One of her breasts is in danger of slipping out of her low-cut top.

'Think I might be sick . . . ' She sags forwards.

Sam jumps up, but Mattie motions him to sit. She helps Daisy up and guides her out of the room. 'Hold on. Bathroom's this way . . . '

Then George is there, on the threshold, arms out. 'Front door was open.' He beams at Sam. 'There he is.'

Sam finds himself crushed to his brother's chest, his glass tilting and slopping liquid onto his shoes. He glances towards the hall. 'You just missed Daisy. Mattie's taken her upstairs.'

'Daisy? Ha! Let me guess. She's completely shit-faced?' George winks. 'She's been making the papers every week. Been seen out on the town with about five different men while you've been in the Priory. Think secretly she's enjoying the attention,' he adds.

They sit at the pine table and Sam takes a sip of his drink. Seeing Daisy out of control makes him even more determined not to slide back into bad habits. They called it a nervous collapse, but substance abuse had made everything worse. Now he's out in the real world he's going to go slow, eat healthily, breathe deeply.

Mattie comes in. 'Out cold in my room. What a drama queen.'

She takes a vegetable lasagne out of the oven, and the four of them sit around the kitchen table. Sam raises his soda in a toast. 'To Mattie,

262

for your food and hospitality — and for dealing with drunk ex-girlfriends. Thank you.'

She blows him a kiss across the table.

'So . . . what's next?' George asks, his voice deliberately casual.

Sam sits up straighter. 'Well, we've still got our remaining contractual obligations to Island,' he says slowly. 'The UK tour and stuff. But after that . . . ' He swallows. 'I . . . I want to go solo, George. Just me and my guitar. See if I can write and play the kind of music I set out to make another lifetime ago.' He's been looking down at his plate. Now he glances up at George. 'Are you okay with that?'

George nods. 'It's what I expected, to be honest. There were some clear signs coming from you — have been for a while.'

Sam scratches his head. 'I don't want to let anyone down, but I need to get back to doing what feels right.'

George leans across and touches his shoulder. 'I've got something to tell you, too. I've bought a farm. In Wiltshire. An old manor house. Acres of land. I want out of the business.'

Sam stares at him in amazement. 'I had no idea. Out of the business altogether?'

George shrugs. 'I miss the countryside.'

'But . . . this hasn't come out of nowhere. You must have been planning it. You never told me you were thinking of quitting.' Sam tries to keep his voice neutral.

George's cheeks colour. 'You were in a bad place before you went into the Priory. You needed support.' He gives Sam a steady look. 'It

263

didn't feel like the right time to discuss my plans to leave.'

Sam shakes his head. 'Jesus, man. I'm sorry. I wish you could have talked to me when you wanted to.'

George grins. 'Yeah, I've been dying to tell you that I'm getting my own fucking peacocks at last.'

Sam stares at him, and then laughs. His stomach hurts with the effort, his muscles contracting and squeezing. When he stops, wiping his eyes, he says, 'Hope they appreciate you beating the shit out of your drums.'

Mattie's eyes widen as she looks from one brother to the other. 'I need another glass of wine,' she says. 'That's a lot to take in.'

Luke leans over to grab the bottle of red wine. 'I don't have any grand announcements myself, I'm afraid. So I'll just keep on drinking. Don't mind me.'

'You are such a complete prick, Luke,' Mattie says pleasantly.

Luke raises his glass to her. Mattie is smiling, but her eyes are empty. Sam wishes he was close enough to take her hand. Instead, he says, 'And another thing, I'm going to need a new manager. Mattie, how would you feel about it?'

'What? Me?' Her eyes open wide. 'But what about Marcus? And anyway . . . I don't have any experience.'

'Marcus and I have parted company. At least, we will as soon as the UK tour is over.' He leans towards her. 'You *do* have experience — you manage a household and a child, and you used to work as a buyer at Liberty. You're great at organising. You're good with people. Brilliant persuasive powers. Good sense of style. And I trust you.'

George knocks his knuckles on the table. 'I think it's a great idea. You'll be a good team.'

'Well . . . ' Mattie glances at Luke, who looks bored. 'I guess River will be at school . . . and I could do a lot from home, right?'

Sam nods.

'Luke?' She looks at her husband again.

He shrugs. 'I can't stop you.'

'Then I'll do it.' She turns back to Sam. 'On one condition. That you go and see Dad.'

★ ★ ★

There's a Hound of the Baskervilles baying before Sam's mother answers the door. He rang beforehand to let her know he was coming. She reaches up for a hug. Under her clothes, he feels the creak of some old-fashioned construction that gives her a semblance of a waist. The dogs crowd him, long tails whipping back and forth, huge heads butting at him.

His mother shoos them away. 'Your father's in the library, dear. I'm so glad you've come. Have a cup of tea first, though, and tell me your news.'

They go through to the kitchen. He looks at the dark furniture and floral wallpaper, long fraying curtains at the windows, worn antique rugs on the floor, surfaces gritty with dust, and sniffs the clinging smell of stale cigarette smoke. He hasn't been home since he left for America.

265

Nothing changes in this house. It looks exactly as it did when he was an unhappy boy back from boarding school.

His mother doesn't mention his breakdown.

'Such lovely weather,' she says, handing him a cup of tea, with saucer and teaspoon. 'I've been champing at the bit to get out into the garden. There's so much to do. Are you going to stay with Matilda for long, darling?'

'No. Not long,' he says. 'Just until I feel ready to go back to the new house. It's far too big for me really.'

'Is it completely over with Daisy?' she asks. 'Such a sweet girl. Even if her clothes were a little on the skimpy side.'

'It's over, Mum. She and I weren't right for each other. I'm a single man again.'

'Well, you're at the marrying age, darling. Don't wait around for too long.'

Sam changes the subject, telling her a few details about the new tour, trying to make it interesting for her. But he's nervous. He wants to see his father. This meeting has been a long time coming, and he has things he needs to say. He pushes an envelope into her hand. 'A little something,' he says. 'For new clothes, or plants for the garden, or both ... ' He runs out of ideas. He's not sure what his mother would spend money on. She buys everything on a housekeeping budget — his father has never allowed her access to a joint account. 'Open it later,' he tells her quickly, knowing that the money will make her embarrassed. But he wants her to have it. Escape money, perhaps. 'Come and stay with me in London any time, Mum,' he says. 'You don't need to ring ahead. I've put a spare key to my house in there too.'

'That's so thoughtful, darling,' she says. 'But you know I can't leave the dogs.' She smiles. 'Or your father.'

★ ★ ★

The library is bright with sunshine coming through the big sash windows. His father is sitting in his old leather chair, a newspaper in his hands. Sam has imagined this moment many times. He's run scenarios through his mind in which he shouts at him, explaining how he ruined his life. But recently, he's seen a new version, in which he holds his father's trembling hand, full of forgiveness, the old man repentant before him.

His father peers over the top of *The Times*.

'Hello, Dad,' Sam says.

'Well, sit down.' His father nods towards another chair. 'Don't stand about dithering. Sun's in my eyes.' A cigarette is burning in an ashtray.

Sam pauses for a second, turning on the ball of one foot. Already the situation is slipping away, and he feels himself returning to the past, as if a chain has appeared on his ankle, dragging him back into his role as the disappointing son. But then he takes a breath and sits.

'Seen your mother, have you?' his father asks, taking a drag and stubbing the cigarette out.

'Yes,' Sam says.

'Hmm.' His father shakes the newspaper out and folds it flat on his knees. 'Your mother would like to see more of you.'

'You know I take her out to tea in London every month?'

His father nods. He leans forward. 'And how have you been?'

Sam swallows. He can't remember the last time his father asked such a question. Warmth spills inside, a gladness, a hope. He moistens his lips, preparing to reply. But his father is already speaking again.

'I hear you had to go to a funny farm.'

Sam's throat closes in shock. 'No. It wasn't . . . It was a place I went to voluntarily. I was very tired. Exhausted. I needed a . . . rest.' He coughs. 'I had a kind of breakdown.'

'You always were weak. A dreamer. I know about people like you, with your long hair and your caterwauling.' His father's mouth turns down. 'You've been taking drugs. You might pull the wool over your mother's eyes, but you can't over mine.'

Heat rushes through Sam, and then icy cold. Horror has his body in a stranglehold, and he sits rigid, unmoving. What was he thinking, coming back here?

'Dad.' He leans forward, an urgent need to speak rushing through him. 'You're right. I took drugs sometimes. I drank too much sometimes. I *was* weak.' He wipes his sweaty palms on his jeans. 'But you've never helped me to be strong. Telling someone they're no good makes them distrust themselves. It takes all their confidence away. If you had given me one word of approval, then — '

'Excuses.' His father scowls, and snaps the paper in Sam's direction, as if he's swatting a fly. 'All your generation do is blame your parents.'

Sam takes a deep breath. 'I didn't come here to argue. I came here to tell you that I forgive you.'

'Forgive me?' His father looks startled for the first time.

'For lying to us for all those years, for making Mum complicit in the lie. For telling me to be a gentleman when all the time you were behaving like the worst of men.'

His father gives a sly smile. 'Tell me, did you and your sisters ever want for anything? You never complained about living in this house, having your meals and your clothes provided. Going on holidays. You didn't like the school I sent you to, perhaps. But it's the best school in the country. The very best. You had every opportunity. And you've ended up being . . . what? A drug addict?'

'No, Dad. I've ended up being a very successful musician. I've ended up making a great deal of money. And the thing is,' Sam rakes his hair back from his forehead, 'even though you don't understand, I still forgive you. Because I need to, for me.'

He stands up. His legs are shaking. He looks down at his father and notices the pouches and wrinkles reshaping his face, the edges of his bony knees pressing through his corduroy trousers. He would have liked to re-enact his original script,

269

holding his father's nicotine-stained hands inside his own. That was a fantasy. He feels weary now that he's said what he needed to. But under his blanket of exhaustion, something else stirs, a bright, turning spark of wonder, because he knows, really knows, for the first time in his life, that he will never hear words of approval from his father. He doesn't need to look for them, not ever. For they will never come.

35

Cat, August 1990

Grace comes to find me in the kitchen. 'Nancy's mum's on the phone,' she says in a breathless voice.

'For me?'

She nods, chewing her lip and fidgeting.

I put down my cup of coffee, walk into the hall and take up the receiver. I don't know Nancy's mom very well. She's from New York originally, works in an office, and always seems in a hurry, rushing around in her smart clothes, calling to me from the window of her big car.

'Catrin?'

I stall. For a horrible second, I can't remember her name. And then it comes to me. 'Hi, Beth.'

'I'll get right to the point,' she says. 'I like the novel a lot. Could you come in for a meeting, say, tomorrow afternoon?'

'Excuse me?' My mind is blank. I panic. She's gotten the wrong person.

Grace has appeared. She sits on the bottom step of the stairs, arms looped around her knees, grinning up at me. I make a what's-going-on? face at her. She just grins harder.

'Sorry,' I say into the phone, clearing my throat. 'You were saying?'

'Grace gave me the manuscript of *The Time-Jumping Detectives* a few weeks ago. I'm

271

afraid it's taken me this long to read it.'

'Grace gave you my book?'

'Yes.' She sounds impatient. 'Didn't you know?'

'No.'

There's a pause. 'I see. I did think it was a little odd to send it through her. So,' she clears her throat, 'I suppose the question is, are you interested in having it published?'

I run my tongue over dry lips, making the effort to steady my breathing. I don't have to think about my answer.

'Good. Then we can discuss it tomorrow. There's more work to be done on it, some edits I'd like to talk over with you. Say four o'clock?'

'Right,' I say, gripping the edge of the table. 'Tomorrow. Yes. Sure.' I swallow. 'Where?'

She gives me the address, and I fumble with the pencil attached to the pad we keep by the phone.

'You don't have an agent, I understand?'

'No.'

'No matter. You might want to find someone to represent you now.'

She's gone. I'm holding a purring phone. I put it down. My fingers are damp. I look at Grace, widening my eyes, shaking my head. 'Holy Toledo!'

She laughs, getting up and coming over to me. 'She loved it, didn't she?'

'What made you give it to her?'

'I told Nancy about it, and when you were out, we sneaked into your study to read it. She said it was great, better than most of the stuff her mum publishes,' she shrugs thin shoulders, 'and

I just had the idea, you know, that maybe her mum would love it too.'

I rub my forehead. 'Wow. I need to sit down.' I fold onto the bottom step. 'You are . . . you are incorrigible, and an amazing person, Grace Dunn. I was preparing myself to send it off and get rejections again, like last time. I just . . .' I look at her. 'I never dreamed it'd be good enough, that it would be possible . . .'

Grace laughs. 'I believed in you.'

Her words trigger a memory. A darkened bedroom in Atlantic City. Sam's hands in mine. I close my eyes, pushing the image away, then open them again. 'Hey,' I say. 'How about supper out tonight, with your dad. To celebrate?'

'Oh.' She steps back. 'Can't. I have a rehearsal tonight. For the show. We're doing the whole run-through.'

'Of course you do. I forgot.' She's playing the lead. Rehearsals have been going on for weeks. 'Maybe this weekend, then.'

I realise it's Wednesday. Leo's squash day. And he said he'd stay for a drink afterwards. He won't be home till late. I have a burning need to go out — to do something to mark this. I'll go stir-crazy on my own at home.

I pick up the phone and dial.

'Good afternoon.' Dougie's voice is official. 'Harpers and Queen, can I help?'

'Dougie, it's me,' I say. 'Something incredible just happened. Can you meet for a drink later, after work?'

'Sounds intriguing.' He pauses. 'I should be through by, say, seven? Call for me in reception.'

273

Grace emerges from the bathroom dressed in her rehearsal clothes. She turns around so I can tame her hair. With a mouthful of bobby pins, I tell her, 'I'm going to meet Dougie for a drink, but I'll swing by and get you afterwards.'

'Sweet,' she says. Her new favourite word.

I don't go back to the house after I've dropped her at Miss Miller's Dance Academy. I'm still in my denim shorts and an old shirt of Leo's, my skin smelling of pond water. I know Dougie will disapprove, but my nerves are too much for walls and rooms.

I drive into town. I love my new driving freedom. Leo made sure I had lessons, and when I passed my test, he got me a little runaround. I slip Sam's album out of my bag and put it in the CD player. The sound of his voice surrounds me. His music fills me with energy, and as I drive, I smile, because I realise we've both fulfilled our dreams, even if we did it separately.

I wonder what edits Beth is talking about, what kind of illustrations the book will have, and when it will come out. I have no idea what sort of money I might get paid. I feel like such a rookie.

I'm too early for Dougie, so I drive slowly across Waterloo Bridge, looking at the wide expanse of river, and park up on the South Bank. Everyone is outside — it's a perfect summer evening. Couples on benches coo at each other. Kids dodge in and out of legs, clutching ice creams. Roller-skaters whizz by. Under the pink-tinged light, the brutalist grey blocks above me take on a softer shimmer. I wander along the river, looking at the water, the boats, the buildings on the other side. There are performers doing tricks; a living statue painted silver stands motionless and unblinking on a box.

It's as I walk past the Queen Elizabeth Hall that I see his face. Those almost-black eyes under dark brows, his long, crooked half-smile. I stop, my mouth dry, my heart thumping. It's a poster advertising a gig by the Lambs. I look at the date. It's tonight. There's a 'sold-out' banner pasted across it.

I turn away, taking deep breaths.

I fumble in my bag, find a pen, tear a blank page out of my notebook. Perhaps it's the confidence of knowing my novel is going to be published, or my reckless mood, or just the glory of the sun-soaked evening, but I want him to know that I'm in London, and that I still think of him. I want a connection. Even one as small as him reading a few scribbled words on a torn scrap of paper.

*Sam, remember me? I'm living in London
now. I'm married. I've heard your songs
on the radio — I know you've made it big
with your music. Just wanted to say well
done. It was what you always wanted.
Hope you're happy. Love, Cat.*

I walk into the foyer. It's eerily empty. Too early yet for an audience to start milling about. I don't know where I can leave my note. There's someone in uniform behind a desk. 'Hi.' I smile a smile that I hope won't make him think I'm a crazy fan. 'I . . . I have a note for Sam Sage. I'm an . . . old friend. Is there somewhere I can leave it?' I turn the small, folded square between my fingers.

He gives me a bored look. 'Just go through to the green room,' he says, inclining his head towards a door.

I look at the door and swallow. 'Oh, right. Thanks.'

I push at it, go along a corridor, down some steps and through another door. There's nobody about. I'm in a dim, deserted room. There are benches, chairs, a sofa with its back to me. A table stands against the wall with unopened bottles of wine and water. I wonder where to put the note.

It's only as I walk around to the front of the sofa that I see him. He is asleep, taking up the length of it. I freeze. Suddenly the air in my lungs is too loud, the creak of my sandals against the floor deafening. I hold my breath, pinching the note hard, as if that could stop me from plummeting through time and space.

He's snoring gently. His eyelashes are dark sweeps over his cheekbones, his lips parted a little. I've kissed that mouth, I think.

I sit on a chair opposite the sofa. I don't take my gaze from his face. Should I wake him? Should I leave the note next to him and creep away? I decide on the second option. I am a coward. And then he opens his eyes.

I keep completely still, my face deadpan, as if I

could scrabble into the centre of myself, hiding in plain sight. He blinks and widens his eyes, shock making his expression comical. It's the trigger for a smile that bursts from deep inside me. And he echoes it, sitting up, raking a hand through his hair in a familiar gesture.

'Cat?' He gives a small dog-like shake. 'I thought I was dreaming.'

He swings his legs around, plants his feet and stands in one easy movement, opening his arms. I walk into them without thinking, closing my eyes. Something that was lost reignites, that feeling I had with him years ago, alive inside me again. As if I've come home. The smell of him is pungent and male, earthy and sharp, like fresh wood shavings. It's almost as if I could open my eyes and find myself in the funeral parlour again with him, with everything still before us.

He squeezes hard. 'What are you doing here?' He's holding one of my hands. 'I can't believe it's really you. Jesus. What a surprise. How did you know where to find me?'

'I didn't,' I say, slipping my hand from his. 'It just . . . happened.'

'Can you stay? For the gig? We could see each other afterwards.' He flicks a glance at his watch. 'The others will be here soon.'

I shake my head. 'I'm already late. I have to meet a friend. And after that, I'm collecting my stepdaughter.'

'Stepdaughter?' He takes a breath. 'Well, how about a coffee then, tomorrow? We're leaving at lunchtime. We're doing a UK tour.'

'Sure.' I nod. 'Coffee. Where shall we meet?' I

277

can't stop looking at him. There are faint lines around his eyes and mouth, but otherwise, he's hardly changed from the boy on the beach in Atlantic City. This is beginning to feel surreal, like an out-of-body experience.

'Our hotel's in Kensington,' he's saying. 'I mean, I have a house here, but it's easier to stay with the rest of the band, and anyway, Mattie's there at the moment, my sister . . . Long story . . . '

'Kensington? What's the address?'

'Yeah, sorry, it's . . . ' He presses his fist to his forehead. 'The Park Grand. Near the Cromwell Road.' He's flustered, but his nerves are making me calm. It's okay, I tell myself. This is bound to trigger emotions. It's probably shock. It doesn't mean anything.

'Got it,' I say. 'Eleven o'clock?'

I recognise the glint in his eyes, the slightly crooked teeth when he smiles. I thought I'd forgotten exactly what he looked like, but all the time, the print of him was there, stamped inside me.

'Great.' I take a step away, still looking at him. 'Break a leg, I guess. I'll see you tomorrow.'

He puts his fingers to his lips, and holds them up in a salute, in a kiss that isn't blown.

★ ★ ★

I'm not sure how I drive, how I find my way to National Magazine House. My fingers tremble against the steering wheel, fumbling as I lock the car, dropping my keys, just missing a disaster

278

down the drain. I clasp my hands as I ask the man on the front desk to tell Dougie I've arrived. Dougie takes one look at my face, and hurries me out of the smoky-mirrored reception into the streets of Soho.

We're in the Groucho Club, at a corner table, two glasses of wine between us, before he says, 'You were late. You're never late. What's going on?'

'Sorry. About being late.'

'It doesn't matter.' He makes an impatient expression. 'Tell me. From the beginning. This incredible thing?' He leans closer, grinning. 'Except I think I've guessed. You're pregnant, aren't you?'

'What? No — no, it's still not happening. In fact, I have a doctor's appointment next week.' I put my hand on my stomach for a moment. 'Just a check-up. Leo's insisting.' I push my hair behind my ear impatiently. 'I was ringing to tell you that my kids' novel is going to be published — *The Time-Jumping Detectives.*'

Dougie gasps and grabs my arm. 'Hen, that's fantastic!'

'Then I saw him. I saw Sam. Sam Sage.'

'What?'

'You know . . . the singer . . . '

'Of course I know who he is,' he snaps. 'The whole world does. What do you mean you saw him? Across the street? On a stage? On screen?'

'In a green room. Just him and me.'

'You're kidding? No! What did he do when he saw you?'

'He hugged me. It was like no time had gone

279

by. He looked the same. It felt so . . . I don't know . . . normal being with him. Even after everything that's happened.'

'Then what did you do? Just chat, or . . . '

'We talked. I can hardly remember what we said now.' I take a strand of my hair and roll it between my fingers. 'I guess I was sort of in shock.'

'And then you just left?' He puts his hands to his head in a pantomime of despair. 'You should have cancelled me!'

'We're meeting for a coffee tomorrow.' I rub the back of my neck. 'I'm surprised he didn't throw me out. He must think I didn't bother to reply to his letters. I've got to tell him. Remember?' I bite my lip. 'Mom burnt them.'

'God, yes.' He rolls his eyes. 'But now . . . Oh my God, this is so romantic.'

'No.' I sit up, tugging at the collar of Leo's shirt. 'It's not romantic. I'm married. And he's probably in a relationship.'

'Don't you read the papers? He and his long-term girlfriend had a break-up.' He looks smug. 'Lots of photos of her in dark glasses, falling out of taxis drunk. That sort of thing.'

I frown at him. 'Just gossip. Speculation. He could have a new girlfriend by now. Anyway,' I shake my head, angry with myself, with the way the conversation is going, 'that's irrelevant. Obviously. It's not going to be anything except . . . except a chance to say a proper goodbye, to set it all straight.' I look down at my lap. 'It's my chance to apologise.'

Dougie sniffs loudly. 'Your cheeks are on fire.

Your eyes are bright enough that the beauty department would be asking what drops you've been using. Or could it be blue mascara?' He leans close, squinting. 'No.' He wags his head back and forth. 'It's him. He's got to you, hasn't he?'

'One coffee,' I say. 'That's all. It's the surprise of it — I mean, it was crazy, seeing him like that, and straight after the news about my book.' I push my hair behind my ears again. 'I have a meeting tomorrow with a publisher.' I offer him a new topic, a distraction. 'What should I wear?'

He looks at my shirt. 'Something clean.'

I'm regretting telling him. He's making it into something it's not. It's my fault. I've stumbled into a confession I shouldn't have made. I finish my glass of wine, and explain that I have to leave to pick up Grace. Dougie sighs and tells me I'm no fun. But, craning his neck, he sees some people he knows at the bar.

We get up from the table. 'Don't say a word about this,' I tell him. 'Promise?'

'Obviously.' He kisses me on both cheeks, and sways through the tables towards the bar, waving at someone.

* * *

As I drive north through the evening traffic, I think about whether I'm going to tell Leo about meeting Sam today, and our appointment tomorrow. It's complicated — he knows nothing of my history with Sam, and there seems too much to explain. I don't want him to feel jealous

281

or anxious. Especially as he doesn't need to. I won't see Sam again. We live in separate worlds.

I drive past Regent's Park, noticing lovers walking arm in arm through the warm night. I look away, keeping my attention on the stop lights ahead. But shouldn't I at least try and tell Leo the truth? I voice the question aloud, as if I'm checking in on it, weighing it up, giving it due consideration. But all the time, I know the answer is no. I want to own this for myself: an hour in a coffee shop with Sam. After all these years, it's not much. But it's mine.

36

Sam, August 1990

His instinct was to hug her and hold her close. Being with her again made him breathless with an uncomplicated happiness he'd almost forgotten was possible. And even though she's been out of his life for years without explanation, and her hair smelled like muddy water, and she's gone and got herself married and acquired a stepdaughter, none of it actually matters.

Last night's performance passed in a blur. Afterwards, he lay awake till the early hours, memories of Atlantic City playing in his head. He's wiped out. He rubs his face, the stubble scratchy, his furred tongue sticking to his teeth. He wonders what reasons she'll give for not replying to a single letter, for just getting on with her life as if what they'd had meant nothing.

He has a strong espresso sent up with room service, a basket of croissants, some fruit. He needs to eat, to feed his brain, perk himself up. She must have seen him on TV or heard the Lambs on the radio at some point, yet she didn't get in touch. He always hoped she'd write or phone or something, especially after 'Ocean Blue' came out. Island Records isn't exactly hard to find. And how long has she been in London? To know she's been here when he presumed she was far away in the States is disorientating. He

283

eats three croissants without tasting them, getting buttery flakes on his chin, and has a long, hot shower. When he's dressed, reception calls.

'Tell her to walk down Hogarth Road, away from the Cromwell Road,' he tells the man on the desk. He has a plan. 'There's a pub on the corner. The Stag and Hounds. I'll meet her outside, in five minutes.'

★ ★ ★

He's wearing his cap pulled down low, and sunglasses. She smiles, showing the gap in her teeth, the little crease above her top lip. 'You're in disguise,' she says in a deadpan voice. 'Anyone following you?'

'There're a few fans hanging around the entrance to the hotel,' he says, feeling suddenly embarrassed. 'I slipped out through the kitchens. Didn't want you getting pushed around or anything. Some of these . . . kids . . . they can get a little overenthusiastic.'

'Sorry.' She flushes. 'I don't even know why I said that — I didn't mean to tease you,' she says. 'I'm just nervous, I guess.'

A long chauffeur-driven car pulls up beside them. She startles. 'It's all right,' he says quickly. 'I ordered it. Will you come with me? I want to show you something,' he explains as he opens the back door.

She peers into the leather interior of the car and turns to give him a quizzical look.

'I know you're not crazy about surprises.'

'You remembered,' she murmurs.

'This is a good one,' he says. 'A good surprise.' They lock gazes. 'Trust me.'

Silently she slides onto the seat. He gets in next to her, and sits with his hands on his knees, hoping he's doing the right thing. He has to keep telling himself that she's married, that everything is different now. He snatches glances at her profile, wishing he knew what she was thinking.

★ ★ ★

'The Heath?' she says, as the car stops in the car park. She seems disappointed.

'Maybe you've guessed already,' he says. 'Or maybe you don't remember . . . but I want to show you the bench. The one I told you about?'

She looks at him with a strange expression he can't interpret. 'I know it well, Sam,' she says in a low voice. She turns to walk in the direction of Parliament Hill. He follows, stumbling over the rough grass, confused, his plan falling in tatters behind him.

When they reach the lip of the hill, the bench is empty, the hawthorn leaves rustling in the breeze.

'I come to the Heath a lot,' she says, running her fingers over the worn armrest. 'I live just around the corner. I found this eventually — took a while, reading all the inscriptions on all the benches. I used to come and sit here. I suppose I thought that one day I'd find you.'

She sits down, and he follows. 'I don't understand,' he says. 'You were looking for me?'

Her expression gives him his answer.

'But . . . why didn't you reply to my letters?'

Her cheeks flush. 'I never knew you sent them. My mom took them and burnt them. I only found out recently.' She looks at him, and then glances away. 'I thought . . . I thought you'd forgotten me.'

He thinks he must have misheard. 'Your mother *burnt* them?'

She nods again. 'She thought she was doing the right thing, however wrong it was.'

He feels sick. Her mother deliberately ruined their relationship. He recalls thinking he could have charmed her, won her around. Maybe he could have. But Cat never gave him the chance.

'You didn't show up at the airport.' He's aware of the tremor in his voice, and swallows hard.

She touches his arm. 'I'd planned to come. Like we arranged. But my dad was arrested. I had to go home. Sort things out. It was an emergency. I had no way of contacting you.' She keeps her hand there, and he feels her fingers burn through the fabric of his shirt. 'Later, I wondered if I could have phoned the airport, paged you or something . . . ' She blinks. 'It was hard to think straight. Then it was a mess — Dad behind bars, arranging lawyers, his trial. He refused bail. Mom lost the plot. All the time, I wanted to hear from you so bad.' Her voice twists. 'I was gutted when you didn't write. When I thought you didn't write,' she corrects quickly.

'Shit.' He takes a long breath and sighs it out. 'If only I'd known . . . If I'd had just a bit of hope, I would have got on a plane and come back for you.'

286

They both sit, silent, numb.

'Why was he arrested?'

'Embezzlement,' she says. 'I told you he was a gambler? He's done his time. Doesn't gamble any more. He's settled in Alaska.'

'And so . . . you somehow arrived in England. How long have you been here?'

'About seven years.'

He stares at her. 'I thought you were still in the US. On our American tour, each city we went to, I wondered if you might be at the concert.'

She gives him a puzzled look.

'I phoned the funeral home,' he explains. 'They said you'd left Atlantic City. I thought you were somewhere else in the States.'

She shakes her head.

'And now you're married?'

'Yeah.' She roots about in her bag and finds a tissue. Blows her nose. 'I got a job over here as an au pair to a little girl. Her dad's a single parent. And . . . after a few years, he asked me to marry him.'

He works to keep his voice steady. 'You love him?'

She pushes her hair from her forehead. 'Of course.' But she doesn't meet his eyes.

He wants to be generous, do the right thing; he should tell her how happy he is for her, but the words won't come. 'We had something good, Cat,' he says instead, shaking his head. 'And we lost it.'

She seems to hold her breath, her eyes wide. Then her shoulders collapse. 'It was my fault. I didn't get to the airport. My mom destroyed your letters.'

'It wasn't your fault.' He grabs at her hands, holds them tightly inside his own. 'I should have believed in you more. I should have known you'd never have ignored my letters.'

She gives a small sob, and tugs her hands back from his. 'I have to go soon. I have an appointment this afternoon. And there's Grace . . . I have things to sort out for her costume, a performance she's doing.' She sits up straighter. 'I can walk home from here.'

'Yes.' He nods. 'Of course.' She has a life that has nothing to do with him. He glances at his watch. His own life is calling, or the thought of Marcus is — because Marcus will kill him if he's late for the bus. 'Look, I've got to go too.'

'Right,' she says, nodding.

He doesn't move. He can't leave her like this. 'I know you're married. But . . . ' He folds his lips together, frowning. 'But can I see you when the tour's finished? I'll be away for a couple of months. I could call when I'm back. I live in London now, so it would be easy . . . Just a coffee, or a walk in the park?' He hurries on, not wanting a negative response. 'We still have stuff to say, don't we? Gaps to fill in? Just as friends.' He swallows. 'What do you think?'

She stares at the view. She takes a long time to speak, and he can picture the band gathered with their bags in reception, the bus out front, Marcus pacing the pavement. A crowd gathering.

'Okay,' she says. 'But don't phone. Write me. Here's my address.' She rips a page from a notebook in her bag and scribbles on it. She looks at his sceptical expression. 'I know. The last writing plan didn't turn out so well.'

He takes the folded page and slips it into his pocket. Of course, he realises he can't phone her at her home; her husband might answer. He jots his own address down and hands it over as he stands up. 'I'm going to have to run back to the car.' He kisses her cheek, inhaling the scent of her skin; not pondy any more, but a suggestion of green sap, and something sweet, like maple syrup. 'I'll see you soon.' He turns away, past the hawthorn bush. He doesn't look back.

What the fuck are you doing, you total idiot? Those are the words Mattie will use when he tells her. She's the only one he will tell. The only one who'll understand, despite the tongue-lashing she'll give him.

He's on the sun-bright path leading downhill to the car park, and the heels of his boots clip the surface as he breaks into a jog and then a sprint. He pounds along, careening around corners, running faster than he's run since he was on the beach in Atlantic City, hand in hand with Cat, escaping the shadowy threat behind them. A laugh bursts from his throat, his hat flying from his head, and he hopes to God that there are no photographers lurking behind any bushes.

37

Cat, October 1990

It's not this Sam that I love. Not the Sam Sage of today — the rock star, the man I saw in the green room. It's who he used to be, who we used to be: the twenty-somethings in Atlantic City, giddy with romance, innocently hopeful, full of plans and dreams. I think I've always been in love with the memory of those people. Seeing Sam again like that, so unexpectedly, was a trigger for remembered feelings to come rushing back. And it was confusing for a moment. But I'm not confused any more. I know where I belong, and who I love.

★ ★ ★

Leo and I sit in the darkness, gazing at Grace as she pirouettes across the stage, chin up, head snapping round as she turns. Her tutu sticks out above taut legs, her arms curve. She looks like a doll, I think, remembering suddenly the dolls on the floor of her room, hacked to pieces. The hall is loud with clapping and cheering. It's an enthusiastic crowd, mostly other parents, family and friends of the young dancers. Grace is curtseying, her cheeks pink, eyes bright.

Leo and I wait outside the stage door with a group of other parents. The fall night has a chill, and I shiver. Leo puts his arm around my shoulders and gives me a brisk rub. 'Why don't you sit in the car, darling?'

Since my body has failed to get pregnant, he's started to treat me like an invalid. The doctor could find nothing wrong. 'I'm sure it's all just a matter of time.' He gave me a paternal smile. 'Stop thinking about it, and it'll happen.'

But our sex life has altered under the strain. Already it's become a kind of chore. Something riddled with anxiety instead of filled with pleasure. Leo takes my temperature every day, knows my cycle better than me, marking my fertile days on the calendar. He's disappointed when, every month, I come out of the bathroom shaking my head.

Grace appears, still wearing the mask of her stage make-up.

'Good job!' I congratulate her.

'Well done,' Leo says. 'Proud of you, darling.'

We walk back to the car, arms linked, a family unit. This is enough, I tell myself. The three of us. I wish it could be, because since meeting Sam, my feelings have changed: I still want to get pregnant, but knowing that Sam and I could have had a life together makes me feel odd about having a child with Leo. But that's ridiculous. Leo is my husband. I can't back out now. He and Grace are counting on me.

★ ★ ★

At supper, Grace looks at us both. She's nervous, I can tell, because she's doing that thing

291

with her mouth, chewing her lips, pressing them together.

'Dad . . . Cat . . . guess what? Miss Miller says I have what it takes to be a professional dancer.'

'Well, that doesn't surprise me!' I tell her. 'You're so good. Do you want to dance as a career?'

She nods. 'More than anything.'

I know how that feels. Want becomes need. The need entered my bones, lives inside me still. I can see it's the same for Grace. Her eyes shine with passion. 'Then we need to talk to Miss Miller,' I glance at Leo for confirmation, 'find out what we should do to make that happen.'

'Just hold on a minute.' Leo places his knife and fork together on his plate. 'I think perhaps Miss Miller should have talked to me first.'

'Oh, she does want to talk to you,' Grace rushes on, breathless with excitement. 'She says to discuss extra classes with her, and I should switch to a dance and drama school. Urdang maybe, or Tring if I want something more classical. I'll need to audition.'

'Dancing's not a sensible career choice, darling,' he says. 'Even if you were to make a success of it, it's short-lived. You're a clever girl. Keep it as a hobby and find something more worthwhile to do.'

'Oh, but please, Daddy,' she says. 'I really, really want to be a dancer.'

I hold my breath, watching her lips tremble. She's staring at him with eager eyes.

Leo clears his throat. 'No, Grace. I'm sorry. I just can't support it.'

'Dad.' She leans across the table. 'Please.'

'Leo,' I say quickly. 'Couldn't we just talk about it? Grace is really talented. And if this is her dream . . .'

He gives me a warning look. 'The dreams of thirteen-year-olds are liable to change.'

'I won't change my mind,' she says quickly.

'I won't either,' he tells her. 'You'll stay at school and take your exams as planned.'

Grace stands up, pushing back her chair so fast that it falls behind her. Her cheeks are flushed, and she's blinking back tears. 'I hate you.' She runs from the room.

I listen to her feet crashing up the stairs. 'Maybe you should go to her?'

He sets the fallen chair upright, and pours himself a rare second glass of wine. 'She'll calm down.'

I begin to rise, but he puts his hand on mine. 'Give her time.'

'But why don't you want her to dance?' I sink back into my seat. 'I don't understand. I mean, we know how good she is . . .'

'I don't want her to be rejected.' His voice has an edge. 'I won't let her know the humiliation of failure — I'd never forgive myself. She's worth more than that.'

A light bulb has switched on in my head. 'You mean, like Elizabeth?'

He nods. 'I don't want Grace following her mother down *that* road.'

'I think you're wrong,' I say quietly. 'Grace isn't like Elizabeth. She's talented. Disciplined. This isn't fair on her.'

293

'Cat, I know you're trying to help,' he tells me. 'But I'd rather you didn't interfere in this. She's my daughter. I know best.'

I sit back quickly. It feels as though he's slapped me. I expected him to be more supportive of Grace, less old-fashioned in his views. But it's his need for control that shocks me most. Although maybe his attitude shouldn't be such a surprise, I realise, not when I think about how he's used to being respected, obeyed without question when he's in the operating room.

★ ★ ★

When I check on Grace, she's a dark shape under the covers, her hair spread over the pillow, the cat curled behind her knees.

'Are you still awake?' I whisper.

'I can't sleep,' she says, her voice husky with tears. 'How can he be so mean? I just . . . I feel like dying. Like throwing myself out of the window.'

'Hey.' I sit down next to her and hold her hand. 'Don't say that. Shall I stay for a bit?'

'Yes, please.' Our fingers entwine. 'Cat?' she asks in a hesitant voice. 'Do you think he'll change his mind?'

'You know your dad. He's pretty stubborn when he believes he's right about something.' I lean closer. 'Grace, just because you can't switch schools, it doesn't mean you should give up. There are plenty of contemporary dancers who get into it in their twenties. Never say never.'

She gives a shuddering sob, and squeezes my hand.

'And your dad's right about you getting your exams,' I add. 'It'll give you options.'

'I don't care,' she says, 'I don't care about anything any more.'

'Hey.' I give her hand a little shake. 'You'll get past this. It feels like the end of the world. But it's not.'

She shrugs. 'Cat . . . about you having a baby . . . is it really going to happen?'

I run my palm over the sheet. 'These things can take time, and it's only been ten months. It's completely normal. I'm going to the hospital for a few tests — your dad's pulled some strings to get me an appointment. I'm sure everything's fine.'

'Having babies can be dangerous, can't it?' There's a catch in her voice.

'Not really, not nowadays,' I add quickly, leaning down to kiss her forehead. 'Nothing for you to worry about.'

Her diary is on the floor, pages splayed. I pick it up and put it on the bedside table, my fingers lingering for a second on the closed cover. She's just turned thirteen, and I wonder what secrets she's scrawled in there, what teenage angst I'd discover. She must have poured out her heart this evening, raging against Leo's decision. I hope it helped.

★ ★ ★

I climb into bed with Leo, and after a quick hug, he turns away from me. It's not one of our nights, and I'm relieved, because timetabled sex is the last thing on my mind. I'm still angry with him for not even considering the idea of Grace dancing. I remember how disappointed I was when there wasn't money for me to go to college; the sense of being left behind that haunted me. Leo's asleep already. It's a talent he has, his ability to switch off, whatever else is going on.

I lie beside him, listening to the rush of air through his open mouth, the slight wet clicking noise he makes when he's sleeping. I twist the plain gold ring around my finger. And very clearly, I hear Mom's voice, *Regret is pointless, Catrin. Best just to make decisions that will save you from the sorrow of it.*

It startles me, that word. *Regret.* I push it away. Regret has no place here, I tell myself, no place in my mind, in my vocabulary. It's only stolen through the cracks in my consciousness, like a thief wanting my happiness, because I had a postcard from Sam. Nothing at all for weeks and weeks. And then a card from Rome.

Home next week. Shall we meet at the bench? Give me the day and time and I'll be there.

★ ★ ★

When I found it lying on the doormat, a prickle of fear shivered across my skin. What if Leo had found it? What kind of reckless stupidity made me give Sam my address? Why did I agree to see him again?

I send a note as brief as his.

Sorry, this isn't going to work. We can't be

friends. It's best if we don't see each other again.

He'll understand it's better this way.

I roll over onto my hip and put my arm around my husband's chest, my face pressed into his back, the fabric of his pyjamas soft under my cheek. I wait for sleep to come for me. A car changes gear outside. The pipes gurgle behind the wall. Leo's heart beats in the palm of my hand. This is where I belong.

★ ★ ★

The hospital waiting room is busy. The woman across from me sits holding hands with a man I guess must be her husband. A woman on my right is crying, her partner's arm around her. I'm here alone, because I didn't want Leo to have to rearrange his patients. And if he'd come too, it would have given the occasion more gravitas than I wanted it to have.

I pick up a magazine and flick through the pages, skimming the text, glossy images sliding by, adverts shouting their messages. I'm not really concentrating on what I'm looking at; I just want to forget the tests I've been through: the prodding and poking into my most intimate spaces, the scan machine swallowing me inside the claustrophobic tunnel of its roaring mouth.

And then suddenly Sam's face is there, looking at me. I shut the magazine with a gasp. Opening it again, I'm staring down at a photo of him, beautiful in a dark jacket with the collar

297

turned up. There's another of all the band members arranged in a group, giving the camera their best poker faces, Sam in the centre, a tiny smile playing about his lips. The article to go with the photographs is titled: *Sam Sage and the break-up of the Lambs. I'm tired of making music I'm not proud of, says the rock heart-throb.*

I feel my cheeks redden, and glance around. Nobody is looking in my direction. I begin to read, racing through the copy, gobbling it down before I'm called in. Sam talks about looking forward to taking a step away from what he calls 'the rock circus'. He says that he has exciting plans for a new solo album. The writer asks him if he'll be keeping the name Sam Sage or reverting to his real name. I stop, and reread the line, feeling dizzy. His real name? And then the facts come tumbling at me: Jack Winterson changed his name to Sam Sage after a rift with his family. His father and mother still live in his childhood home, a six-bedroom house in Berkshire. The drummer in the band is his long-lost half-brother.

'Catrin Dunn?' A nurse is standing at the front of the waiting room.

I give a guilty start and close the magazine, tossing it onto the table. I follow the nurse into a small room, where a male consultant gestures for me to sit down. The look on his face is grave. I am trying to get over the shock of Sam's lies. But seeing my consultant's expression, a beat of fear has started in my belly, drowning everything else. My mouth is dry; I wait for him to speak.

'Isn't your husband here, Mrs Dunn?' he asks.

I shake my head, wishing that Leo had come.

'It's your fallopian tubes, I'm afraid,' he says. 'I'll show you on the scan images in a moment, but suffice to say, they are blocked.'

'Oh.' I have a moment of dizzying relief. Nothing life-threatening. Surely this can be fixed? 'Can't you unblock them?'

'It's not that simple. There are operations,' he says slowly, 'but they're not always successful for tubes as badly damaged as yours. And . . . ' he pauses, 'there would be a risk of an ectopic pregnancy.'

'I don't understand.' I frown. 'Why are they this badly damaged?'

'There are various reasons for blocked tubes, and, as was your own experience, usually no symptoms. In your case, we think it was the ruptured appendix you suffered as a child. The damage was done then.'

'My appendix?' I'm startled, my hand moving to the scar hidden under my clothes. 'So all this time . . . I couldn't have got pregnant . . . ' I swallow. 'Isn't there anything else we can do?'

He taps his pen on the blotter. 'There is the possibility of IVF, as that bypasses the fallopian tubes. But that's a discussion to have at a later date . . . ' He pauses and looks at me over his glasses. 'And one you will no doubt want to involve your husband in.'

★　★　★

As I walk towards the Underground station, my head is muddled with new information. The idea

299

of an operation scares me, and I don't like the idea of IVF either, guessing it will entail more poking and prodding, and sex itself becoming redundant. There is already a new tension between me and Leo, a sense, however faint, of a kind of failure on our part to produce a child together. I hazily imagine that IVF will involve Leo having to lock himself in a room with porn magazines and tissues, and passion will be put on hold while we become a science experiment.

I ride the Tube home. The darkened mirror of the train window reflects my pale face. Sentences from the magazine article reel through my mind, and an anger fills me, an anger that wipes away my thoughts about my damaged insides and the puzzle of what happens next for me and Leo and our baby plan. *No lies*, Sam promised me in that hotel room in Atlantic City. I told him everything about my childhood: my dad, Frank. He chose not to confide in me, and instead to lie. He's come back into my life years later, risking the happiness I've worked hard to build, and all the time, he knew he'd been dishonest from the get-go.

Shock and anger curdle in my guts, making me queasy. I'm not sure how I'll eat any supper, how I'm going to talk to Leo about the results of the test, keep a clear head to discuss the possibilities of operations and IVF, when there's this secret fury burning inside me.

I need to see him again. I was wrong about that. I'm going to send a second note cancelling my other message, naming a time for us to meet.

I want to be looking into his face when I ask him why he lied to me.

*　*　*

At home, Leo's mad that I went to my appointment alone. He wants to know every detail of what the consultant said, but it takes me a while to get my words out, my mind still spinning with the shock of Sam's lies and the shock of the news about my damaged reproductive organs.

Leo rubs his chin and says that IVF is the obvious course of action. 'How do you feel about the idea?' he asks.

Right at this moment, I'm feeling a little bit like one of his patients, so I reach for his hand. 'I need to find out about the drugs I'd have to take,' I tell him. 'What side effects they'd have.'

He lets go of my fingers. 'The process is all very straightforward nowadays,' he says. 'No side effects worth worrying about.' He stands up, nodding. 'I'll make some calls in the morning,' he says. 'Find out who we should be seeing. The best man.'

'Or woman,' I say. But he doesn't hear.

I can't sleep for worrying about the process Leo and I are about to embark on, and when I shut my eyes, sentences from the magazine flash up, Sam's lies repeating again and again.

38

Sam, October 1990

Her first note is a shock.

> *Sorry, this isn't going to work. We can't be friends. It's best if we don't see each other again.*

He reads and rereads the words, hoping that they'll magically metamorphose into something different. What made her change her mind? He spends the next day wondering what he can write back to make her reconsider. And then it occurs to him that the reason she's backing out must be because she still has feelings. So when the second note arrives saying she's changed her mind again, telling him to come to the bench, his thoughts scatter and swirl like leaves, catching on possibilities, trembling for a second before being torn away.

The UK tour was a strain; carrying on with the same old set list when he knew the Lambs were over. He got back to London a week late, because at the last minute he had to fly to Rome to do a photo shoot for a men's magazine. The date Cat's suggesting in her second note means he's had to cancel an interview, rearrange an appointment. He remembers her plan of meeting on the beach in Atlantic City after she'd finished work, how vague it seemed, how unlikely. He'd been convinced she wasn't going to show, but she did. They found each other on that wide slice of sand, the ocean beating against the shore.

*   *   *

He walks uphill, pulling his coat tightly across his chest, leaning into the wind. The Heath is a patchwork of gold and russet, the grass a haze of yellow in the dull light. Cat is already waiting for him on the bench, a silhouette against the hawthorn. It makes his throat dry, seeing her, his heart bumping against his ribs as he hurries up the steep slope towards her.

She doesn't smile. He's sweating beneath his thick coat. He'd like to take her in his arms, but she keeps her hands in her pockets, her shoulders stiff.

He sits next to her. 'Hi,' he says. 'It's good to see you.'

He notices her mouth tighten. 'Why did you lie to me?' Her yellow-blue eyes are fixed on his.

His body is rigid. 'What?' He swallows.

'I read an article in a magazine,' she says. 'Your parents aren't dead. And your real name . . . ' she balls her fingers into fists, resting them on her knees, 'is Jack.' She sounds the word as if it tastes bad. 'Jack Winterson.'

He feels winded. He can hardly catch his breath. 'I should have told you,' he manages. He has to try and explain. 'I was an idiot not to. Only I'd just discovered my dad had been keeping another family.' His chin trembles. 'It

303

was a shock to realise my life was built on a pretence . . . the whole of my childhood. That's why I was in the States. I needed time to think. I'd decided to change my name.'

'The first thing I did when I got here,' she says quietly, not looking at him, 'was to go through the phone book.' She snaps her head round to stare at him. 'I tried to find you. I rang every Sage. But I didn't have a hope, did I?'

His eyes sting with the pain of understanding. 'Do you remember that I said I wanted to tell you something?' he asks. 'When you came to the airport. It was this. I was going to explain before I went back to London.'

She stares at him.

'And the letters,' he says. 'When I couldn't tell you in person, I explained it all in writing. I thought that was why you didn't reply. I thought you were angry. I wrote again. I apologised. I sent you a song.'

Her face crumples. 'Oh God.'

He puts out his hand to cover one of hers, but she pulls away. 'Don't,' she whispers.

'There's something else,' he forces himself to admit. 'I had a girlfriend when I met you. We'd grown apart, and I was going to end it anyway, even if I hadn't met you. But I should have told you.'

Cat doesn't say anything.

He scratches a fingernail over the grainy wood of the bench.

'It doesn't matter.' She makes a sound in her throat. 'It all happened a long time ago.' She gets up from the bench and walks a couple of paces

304

away. 'I meant what I wrote in my first note. We can't meet again.'

She stands on the lip of the hill with her back hunched, her arms wrapped around herself. Her hair is tugged by the wind, the yellow and brown strands wild and tangled.

He stands and walks towards her, uncertain of what he can do or say to make this better. He has no words, so he does what he's been wanting to do since he first saw her: he puts his hands on her shoulders and turns her to face him, holding her close, breathing in the scent of her unruly hair. He expected resistance, fury even. But she goes limp, her body collapsing against him.

'My love,' he murmurs.

She pulls away and wipes her nose on a tissue she finds in her pocket. She steps further back, putting distance between them, her breath appearing and disappearing in the chill air.

'I wish . . . ' he says. 'I wish we could turn the clock — '

'But we can't,' she interrupts. She holds herself tall. 'We messed up. And we can't put it right.'

'Can't we?'

'No.' She glances down. 'No.'

He goes back to the bench and sits, elbows on knees, head in his hands. He feels as though he's fallen out of time, out of his life; he's rooted to the bench, unable to move, while his life — the wrong life — is carrying on without him. His mind goes blank. He senses her presence, knows she's sitting next to him. She puts her hand on his. Her fingers are gentle.

He sits up and looks at her. 'What are we going to do?'

She gives a small, bleak smile. 'Nothing,' she says. 'Carry on with our lives. Our separate lives.'

Sam thinks his chest is going to explode with pain. The thump of it is too huge for his heart to manage. The thought of walking away from the bench and never seeing her again is impossible.

'I've got to go,' she says, glancing at her watch.

'Already?' Panic seethes, making him feel sick. 'Can I see you one more time?' he asks.

She shakes her head. 'I'm married.'

'You're talking about duty — '

'Call it what you want,' she interrupts. 'All it means is doing the right thing.'

'But I'm not asking you to do anything wrong,' he argues. 'Meet me here tomorrow, please? To say goodbye properly?'

Her expression wavers and he glimpses her doubt. 'Cat?' he says quickly. 'We've hardly had any time. Let's have a couple of hours together, without being angry or afraid.' His mouth is parched. He's more nervous than when he's standing in front of thousands of people. 'We've got all the explanations out of the way now. The hard part's over. So we can just . . . be us for a little while. Be friends, I mean. Because I thought we were. I'd like to catch up.'

She makes a noise, a kind of groan, and sits with her arms tightly folded, and he knows enough to say nothing. Then she lets her arms fall and bows her head. 'All right. Tomorrow. Here.'

He nods.

'But that will be the last time.' She stands up, and she's careful not to touch him. She shivers. 'Bye.'

'Bye.'

They are awkward as teenagers. He watches her walk away, and as she disappears behind the hawthorn leaves, he collapses back onto the wooden slats. He stares out at the shimmer of the city without seeing it, the pain in his chest subsiding to an ache, strength returning to his limbs. He thinks of the possibility of just remaining here, waiting all night for the next day to come, for the appointed hour. But he's already getting cold, and his dried sweat is itchy. He lumbers to his feet, and his fingers touch the back of the bench for a second, tapping it lightly. He's humming a tune. A fragment of an idea. He's impatient to pick up his guitar, get it down before it's lost.

It's her. Cat. She does this to him, pulls him deep into himself. She always has. It's where all the best music lives: right at the core. He still has tomorrow, he reassures himself, hurrying towards the path. One more time to see her and hold her, and convince her to change her mind. Because they belong together. It's just the way it is.

39

Cat, October 1990

Lying next to my husband's dreaming body, his skin scorching me, I want to turn and kick out at the sheets, get some air. The marriage vows we made to each other thread in and out of my mind, the memory of my fingers grasping my bouquet too tightly, and then in the taxi, the way he picked confetti out of my hair. *You are happy, aren't you, darling?*

We're a team, Leo and me. And now our relationship's going to be tested just trying to get pregnant. I shouldn't see Sam again. But it's only a couple of hours, in daylight, sitting on a bench on the Heath.

I wake to the alarm, my heart racing at the clanging interruption, the scattering of another world.

★ ★ ★

Leo's empty cereal bowl is on the table. The cat jumps up, hopeful for milk. I shoo it away. 'There you are,' my husband says, looking up from his newspaper and kissing my cheek carefully. 'How are you feeling?'

'I'm not ill,' I remind him as I pour kibble into the cat's bowl.

'I know that,' he says gently, taking his jacket

308

from the back of a chair. 'But it must have been a shock to find out about the damage your ruptured appendix caused. These things take time to sink in.'

'Yes. Sorry.' I put a hand on my forehead. 'I just feel a bit . . . touchy, I guess.'

'Understandable. Look, I have to run. See you tonight, darling. I'll call you later with the details of our first hospital appointment.' He drops a kiss on my cheek. 'Exciting!'

Grace comes into the kitchen in her school uniform, back-pack slung from her shoulder. 'What's exciting? What hospital appointment?' she asks, as Leo leaves.

'It seems I have a problem with getting pregnant. So your dad and I are going to talk about maybe having IVF.'

'What's that?'

'A very clever way that doctors can give people a chance of getting pregnant by fertilising an egg outside the body and then putting it back in.' I wipe the drops of spilt milk from the table.

She frowns, biting her lip. 'Will it be painful?'

'Maybe. Not much.'

'I want a baby sister,' she says slowly. 'But not if it's going to hurt you.'

'No,' I tell her quickly. 'It's fine. We'll give it a go. But it may not work — I don't want you to be disappointed.'

'I won't be,' she says in a quiet voice, and bends to give Fat Mog a stroke.

It's then that I see a small red slash on the inside of her wrist. 'Ouch! Did you hurt yourself?'

She straightens up, and turns away, pulling her cuff down. 'Oh, this? It's nothing. Mog scratched me by mistake.'

'Did you put antiseptic on it?'

'Mmm. See you after school,' she murmurs over her shoulder.

'Grace?'

She's gone. I stand alone in the kitchen and put my hands on my belly. Something that was supposed to be simple has turned into something complicated. And now there's Sam, twisting the complication into a tangled knot. I have a flash of memory back to the ball of wool I untangled for Grace, standing in that rainy graveyard.

I look round at the soggy cereal and dirty cups, the dishwasher blinking under the counter, needing emptying. I feel disengaged from it all, as if I'm looking at a film. I put the dishrag on the side of the sink and wipe my hands on my dressing gown. I'm seeing Sam today. It's strange to hold that fact inside me, here in the heart of my home. Everything else falls away. I don't want to think about hospital appointments, or what to cook for dinner tonight; I only want to be with him one last time. I look at the clock on the wall and count the hours before I can start to walk towards the Heath, towards our bench.

★　★　★

He jumps up when I push past the hawthorn leaves. 'Got here ridiculously early,' he says sheepishly.

We smile at each other, suddenly shy. We sit on

the bench and look at the view. It's brighter today, the low sun warm on my face. 'How are we going to do this?' I ask.

He raises his palms. 'Let's just be ourselves. No pressure.'

I give a short laugh. 'Easy to say.'

'I know,' he says quietly. 'But we can try.' He takes a deep breath and I sense his shoulders relaxing. 'I started a new song yesterday. After we met.'

I turn towards him. 'That's wonderful.'

'It's you, Cat,' he says. 'You inspire me. What we have together inspires me. Always has.' He rubs a thumb over a mark on his jeans. 'Did you like the song I wrote — the one about us in Atlantic City?' He hums the tune, singing a few bars. 'Our first hit. It was the start of it all.' He smiles. 'At the time, I thought you might hear it and . . . understand.'

I push away a ticklish strand of hair. 'It came out years after we were together.'

'You didn't read the lyrics? They were printed on the inside of the CD cover.'

'Yes, but . . . ' I shrug. 'I couldn't be sure it was really about me.' I glance at him. 'I couldn't think why you'd write something like that, but not keep in contact.'

'Shit. Yeah.' He scrubs at his face with his fingers. 'If you didn't get my letters, I can see why you'd be confused,' he says. 'This new song in my head is about us too — about being separated and finding each other.'

'For your new album?' I angle my body to face him, warm from the knowledge that I inspire

311

him to write. 'Are you nervous about going solo?'

He shrugs. 'A bit. But it's different this time.' He gives a half-smile. 'I want to write something I'm proud of. I don't need a huge audience. I just need to be able to survive on my work.'

'I'm glad,' I say. 'And you've made loads of money already, haven't you?'

He laughs. 'We did all right,' he agrees. 'Although we had to pay the record company back for money spent on videos and things. And boy, did we do some over-the-top videos.'

He takes my fingers in his and squeezes. The shock of his skin against mine makes me flinch, then, with a small shudder, I let my hand lie quietly inside his. My whole arm feels tingly. I want to lean into him, put my head on his shoulder.

'A hundred years ago,' he says in a different voice, low and intimate, 'there would have been cattle grazing here, locals coming to dig up sand, collect wood for their fires. Just think, we could have been a couple with a smoky cottage to go back to, standing out here, feeling the sun on our faces, the scent of the new ponds in the air. Me reaching for your hand, kissing you, your hair, your mouth, and not caring who saw.'

I can't speak. I slide my hand away from his. He doesn't stop me.

He clears his throat. 'You know, Guy Fawkes and his gang planned to watch Parliament blow up from this vantage point,' he says, 'and there's a myth that Boudicca's buried here.'

'Boudicca! Are you making this up?'

'I used to love reading guidebooks — finding out stuff about places I was visiting. The last few years, I've hardly known what city I've been in.' He shows me a battered book from his coat pocket. 'I found this in a second-hand shop near the Tube station. *Hampstead Heath: The Walker's Guide.*'

'Very sex, drugs and rock 'n' roll,' I say, laughing.

He makes a comedy face and pretends to grab me. I leap up and run down the hill; the boggy ground slurps at my heels, the tussocks of grass make me stumble, but I crash on down the steep slope. Cold air rushes into my lungs and my cheeks sting. He's coming after me; I hear the gulp and splatter of his boots in the mud, the rustle of his coat. And then the thump of his body against mine. He's got me around the middle, holding tight. We're laughing, nearly falling. I twist around to face him, trembling, hands flat on his chest to push him away, but he drops his face towards mine and our mouths meet.

It's as if we're back in Atlantic City, crouching between two parked cars, kissing for the first time. Except I know this man, this mouth, this tongue. We kiss for a long time, and then we stand in the mud, holding each other. I never want to let go. The noises of the park hum around us: leaf whisper, distant voices, birdsong, the far-up zoom of an airplane. I let my arms slacken and move away a little, giving us space. 'That wasn't supposed to happen,' I say quietly.

'Cat.' He takes my hand and presses it. 'I want to be with you.'

I screw up my face, frowning. 'I'm — '

'I know,' he says quickly. 'I suppose I'm asking if . . . if you're happy with him. Really happy.'

'Happy?' I duck my head. 'It's not that simple, Sam. It never can be. Not any more. Two people count on me.'

I don't want to discuss Leo with Sam. It feels wrong.

'But you're talking about duty again.' He gives an impatient shrug. 'Are you going to let duty dictate the rest of your life? What about what *you* want?' I hear the rasp of his breath. 'You know what happened with my dad, how he made me believe I owed him my life.' He holds my arms, looking into my face. 'It wasn't until I met you that I found the courage to stop — to just be myself.' He shudders. 'Fuck duty, Cat.'

'This is different,' I say. 'You know it is.'

His face crumples, and he lets go, turns and trudges back up the hill towards the bench. I follow, stumbling next to him. 'I made a promise,' I say. 'Don't ask me to break it. It's not fair.' I bite my lip. 'You said you wouldn't do this.'

We sit down. He rubs a hand over his face, rough fingers pushing at his skin. The rasp of stubble. 'I'm sorry,' he says.

Neither of us speaks for minutes. I touch the engraving on the back of the bench, '*Still sitting here beside you*,' I read aloud, '*come rain or shine.*'

'Yeah,' he says, with a small smile. 'Makes me

shiver. Weird, isn't it? It's the same idea as the one in Atlantic City — the one with your brother's name.'

I rest my hand on the wooden back. 'As soon as I found this bench, I knew it was the right one. The words made me feel at home, as if I belonged here.'

'We should have an inscription too,' he says.

I tilt my head. 'For Cat and Sam, who found each other and lost each other and found each other again,' I suggest.

He purses his lips, 'Not bad. Not bad at all.'

I fold my arms, laughing, relieved by his humour. 'What would you have?'

'Sam and Cat's bench.' He gives me his crooked smile. 'And then, in capitals: Keep off!'

'Not very public spirited.' I slap his knee lightly. 'Or poetic. I found one once that said, *In memory of Joe, who hated this Heath and everyone on it.*'

He laughs.

'What do they mean to you?' I ask. 'Words on benches? You're the only person I know who has the same obsession as me.'

He traces the engraving with one finger. 'They're a testament, I suppose, a testament to love, in all its foolish bravery. The risk of it, the knowledge of the danger it puts us in, when anyone we love can be taken from us at any moment.' He pauses, a little frown between his brows. 'And then there's the way we can be let down, betrayed, deceived, and yet we still dare to love, to give ourselves to other people — not just lovers, but children and friends and parents.' He

315

looks at me. 'All that love, all that courage: that's what those little plaques mean to me. It's what connects us, I guess — the impossible decision we make to love and go on loving, despite everything.'

Speechless, I nod.

'And you?' he asks.

I clear my throat. 'When . . . when I'm reading someone's name on a bench, I imagine them sitting there. I know I'm in a place that meant something to them, and for a moment, it's as if they're there with me. And even though I never knew them, I remember them. Sounds weird, I know . . . '

He shakes his head.

I lift my shoulders, wanting to explain. 'It's such a simple thing, isn't it? A bench in a park. Something we walk past without noticing most of the time. But it's as if those words — even basic names and dates — kind of resonate with the beautiful bits of what it takes to be human.'

'Cat,' he says, his voice breaking.

My chest tightens, clenches like a fist as I stop myself from reaching for him. Instead, I push my hair back behind my ears, angle my face away.

He understands at once, shifting a little further from me. The air between us is tight with the effort of not touching.

'Tell me what you do.' He's trying to sound normal. 'I mean in your everyday life,' he adds. 'I want to be able to picture you going about your day when I'm not with you.'

'I look after my stepdaughter, Grace.' I close my eyes for a second, knowing that we need to talk our way back into our separate lives. 'I swim here — in the ponds. I love the feeling of swimming outdoors, the mud, the greenery, the air on my skin. I do it all year round. In the winter, we break the ice. And I write for about four or five hours a day. I'm a children's author now,' I tell him. 'I have a two-book deal. My first is coming out next year.'

'Your first novel! Why didn't you say before?' His eyebrows shoot up. 'I've been looking for your name in bookshops, and now it'll be there, where it belongs. What an achievement.'

'Well, I'm not a superstar like some people I know . . . '

'I didn't think Americans were supposed to be modest.' He drapes his arm around my shoulders and squeezes me tight. 'A children's book? You rock, Cat. Always have. Sometimes you just need to say: fuck it, I did it. Take that, world.' He sweeps his other arm towards the view.

He lets go and we sit looking down the slope towards the woods, the distant cityscape and the world beyond. The weather is colder; a slight mist haunts the air, seeps into my bones. I shiver.

'Do you think we would have made it?' he asks. 'I mean, if we'd stayed together?'

'I don't know,' I say. 'I guess all the ordinary stuff would have fallen on our shoulders sooner or later, all the domestic details of sharing a life.'

'I think we would have made it,' he says quietly. 'I think we would have been bigger than that.'

I don't answer, because there's nothing I can say that would make me feel any better, nothing

317

that wouldn't be disloyal to Leo.

'Is this really goodbye?' Sam murmurs.

'What else can it be?' I lick dry lips. 'We can't have an affair.'

'How about we meet, I don't know, once every six months, once a year even?' He says it so quickly that I know he's already thought about it. 'Just so we don't lose contact,' he adds. 'But you couldn't call it an affair.'

I sit up, back straight, my hands caught between my knees. The suggestion rolls around inside my head, and everywhere it touches feels good and possible, and better, so much better than the endless loss of him. But then I remember my conversation with Leo last night, the disappointment in Grace's voice this morning.

'No,' I tell him. 'It really is over, Sam.'

'But . . . I'm going out of London for a while to work on my new album,' he says. 'That takes us into next year, and — '

I stop him. 'You don't understand. I'm trying to get pregnant. We're trying to get pregnant, Leo and me.'

He stares at me, shock wiping his features clean.

'So . . . it's impossible.' I blink away tears. 'I can't see you again.'

He looks as though he's going to say something else, argue perhaps, but he doesn't. He sits with his hands over his stomach, as though what I've said has winded him, stolen the breath from his body; then he takes my face in his hands, cupping my chin and cheeks, and looks into my eyes. We stare at each other. He kisses my mouth, once, briefly.

'I want you to be happy.' His voice is husky. 'I hope you find what . . . what you truly want.'

I manage a nod, placing my fingers over his.

'I will think of you,' he says. 'Every day.'

Our foreheads touch, and then we move away.

Part Four

GONE BUT NEVER FORGOTTEN.
WE LISTEN FOR YOU STILL IN OUR HEARTS.

40

Sam, April 1991

Sam is rewarding himself with a glass of wine. The clocks have recently gone forward, and the gift of evening light lies on the flagstones, bleaching them. There's no noise. Not even the ticking of a clock in this large, comfortable sitting room. The faint baaing of sheep and the trill of birdsong drifts through the slightly open window.

He closes his eyes, letting the taste of the wine linger on his tongue. As soon as they broke from the session, George disappeared off to see his rare-breed sheep, River clutching his hand, his Border Terrier trotting after him. From the kitchen comes the sound of Mattie chatting with George's girlfriend. Delicious cooking smells waft through, accompanied by laughter.

George's farmhouse is a seventeenth-century Jacobean manor. It's a huge, rambling place, with twisting corridors and staircases, ancient wooden beams above open stone fireplaces. Mattie swears she saw a ghost one night when she got up for a pee.

George hasn't given up the music business, not completely; he's installed a recording studio in his coach house. He rents it out to musicians, sometimes even agrees to lay down a drum track, as he's doing at the moment on Sam's first solo album.

Mattie puts her head round the door, a glass of wine in one hand and a bowl of crisps in the other. 'Here you are,' she says, padding over to the sofa. 'This house is so big, it's impossible to find anyone.' She offers the bowl of crisps. Sam shakes his head.

'You should eat more,' she says. 'You've lost weight.'

'Not sure crisps are a recommended source of nourishment.' He raises an eyebrow at her. 'I'm glad George has found someone,' he adds. 'You like her, don't you?'

Mattie nods, takes a sip of her drink. 'Yeah. She's nice. Good cook, too. Speaking of which — supper will be ready in half an hour.' She kicks off her shoes and curls her feet under her, settling on the deep cushions next to him. 'And what about you? Are you still thinking about her?'

He nods.

Mattie sighs. 'Wish you'd never met her again.'

'Don't say that.' He tightens his grip on his glass, sits up straighter, recrossing his legs. 'I can't stop hoping that maybe she'll leave her husband. You left Luke.'

Mattie sighs again. 'I know. And it was the hardest thing I've ever done. I wouldn't wish that on anyone.' She leans closer to him. 'It's time to move on. There are a whole load of women out there, single, available women, who would sell their grandmothers to have a chance with you.'

Sam looks out of the window at the daffodils and the bright lime of the new buds. 'She's just . . . she's just the only woman I want to be with. That's all.'

324

'Sam, come on! There's no such thing as 'the one'. That's a fairy tale. Something people like you make pop records about. Falling in love is actually just a glitch in our brains that doesn't last. Picking someone to have a relationship with? That's different — it's about making the best compromise.' She holds up a placating hand. 'I'm sorry you've lost her, I really am. Only she's trying to get pregnant, Sam.' She looks at him earnestly. 'With her husband. Maybe she already is.'

The thought of Cat pregnant with another man's child pushes into his mind, and he turns away from his sister. 'I understand you're trying to protect me, but I can look after myself.'

She sighs. 'Point taken.' She takes a sip of wine, munches a crisp. 'Changing the subject — I thought the session sounded incredible today.'

He smiles, relieved. 'Thanks. Yeah. It's going in the right direction.'

In his head, the song he began at the bench begins to play. It's nearly finished. He thinks it's as good as 'Ocean Blue'. Better. Excitement makes his hands tremble. He sets his wine glass down carefully on the coffee table. Just in time, as River comes crashing into the room, leaping onto the sofa between his mother and uncle, bouncing over them, full of stories about petting the sheep.

The sharp pain of his nephew's trampling feet jolts Sam into the moment. He folds River in a bear hug, growling into his squirming belly, inhaling scents of boy and sheep, fending off sharp elbows and knees. He needs this physicality — needs to be pinned into the present. The only other time it happens is when he's in the studio, when there's nothing but the music. Outside that, there's always a part of him absent, a part of him with her.

May 1991

It wasn't hard to discover where Cat's book launch was happening. He rang all the local bookshops, and struck lucky with the Hampstead Waterstones. They gave him the date, but said it was invitation only. He has no intention of inviting himself along; he's sure her husband will be there. But the temptation to glimpse her celebrating the publication of her first novel is too great to resist.

He makes sure he's outside the shop after all the guests have already entered. With his hat pulled down and dark glasses on, he allows himself to pause for just a few minutes, squinting through the window display into the back of the store, where people mill about with glasses in their hands.

He searches for her, his gaze rolling quickly over strangers' faces, until she's there, like a subject in a camera lens: radiant, smiling, gesticulating with her hands as she talks to someone. He absorbs the fall of her hair across her cheekbones, the shape of her neck as she turns. He smiles at her joy. 'Well done, my love,' he whispers. 'You rock.'

326

He realises that all the books in the window display are copies of her novel. He wants to pick one up and turn the pages. He moves away, head down, hands in his pockets. He'll go back tomorrow and buy a couple. Maybe there'll be some signed ones. It was enough, he thinks, just to glimpse her.

But as he walks away, his throat feels sore, as if he's coming down with something.

41

Cat, May 1991

There's a party to celebrate my book launch in the local branch of Waterstones — a small gathering of friends — with the bonus of having my book in the store window for a week.

People chat between the shelves of books, glasses in their hands. My publisher makes a speech. Beth tells the story of Grace giving her my original manuscript without my knowledge. She relates that first confusing phone call. It makes everyone laugh, and she raises her glass to Grace, and then to me.

Dougie comes up after I've said my few words of thanks.

'Well done.' He kisses both my cheeks.

'Glad that's over.' I roll my eyes. 'My mouth went dry, and my tongue wouldn't work properly.' I grimace. 'I didn't sound too bad?'

'Don't be silly. You sounded great.' He puts his head to one side. 'You should be proud of yourself.'

'I feel lucky,' I say.

He makes an exasperated face. 'You wrote the book, darling.' He flicks his gauzy scarf behind him. 'What's with you? You look like a wet afternoon.'

'I just have a bit of a headache.' I look at the floor. The new fertility drugs have kicked in, and they're making me sore and bloated.

I don't dare let him see my eyes. Dougie's too sharp and he knows too much. He's the one person who might decipher my expression, reading my real thoughts, asking me questions I can't answer. Leo makes his way across the room and takes my arm, leaning to shake Dougie's hand. I watch Grace with Nancy in the corner, smiling and whispering.

I catch something at the corner of my eye, and take a sharp breath. I thought I saw Sam. I gaze around. He's not here. Of course not. But I'm imagining the feel of his body as he takes me in his arms, tilting me off my feet. He gives me that wide crooked smile. 'Let's get out of here,' I hear him say.

★ ★ ★

There's a giant bouquet of white roses on my bedside table, a present from Leo. The smell of them infuses the room with an overpowering heady sweetness. The perfume makes me remember Elizabeth's funeral. Those heaps of white flowers. The rain. The beginning of all this. My marriage. My life here with Leo and Grace.

When Leo gives me a goodnight hug, he asks, 'You all right? You seem . . . unhappy.'

'Just tired,' I say, wrapping my arms around his back.

'Well, you could stop writing,' he says. 'You've achieved your goal — got a book published — which is wonderful. But now it's time to focus on getting pregnant. You won't be able to juggle being an author and a mother of a newborn, will you?'

I don't say anything. But he doesn't know me at all if he thinks I'm going to stop writing.

★ ★ ★

This morning, I stand in my bra and pants so that he can give me a shot in the stomach. 'Take a breath,' he says. 'Good.' He slides the needle into me. 'All done.' He pats my shoulder.

The injections go into belly fat. They don't hurt. I could give them to myself, but Leo insists on doing it. He's written out charts with all our appointments at the hospital: the ultrasounds, the transferring of embryos. He takes my temperature and pulse, gives me advice on what I should eat, makes me go to bed early. It's not for ever, I tell myself. I'll get pregnant soon and then he'll back off. He can't help wanting to control everything when we're in the medical intervention stage.

Loud music comes pounding through our bedroom wall. Grace has turned into a full-on teenager. She stays locked in her room, playing her CDs, painting her nails green or blue. She's perfected the sulky pout, the dismissive eye-roll as if she's been taking classes. 'Talk to the hand' is her new favourite phrase. I miss my chatty, smiley child.

'I have a good feeling about this round,' Leo is saying. 'Just think, one of them could be our son.' He frowns at the blaring music. 'It's not on,' he says.

'It's fine,' I say.

'No, it's not. I'm fed up with her moods. She needs to be more considerate.'

I start to get up, but Leo motions me to stay. He leaves the room. I hear him knocking and telling Grace to turn the music off. There's a slammed door and then ringing silence. I hear his feet moving quietly on the stairs. He hates to shout.

September 1991

Summer's over. I'm still not pregnant.

November 1991

As I struggle to pull Grace's duvet from its cover, I catch sight of Fat Mog, curled under her desk. He didn't come down for his breakfast. I make chirping noises, watching for the flicker of his ears. The duvet slithers onto the carpet. I reach for the clean cover.

There was no ear-flicker, and I have a sudden clutch of anxiety. 'Mog,' I call. 'Hey, kitty. Greedy-guts. Want some breakfast?'

My breath quickens as I kneel by him. The softness beneath my fingers radiates cold. Under the rug of his fur, his body is stiff. I peer at his face. His eyes are dull, unseeing. 'Oh Mog . . .'

I find one of Leo's old shoeboxes and line it with tissue paper. It's only just big enough. I tuck Fat Mog's tail inside, and bend his paws to fit. I spend the rest of the day dreading the sound of Grace's key in the lock.

Her face crumples when I tell her; she lets out a long wail, her hand over her mouth. I put my arms around her, cradling her head. 'I'm sorry, sweetheart,' I whisper. 'I'm so sorry.'

We bury him near a silver birch at the bottom of the garden. The ground is hard, and it takes both our efforts to dig a hole. She's silent, red-faced, hiccuping with sobs. All her new-found bravado has gone. 'Let's give him a lovely grave,' I say. 'In the spring, we could plant something beautiful over the top.'

Leo is working late. My body is tight with resentment, even though I know it isn't his fault, that he hasn't deliberately stayed away. It's just he's away so much, for work, and all those hours spent playing golf. I thought I'd got used to it. I tell myself it's just the hormones. I need to get a grip.

Grace goes to bed early. She's begun to shut her door at bedtime, but this evening she lets me sit beside her.

'Do you think the IVF will work?' she asks.

'I hope so,' I tell her. 'People often get pregnant on the third try. We'll have to wait and see.'

Her diary lies open on the sheet next to her. 'You're so good at keeping up with it,' I say. 'Remember the first one I got you, for your birthday?'

She nods. 'Makes me feel . . . better. To write things down.'

'Me too.'

She puts up her hand to take the elastic band from her ponytail, and the sleeve of her top slips down, showing the nub of her wrist bone and a

332

thin red mark beside it.

'Did Mog scratch you again?'

Her fingers move to the place, and her mouth trembles. 'His claws got long. It wasn't his fault.'

'No. Of course not. He loved you.' I tilt my head to see the scratch. 'Shall I get some antiseptic?'

'No, it's fine. I did it already.' She lies down. 'Goodnight, Mum.'

I catch onto that one word, and something opens inside me; an expanse of hope, of possibility. 'You . . . you called me Mum.'

She rubs her swollen eyes. 'Do you mind?'

'Mind?' I lean forward to kiss her cheek. 'Grace, I've wanted to hear you call me that for a long time.'

I go to the door to switch off the light. 'Love you, bug.'

March 1992

I take the familiar little white stick into the bathroom with me. It's blank, white as virgin snow. Not even a hint of blue. I don't cry. I drop it in the trash and wash my hands. The truth is, there's a part of me that's relieved. I could never say that aloud. I guess I've lost trust in Leo to do the right thing, for me, for Grace.

August 1992

Leo and I sit in the new private consultant's room like children before a headmaster's desk.

The doctor glances up from our notes. 'I'm sorry, but in my opinion, it's not advisable to continue with more IVF cycles,' he tells us. 'I feel that the negative impact of the procedure now outweighs your chances of success.'

Relief falls through me like a weight of water, tension washing out of my body. I slump back against my chair.

'But we can find the funds for more,' Leo is saying. 'People do continue having cycles beyond this point.'

The consultant shifts his heavy shoulders. 'Statistically, the chance of success is going down.'

'So if you're advising against further IVF,' Leo says, the slowness of his speech betraying his impatience, 'perhaps now is the time to talk about the operation.'

The consultant purses his lips and places his fingertips together. 'I wouldn't advise it,' he says. He glances down at my notes again. 'At thirty-six and forty-one, your ages are working against you. You must understand, the operation can't offer any certainty. And there could be further consequences, as I believe was originally outlined to Catrin. For example, the increased chance of an ectopic pregnancy.'

I glance at Leo. His face is red, and I can tell he doesn't like the way the consultant is treating him; despite being a friend of a friend, this man is not behaving as if they're equals. 'I don't think we can dismiss the possibility of surgery,' he says. 'Not without further advice.'

There used to be hope in Leo's face when he

334

slid the needle into my stomach; now it's more like determination. This process has changed him, or maybe it's just shown me what he was really like all along.

'No.' I press my nails into my palms. 'I'm not having an operation.'

'Of course, darling. It has to be your decision,' he says carefully.

But when he places his hand on my arm, my skin shrinks from his touch.

Outside the consulting room, he says, 'The man's an idiot. We'll get a second opinion.'

Anger flares. 'Listen to me. We've got one child already.' I tug at his sleeve. 'She's a teenager. She's finding life difficult. I worry about her. Our focus should be on her, not trying for something that doesn't exist.'

He nods, but he's not really listening.

* * *

Sometimes I write Sam notes. They say, *Please come, I need to see you.* Or, *I've changed my mind. I have to be with you, whatever the cost.* They ask him to forgive me, to come and get me, or to meet me at our bench. After I've written them, I rip them into tiny, tiny pieces and push them deep into the trash.

42

Sam, January 1993

Sam stands beside his mother, supporting her elbow. The priest raises his hand: 'May his soul and the souls of all the faithful departed through the mercy of God rest in peace.' Sam's mother gives a sob, pressing her hanky to her mouth. A week ago, she phoned Sam in the early hours. A massive stroke, she said. His father had been dead on arrival at hospital. Now Sam watches the coffin swinging slowly into the grave. His mother's handful of dirt makes a scratching sound as it scatters across the lid.

He remembers Cat leading him into the funeral parlour, the different kinds of coffin on display, her insouciance amongst these practical necessities, how he admired it, even as his own fear of death thundered through him. Back home in London, it would take him less than half an hour to reach her. His Nokia sits in his pocket, redundant. He doubts she has a mobile, and he doesn't know her landline number. But he can't call her even if he did.

It's silly to want to tell her the news. She didn't even meet his father, believed until recently that he was already dead. So it doesn't make sense to want to share this with her. But he does, more than anything.

336

At the wake, Sam accepts condolences with a fixed smile. When George and Mattie appear at his side, he breathes a sigh of relief. 'Thank God. The polite nodding was giving me neck ache,' he says. 'Who knew we had so many distant relatives?'

Mattie rubs red-rimmed eyes. Sam puts an arm around her shoulder, giving her a squeeze. George's ruddy cheeks are dimmed. 'Mum wanted to come,' he says, 'but she thought it would be difficult — upsetting for your mother and all of you. I stayed with her last night. She cried for hours.' He scratches his head. 'We humans know how to make a mess of our lives, don't we?'

Mattie holds onto his elbow. 'I'm sorry.'

'Mum's devastated too,' Sam says. 'This has really hit her hard. Her loyalty to the old bugger is beyond belief.'

'She loved him,' Mattie says. 'And who are we to question that? What do we know about what went on between them? Or between him and Maureen? What goes on between any couple in private?'

George raises his glass, 'To James Winterson, our father. Whatever else, he gave us life.'

Mattie smiles and chinks her glass against his. 'And each other.'

Sam touches his own glass to his siblings', holding it by the stem so that the delicate bowl makes a true ringing sound.

'I read a review of the album the other day,'

George says, 'in the *Guardian*. What was the phrase they used ... ' He presses his lips together, tilting his head. 'Uplifting and beguiling. I think that was it.'

Sam nods. 'The press have been kind. Mattie's arranged some UK gigs. Small venues.' He takes a sip of wine. 'Everything's on a different scale now and I feel better for it.'

'And you've moved into your new house, I hear?' George asks Mattie.

'River and I are installed in a sweet house in the next street to Sam. Not quite a cottage, but nearly. You should come over.'

'It's great to have you guys so close,' Sam says.

Mattie laughs. 'You might just begin to regret it when he gets old enough to pop round to Uncle Sam's on his own. I can predict he'll want your place to be his hangout pad. It'll certainly impress all his mates.'

'Sounds like fun.' Sam smiles, scanning the room for his mother.

★ ★ ★

She's in the library, curled up in his father's favourite chair, a burning cigarette between her fingers, the dogs waiting anxiously beside her. Sam sits on the sofa opposite and leans forward. 'Can I get you anything?'

Her lipsticked mouth wobbles. 'I keep thinking he's in the next room. About to walk through the door.' She blinks and swallows, regaining control. 'I have something for you.' She searches her pockets and presses an object into his palm.

Heavy, cool, silver. His father's watch.

'I'd like you to have it,' she says. She leans over, crushing her cigarette into an ashtray, and pats his knee. 'He was a difficult man, I know. But he loved us. It wasn't obvious, but he did — despite what you think.'

Sam clasps the watch, circling his thumb over the smooth face. His mother gets up, the dogs struggling to their feet, ears pricked for the sound of her voice. 'Better get back to it,' she says, pushing her chest out. As she passes, she touches the top of his head like a priest giving a blessing.

He fastens the watch around his wrist, the new weight strange against the bone. He listens to the sound of the clock on the mantelpiece and imagines he hears the whisper of the pages of *The Times* turning, the smell of his father's aftershave: a man who had two families.

Is he just as guilty? He's learnt that living without hurting others is harder than he imagined. He doesn't have a wife and children to betray, but Cat is married, and there is a child. When they met again, he carefully avoided asking any questions that would make them into real people. All he knows is that the husband is called Leo and the girl is Grace. He has no information about the man's job, no details of either of their physical appearances, foibles or habits; he doesn't know what makes them laugh, or the way their voices sound. It's as if not-knowing is a method of erasure. A way of pretending they don't exist.

339

And now, he thinks with a jolt, there could be a baby.

★ ★ ★

Sam avoids Hampstead Heath. But he walks in other places: Battersea Park, St James's Park, Green Park, Highbury Fields. Today he meanders through Hyde Park, stopping by bench inscriptions that catch his interest. He scribbles them down in his notebook, letting the ideas that come from those brief lines float and flicker inside him, until something catches and he begins to hear a song. He stops and watches a young woman walk past, her new baby slung in a papoose across her chest. Could Cat really be pregnant? Could she have had a baby by now? He's sure he'd somehow have a feeling about it, and he doesn't. He takes a seat for a moment, absorbing the ebb and flow of the park: dogs with smiling mouths, some kids playing catch. He notices a couple lost in each other on a nearby bench, and feels that familiar tug inside him. It's as if he's tethered to her. Wherever Cat is, whatever she's doing, he knows the connection between them will not break, will not snap or even fray, but will hold tight, binding him to her.

On his way out of the park, the last inscription he stops to read startles him. Under a woman's name is a short, simple sentence: *She is not far away.* He looks up involuntarily, and glances around. She's not there, of course, but he can't help feeling that the inscription was a message.

340

So when the next day an envelope arrives addressed in her writing, it's as if he knew she'd be contacting him. He tears it open: *Please come, it reads. I need you. I'll be at our bench tomorrow at midday.*

43

Cat, January 1993

It's raining. I get to the bench first, afraid he's not going to come. Then I hear movement through the wet leaves. We're in each other's arms. The push of his tongue against mine. The soft give of his mouth. All the tastes and shapes and textures of him living in me again. Relief stings my eyes.

Rain falls onto my skin, trembling in tiny mercury beads over our coats. It shines inside our hair. He sits down and I'm in his lap, arms around his neck. I examine tiny details of him: the close-up whorl of his ear, dark hair springing from follicles, a small pimple on his cheek, a pale scar shaped like a torn petal at the edge of his jaw. The skin behind his ear is pinker than the rest of his neck, the surface slightly rough. I run my finger over it, and he shivers. I lick raindrops from my lips, blink them from my lashes.

'You came,' I say.

'Of course,' he says. 'I got your note. Of course I came.'

'I didn't know if you were in the country.'

He kisses me with cold lips. 'Come home with me,' he whispers.

'I can't.'

He pulls back from me, forehead wrinkling.

'We can't talk here — we need to get out of this downpour.'

The slippery, wet feel of his hair is against my mouth.

'We'll drown if we stay here much longer,' he adds, his attempt at humour making his voice crack.

Our hearts are thudding. His lungs are working fast, as fast as my own. I can feel the rise and fall of his chest through his coat.

'Cat?' His voice is tight. His arms tremble against me.

In answer, I slip off his lap and stand, holding out my hand to him. I see myself reflected in his dark irises, my own desire and fear mirrored back at me. The uncertainty of our lives stretches out, unmapped and unknown, impossible to grasp, but our desire for each other is real, tangible as rocks. He puts his hand into my outstretched one and we walk away from the bench and down the hill towards the road.

He hails a black cab, and we bundle inside. Panic races through my veins, but at my centre it feels right, going home with him. We hold hands all the way, without speaking.

★　★　★

The cab pulls up outside an elegant flat-fronted Georgian house. I stare at it while he pays the driver. Inside, I have a vague notion of luxurious fabrics, recessed switches and down-lighting. There are hardly any personal touches. It's more like a hotel than a home. Now that we're here, he

343

seems nervous. 'Do you want a drink . . . or anything?'

'No. Thanks.'

'What's going on?'

Small puddles are forming around our feet. I shake my head. Being with him after so long, I just want to bury myself inside him, speak to him with touch. Slowly I begin to undo the buttons of my sodden coat. He watches as I shuck it from my shoulders, letting it drop onto the parquet. My pulse is bumping in my ears as I yank my sweater over my head. My fingers move to the zipper of my jeans. He makes a small noise in the back of his throat and grabs my hand.

'Upstairs,' he manages, as he pulls me towards the stairs. On the first floor, he turns a door handle. He's ripping off his shirt. A button pings onto the carpet. My fingers fumble with hooks and fastenings; I bend to pull off my socks. The world has shrunk to this — the two of us getting naked in a room. My skin is alive with yearning, my stomach a knot of nerves and need. A trail of dropped clothes leads to the bed. He gets his foot caught inside one leg of his jeans, and hops, arms flailing, before he crashes over the mattress. He manages to extricate his foot, holds out his arms to me.

It's the first time we've seen each other naked since Atlantic City, the first time we've been in a bed together since that night in the hotel. All the years in between haven't taken away our familiarity. My body knows his body. There are small changes, and I explore these with my eyes and fingers and mouth. His chest is a little broader, the muscles in his arms feel denser, less sinewy, his neck thicker. The few hairs on his chest have multiplied. I can tell he's making similar discoveries in me. Although I've stopped the fertility drugs, my belly is still swollen. He runs his fingers over it tenderly, then takes my face between his hands and looks into my eyes. 'I don't know how you do it — this thing you do without trying,' he says. 'But I'm only me when I'm with you.'

He holds himself above me, and moves purposefully downwards, kissing my throat, collarbone, breasts, stomach, my scar, hip hollows, pubis. I tangle my fingers in his hair and close my eyes.

⋆   ⋆   ⋆

We lie in the big bed, tightly wrapped around each other, my head on his shoulder. His chest moves up and down in a steady rhythm under my cheek. He hasn't pulled the drapes. It's stopped raining, and a shaft of winter sunlight makes me screw up my eyes. The sun fades as cloud shadows trail darkness over the roofs of the houses opposite, and a chill settles on my skin. Cramp stabs at my calves.

'What's the time?' I mumble.

He picks up a heavy silver watch from the bedside table and squints at it. 'It's only been a couple of hours. Don't leave yet. What's going on? Why the note — why are we here?'

I wiggle my toes, trying to shift the cramp. I'm

shivering, and he rubs my arm, tucks the duvet tighter over my shoulder.

'Cat?'

The truth is simple. Selfish. I wanted to see him because I was miserable. It was pure blind need that made me send the note. But now I realise he might think I'm leaving Leo.

'I'm sorry,' I tell him. 'I'm sorry for making you come.'

'I don't understand. What's going on?' He turns to look into my face. 'You're not pregnant?'

I shake my head. 'I can't get pregnant. We've been trying IVF. It didn't work.' I feel a sob push into my throat. 'It's shit, the whole process . . . invasive, uncomfortable, undignified. And every time they put those embryos in you, you can't help hoping . . . then it fails and you feel it's your fault — that you're the failure.'

'I'm sorry,' he says quietly. 'So now what?'

'I don't know.' I push my face into his neck. 'I'm tired of it all — the injections and procedures and tests — and I don't even think . . . ' I fight to control my voice, 'I don't think I want a baby any more.'

'If it's not right, then don't do it,' he says.

'I worry about Grace,' I say. 'She's an only child. She was really excited. She wanted a sister. I've failed her. I've failed Leo.'

He rubs my shoulder. 'It's not your fault,' he whispers, tightening his fingers against me.

I look at the clouds, darkening and moving faster across the rooftops.

'If Leo loves you,' Sam says slowly, 'then he'll understand. He won't want you to go through any more medical stuff — he'll respect your decision.'

I wish I believed that.

'I don't know anything about him,' Sam's saying. 'I realised that a while ago. I never even asked you what he does for a living.'

'He's a surgeon, an eye surgeon.'

There's a pause, and I hear him swallow. 'An eye surgeon?' He sits up beside me. 'Where did you meet him?'

'In Atlantic City,' I tell him. 'I met him when I was helping at that funeral — the one you came along to afterwards, remember? It was his wife, Elizabeth, we were burying. I helped out with Grace. Then something he said made me realise they were looking for a nanny, and when you didn't write, I asked for the job.'

Sam is running his fingers through his hair, raking his nails over his scalp. 'Hang on. You're married to him? *That* man?' He pushes the heels of his hands into his eyes. 'But I met him later, in London . . . He operated on my brother. Saved the sight in one of his eyes.'

'That's . . . that's weird.' I put a hand on Sam's forearm, the twist of muscle. 'So you saw him at the hospital and recognised him?'

'Not at first. Later.' He lets his breath out in a long whoosh of air. 'When I got home, I remembered who he was. But I had no idea that . . . ' he breaks off, 'that he was going back to you.' He shakes his head. 'I didn't know at that point that you were even in London.' His voice is jerky. Hoarse.

'Are you all right?'

He clears his throat and nods. 'It's just a . . . shock. I can't believe I didn't know who he was . . . '

'Does it make such a big difference?'

'I've got this image of his face in the hospital as he walked past me. Earnest and busy. And kind.'

'I never said he was a monster.' I let my fingers slide away from his forearm, then slip out of bed, pick up my knickers and step into them. I find my bra, put it on backwards and fasten it, turn it around the right way and push my arms through the straps. 'He's a good surgeon. He makes a difference to people's lives.'

Sam is out of bed, and his arms are around me. 'Don't leave,' he's saying. 'I needed to know who he was. And now I do. It doesn't change how I feel about you. It just makes everything seem . . . even harder.' He breathes into my hair. 'I love you, Cat.'

'I love you too.' I bend down to pick up my jeans. 'And this . . . thing, this love we have, it makes me feel like crap most of the time.'

'You're leaving again?' Sam says. 'After . . . this.' He waves towards the crumpled bed. 'What, so that's it?' His voice hardens. 'You needed a shoulder to cry on, and now you're done?'

'It's not like that,' I say. 'I miss you. It's like being permanently homesick. I stop myself from doing anything about it. But I had a moment of weakness. The IVF didn't work. Years of struggle have ended in this sad little full stop . . . and now the only chance is to have an operation. Except I don't want one. We have Grace. She's more than enough for me. But I seem to be on this . . . this baby-making conveyor belt, and I want to get off. And the person I wanted to talk to about it was you — even though that doesn't make sense.' I stop, breathing deeply. 'Nothing makes sense. Everything's back-to-front, because . . . because if I were able to have a child, I'd want it to be yours.'

He says nothing, hanging his head. 'My dad died,' he says quietly. 'And I couldn't tell you. You're the only person I want to speak to most of the time. My life is going past and you're not there to share it with — not even as a voice on the phone.'

Grief sits hard and heavy and familiar in my belly. 'I'm sorry about your dad,' I say. 'I . . . I wish I'd been there for you. I should never have sent you that note.'

'Remember when we talked about what would have happened if we'd stayed together? And you said the domestic details — the ordinary things — might have finished us? Well, I want ordinary with you, Cat. I want humdrum. I want to see you every morning with puffy eyes and dirty hair. I want to pick up your socks, listen to you moan. I want to look after you when you're feeling ill.' He doesn't look away from me. 'I want you to meet Mattie and George. I want to take you out to dinner. Have you there at a gig, so I can smile at you in the wings and see you smiling back. I want to go into a bookshop with you and buy one of your books and tell the person behind the till: look, this woman beside me, she's the author.'

I shake my head. 'Stop . . . ' Tears jam in my throat.

'Tell me we can be together. One day.' His voice trembles. 'Jesus, Cat. Tell me it'll happen.' He grasps my arms above the elbows and makes me look at him. 'Tell me there's some hope. Give me that, at least.'

My gaze tries to veer away from his; his eyes sear right through me. I hold steady. 'I'm sorry. I can't . . . I can't promise anything.'

★ ★ ★

I should never have asked him to meet me. I should never have gone to his house. It wasn't fair on any of us. I'm making mistakes. Most days I just feel stunned, kind of numb, as if I've been doped, or hit on the head.

Dougie asks to meet me for a coffee. When we're sitting down, he pushes a folded-up newspaper across the table. In the gossip pages, there it is, a blurry photo of me leaving Sam's house, and Sam in the doorway without his shirt. *Ex-Lambs lead singer Sam Sage and mystery girlfriend*, the caption reads. I drop the paper like the words are written in acid. I want to get up, run, keep running.

Dougie tells me not to panic, that nobody will recognise me. My head is turned away in the picture. He only knows because of what I told him before. He leans close and asks if I'm seeing him — if we're having an affair.

I feel sick at the thought of other people's

speculation; it makes what we have seem sordid and wrong. Only I can't stop re-imagining that afternoon in his bed, reliving the seconds, the moments, the way he touched me, the way I felt in his arms, just like I used to — that feeling of being at home. I gave him hope and then took it away. How can he forgive me?

44

Sam, September 1994

Her smell faded after a few days. Even when he pressed his face deep into the pillow and inhaled. It's a long time now since Cat was in Sam's bed. He was angry and hurt after she left, confused that she'd asked for him then walked away. But later, he realised how difficult it would be for her to leave a family, a child. He thinks about her gambling father, how they continually moved from one city to the next, and how precious a real home must be, how hard to destroy it.

When Ben calls and says he has tickets for a new show in the West End, Sam says to count him in. He accepts most invitations that come his way. Or he walks around the corner to spend the evening with Mattie, helping River with his homework, sitting at their kitchen table.

★ ★ ★

He arrives at the crowded foyer of the Prince Edward in Soho with five minutes to spare. He squeezes past backs and elbows to get to Ben and his wife Boo. 'This is Janie,' Ben says. 'A friend of Boo's.'

A petite woman holds out a bejewelled hand. Sam takes it, and gives her a polite smile. Her bones feel fragile inside his grip. Several large rings bite into his palm. A bob of shining black hair swings in perfect symmetry at the line of her pale collarbone.

Sam turns to Ben and gives him a meaningful stare. He's asked him not to arrange blind dates. All his friends do it. None of them, except Mattie and George, know about Cat.

In his Armani jacket, Ben looks very different from the skinny punk living in the Brixton squat. He's an estate agent now. He always had a practical self-interest, a chameleon-like ability. He and Boo live in a five-bedroom house in Clapham with their twin boys. They laugh about their punk days.

Janie tells Sam she works as a finance director for an IT company. He struggles to think of suitable questions. He's relieved when the warning bell summons them to their seats. He'll make his excuses straight after the show, slip away home.

'This was a big hit on Broadway last year,' Boo is telling them as they settle in the plush red splendour of the stalls. 'I love Gershwin,' she adds.

In the interval, Janie murmurs, 'I hate musicals. But when Boo said you were coming, I wanted to meet you.' She touches his sleeve with red-tipped fingers. 'I admire your music. The stuff you're doing now especially.'

Sam's mouth is dry. He's furious with Ben for putting him in this situation. He waits for her to remove her hand, then shifts his weight back onto his heels. 'Thanks,' he says vaguely.

When Janie and Boo disappear into the

ladies', heads together, Ben gives Sam a glass of wine. 'She's a bit of a babe, don't you think?' he says. 'She earns a fucking fortune, but get this, she works as a Samaritan in her spare time. She's been to your gigs. She was very keen to meet you.'

'I asked you not to do this,' Sam says.

Ben grins. 'Come on, mate. Everyone's wondering when you're going to settle down. I saw that photo in the paper last year. Your mystery girlfriend. How come we never met her? Was she a hooker? No shame in that. But people want to see you . . . happy.'

'Trust me, there's more to care about in this world than my love life. Janie seems like a nice person. But she's not for me.' Sam glances away, finishes his wine in one long swig and goes to the bar. 'Same again,' he says.

★ ★ ★

Sam groans. His throat is parched, his mouth tacky. Cardamom and garlic, alcohol and sweat seep from his pores. There's an unfamiliar perfume too, on his skin, on the sheets. Black hair fans across the pillow next to him. Janie turns over, yawning. Sam keeps very still, as if she might not notice him.

'Morning,' she says, their faces inches apart. She grins.

'Hi,' he says, shuffling back and pushing up onto one elbow. 'Um. Yeah. Morning.'

She stretches. 'I'm starving. Do you have any food here? Or shall we go out and grab a

354

croissant and coffee somewhere?'

'Actually,' he licks dry lips, 'it's pretty late, and I've got . . . stuff to do.' He sits up. 'I should really get going . . . sorry.'

'Oh.' The smile fades from her mouth. 'No. Of course. I should too. Get going.' She sits up, tugging the sheet around her narrow torso, her small breasts.

Sam blinks. He has little memory of what happened last night. An Indian meal. A lot of wine. Ben offered him a bump of snow in the lavatory. Then somehow he ended up in Islington with Janie. They had sex. The smell is everywhere, clinging like a stain. Janie's perfect hair is mussed, flyaway strands standing up over the crown of her head. He feels like a shit.

'Look,' he says. 'I really am sorry. This shouldn't have happened.'

'Why not?' she asks, raising her pointed chin.

'Because I'm in love with someone else.'

'Oh . . . ' She shifts further away from him. 'Who?'

'Someone I've known for a very long time. She's married.'

She raises an eyebrow.

'I know.' He shrugs. 'A cliché, right? I'm an idiot. Or a bastard. Or both.' He pushes at his eyebrows, stretching them upwards. 'I shouldn't have told you. But I wanted to be honest.'

Janie doesn't say anything for a moment. She rubs her knuckles, twists her rings around her fingers. 'Thanks, I suppose. For explaining.' She shuffles over to the side of the bed and wraps the satin bedcover around her. 'I can't say I don't feel a bit of an idiot myself, but . . . I don't regret it.'

Her understanding makes Sam feel worse. He waves a hand towards the bathroom. 'Have a shower. Take your time. I don't have any food in the house, but I do have a stupidly expensive Italian espresso machine, if you want a shot of caffeine.'

'Thanks. I'll just get going.' She takes small steps around the room picking up items of clothing with difficulty, hooking silky red things, a pair of strappy high heels. She turns at the door to the bathroom, clothes clutched to her chest. 'You *are* a bastard, by the way. But I won't say anything to anyone.' She swallows. 'About what you told me.'

Sam sits with his arms wrapped around his knees.

'Actually,' she says, 'I feel sorry for you.' And she disappears into the bathroom.

★　★　★

After Janie has left, he downs a strong espresso and pushes his feet into his old trainers. Ignoring his thumping head, he leaves the house and runs through the streets, finding his pace as he lopes along the long drag of Holloway, under scruffy autumnal trees, and then through a brief green space. He pants and struggles up the elegant hills of Highgate, the burning in his legs like a fire in his veins. He sees the gate to the Heath and sprints through. Running to the top of Parliament Hill, he staggers to a halt, his hands on his knees, gasping for breath. You're hurting other people and you're wasting your life, he tells himself. So what are you going to do about it?

It has to be more than words this time, he admonishes himself. Letting her go has to come from the very centre. Like the forgiveness he eventually felt for his father, it can't be forced. Can he somehow find a way to leave his love for her behind? He wipes his sweating brow with the edge of his T-shirt. Perhaps if he saw her with Leo and the child . . . who, he supposes hazily, must be a teenager now . . . if he saw them together as a family, perhaps it would make him understand her real life properly. He doesn't have a clue who she is in that other world. He's completely shut out. Seeing her being a mother, a wife, might mean he could finally give up hope.

He makes his way slowly towards the bench — their bench — to sit on it one last time.

45

Cat, September 1994

Leo and I face each other across the bedroom.

I'm trembling. 'No,' I tell him. 'Why are we even talking about this again? We agreed. I'm not having an operation.' I try to stay calm. 'I haven't changed my mind.'

'But we've come so far . . . '

'Where? Where have we come?' I stare at him. 'I can't see that we've got anywhere. You of all people should know that. I mean, not just as a doctor, but as my husband. You saw what the drugs did to me. You know we gave up making love because . . . because we were both too tired and depressed to bother any more, and we've never got back to normal since.'

'It wasn't that bad,' he says. 'It was for a good cause. And now we're older, this could really be our last chance.'

'I can't do it any more. I'm thirty-eight. We're a family already. We have Grace.'

'You're tired, I can see that,' he says, his tone softening. 'Maybe you just need a break. A proper holiday. How about going somewhere long-haul? St Lucia? Mauritius?'

'No,' I tell him, my voice rising. 'You're not listening. You're . . . obsessed with making this happen. And it's not going to. You need to accept that.'

'I'm trying to listen. Don't be unreasonable, Cat,' he says. 'Calm down, or Grace will hear you.'

'It's not your body, your life that was hijacked for years. If it *had* been, I'd like to see how reasonable you'd feel!' I tell him, anger pushing through my words.

'Darling,' he says, holding up his hands. He looks concerned. 'Just take a deep breath.'

His bedside manner feels like an insult. He's approaching me with his arms out for a hug, but I can't breathe — my lungs are flailing inside my ribs, bones tight as a corset. My hands fly to my throat, pulling my shirt apart.

As he reaches me, I twist away. He exclaims in surprise.

I'm hurrying onto the landing. All I can think is that I need air. Grace looks up at me from her open bedroom door, eyes wide. I can see that she's upset. She must have heard us. But I can't stop. I need to get out of the house.

As I run downstairs, I slip a few steps from the bottom. My feet go from under me, and I fall onto my behind, bumping down the rest of the stairs, landing in an undignified sprawl. Shaken, I stand up gingerly and test my ankle, rub my spine where I know bruises are already seeping through my skin. But there's no real damage done.

'Mum!' Grace's voice wails from the top of the stairs. Her face is white with shock.

'I slipped,' I call up to her, trying to sound normal. 'I'm not hurt. Don't worry.'

'Where are you going?'

'Just out. I'll be back,' I call. 'I need a walk, that's all.'

'Cat?' Leo's voice floats down to me.

I'm pulling the door open, and as I step onto the pavement, something in my chest releases. I'm walking to the Heath, striding uphill as fast as I can.

★ ★ ★

I get to the top, out of breath but already feeling better just knowing I can sit on our bench and have solitude in a place where I feel close to him. Maybe I can make some sense out of my confusion, pick apart the elements of my frustration and unhappiness. But with a jolt, I realise somebody else has got there first. I can see their shape through the hawthorn leaves. A pointless rage fills me, and I nearly turn away; but I need to sit on those familiar wooden slats. Perhaps the stranger will leave.

As I push past the leaves, I know instantly. Shock turns my body cold, then hot. My heart batters against my ribs. Why is he here? He sits facing the view, unaware of me. I'm scared to speak. He's lost in his thoughts. I have no idea what those thoughts are, or how he'll react when he sees me.

I approach softly, and he looks up, his face blank with disbelief. 'Cat?' His voice is tight. He gets to his feet, standing as if braced for disaster. 'What are you doing here?'

I remember last time. My note. My walking away. I don't deserve for him to be pleased to see

360

me. I'm shaking, every bit of me filled with yearning, but I shift uncomfortably from one foot to the other. 'Sam . . . I . . . Do you want me to go?'

He moves his head, staring at me. Then his expression changes to concern, and he steps closer. 'What's the matter? Is something wrong?'

I open my mouth, but words won't come.

'Are you all right?' Fear makes his voice tense.

I manage a nod. He reaches out a hand and touches my cheek. 'Cat?' The word is soft in his mouth. More than a question.

I bow my head, unable to meet his eyes. My legs won't hold me. I sink onto the seat, and he sits next to me. I slip my fingers inside his. We stay like that, looking out over the view, hands joined. September has turned everything dusty yellow and faded green. But I don't feel connected to the Heath or the day; it's as if we're inhabiting a separate world. He shifts closer, and my head sinks onto his shoulder, my cheek against the thin material of his top. Stress lifts away, tension leaving my body like condensation. The physicality of him a key, unlocking me.

'You've been running,' I murmur, looking down at his bare knees. 'You're going to get cold.'

'Mmm.' He has his arm around me.

'Why is it that it's always the same between us, even when we haven't seen each other for ages?'

'I don't know,' he says. 'It's just the way it is.'

I pull away. 'I . . . I'm going to leave Leo.' As I say it, I know it's true.

He goes very still, his face impassive.

'Trying for a baby has broken something between us — a kind of trust. I don't want to leave Grace. But she's sixteen. I think she'll cope. I was afraid that perhaps I wouldn't be able to see her any more if I left — because I'm not her real mom.' I'm almost breathless with words rushing out of me. I lean forward, rubbing my forehead. 'Only Leo isn't a cruel person. He wouldn't stop me from seeing her.'

Sam still says nothing.

'Leo will already have gone to the hospital. But tonight, I'll tell him.' I dare to look at Sam. 'I don't . . . presume anything. I don't have any expectations. Maybe you don't want to be with me any more. Especially after last time. What I did . . . it was unforgivable.' I scrub at my eyes. I mustn't cry. 'I don't know if you're with anyone or . . . anything.'

The air slurs and slows around us. We are fixed to the bench, side by side, stupefied by my words. I'm suddenly certain that he's found someone else, that she's waiting for him at his house. Why doesn't he say something? He takes my hand again. I think I hear the thud of his heart. Feel it knocking at the surface of his skin, his pulse colliding with my own at the place where our hands connect.

'I love you,' he says quietly. 'Always have. Always will.'

I squeeze his fingers. Tears spill from my eyes.

'Will you phone me?' he says. 'After you've told him — so that I know you're okay?'

I manage a nod.

'Here's my number. It's a mobile, so you can

reach me anytime.' He presses a piece of paper into my hand, then kisses the top of my scalp, at the parting of my hair. 'I think you're brave.'

'This is the worst thing I've ever done,' I tell him.

'It's the beginning,' he says. 'If you want it to be.'

★ ★ ★

My fingers tremble as I slot my key into the lock of the front door. I've turned this metal shape countless times, but now I feel like a thief. The hallway looks different, as if I'm seeing it with a stranger's eyes. Already, I don't belong. I wonder if I should pack a case. Prepare. But how *can* I prepare for this? Then I see Grace's rucksack on the floor, her sneakers kicked into the corner. I frown. How come she's still here? She should be sitting in class by now. 'Grace?' I call.

I go upstairs, my hand sliding along the banister. 'Grace?'

She's not in her bedroom. The bathroom door is shut. I put my ear to the wood and knock. 'Grace? Are you okay?' Silence washes back at me. I knock again. 'Bug? Are you feeling ill?'

Something is wrong. I feel it like a hand around my heart. I turn the handle and push with all my might. It's not locked, and I stumble into the hot, steamy room.

Grace is in the bathtub. It's full to the brim; she's suspended, floating, head tipped back, exposing the delicate curve of her throat. The faucet drips onto her bobbing toes. Her long hair

363

is plastered to her skull. It hangs in ropes around her shoulders, merging with the water in a sodden mass. The water is cochineal, tinted with seeping strands of red, drifting into pink. The colour flows from openings in her wrists: two little bleeding mouths.

'Grace!' I'm kneeling by her, picking up her limp wrists, wrapping them tightly with whatever fabric comes to hand, pressing down hard. 'Grace!' Her eyelids flicker. 'Thank God.'

I don't know what to do. I mustn't stop pressing against the oozing slits, but I need to phone for an ambulance. Sobbing, I attempt to pick her up. I bend over the tub, managing to get one arm around her upper back, and slowly lever her towards me. Water slops everywhere. She's heavy and inert, impossible to gather. As soon as I raise her torso, gravity adds new weight to her slack limbs. I struggle; my feet can't get traction on the wet floor. My muscles strain. Her head lolls, shoulders slithering away from me, and she slips back. I fall to my knees. I can't do this. I pull the plug, letting the water drain away. Carefully I place her arms on either side of the bathtub. The windings of fabric are crimson.

Scrabbling to my feet, I run for the door, for the phone in the hall. I slip on puddles of water and blood, crash down, get back up. 'Stay awake, Grace,' I shout over my shoulder. 'Don't move. I'm calling for help.'

The voice on the end of the phone is calm and matter-of-fact. She takes the address and asks me questions, about Grace, about the wounds, whether she's breathing, where she is. I am given

364

instructions. I go back upstairs, taking them two at a time, panting, my head full of urgent commands. I must elevate her arms above her heart, keep the sodden towels in place, find more to wrap around. I must keep applying pressure. And there's a pressure point on the inside fold of the elbow, the voice told me; press there too.

I don't have enough hands. I push the pads of my fingers down through layers of towel, hoping I've found the right places. I lay a hand on her forehead briefly. It feels cold. The bath's drained away, leaving her stranded; her body looks shrunken, broken, skin softened, swollen like dough from being in the water. I gasp as I see the inside of her arms and thighs, both places marked with a cross-hatching of old wounds and some fresh raw ones. A razor blade glints, washed up onto the plug hole. I keep talking to her. 'Stay with me. Don't leave me, Grace. I'm here, sweetheart. I won't leave you. I'm not going anywhere.' Her eyelids flutter, lashes making starred points against her pale cheeks. I kiss her shoulder, her forehead. 'I'm sorry,' I tell her. 'I'm sorry.' She moans.

Sirens sound outside.

* * *

Leo finds me slumped on a hospital chair, my head in my hands. He pulls me into a hug, his face white and strained. 'What news?'

'She missed the arteries. The cuts weren't deep enough.'

365

'Thank God.' His mouth contorts, chin wobbling.

'They said to wait while they stitched her . . . ' I trail away as I realise he's stopped listening.

He's looking around him in a distracted way. 'I need to find out who the senior doctor is,' he says. He stalks down the corridor purposefully. I watch him talking to a nurse in a low voice. He carries an air of authority here. This is his world.

We are shown into a private room. Grace is lying in bed, very straight and small under the neat covers, her lower arms and hands wrapped in bandages. To my relief, there's no sign of blood. When we come in, she looks up with red eyes. 'I'm sorry,' she whispers.

'Shh,' Leo says, sitting by her side. 'We're just so relieved that you're still here with us.'

I smile, bending down to kiss her cold forehead. Leo touches the tips of her pale fingers, tears dripping from the end of his nose. He takes off his glasses and wipes his eyes.

'Daddy,' she says, her voice trembling.

I swallow hard and put my hand on his shoulder. 'I'm going to wait outside,' I tell them. 'Let you two have some alone time.'

I watch them from the doorway, father and daughter, their faces close. I feel isolated, separate, and it makes my bones ache. I can't cry. My grief is complicated, riddled with guilt, sharp with horror. It lodges in my chest, bird-like, trapped, wings flailing.

* * *

366

At home, Leo pours us large whiskies. 'A nurse will stay with her tonight. Suicide watch. We'll talk to the psychiatric team tomorrow after they've assessed her.'

'Was this a cry for help?' I take a sip, grimacing at the peaty sourness. 'Or did she really mean to . . . to kill herself?'

'I don't know.' He shakes his head. 'She would have needed to cut deeper and harder to make the attempt successful. But maybe she didn't know. She's not a medic. And it would have hurt like hell to do it.'

'She left the bathroom door unlocked,' I say. 'As if she wanted to be found.' I think about those marks on her wrists. I should have investigated further, examined the injuries. 'A while ago, she had a couple of scratches on her arm,' I admit to him. 'She told me it was the cat. But now . . . I think they must have been made by her. She's been cutting herself for a long time.'

'What?' He snaps his head up, staring at me. 'Why didn't you tell me?'

'Because I didn't think there was anything to tell.' I keep my voice steady. 'As far as I knew, the cat had scratched her a couple of times. The marks didn't look bad — and I never thought for a moment she'd done them herself.'

'Maybe you needed to be a little more alert. She was in your care!'

'I made a mistake,' I say, bowing my head. 'She was obviously hiding things from me — from us — and I didn't understand.'

He leans away from me. 'I've done everything

367

I can to . . . ' he swallows, 'to be a good father.' He rubs his eyes. 'If we'd asked the right questions . . . been more understanding . . . maybe this wouldn't have happened.'

I want to tell him how passionately I disagreed with the way he shut down Grace's dreams of dancing. I want to tell him he has a problem with control, and how it's pushed us apart, affected his relationship with Grace. But now is not the time. So we sit at the kitchen table in silence, the bottle of single malt between us. Everything is unravelling. And I feel tainted by guilt.

'Did she tell you anything in the hospital?' I ask quietly. 'You were with her for a long time.'

He turns his glass in his hands. He looks exhausted, emptied out. 'She's been blaming herself for her mother's death,' he says in a monotone.

'What?' I look up.

'She thinks she killed Elizabeth.' His mouth tightens. 'What we didn't know was that Elizabeth fell because . . . because she tripped over Grace's dolls. Grace had been playing with them at the top of the stairs. She'd been giving a tea party with little plastic cups and plates.' He stops and unhooks his glasses from his ears to wipe a hand over his eyes. 'The phone rang in the hall. Elizabeth hurried to get it. She told Grace to move out of her way. As she tried to get past, her foot got tangled up in the dolls. She slipped on the plastic saucers and cups. Then she was . . . falling. When she didn't get up, Grace sat by the body, talking to her.'

Leo stops. He makes an effort to force saliva

down his throat. 'She says she didn't really understand then that her mother was dead. But she understood it was her fault. That she'd done a bad thing. Then she got frightened . . . frightened that she would be in trouble and . . . and that I would . . . ' he stops again, clearing his throat, 'that I would be angry.' He breathes out loudly. 'She put her dolls back in her room. Cleared away all traces of the tea party. She never told anyone.'

'My God.' I pinch the flesh of my lip between my teeth, then reach across to touch his hand.

He blinks and looks up at me. 'I was wrong to protect Grace from the truth about Elizabeth. To let her believe her mother was perfect — some kind of saint.' He has a deep frown between his brows. 'In the hospital just now, I told her the truth, that Elizabeth was a drunk. That she'd been drinking heavily that day. She would have been careless, sloppy, easily unbalanced. I told her it wasn't her fault. That I would never be angry with her. Never.' His mouth jags and droops. 'We both made mistakes, Cat.'

He drops his forehead onto his arms, folded on the table. His shoulders shake. I crouch by his side and murmur to him, patting at his arm.

★　★　★

We lie in bed, shivering and exhausted, holding each other, exhaling whisky fumes into the darkness. Leo falls asleep first; after his breathing settles, I lift his arm away from my chest carefully and slip out from under it. I pad across the floor, feeling my way. In Grace's room, I switch on the light. Her diary is lying on the carpet, unlocked. I sit on her bed, take a deep gulp of air and open the pages. Sentences rear up at me. I flick through, spanning years of her secret thoughts. What I read makes me clamp my palm over my mouth to stop the noise that's building in my throat.

I'm BAD. I don't deserve to LIVE. It's my fault Mummy's dead. I killed her. I made her fall down the stairs. I can't forget the sound she made when she landed. The nightmares won't go away. I see that look on her face when she fell — over and over. Why won't it stop?

Dad will hate me if he finds out. I hate myself. I am a bad person. I should be punished.

Cat and Dad are getting married — I wish I could call her mum. Sometimes I feel happy. And then I remember. Dad and Cat are going to have a baby!!!! I want a sister so badly.

When Cat has the baby then it will make every-thing better. We'll call her Sally and I'll tell her stories like Cat told me.

Dad won't let me go to dance school. I want it more than anything. More than a little sister even. I hate him.

Nothing matters any more. I don't care about living. What's the point?

370

Dad and Cat are arguing. It's my fault. I should never have asked for a sister. What if Cat dies from having a baby? I will be a double murderer. I made her do this.

Nobody smiles any more. Everything is going wrong and it's my fault. My fault. MY FAULT.

I SHOULD KILL MYSELF. EVERY-THING I TOUCH TURNS TO POISON.

Sometimes the letters are scratched so hard into the paper that it's ruched and torn, stabbing through onto the page underneath. Ink spots blot and obscure words. There are bits of text, whole chunks, that read like any normal teenager's diary: talk about pimples and boys and friendships, long tracts relating details of parties and an argument with Nancy, lists of clothes she wants to buy with little illustrations next to them. Then it starts again, the terrible self-blame, the hatred, the idea of suicide discussed, the need for it getting stronger and stronger. A photo of Elizabeth has been glued onto the inside of the front cover, greasy with lip prints.

I snap the book shut. She left it unlocked for a reason. I didn't understand. I failed her.

46

Sam, September 1994

He has an urge to run after her, lurching down Parliament Hill, skidding across footpaths, so that he can trail behind, following her home like a stray dog. Back to a house he's never seen. He wants to stand outside, under the shadow of a tree, to be unobtrusive but poised to act if need be, in case — in case what? In case Leo turns violent? The mild bespectacled surgeon that Sam remembers looked as though he didn't have an aggressive bone in his body. But people can surprise you.

It might take hours before Cat calls him. It might not be until tomorrow. He doesn't know what to do with himself while he's waiting.

★ ★ ★

Sam presses his finger on the buzzer, and the familiar ringtone of Mattie's doorbell peals. After a few moments and some muffled swearing, she opens the door part way, peering through the crack. 'Hi.'

'Are you ill?' he asks, observing his sister's flushed cheeks and dishevelled hair.

She shakes her head, glancing behind her, and then back. 'Not a good time.'

There's a noise on the stairs, a male voice.

'Come back to bed, baby.'

Sam widens his eyes at her. She narrows hers at him.

'Where's River?'

'With Luke.'

She hovers, her fingers remaining on the edge of the door. Then she seems to see him for the first time, focuses and frowns. 'You all right?'

He digs into the deepest part of himself to drag the fragmented, spinning bits of himself back together. He holds them there for the time it takes him to say, 'It's not the postman in there with you, is it?' He raises one eyebrow. 'Milkman? I did warn them about you.'

She laughs, 'Goodbye, Sam,' and shuts the door.

★ ★ ★

It's the longest night of his life. He walks clutching his mobile in his hand; trudging south, he passes pubs and restaurants noisy with the clatter of cutlery and conversation. He skirts around the opera crowd at Covent Garden, their privilege covering them like gilded capes. He crosses Waterloo Bridge, stopping to stare down at the dark river, surface streaked with oily reflections, littered with the ghosts of city lights. He makes his way along the South Bank, remembering the day she found him sleeping in the green room at the Queen Elizabeth Hall. He re-crosses the river at Blackfriars. He checks and rechecks his phone in case he's missed her call. A train rumbles across the bridge, lights flashing on and off as windows pass the struts.

He limps northwards, a blister on his heel, heading for Rosebery Avenue. A fox slinks from behind a bin. As the hours pass, there are fewer people, and they're changed by booze or drugs or desperation. They stare with sullen, empty eyes, or stagger and shout. Groups gather outside kebab shops and chippies, eating with feral, mindless hunger. Homeless people are bedded down under a bridge, cardboard carefully arranged as windbreaks and pillows. Sam puts his hands in his pockets and realises that he doesn't have his wallet on him; he has nothing to give.

*   *   *

It's not until the next morning that she phones. She wants to meet at their bench. 'Soon as you can get there,' she says. Her voice low, expressionless. 'I can't speak now,' she says. 'I'll explain when I see you.'

It's all wrong. What is there to explain? Sam feels sick.

*   *   *

She's there, hunched, staring into the distance.

He sits beside her. 'What is it . . . what's happened?'

He's shocked by her raw, swollen eyes. She pushes a strand of limp hair from her forehead. 'Grace tried to kill herself last night.'

Sam is cold. 'What?' he gasps.

374

She shakes her head. 'I didn't tell Leo that I was leaving. I couldn't, because after I left here, I found . . . ' She takes a gulp of air. 'I found her with her wrists cut, in the bath.'

'Jesus.' He rubs his forehead. 'Cat, I'm so sorry. Is she going to be okay?'

'The wounds weren't deep enough . . . to be fatal.' She balls her hands, keeps them on her knees. 'She's in hospital, being assessed to see if she needs to be moved to the psychiatric ward. It's complicated. She's been blaming herself for her mom's death. Suffering in silence all these years.'

'And us?' His voice is just a thread of sound.

She shakes her head. 'I can't. We can't.' She moves her head slowly on her neck.

He puts his hand on one of hers, folding his warmth over her cold skin. 'I can see . . . that things are difficult and you need to wait a bit longer, but — '

She tugs her hand away. 'No more waiting, Sam. It's not fair . . . on anyone. I'm not going to leave her. Not now. Not ever. I can't.'

'But you said that you and Leo shouldn't be married.' He tries to make her look at him. 'Never mind about me. If you stay with him, you'll be unhappy. For the rest of your life.'

Tears leak along the line of her nose, collecting above her top lip. He wipes them with his fingers. 'Listen,' he says. 'I'm not going to accept this. I can't.'

Her blurred eyes meet his. He pulls her towards him, holding her tight. She's stiff and unyielding. Her hair smells of hospitals. 'Cat,' he whispers. She gulps and wraps her arms tightly around him, burying her damp face in his neck. 'Give it a bit more time, let the shock settle, and then we can talk,' he murmurs into her hair.

'No.' She struggles, disentangling herself from his embrace. 'Grace needs me. I'm not leaving her. I promised.'

'Then . . . Okay . . .' He flails around for something to hang onto. 'We'll give it longer — two years? Five years? We'll meet in five years.'

'No.' She puts her palm to his cheek, holding it there. 'I don't want you to be alone. I don't want you to spend years waiting — it's crazy.'

'It's my life,' he says quietly. 'My choice.'

She shakes her head, mutely.

'All right.' He takes a deep breath. 'I'll meet you here, on our bench, in ten years' time.'

'What?' She closes her eyes, then opens them again. 'Sam. No. We'll be in our forties. We'll be . . . nearly fifty.'

He nods. 'Exactly. And Grace will be grown up. We'll meet, and if I've met someone else, or if you're happy with Leo, then that will be the very last time.' His voice is flat and tired. 'But if not . . . then we'll be free for each other. Ten years, Cat.' He leans closer. 'I have faith in us — the way we feel about each other won't change.'

'You really want that? To wait for years and years?'

'If I have to.'

'But what will you do?' She gazes around her, as if the answer is floating in the air, caught in the branches of distant trees. 'What will you do in all that time?'

376

He shrugs. 'I don't know. Does it matter?' He rubs a finger over a stain on his sleeve. 'Maybe I'll sell the house. Maybe I'll travel. There are plenty of places I want to visit — Greece, Albania, Mali — places I'd like to work with local musicians.' He touches her hair. 'Don't worry about me.'

'I'm sorry.' She fishes in her pocket for a tissue. Blows her nose. 'All I've done since we met is ruin your life.'

'Best thing that ever happened to me was meeting you.' He smiles. 'You are the music, Cat.'

She touches his face.

He lets her go first. Watches as she stands up unsteadily, as she blinks and turns her head away from him, setting her gaze towards her other life. He keeps watching until she disappears behind the hawthorn leaves. Then he stares at the shape she's left behind, the absence, the gaping hole.

47

Cat, July 2001

'Grace Dunn.' Her name sounds clearly through the hall. Over the heads of other parents, I watch my daughter as she mounts the steps to the podium to collect her philosophy degree. She makes her way back to her seat with composure, gliding across the floor, clutching that precious roll of paper to her chest. Her eyes scan the crowd, seeking us out. Leo and I put up our hands simultaneously and wave. She grins.

I'm proud of her, of the choices she's made. She kept dancing, but now she's set on working in the charity sector; she's off to be a paid volunteer teaching in a school near Bangalore next month. She's had a tattoo inked onto her shoulder of a large brown and yellow eagle, wings spread in flight. Leo was horrified. I thought of Sam's musical notes, and asked her what the eagle stood for. 'Freedom,' she replied. She put her fingers on her shoulder, touching the place like a friend. 'And it reminds me that I'm stronger than I think.' Just under her sleeve, I caught a glimpse of her wrist, her scars still visible.

The three of us have dinner, and after we've toasted her with champagne, she goes off to celebrate with her friends. She's staying on in Bristol for a few more days: more parties, time

378

with her boyfriend, packing up her room and shared house. I'm going to drive down again at the weekend to bring her and her stuff back to London.

It's late when we leave the restaurant. It'll take us nearly three hours to drive back to Hampstead. Leo has consultations in the morning, needs to get home. He takes the wheel, and I sit in the passenger seat staring into the darkness, the rush and roar of the motorway making me sleepy. Headlights flash as they pass, red tail-lights moving in an ever-changing pattern. I force myself to stay awake to keep Leo company, although he's listening to a political programme on the radio, eyes fixed on the road. Despite the warmth of the car, I shiver, aware of a sudden prickling across my skin, the realisation that something changed today, irrevocably. Grace's ceremony, our dinner, even this journey: they all mark the end of a phase in our lives. Sadness and nostalgia have settled inside me, but now there's a sense of urgency too. My stomach lurches. I squint into the darkness, and it's as if a locked door swings open before me.

Leo and I don't speak as we go through our separate bedtime routines. As I pull back the covers, I glance down at the cupboard below my bedside table where I keep my diaries, two volumes charting my life, tracing the story of me and Sam. I think of our last meeting at the bench, and our plan to wait for ten years. The truth sits inside me like a stone, worn by time and knowledge to a fine, smooth shine. I can't keep it secret any more. There's no mistaking the care I feel for my husband, for the life we've made together. But there's someone else who will always be first in my thoughts, first in my heart.

Leo gets into bed, his pyjamas buttoned to the neck, his breath minty with mouthwash.

'Leo,' I say, 'can we talk?'

'Not now, Cat.' His hand hovers over the light switch. 'You know I've got an early start tomorrow.'

'I just . . . I need to tell you something.' My pulse is racing. I didn't plan for this to happen, but there will never be a right time to tell my husband that I want to live separately from him.

I fumble around the words to explain that we're more like room-mates than husband and wife; that we both deserve better. As he listens, his expression changes from irritable to disbelieving. He shakes his head, dismissing everything I've said. 'Don't you think, at our age, that being friends is more important than passion?' His voice is calm and steady, a little patronising.

'It could be,' I tell him. 'But no. Not for me.'

He sighs, making a point. 'Get some sleep, darling. You're tired. It's been an emotional day. We can talk about this another time.'

'No,' I say. 'No, I'm sorry. It can't wait.'

Every nerve jumps, my body alive with a drumming fear. I've just done the unthinkable, leapt into the void, told him that we should separate, but Leo thinks he can make it go away with a pat on the hand and some practical advice. I remember Sam telling me I was brave when I first resolved to leave Leo, all those years ago. I didn't feel brave then, and I don't now. My hands shake, and I'm shivering.

I have to find a way to explain properly, to tell him everything. I try again, starting at the beginning, in Atlantic City. At the mention of Sam, Leo sits up straighter, puts his glasses back on. I don't leave anything out. He waits for me to finish. As the story unfolds, I feel him shrinking from me, the air between us becoming thin and tight.

'So . . . even when we were trying for a baby — even then — you were thinking of this other man. Jesus *Christ*.' He thumps his fist onto the bed.

I flinch. But after that one outburst, he doesn't rage and shout; instead he covers his face with his fingers, head bowed, sitting silent beside me.

I want to touch him, but I know I mustn't. I curl my fingers back into my palms. 'I'm sorry,' I say.

'Did you ever love me?' he asks, raising his head. He looks at me with searching eyes.

I nod. 'Yes. I did. I do.'

'But not like you love *him*.'

'No. Not like that.' My words are brutal. I'm horrified by them — but I can't stop them.

'Where is this man?' His mouth turns down. 'Is he in London?'

'I don't know. I haven't seen him since Grace . . . since she cut her wrists. Last time I saw him was when we arranged to meet in ten years' time,' I say.

'So there's been no communication between

381

you for, what, seven years?' Leo's voice is hard.

I move my head.

'The whole thing sounds like a fantasy.' He folds his arms. 'How do you know he's going to turn up?'

'I don't.' I stare at my hands. 'But whether he does or not, it doesn't change this — us; it doesn't change the fact that it's . . . it's time we accepted that we're not good for each other any more.'

'You seem very sure of that.' He rubs his hand over his forehead.

'I think . . .' I lower my voice. 'I think you know it too.'

He frowns. 'You lied to me, Cat. You've been dishonest. But . . . I still want to at least try and save our marriage.' He looks at me as if I'm a stranger. 'Don't you?'

I should agree with him. I should tell him that yes, we can talk more, see a therapist. But now that I've spoken the words, relief fills me. An extraordinary, head-spinning relief. There's no going back, there's nothing that will change this.

He waits for me to speak, but it's the look on my face that gives him his answer. His mouth turns down, and he nods as if something has been decided. 'Your mind's made up, isn't it?' He clears his throat, sets his shoulders. 'If this is really what you want . . . ' He looks at me with a hurt gaze. 'But you should be the one to tell Grace.' He turns away from me. 'I hope for your sake she forgives you.'

He takes off his glasses, and rubs his eyes. His face is naked and vulnerable without them. He looks exhausted and old. I wish there was something I could say to make things easier, better. But I've ripped up the worn fabric of our marriage, and a gale is blowing through, bleak and cold. There's no access to our familiar comforts, our consoling platitudes.

He's staring blindly towards the door. 'I want . . . I want to be alone.' His voice breaks.

I expected more anger, more of a fight. He's let me go.

He continues to look towards the door, his features rigid. I slip out of bed. Coldness has always been his weapon; it's what I deserve. I make up the single bed in my old room and crawl into it, feeling ancient, tired. The hurt I've inflicted on Leo has drained all my energy. I curl up, shivering, hugging my knees. I am dry-eyed, miserable, but I know that whatever happens in three years' time, Leo and I don't belong together any more.

★　★　★

It hurts. I knew it would, when we finally parted, but it's worse than I could have imagined; every part of me is alive with a kind of wrung-out aching pain, as if my internal organs are being squeezed and squeezed.

★　★　★

In Bristol, at the weekend, after we've packed up the car with her boxes and cases, Grace and I go for a coffee and sandwich before the drive home.

'There's something I need to tell you, bug,' I say, my stomach knotting. 'Your dad and I. We're . . . separating.'

She holds her mug between her hands, frowning into its contents like a fortune-teller. Then she nods. 'You waited for me to finish my degree?'

It wasn't what I was expecting her to say. I swallow. 'Kind of.' I lean across the table. 'Actually, there wasn't a plan. It just happened. I don't think we've been truly happy for a while.'

'No.' She looks at me, her face suddenly older and wiser. 'I can see that.'

I take a deep breath and let it out. I remember so clearly when she surprised me before the wedding, telling me tearfully why she couldn't call me mom. Now she's surprising me again. She has questions, practical questions, which I do my best to answer.

'Dad and I, we don't want this to get ugly,' I try to reassure her. 'We've agreed to separate. There won't be any need to go to court or anything.' I touch her hand. 'It will be hard. For all of us. But I truly believe it's for the best.'

In the car, she cries quietly, looking away from me, sniffing. I hand her a tissue and she takes it silently, blowing her nose.

I haven't mentioned Sam, because Leo asked me not to. 'She needs to deal with the fact that we're separating first,' he said. 'And this man . . . Sam Sage . . . may not reappear in our lives,' he added grimly.

I agreed, because it seemed only fair, and I knew he needed to claw back some control, to set limits and rules.

My tiny terraced house in Gospel Oak is still near enough to the Heath for daily swims. The neighbourhood is mixed, the sidewalks dirtier, the shops more eclectic, creating an energy, a buzz that was missing in the long, sweeping, elegant road I've left behind. As I arrange my ornaments and books on shelves, put my few pictures on the walls, I have a sense of rightness.

The days pass, and I work in my study looking out at the square of muddy grass that passes for a garden. I swim and walk. Grace is away in India. When she's in London, she'll share her time between her father and me. Leo is reserved with me, polite. He holds himself stiffly, as if he's standing behind an invisible protective barrier, and he never touches me. It will take a long time to reach something more relaxed and friendly. Perhaps we never will, but we've achieved what we agreed we wanted, at least as much as it's ever possible: a civilised divorce.

★ ★ ★

I want to contact Sam. Three years early. I sit down in my kitchen and try his cell. My fingers shake as I dial: *Sorry, the number you have dialled has not been recognised.* I try again, and get the same mechanical voice. I call his music label. The receptionist seems confused when I ask to speak to someone about Sam Sage. Eventually a voice comes on the line. They tell me that he's left the label. He's gone off grid, they say. I remember that his sister is called Mattie, and try finding M. Winterson in the directory, but she's not listed. Maybe she goes under a different surname.

At his old house in Islington, there are different curtains at the windows. The door is painted red, not grey. I stand on the doorstep, my heart hammering in my ears as I ring the bell. A housekeeper holds the door part open, looking suspicious. She shakes her head when I ask if she has a forwarding address for the previous occupant.

As I walk back to the Tube, rain begins to fall, light and misty, dampening my skin, darkening my coat. Disappointment hollows me out, and I drag my feet, suddenly exhausted. I falter to a stop on the sidewalk, and people mutter in annoyance, stepping around me. I stare into the blank, wet sky, watching pigeons flutter from a ledge. From their outspread wings, a feather falls, landing grey and lost at my feet. I bend to pick it up. As I turn it between my fingers I wonder: shouldn't I be able to feel something? Intuit something about what he's doing and where he is? I close my eyes, concentrating. But it's like that time in Atlantic City when I was waiting for his letters, as if he's stepped off the edge of the world.

48

Cat, September 2004

My cell phone rings. I sigh, taking my hands from the keyboard, wrenching myself out of the scene I'm in the middle of writing. The word I was searching for hovers, then disintegrates like ash before I can grasp it. Damn. Without looking away from my computer screen, I fumble for my shrill, demanding phone.

'Hi,' I say, clicking the ON button.

'Mum?'

'Sweetheart?' I hold the phone closer to my ear. 'Bug, how are you?' My eyes move to the photo of her pinned to my cork board. She's just started a new job in Nairobi with the VSO. The line crackles. 'Just checking in,' she says. 'Can't talk now. Just wanted you to know that everything is fine. The people here are really nice. I'll call again next week for longer.'

'I'm so glad to hear that,' I say. 'It'll be good to have a longer chat.'

'I know,' she says. 'I miss you. Shame it's so expensive to call. But . . . if you need me, Mum, my mobile works most of the time.'

'I'll be fine, darling. Don't worry about me. Stay safe. Love you.'

'Love you too.'

I sit with the little black Nokia in my hand. Odd to think it's the conduit for a connection across the globe — from one world to another, from her to me — and I try and imagine the place where Grace is right now, the heat, the parched earth, the unknown shapes of a foreign city. The words on the computer screen in front of me seem less important, reduced somehow. Grace's voice has tipped me out of my story. She'll be twenty-seven next month, the same age I was when I met Sam.

★ ★ ★

September. Ten years have gone by, made up of days and weeks and months and years, a stacking-up of small, ordinary things: shared meals and solitary swims, vacuuming and writing, sickness and arguments, holidays, reading in bed and visits to the cinema. A life. And now, the date that seemed impossibly far is almost here. It doesn't feel real. Sometimes I'm afraid I imagined it. I scan newspapers and magazines for anything that might give me a clue as to what he's doing — who he's with, where he lives. But as far as I can tell, he's still off grid, disappeared from public view. He must be travelling. I remember how, at our last meeting, he listed some countries he wanted to visit.

His songs sometimes get played on the radio. Tracks from the Lambs and his solo work pop up on various stations. When 'Ocean Blue' gets airtime, I quit what I'm doing, turn up the volume.

Ten years. Will he remember? Will he come?

And if he does, what will he think of the forty-eight-year-old me? Will he still want me?

★ ★ ★

I stand in front of the long mirror in my bedroom and look at my reflection, scrutinising the changes. There's grey in my hair, enough for me to notice when I run a brush through. Fine lines etch my forehead, crinkle at the edges of my eyes. My waist is thicker. I touch my chest, where sun-damaged skin mottles darker brown. Blue veins scrawl over my thighs. But I've never had a child, and daily swimming and long walks across the Heath mean I've kept in pretty good shape.

I scribble some sentences in my diary, stop and flick back through the pages to the beginning of the volume, to the time straight after Grace's suicide attempt, to the days when I could do nothing more than function, each hour like another stepping stone across an endless river. And then the divorce, and the days after that, a different kind of hard, but getting better as we settled into our new, separate lives.

I close the diary and put it back, next to its companion. The pair of them charting my life for two decades. I go down into the kitchen and make another cup of tea, then return to my desk to try and get back into my children's novel. *The Time-Jumping Detectives* ran into an eight-part series, and then a TV show. I'm experimenting with a new idea about a race of children who live underwater, like a modern *Water-Babies*, but with more adventure.

Dougie and I eat Vietnamese noodles in a little restaurant in Soho. You have to bring your own wine, and the line of hopeful customers stretches down the block. He's editor of *Marie Claire* now. Lives with his photographer boyfriend in a house in Hackney. We try and meet for supper once a fortnight to catch up.

'Did you see that story about the Fathers for Justice campaigner?' he asks, adding soya sauce to his food. 'Scaled the fence at Buckingham Palace dressed as Batman.'

We slurp from our bowls and discuss Batman on the Queen's balcony and the righteous cause of divorced fathers. He refills my glass and tells me about the latest drama between him and his boyfriend. 'How's Leo nowadays?' he asks, dabbing his mouth with his paper napkin.

'He and Ann seem happy. I'm glad he remarried.'

'You still see him?'

'Yeah — we meet up sometimes, and we talk on the phone. Sharing Grace will always connect us.'

Dougie sits up straighter. 'So, isn't it that time — you know, the ten-year thing you arranged with Sam? Isn't that coming up soon?'

I put my glass down, my fingers suddenly shaky. 'You remembered?'

Dougie's the only person who knows, but I haven't talked about Sam for years, not since a drunken evening after it happened, when I needed his elegant, bony shoulder to cry on.

He rolls his eyes. 'I'm not going to forget something like that. It was the most romantic thing I'd ever heard.' He gives me an intense look. 'So?'

'It's this month. I don't know if he'll show . . . It's been so long.' I push my bowl away. I'm not hungry any more.

Dougie reaches across the table and takes my hand in his. 'He'll be there, hen. I know it.' He squeezes my fingers.

* * *

The pond is the only place I could think to come for the courage and clarity I need. Freezing water will do that for a person. I have missed Sam for so long; the missing has been like a creature hiding inside me, between the slots of my ribs, in the base of my throat, inside my fingers and toes. But now it's crawling out, letting itself be known with urgent roars and pleas; it's stretching to fill all the spaces, taking me over.

I swim and swim. After my laps, I'm panting, exhausted. I put my feet down on the muddy bottom, toes pressing into thick, sludgy sediment, and wade through the weeds towards the ladder. My skin is pimply with cold. I'll sleep tonight, I think, after this. A sharp prick under my foot makes me wince. As I climb out, I leave bloodied prints on the scuffed wooden boards. I bend down and examine the small tear in the sole of my left foot. It's not too deep. I make sure to wash it out under the shower. When I get home, I stick the edges together with a Band-Aid. The cold water has left me chilled. Shivering.

★ ★ ★

Counting down the days to our meeting date has become unbearable. I try to lose myself in work, and when that fails, I spend a whole day rearranging the linen cupboard and clearing out my wardrobe. Anything to make the seconds pass. But I'm coming down with flu. All the signs are there. I have a pounding head, and achy bones; I feel hot and cold by turns. I make myself lemon and honey, pour in a slug of single malt. I shouldn't have gone swimming.

I have to get well before I see Sam, before I feel his arms around me, his cheek against mine. Before I tell him, I'm here. I'm home. With you.

In bed, the duvet twisted over me, I sleep and wake and sleep again.

Hello, little sister, Frank's voice whispers. *It's been a long time.*

I open my eyes, puzzled, staring up into the gloom. I thought Frank was sitting on my bed. I felt his hand on my forehead.

I'm not sure what day it is, or how much time has passed. I try to get out of bed, but it hurts to stand and the room spins. I'm so thirsty. My skin is scorched, clammy. It's agony to move, or open my sealed lids; my eyes shrivel in dry, gaping sockets. I sleep again, falling into fragments of memory. Or perhaps it's real, the past, present and future colliding, crushing me.

Sam is standing by the bench. I see him turning his head to look for me. I stand on tiptoes and wave. *I'm here*, I try to call. *I'm coming!*

I reach out to him, but hawthorn leaves obstruct my way, rustling in a thickened wall of leaf flesh. I try to battle through, but the leaves multiply and multiply. I'm sobbing and struggling, caught up in the branches. Thorns pierce my hands, stab my face, tear my skin.

This is what I deserve, a voice says. *I'm a bad person. I don't deserve to live.* No! It's not my voice. Those are not my words. I don't want to die. I want to live.

And then someone is saying my name over and over.

49

Sam, September 2004

Cutting across woodland, squelching onto open ground, boggy with recent rain, he approaches the bench from the front instead of going past the hawthorn. He wants to be able to see it from a distance. He wants that advantage. After all these years, with no communication, he is afraid of disappointment. But he believes she'll come.

When he looks up, shielding his eyes from the glare, gazing towards the top of the hill and the silhouette of the bench, he realises with a heart stutter that she's there. He digs in with his toes and sprints up the steep slope, head down, arms pumping at his sides as if he's in a race.

When he reaches the top of the rise, he understands that his eyes have tricked him. It's a stranger sitting on the bench. A young woman with dark hair. In all his imaginings, he never once pictured another person on those wooden slats. He worried that Cat wouldn't show. He thought of all the scenarios that might play out if she did come. But now this — this impostor, this trespasser, this young woman sitting just where Cat should be. It confuses him.

He's panting, and he stands catching his breath, running a hand through his hair, pushing it off his forehead. The young woman is looking at him expectantly, as if she knows him. He glances at her again, at her neat features, her tanned skin — which looks odd under the flat autumn light — the loops of coloured beads around her neck, the clutch of silver bracelets at her wrists.

'Sam?' she asks.

And then he knows, he knows who this stranger is.

He sits beside her on the bench, gathering his scattered wits, trying to suppress the fear unravelling in the pit of his belly. 'Grace?'

She nods, twisting her bracelets around.

'Did . . . did Cat tell you about me?' He keeps looking at her face, trying to read her expression. 'Did she send you?'

'No.' Grace gives a small shake of her head. 'I had no idea about . . . you and her. She never mentioned your name.'

'Then . . . how . . . '

She picks something up from the bench beside her. A battered book with a blue cover. She rubs her hand over it. 'Her diaries. They were in her bedroom. Two volumes. And after she . . . when she wasn't there . . . I . . . I wanted to feel closer to her. So I read them.' She fights to control her face. 'Once, a long time ago, she read my diary.'

'Hang on.' He shakes his head. 'After she . . . what?' Fear slips from his control, surging through his body. He puts a hand over his mouth to stop himself crying out. Taking deep breaths, he manages, 'Is she all right?'

'It took me a while to find the bench,' she says. 'It's described in the first diary.' She hugs the book to her chest. 'The hawthorn. The hill. The

395

view. I worked it out in the end.' She touches the back of the bench. 'And then I read the inscription, and I knew it was the right one.'

'Grace, please tell me what's happened to Cat.'

She stares out at the view.

'Grace?'

She startles, and looks at him as if remembering why she's here. 'It happened at the pond,' she says. 'She'd been swimming. She trod on . . . something sharp . . . ' She touches her mouth with a trembling hand. She doesn't look at him, but out towards the horizon. 'She was alone in the house. All alone . . . ' Her voice cracks. She gulps. 'She got blood poisoning. Sepsis.'

'What?' Sam clutches at her arm. Grace looks startled; he withdraws his touch, clamps rigid fingers around his knees. 'Where is she now?' He speaks clearly. He understands that he needs to be gentle, even though he's desperate for clarity.

'Her friend Dougie found her. He was worried when she didn't answer his calls. He alerted the police and they broke in.' She's crying, cheeks shiny with wet, snuffling and sniffing. She fumbles for a tissue in a pocket.

'But . . . I don't understand . . . Where was your father?'

She gives him a puzzled look. 'They divorced. Years ago.' She rubs her eyes. 'I wasn't here either. I was in Africa. She'd been alone for days . . . '

'Where. Is. She. Now.' He has to stop himself from shouting, from taking hold of her by the shoulders and shaking the answer out.

Grace wipes her eyes and blows her nose. 'She's in the Royal Free.'

'In hospital?' He feels sick with relief.

'She's on an antibiotic drip. She had an operation. They saved her life. We thought . . . I thought she was going to die.'

Sam's shoulders slump, his hands drop, dangling between his legs as he leans forward, staring at the leaves twisting and falling through the air. He feels as though he's falling with them, weightless, fragile.

'She was planning on coming here,' Grace says. 'To meet you. She wants to be with you. I read it in her diary. That's why I'm here, to take you to her. She doesn't know. I wanted it to be like . . . I don't know . . . a surprise. A gift.'

He blinks away the tears stinging his eyes. 'I thought you'd be angry,' he says. 'About us.'

'It was a shock, at first. But it explained a lot of things. And after the divorce, she never wanted to meet anyone else. She was waiting for you. She loves you.' Grace swallows a sob. 'I know . . . I know what she did for me, what you both did for me. All those years apart from each other. Now I just want her to have the chance to . . . to live the right life.'

They stand up from the bench, Sam's fingers trailing the sturdy wood, the engraved inscription.

Then they walk away, down the hill, towards the city, towards a bed on a ward in a hospital, and a woman who is waiting there.

50

Cat, September 2004

I am tethered to the bed by a drip in my arm; clear liquid slides into me, chasing away the poison, making me better. The ward is airless, windows sealed against the outside. There are five other women in here with me, breathing and moaning and chatting to each other. From my bed, I have a view of sky, empty of everything except clouds. The ward must be at the top of the hospital.

The first thing I asked when I came round from the operation two days ago was the date. The answer I was given made me let out a wail, and a nurse patted my hand. 'You'll feel better soon,' she said. 'You need to rest.'

'No,' I muttered, my mouth dry, not working properly. 'You don't understand . . .'

I couldn't explain that I was going to miss an appointment I'd waited ten years to keep. It's today. I imagine him sitting on our bench, narrowing his eyes as a figure starts up the hill, turning his head expectantly when the leaves behind him rustle. And I can't bear his disappointment. He'll wait for a time, and then he'll disappear; I'm frightened I'll never be able to find him.

Sam, I'm here. I'm right here, thinking of you with every fibre of my being.

I can hardly breathe. The pain of losing him is

a weight on my chest. Deep inside, I'm screaming and kicking, but I'm stuck in a sick body on a bed, the unchanging hospital routine revolving around me: three daily meals, the drug trolley, the snack trolley, the consultant's rounds, visitors trickling in with flowers and smiles of commiseration. The woman in the next bed asks what happened to my foot, and offers me a sweet. My consultant stops by, peering over his notes. I can't concentrate. Can't hear their words properly — can't give the right answers. I want to yank the needle out of my arm, swing my bandaged foot to the ground and limp down the anonymous corridors, heading for the Heath with my hospital gown flapping behind me. I ball my free hand into a fist, squeezing in frustration. But I'm so weak I hardly have the strength to curl my own fingers.

I don't believe in fate. I just know that if it does exist, it's determined to keep me and Sam apart. I've stopped fighting. It's over. Only now do I realise exactly how hard it's been to exist without him, to keep smiling and working and caring for Grace and Leo, to keep moving forward through the years, gleaning sweetness from the days, when my insides were aching with loss. Even when it was very far away, this day kept me going. I've run it through my imagination a million times — us meeting at the bench, who gets there first, who says what — but I never thought I'd be too sick to go. I turn my head on the pillow, a single tear sliding along the side of my nose.

I must have dozed off. I wake to see Grace

peering down at me. She wears an expression of concern on her tanned face. When she appeared at my bedside yesterday, tearful, and tired from the journey, I was stunned. It was a wonderful surprise to have her with me, but I feel guilty for dragging her home.

'Sweetheart.' I blink and struggle to sit up, and her young, strong hands are at my back, silver bangles jangling; the smell of the outside is caught in her hair. I inhale the scent of cold leaves and damp earth; it acts on me like another medicine.

'Mum,' she says. 'I'm . . . I'm not alone. There's someone here to see you.'

'Oh.' I touch my straggly hair, combing my fingers through it. 'Who?'

She has a strange look on her face, a look of anticipation. I can see now that she's nervous. She's doing that thing with her mouth, moving it around, biting her lips, folding them inwards.

'Grace?' My heart has begun to kick in my chest. She's backing away.

I look past her, over to the entrance, hungry for the impossible.

A figure steps into the ward.

Sam. His name catches in my throat. The world slows, the room and everyone in it disappearing as he moves towards me, pushing his dark hair off his forehead in a familiar gesture, his long, crooked smile fixed on me.

He's beside me, and he takes my good hand and raises it to his mouth. He kisses it. His lips are warm and dry. He's real.

'How?' I ask.

He lays his cheek against my hand. 'Grace,' he answers. I don't question him any more. There will be time later, I think. All the time we need.

He sits down beside me, and we look and look at each other, as if we're silently rerunning the years we've been apart, reliving them at impossible speed, spinning past the ghosts of our old lives. Staring into his face, I glimpse fragments of his time without me: there he is in a dark bar with his guitar, playing to a crowd of locals; on a lurching bus on a winding mountain road; camping out in a hut on the edge of a desert, firelight reflected in his eyes. He touches my face, tracing the lines of my bones, learning the subtle changes, the softening of my jaw, my wrinkles. I do the same to him. We smile. We have always been rushing towards this.

I shuffle across the mattress as far as I can, and he manoeuvres himself onto the bed, careful to avoid my sore foot and the snaking line of the drip. With his arms around me, I lie against his chest, like I did all those years ago in the funeral parlour, and push my face into his neck, burying myself inside the smell and taste of him.

The curtain swishes closed around the bed, tugged by an invisible hand. Light gleams through thin fabric. 'Cat,' he whispers, and in my head I thank my daughter, thank whatever invisible forces in the world led her to him, and him to me.

Then there is no more thinking. There's just the relief of being held, of being home, the two of us lying together in silence, marking this moment, before the rest of our lives begins.

Epilogue

Standing at the top of the hill, by the bench, Grace claps her hands. 'It's time! Come along!' and her three grandchildren wheel around in the long autumn grass, the dog at their heels, and bound back up the hill towards her, laughing. Her own daughter, now in her late thirties, takes her arm and gives a supportive squeeze.

As she waits for them to gather around, Grace glances at the view, thinking how different it would have looked to Cat and Sam back then. Today the skyline bristles with shining towers. But she supposes the Heath itself has remained almost exactly as it has been for hundreds of years. She and her husband inherited the white gothic house after Leo retired. They'd lived abroad for a long time; it felt good to come home to this place.

She looks around at the expectant faces of her daughter and grandchildren and smiles. 'We all know how much Sam and Cat loved this place,' she tells her audience, 'and the inscription meant something to them. So when the chance came to take this bench over, I thought really carefully about what it should say.' She blinks away the blurring of tears. 'They had thirty years. They travelled and lived and loved. They wrote music and books, and spent time with us, and grew old

402

together. We miss them.' Her voice breaks. She glances at her youngest grandchild, who's beginning to fidget, and makes an effort to smile. 'Okay, who wants to see what's under here?'

'Me!' they all shout.

She stoops to take hold of the scarf draped across the bench. It's a large square of multicoloured silk that once belonged to Cat, soft and worn from use.

'Ta da!' She whisks it away, revealing the seat underneath, with its fresh inscription picked out in the wood.

Her daughter lets out a sigh. 'It's beautiful, Mum. They would have loved it.'

The children clap. The littlest one clambers up onto the slats, where she pokes her fingers into the pale lettering, tracing the words.

Grace looks at the bench, her breath held in her lungs, because she sees them there as if they are flesh and blood, their heads together, murmuring to each other, fingers interlinked. Then they are gone, and her granddaughter is there instead, smiling up at her. She scoops the little girl into her arms, kissing her plump cheek before placing her on the ground. She wonders if the invisible ghosts of all the people who talked and walked and loved in this place are here too, whispering around them, their laughter rustling the leaves.

The two older children are playing with Cat's silk scarf, waving it in the air, setting the colours dancing. Grace smiles. 'Come on, you lot,' she calls. 'Let's go home.' She gestures in the direction of the valley. 'There's cake for tea.'

The two women walk slowly down the hill, arms linked, with the children and the dog racing ahead before them through the rough yellow grass.

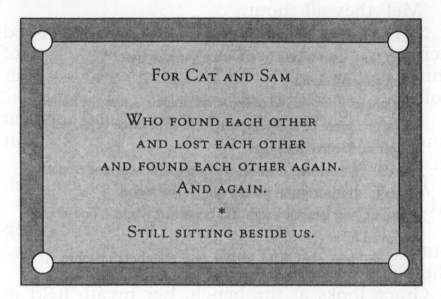

FOR CAT AND SAM

WHO FOUND EACH OTHER
AND LOST EACH OTHER
AND FOUND EACH OTHER AGAIN.
AND AGAIN.

*

STILL SITTING BESIDE US.

Author's Note

I spend hours walking my dogs in parks, through woods, on heaths, and along river banks, and whenever I come across a bench, I stop to read the inscription. It's a compulsion which I now share with my characters in this novel, Cat and Sam. Like them, I peer closely at the engraved lettering, hoping for inspiration, hungry for a story; sometimes the words I find are uplifting, sometimes tragic, sometimes they make me laugh, but however unassuming or profound, they are always resonant with the human ability to love.

Unlike a headstone, a bench can be placed somewhere that meant something to the person it's commemorating. That powerful combination of words and place is a kind of magic, making a simple wooden seat suddenly potent with meaning — you can almost hear lost laughter and conversation, sense someone's solitude and stillness. But a bench is also a practical object, allowing others to make their own memories sitting in the same place, creating over time a layering of different meanings. And so a bench becomes a gift to strangers — to a whole community — a symbol that stands, not just for the person that's gone, but for our faith in the future and in each other.

The inscriptions in this novel are quotes from

benches I've come across on my walks in the South of England. In the interests of privacy and brevity, I have left out names and dates. The bench inscription on p.5 is from *Hamlet* by William Shakespeare, Act 4, Scene 7.

Acknowledgements

A huge thank you to my editor, Emma Beswetherick, and the following people at Piatkus who do so much for me and my books: Jo Wickham, Hannah Wann, Kate Hibbert, Andy Hine, and Helena Doree. And thanks to Jane Selley for thoughtful copyediting.

Thank you, as always, to Eve White, and Ludo Cinelli, at the Eve White Literary Agency.

Thanks to Sara Sarre, Alex Marengo, Mary Chamberlain, Viv Graveson, Cecilia Ekback and Laura McClelland for reading early versions and giving invaluable feedback.

Big thanks to Andy Hank Dog for his stories about the music scene in London in the 80s and 90s, and for explaining the subtleties between different types of guitar and amp.

And finally, my family, Alex Marengo, Hannah Hayward, Olivia Hayward, Sam Hayward, Gabriel Marengo, Ana Sarginson, and Alex Sarginson. Your unfailing love and support means everything to me.

While researching crematoriums, a book I found particularly helpful and truly fascinating was 'Smoke Gets In Your Eyes' by Caitlin Doughty (Canongate Books, 2015).

We do hope that you have enjoyed reading
this large print book.

Did you know that all of our titles
are available for purchase?

We publish a wide range of high quality
large print books including:
Romances, Mysteries, Classics
General Fiction
Non Fiction and Westerns

Special interest titles available in
large print are:
The Little Oxford Dictionary
Music Book
Song Book
Hymn Book
Service Book

Also available from us courtesy of
Oxford University Press:
Young Readers' Dictionary
(large print edition)
Young Readers' Thesaurus
(large print edition)

For further information or a free
brochure, please contact us at:
Ulverscroft Large Print Books Ltd.,
The Green, Bradgate Road, Anstey,
Leicester, LE7 7FU, England.
Tel: **(00 44) 0116 236 4325**
Fax: **(00 44) 0116 234 0205**

Other titles published by Ulverscroft:

THE STRANGER

Saskia Sarginson

We all have our secrets. Eleanor Rathmell has kept one her whole life. But when her husband dies and a stranger arrives at her door, her safe life in the idyllic English village she's chosen as her home begins to topple. Everyone is suspicious of this stranger — except for Eleanor; and her trust in him will put her life in danger. Nothing is as it seems — not her dead husband, the man who claims to love her, or the inscrutable outsider to whom she's opened her home and her heart . . .

THE OTHER ME

Saskia Sarginson

London, 1986: Klaudia is about to start high school. She's embarrassed by her German father, unsure of what he may or may not have done during the war . . . Nine years later, Klaudia has given herself a new identity, having run away from her old life and a terrible secret buried at the heart of her family. Now living in Leeds, she is Eliza, a young woman in love — with her life as a dance student, and with her boyfriend Cosmo. But when her mother dies and she is called home, she can no longer deny her roots, even if it will cost her everything. The past has a way of staying with you, and Eliza knows she must face it head-on if she is to ever be truly happy . . .

WITHOUT YOU

Saskia Sarginson

Suffolk, 1984: When seventeen-year-old Eva goes missing at sea, everyone presumes that she has drowned. Her parents' relationship is falling apart, undermined by guilt and grief. But her younger sister, Faith, refuses to consider a life without Eva; she's determined to find her sister and bring her home alive. Close to the shore looms the shape of an island — out of bounds, mysterious and dotted with windowless concrete huts. What nobody knows is that inside one of the huts Eva is being held captive. That she is fighting to survive — and return home.

THE TWINS

Saskia Sarginson

Isolte and Viola are twins. Inseparable as children, they've grown into very different adults. Isolte is a successful features writer for a fashion magazine with a photographer boyfriend and a flat in London, while Viola is desperately unhappy and struggling with a lifelong eating disorder. What happened all those years ago to set the twins on such different paths to adulthood? As both women start to unravel the escalating tragedies of a half-remembered summer, terrifying secrets from the past come rushing back — and threaten to overwhelm their adult lives . . .